# MEN

# AND

# APPARITIONS

ALSO BY LYNNE TILLMAN

*Haunted Houses*

*Absence Makes the Heart* (stories)

*Motion Sickness*

*The Madame Realism Complex* (stories)

*Cast in Doubt*

*The Velvet Years: Warhol's Factory 1965–1967*

*The Broad Picture: Essays 1987–1996*

*No Lease on Life*

*Bookstore: The Life and Times of Jeannette Watson and Books & Co.*

*This Is Not It* (stories)

*American Genius, A Comedy*

*Someday This Will Be Funny* (stories)

*What Would Lynne Tillman Do?* (essays)

*The Complete Madame Realism and Other Stories*

# MEN

# AND

# APPARITIONS

A NOVEL

# LYNNE

# TILLMAN

Soft Skull  New York

Copyright © 2018 by Lynne Tillman
All rights reserved

First Soft Skull printing: March 2018

Library of Congress Cataloging-in-Publication Data
Names: Tillman, Lynne, author.
Title: Men and apparitions / Lynne Tillman.
Description: First Soft Skull edition. | New York : Soft Skull, 2018.
Identifiers: LCCN 2017038235 | ISBN 9781593766795 (pbk. : alk.
   paper) | ISBN 9781593766849 (ebook)
Classification: LCC PS3570.I42 M46 2018 | DDC 813/.54—dc23
LC record available at https://lccn.loc.gov/2017038235

Published by Soft Skull Press
1140 Broadway, Suite 704
New York, NY 10001
www.softskull.com

Soft Skull titles are distributed to the trade by Publishers Group West
Phone: 866-400-5351

Printed in the United States of America

10 9 8 7 6 5 4 3 2 1

For Richard Nash
without whom . . .

We must learn to be surprised.

—RABBI ABRAHAM HESCHEL

Mystery is a great embarrassment to the modern mind.

—FLANNERY O'CONNOR

# MEN

# AND

# APPARITIONS

## PROLOGUE

The end doesn't depend on the beginning, it upends beginnings, also provokes new ones. If the end comes, it's to one person, and could spark beginnings in others.

The beginning starts in history, not as a single event, though every birth is singular, and every death, also, but death and birth repeat themselves, the way history does, until no one remembers. —Ezekiel H. Stark

## SELF-NARRATION, OR WILDNESS OF ORIGIN MYTHS

The universe heaves with laughter, and I'm all about my lopsided, self-defining tale. How I came to be me, not you, how I'm shaping me for you, the way my posse and other native informants do for me, how I'm shape-shifting. I'm telling you that I'm telling you; my self is my field, and habitually I observe, and write field notes.

Ethnographer, study yourself. Ethnographer, heal yourself.

There was a no-time, with time outs—a long time ago, Way Before Now. Space and time, on a continuum, bend in relationship, and I imagine that soon I will, in some sense, return to the past. Whenever I want.

Routine settles, creeps in: I've performed the same acts for thirty-eight years, like eating breakfast. You were eating breakfast, you have been eating breakfast, you are conjugating breakfast ever since your mother set food before you, and now you're feeding yourself only if you shop for it, or maybe you went back to the land to raise it, but not everything, you don't and can't raise everything. I was damn fortunate: meals appeared regularly, I'm no ingrate. That was part of "my home."

You were spoon-fed, and it landed plop on the floor, or you the baby threw it. Bad boy. Throw a tantrum, make a mess, soon you have to clean it up—break it, buddy, it's yours, in pieces, because you are responsible; and, true, things go to pieces when not actually broken. Abstractions get broken. Ideas get broken. I have seen the best minds of my gen . . . Me talking 'bout the flawed life, totally.

Going to sleep, that gets tired, ha, the regularity, and boredom might cause my chronic insomnia, so it's cool when you don't know you're falling asleep, then you wake up and the TV is on. You open your eyes, weird. To dream becomes the best reason to sleep, especially if you do (I do) conscious dreaming, and get to choose: a dream becomes a podcast or movie. Otherwise, nightmares pit REM sleep with terror.

I listened to a podcast of an old TV news program and heard a Soviet and Russian historian, Stephen Cohen, argue with a total jerk. Completely exasperated by the fool, Cohen finally said, "With all due respect, you don't know what you're talking about." I swallowed the moment like a hallucinogen. That's so fucking rare . . . it tears up Max Weber's cage.

That's my goal, to tear it up. Me, especially.

I don't get high anymore, antidepressants keep me sort of level, and don't combine well with recreational drugs. Living drug-free is a sort of high, except clarity can get ugly.

My analyst suggests that I elongated my kid-hood by delaying leaving home. No big deal, really typical.

I suffer from abulia, which my analyst says is an abnormal lack of ability to act or make decisions. I like the word. So, I say to my analyst, "Abulia . . . I'm another Hamlet. Look what happened to him." I dither, weigh both sides, make lists, advantages, disadvantages.

My mother was a permissive parent, finishing college in the mid-sixties, and didn't want to parent like her uptight parents who let her know she was on her own. Mother had a small trust fund from her maternal grandmother, and did an M.A. in English, then met a man who became her husband, my father, and started a family, as they put it. Father didn't drink then, I mean, excessively. They had us, spacing Bro Hart and me, then an accident—Little Sister—she had to have been. Father, I don't know what his wishes were, but I don't think he fulfilled something in himself. Anyway, he became a functional drunk; Mother kept loving him, maybe. Takes all kinds. He was absent for me, hooked up to his necessaries, like to a breathing machine. I'd come home after school or tennis lessons, walk over to the couch, and his watery eyes were just pools.

Staring at photographs of him when he was young, when

I was young, comforted and bothered me. Here was evidence of a bright-eyed guy beside the dull living person I knew, and it was discrepant, though I wouldn't have said it like that then, couldn't put the two together, it didn't compute that the boy had turned into this man, my father.

In childhood, desires and passions are seeded. In adulthood, they flower into interests and manias.

## PICTURE: ME IN A FRAME (FRAMED)

My frame of reference is cultural anthropology. Clifford Geertz says that "doing ethnography is like trying to read (in the sense of 'construct a reading of') a manuscript . . ."; that "culture is public because meaning is." I do ethnography by working with photographs; also with the human absorption in images, and with the many forms and senses of image, creating an image, loving an image, etc. My specialty— family photographs.

Images don't mean as words mean, though people (and I) apply words to them.

Photographs can create images, but they are not images per se, they are things, a physical object. An image doesn't have to be based on a photograph. It is a mind-picture, or an image is a picture in the mind. A photograph may inspire or foment an image or images. An image is a concoction, often manufactured, meant to create a way to be seen, viewed, understood. It can be aerie faerie, a phantom, phantasm.

Can an image built out of self-consciousness lie?

I wear a brimless hat, because it's cool. Does it tell a lie about me?

I take a photograph, I don't take an image.

(Unless I'm a vampire. Haha. Vampires don't look like the ones on TV, the living dead are regular people, who suck you dry.)

A mind is not a brain. Or, a brain is to a mind what a photograph is to an image. And they can be conflated, brains and minds, images and photographs, and sometimes I do it too.

Virginia Woolf—Mother's fave—says that words also can't be pinned down: "[Words] do not live in dictionaries . . . they hate anything that stamps them with one meaning or confines them to one attitude, for it is their nature to change . . . It is because the truth they try to catch is many-sided, and they convey it by being themselves many-sided, flashing this way, then that. Thus they mean one thing to one person, another thing to another person."

But a photograph doesn't own even a wayward dictionary, though semioticians work it, finding ways to read one. Even vertiginously, words have definitions, to name and re-name objects in a cascade of tautologies. A synonym loops, loop de loops.

The antique game of telephone: the last to hear, in a string of listeners, will have (hear) an entirely different story from the first.

Looking can be benign or malevolent; looking entails everything human, and our instinct to look keeps us close to our evolutionary partners and antecedents in crime and development. If a deer spies a human, it will determine its level of threat. A deer runs if an unknown creature gets closer than what it perceives as safe. And deer are stupid, nice to look at but dumb as doors.

Now, people are stealthier in their observations, but the same principle applies: the need to clock others. A stranger enters a room, a group of familiars note her or him, no one moves, a second, thirty seconds pass until one brave familiar strides across the floor, to the door. The stranger introduces himself, and the familiar brings the stranger into the room, and soon others come closer and sort of sniff him. If no one moves toward the door: stasis, unless the stranger boldly enters and quickly identifies himself—I'm Michael, Donald's friend. Imagine if the person entered but didn't identify himself. Discomfort would be fierce.

Who is a perfect stranger? Is there a "complete stranger"?

Humans assess others shoddily, errors in judgment they're called. People can be poor at sniffing out an enemy, lack discernment, even common sense, and fail at comprehending dangers, signs. Supposedly our big brains allow for more choice, for being sensible, and are capable of complex thinking, etc. Other theorists work diligently on this problem; for one, economists, who analyze rational and irrational consumption patterns.

Just saying, as a person who studies groups: people fall in love with the wrong people, make the wrong friends, trust the wrong bank manager, and associate with hurtful, vengeful people.

Wolf families have a scapegoat; no wolf picks on any other wolf except an outsider (exogamous) male who tries to pick off the pack's females or eat its cubs. A fight happens then, often to the death. Otherwise, it's the scapegoat who's pushed around. He or she eats last, even when he's the brother, say, of the alpha who eats first. No mercy for a scapegoat.

In human groups, scapegoats exist to keep the tribe united.

Call human scapegoats "victims."


Generally, people drop imprecise clues. Unlike other animals that mark territory with piss or rub scent on trees, human displays or signs can mystify, at least be ambiguous. The worst, the most troubled and damaged, might be the best at keeping their worst signs on the down low. Yet an extremely foul-smelling human on a train clears the car. Imagine if untrustworthy lovers gave off a specific odor.

A traditional sign, the wedding ring, signifies as few contemporary interpersonal and social signs do. But it also has scant weight in some Western circles and might even encourage a "free-ranging" male or female to pounce onto someone's spouse. No consequences. Haha.

When I was fifteen, I met a philosopher, ninety years old, and, half-kidding, asked him, "You're a philosopher, so, what do you think about?" He was kind to a smart-ass high school boy, answered seriously, I thought, with a twinkle in his eye, because I don't know what else to call it—a glint? The philosopher repeated my question, seemingly asking himself: "What do I think about? Love. I think about love, I always think about love."

Love—platonic, romantic, sexual—appears in human–animal stories, and mine. A common trope, the love dope. Kidding. The grand passion, *l'amour fou*, mine is long running and deep, if mad love can run the distance. No kidding.

People repeat themselves, usually don't know it, and I hate repeating myself (but if I didn't, who would? Kidding), but no one is considered herself, himself, without doing it. Consistency = repetitive behavior. A groove grinds itself into the brain, a beat or melody runs the neural pathways. On repeat, repeat, repeat. The most popular songs, the most repetitious: "All about that bass, 'bout that bass." Can't stop singing it.

The mind fuck.

Does the way you fall in love /

go the same way /

love on repeat or replay?

Similarly, family attitudes, though they aren't obvious like rhythms and lyrics, get beat into us. Neurosis and Love are grooves, and they get deeper.


## FAMILY MATTERS

I began life, comfortably.

The family lived in a large 1960s pseudo-architect modernist ranch-style house: five bedrooms, parents on one end (and Mother's office), children the other side, bedrooms of same size for Bro Hart and me, but Little Sister—hers had more windows, sore point—and walls of picture windows in the living and dining room areas, slate floors, an open kitchen with an island, floor to-ceiling stone fireplace, and we were sort of in the country. Outside Boston, near Beverly. John Updike territory. Nice family place, if you didn't know the family. Just kidding.

Mother—Ellen Hooper Stark—edited manuscripts, histories, political science, biographies and memoirs, of intellectuals, she said. I was about seven when she explained it. Little Sister was one and a half, not yet talking, weird for a girl. (The term then was "delayed talker.")

Mother, what's editing?

Making writing better, checking information, correcting grammar, and being fair to the text.

Fair?

Mother believed she perfectly fit in the great line of judges who never made it to the bench. When she explained critical issues—This is critical, she'd say—like about editing, cleaning up my room, and the man I should be when I grew up, she gazed at me meaningfully; the knowledge imparted was the MOST important thing in the world. Her expectant look bewildered and dazzled me. What if I didn't get it then—would I ever? Would I succeed in life? Mother worked herself up deciding how often to repeat the same info, and whether repeating it would be counterproductive or what.

Mater of grammar, fact finder, and syntax investigator labored in abstractions; before I was born she'd been an editor at a press in Boston; then with two little boys, she decided to freelance, edit books at home, in her sacred office.

We children weren't allowed to enter if the door was shut, except for emergencies. I grew up believing in the urgency of matters behind that door, out of sight, and when I grew up, I could also shut a door and keep everyone and everything OUT. I could cut you all OUT. Father's leaving for his law office had less value, because he left, and it was the house, the home, that mattered, Mother's territory and mine: it had all my things, and hers. That's an idiomatic comfort phrase: my things. I don't use it much now, too babyish, greedy, and self-exposing.

Sometimes Mother drove to Boston to discuss work with a publisher, or get out of the house and away from us, I knew that, then later she toted not-yet-talking Little Sister to another professional, and another—neurologist or psychologist or psychic.

Some think I became a cultural anthropologist because of them.

Spiritualists litter (kitty litter, kidding) Mother's ancestral line, with which, she maintained, she felt mystically connected. More, later.

## FACE VALUES

Family photographs were the subject of my dissertation and first book, *You're a Picture, You're Not a Picture*. I analyzed how families picture themselves through their own photographs, what that picturing implies in terms of association, sibling order, gender relations, etc. How does the sociology of the American family—for instance, birth order—affect pictures, and does that "fact" become an image for the family?

Narratives grow with and in time, the family story about

what and who came when. If Little Sister had been the oldest, would she have spoken more? Father was the baby in his
family, did him no good. The qualities that make the baby
appealing just made him arrogant. Mother, though younger
than Clarissa, couldn't be the baby. Clarissa needed so much
care, hot-wired the way she was.

Whose "I"/"eye" can be trusted? From what I learned in
my family, I don't trust anyone in front of or behind a camera,
but I keep my bias out of it. Kidding.

Is trust an issue in art, and if so why?

I interviewed over a hundred families across America,
and chose pictures from their stacks, or they did the choosing. They told me who was who, and what, what was going on, and weird narratives spilled out. I inferred meanings,
as an ethnographer, sorting through the consonances and
dissonances, and what the gaps meant, if anything. A picture can actually tell you very little, which is why Thematic
Apperception Tests (TAT) invented by psychologists in the
1930s still appeal, at least in research. The open-endedness of
pictures has been utilized to study the mystery of perception,
emerging from an individual human psyche, as the subject
sees into a picture what is not there. One can't read an expression as a revelation of character or personality; it is just
temporal, an affect, often for the camera.

Behind so many smiles, I see: Eat Shit, Asshole. But then
that's me.

The concept of family resemblance is reasonable, given
genetics, but it's peculiar, because what makes a resemblance
isn't clear, there's no feature-by-feature similarity. Most of
us in families share a resemblance. Fascination with the

"family other"—a neologism I coined in an early pubbed article—is dulled by the other's being related by blood; yet what's near can be farther (what's in the mirror is farther than you think), because up close, we're less able to see each other. I don't look like my brother, but everyone says I do. I feared Bro Hart. He wanted to kill me at birth. Reaction formation, correct.

Often we hate our siblings, our blood, who might be our murderers. The Greeks, Shakespeare, et al.

A family's secrets appear as absences and exclusions, erasures and deletions. A first marriage was annulled: no photos. A child given up for adoption, no pix of the pregnant mother. The not-there, un-pictured life—think about it, an un-pictured life—or invisible story, hangs around the edges of albums, obscene, out of sight, off screen, you name it. Still, it functions along with the already-silent conversation of non-speaking pictures.

The incapacity to see—SEE—resides within the self, a condition I half-jokingly call The Fault Dear Brutus syndrome. I'm sampling Shakespeare's *Julius Caesar*, Cassius saying: "The fault, dear Brutus, is not in our stars, / But in ourselves, that we are underlings."

Don't tell Americans they're underlings.


## DOMESTIC VISUALS

Where are all the amateurs who do it for love, where have they gone?

In baseball stadiums, couples know, when the camera spots them, they should kiss, and they do. For love. For love of the camera.

I lusted after these so-called unposed moments, ephem era, even a lunch box called "The Remains of the Day," in the movie *Waiting for Guffman*. Kidding.

My unguarded moments are not cool.

In found family albums and pictures lent to me, picked up or bought at sites for collectibles and common relics, I studied/saw a quality I want to call straightforward, pictures uncomplicated by ideas about art or self-presentation, some bearing the self-consciousness of their subjects.

When I looked at art photography, posed and unposed, I was drawn to artists who shot families and their familiars, like Carrie Mae Weems, Catherine Opie, Mary Kelly, especially her *Post-Partum Document*, and Mitch Epstein, his book about his father, which aligned with my childhood obsession. Later on, that entered into my dissertation on family photo albums and amateur pictures creating the family image of itself, and for society.

Artist vernaculars impressed me: Warhol's photo-machine pix and Polaroids, Stephen Shore's visual travel diary, Susan Hiller's *Rough Seas* postcard collection, and Gerhard Richter's massive *Atlas* project, in which he attempted to include every kind of image, or the impossibility of the totality.

When artists incorporate or appropriate unsophisticated or naïve work in their work, a double consciousness plays that game. Or, to say it another way, the artists are presenting visual meta-fictions.

Four "amateurs" represent how people pictured themselves—these date from the 1930s through the 1950s—
displaying attitudes through their stances, for one, and
approaches to being photographed. Two of them feature
people and their pets; one, a woman is in front of her house;

and the other "stray image," two men, one in a U.S. army uniform, the other civilian dress.

The soldier has his arm about the second man's shoulders. Both men stand stiffly, neither smiles for the camera. They perform a "reluctance to be photographed." Palpable discomfort especially rests in the body of the civilian; the soldier's inclination—his capped head inclines toward the civilian—establishes familiarity: these men are "close" or know each other. Grimness, pictured—and resolve. The photographer stands at a medium distance, and has centered the men in the frame, the sloping roof of a brick building aligned with the civilian's forehead. It is a stark image. Is he going to war? Is the glumness of the civilian significant? Or, is it only that he can't stand being shot? I can't know, it's a mystery no one now can solve.

Their seriousness before the camera arrests me most. The two men, soldier and civilian, mean this picture to count, to represent their earnestness.

Contemporary men don't pose that way. For one, the ubiquity of images has made picturing selves less significant. With the speed of the digital, a casual attitude arrived: this wasn't going to be the only picture, loads would come, and many to delete. Our fast images: tossed away, worthless. Also, contemporaries maturing in an intensely pictured world experience the camera like a pet.

A woman in her forties or fifties stands in front of her house, presumably hers, unless she's a servant, which doesn't seem the case, because of the modesty of the house (though it could be servants' quarters): she's wearing a full, white apron. She has long arms, they dangle or hang next to her body, and settle at mid-thigh. The apron covers most of her short-sleeved, summery print dress. Her shoes date the photograph, probably the late 1930s or 1940s. (Mother will know.) Her hair is parted in the center, flat to her head, no frills whatever about her person; she wears wire-framed glasses, which go in and out of style. I'd call her a plain woman, and this a plain picture. She appears serious, at least about having her picture taken, but her body looks relaxed. Still, there's nothing casual about her or this picture. It was posed. That she would take a picture with her apron on says something about class, her "plainness," determination, sense of herself. No fussing for picture-taking. She's the picture of neatness.

An image: "picture of neatness."

In a color photo, a woman is seated beside her dog, both on kitchen chairs. A homely scene, the woman wears a half-apron (in the age of aprons), and, behind the two figures, appliances including a coffee pot and washing machine. The dog is holding up one paw, while one of the woman's hands is raised above the other (that one lies in her lap). To the left of the frame, a part of another figure, an arm, apparently a man's, in a long-sleeved plaid shirt. What is striking: the parallel pose of woman and dog, their equal status in the frame.

In another, dated on its back "1948," a kneeling boy of twelve or so and a white kitten sitting on a wooden dinner table chair. My first take: it could be an artist's. Why? Notice the frame within the frame. The boy stares out, not without expression but one that isn't legible; his face is poised between the chair's back slats. The white kitten, foregrounded, sits remarkably still and calm, while the boy looks at it with fascination or curiosity. Behind the boy, a telephone pole, a house with a porch, all indicate a neighborhood. The chair dominates, its top cuts the plane in half. This accidental framing, I imagine it was an accident, makes it a picture, not a snapshot or family photo, but something more. The composition is disorienting, unexpected, with several special elements that call to the viewer's eye.

"Naïve" or amateur shots can be differentiated from current artists' renderings of supposed unposed moments because of framing, sure, but also by attitudes toward what's permissible in a picture, what a picture should be, and how people should act for or look in one, present themselves for the record.

Pictures become a memory for which you have no actual memory. Pictures augment memory's elusiveness, how much more is forgotten than we think. A pictured moment has resonance to me, not as a fact of life but as an impression from a time in which THIS behavior happened, etc. Some artists don't title works—Barbara Kruger doesn't. Her work uses text and image (text as image), and, for one thing, the text acts like an internal title. Other artists might number a piece or title it to direct interpretation or a way of looking. A caption or subtitle shapes a picture, but a picture wants to resist finitude.

## DOMESTIC VISUALS TOO

I was totally conscious, as a little kid, of life passing, and when I saw a brilliant fall leaf hanging from a tree about to drop, seeing it from a car window, I thought, I'll never see that leaf again, and felt sad, and I don't know why, at four years old, I felt such loss.

The French, right, have a smart phrase: *nostalgie de la boue*.

In our family's albums, "leaves" were glued on pages (leafs) or set under plastic, and maybe I experienced something like D. W. Winnicott's "holding," far from consciousness. The ephemeral was transformed into a document that turned into a monument to memory and "truth." There it was, Mother as a girl.

Samuel Beckett: "All art is the same—an attempt to fill an empty space."

I'd lost nothing, nothing I was aware of, only what everyone loses when the amniotic sac bursts, and you, fetus, drop, get pushed through a tight vaginal canal, and thrust into unexpected environs.

We didn't know.

Now, always, trying to fill the emptiness.

I spent, spend, hours, weeks, months, from my young life on, with pictures, absorbed by their mysteriousness, there yet not there. WHAT IS THERE?


## ETHNOGRAPHIC VALUES

Ethnography focuses on actual people. "Real" people in "real" situations. That's how I articulated it to myself. I wouldn't just be rocking in my own head, limited, but my mind could spread out. Ha.

No escape from patterns and systems, no exits. Nothing, and no one, resides outside a system; that's the way it is. Nothing outside the inside, the inside is also outside, etc.

The Unabomber, a solitary man hiding in a house in the

wilderness, mailed explosives through the U.S. Postal Service. His wish for recognition or "success" led him to publish a manifesto in *The New York Times*. Theodore Kaczynski, a so-called lone wolf, had typical human needs, and they doomed him. His sister-in-law recognized his writing, his philosophy, and reported him. If he hadn't demanded publication, threatening to kill more people if the *Times* didn't publish it, he might never have been caught and jailed.

Maybe he wanted to stop his murdering, maybe not.

Deluded, but horribly effective for a while.

In 2007, Sicilian police reported finding Sicilian Mafia boss Salvatore Lo Piccolo's list of Ten Commandments for how to be a good gangster.

No one can present himself directly to another of our friends. There must be a third person to do it.

Never look at the wives of friends.

Never be seen with cops.

Never go to pubs and clubs, etc.

My fave commandment: The people who can't be part of Cosa Nostra are those who have a close relative in the police. Also, anyone who behaves badly and doesn't hold moral values.

People delude themselves; but delusions are based in a general culture, and dissension responds to and appears in recognizable forms. Totally disturbing. Sometimes I believe that, with will and effort, I can overcome and think for my-self. But what is that, who is it thinking? I think in a common language. Writers will infrequently find unique articulations.

I don't mean I want to metamorphose into a wild child, which might be cool, but discover what I think, if capable of purging my mind of certain images that determined, even predetermined me.

A THOUGHT is an effect of a specific education and its environment.

For cohesion, people need to play ball in the same concep-tual park, and make systems for survival, structures like eating three meals a day. People follow that here. Some skip a meal. No biggie, really, skipping a meal still recognizes the system.

Individuality is a necessary fiction. But why? Why do people seek to know their own minds, when knowing won't change them; people think they're right, right? Outcomes and events are often coincidences, unplanned, and may be appealing or unappealing, but humans imagine they can plan—plot—their lives more than they can. Some schedule their hours as if running an army, this must be done now or then; if a friend changes an appointment on one of these characters, their foundation crumbles. They become enraged at the "un-settler." (My term.)

People desire the un-plannable: money and success, hap-piness, love, health. A person's "fate" is traduced by conse-quences that are not predictable.

Accidents of fate, and happenstance, make us who we are. Take Oedipus: he knew but could not accept his fate, which crushed his sense of individuality, of opportunity. He couldn't make his own way. Greek hubris depended upon people imagining freedom from fate, or consequences, from what could be called social and cultural mandates.

## FAMILY TALES

There's a story in my family about Great Uncle Ezekiel, who didn't know, until he was eighteen and married to Margaret, that women went to the bathroom. It's always told with that euphemism. Uncle Ezekiel belonged to my father's side of the family. My father told it to my older brother, Hart, when he was thirteen, then me at thirteen—a father-son rite of passage deal—and his two brothers told their sons, then their daughters, when everyone loosened up about girls.

My parents told loads of stories about their upbringing—up 'til the point when they couldn't make sense of them, or why they were telling us, which reminded them. They shouldn't have had children. Three of us shouldn't have been born. "But we had YOU. We love you." Sensible people/parents: they waited until the best time, they said, to have the best children. All that pimping their gene-carriers' supposed exceptionalism, and they bestowed upon us "unique monikers." I'm Ezekiel (Father's great uncle, also a sixth-century prophet); Hooper (maternal surname, related by marriage to the Adams family); Stark (paternal German-Jewish-English-Unitarian, or neutralists). In grade school, my name rhymed with everything dumb. Brother Hart Adams Stark glories in his, imagines he's special, like Hart Crane, the writer. Bro Hart is just a pathologist who suffers from what psychiatrists call taphephobia: he's totally afraid of being buried alive. No one knows why.

Little Sister doesn't dwell on her signifying handle: Matilda (Tilda) Hooper Stark. Not publicly. (Matilda was the name of a great great great Hooper aunt.) She doesn't mention a lot, because she suffers from selective mutism, so she can talk with us, family, close friends, otherwise she's mostly silent. She couldn't speak at school and with strangers—now she says mostly she doesn't choose to. She talked when she was moved to talk, like a Quaker. When we were kids, I believed she chose not to talk.

Her shrink believes she suffers from alexithymia—trouble experiencing, expressing, describing emotional responses. Which may be one reason she speaks selectively, or the reverse. A while ago, I read about it in the *Times*. "People who are confused about the sources of their own emotions . . . tend to report little benefit from a burst of tears, studies have found."

When Little Sister cries, it doesn't sound human, more like she's choking.

She's six years younger. Ten years younger than Hart. That's the spread. I understand her better now, identify more, though identification can also be mis-identification. In some way I always felt close to her, though she blames me for talking too much when we were kids, and not giving her a chance, which is probably true.

Little Sister is another twist or tangle in the family wiring.

I'm the middle child, so I blame top and bottom, squeezed and dislodged by both. I can play that card.

Yeah, I'm cool.

•

Ethnography isn't a nineteenth-century discipline anymore. There's rigor, or solemnity, about approach and methodology, sure, but there's a restive criticality in our fractious field about subject/object relationships; objectivity itself, challenged especially by postwar theories, e.g., post-structuralism; and, straight up, the field's been upended, blasted, or maybe for some lies in ruins. Optimistically, it's been helped by its contradictions and differences, and these might lead to more Ph.D.s, which is cool, because it keeps everything moving (primarily for jobs).

My focus on images in, by, and of the family includes sexual and gendered behavior and relationships as understood in those pictures. I'm thirty-eight, an assistant professor in an Eastern university I'll get associate, tenure, if I don't piss off the department stiffs by being "too clever." Have to walk the walk, then like everyone else who's tenured do the big fade.

Cultural Studies scored during the 1990s; since then, the academy's star is like life in Warhol's Factory, who's up, who's down, a guessing game. There's been lots of theoretical work on masculinity, which probably got me thinking about men my age. Many moved into it, and some have shifted to transgender studies—Humanities, that department is disappearing, a sideline to the main game, Tech, Science, Abject and Obesity Studies. Sort of kidding. Let's say, the older fields are in as much flux as what they study, transitional objects and subjects. But strangely we proceed, no Sundays off in the post-1960s academic and not-so-academic civil wars.

A cultural anthropologist reflects on differences, similarities, patterns, problems, gathers information, takes notes, keeps a journal—makes field notes—is an observer and a writer; we look at how human beings act and collaborate or not. We try to make sense of "why." We study others and increasingly ourselves, and what customs and behaviors do for the society that enacts or supports them.

According to Geertz, ethnographies are also interpretations: "We begin with our own interpretations of what our informants are up to, or think they are up to, and then systematize those."

Ethnographers study commonalities among cultures, societies, the essentials, the basics: people need to eat, find shelter, procreate, etc. The differences in values, rituals, kinship relations are works of creation, born from, in part, basic needs and social conditions, etc., but adaptations and specifics range widely. A multimillion-ring circus, in Venn diagrams, unreadably dense, subsets and sub-subsets crisscrossing, is seemingly infinite. An ethnographer, again following Geertz, makes an intellectual effort toward thick interpretation (see later). I interpret with as much complexity as I can bring to the worlds I observe.

Culture is only the pattern of meanings embedded in symbols, thus spake Geertz. Primitive doesn't mean "primitive"; "we," "they," all pronouns have begun to act the way pronouns are intended: they shift. They, them, us, we, you can be anybody—we can all be subjects and objects of investigation, and are. Everything and everyone's being studied, from Tokyo post–3/11/2011, senior centers, the Sydney beach scene, London clubs, Borneo mating habits, Brazil's plastic surgery industry, Samoan society since WWII, NYC's gangs, etc. Etcetera. Almost anything goes under the knife.

I view society through images, in words and pix, in how individuals see themselves, in past and present tenses, and with what they identify, which are also images. That's my gig.

I started out in the field, I mean, got name recognition,

presenting a paper at a conference: "We are The Picture People." I began: "I name us Picture People because most special and obvious about the species is, our kind lives on and for pictures, lives as and for images, our species takes pictures, makes pix, thinks in pix. It exists if it's a picture and can be pictured. Surface is depth, when nothing is superficial."

Brought down a shaky house.

## LOOKING FILLS TIME

Pictures demand mental space and time.

In photographs, unguarded moments lend themselves to interpretation, and also to obliquity. An unwitting gesture doesn't reveal the person. Maybe there's more paradox to unposed moments, though; I hope to make something of those. But to pin down ambiguity, how weird is that. Ethnographers toil there, our milieu, especially those of us dedicated to thick description, where meaning exists in situ.

It's ineluctable. A picture describes, say, but never defines. An accidental pose can tell more, we often suppose, than a studied one; Freud made a lot of the unconscious of the accident, especially a word slip. But subjects in a candid shot, accidents— not the same. Think about "truth" or revelation in Warhol's *Screen Tests*, his silent or oxymoronic still movies: he focused on a person for a three-minute 16mm roll, and dared the poser to drop the pose (like a fetus through the birth canal). He didn't make posing easy, he wasn't looking for poise. His subject must breathe, creating movement, though each sitter was challenged to perform stillness. Weird, as if each sitter might be an Empire State Building. A psychological experiment, sure. Doing this kind of film, Warhol invoked early photography that required posers to sit still for a long time. Neck guards were invented to hold the poser's head straight, immobile. Warhol's poser had no guards other than his or her guardedness.

OK, the pose drops, but no essential truth is revealed. Unless one thinks that beneath the pose or the surface lies a greater truth. We've been led not to trust people's appearances, because, it's suggested, an essential truth about people can't be seen at all or easily on the surface. A lie is different from an appearance. Conscious liars know they are lying. But everyone has an appearance, which can't lie, even as appearances change and are chosen. They are not lies. A surface is not a lie.

About a photograph: its surface is its depth; there can be no single, correct interpretation; its depth rests on the surface, and, when you recognize that it can't be read absolutely, it opens up as its own thing. Not revealing anything but itself. Another paradox.

G. E. Moore's famous paradox: What can't be said in the present tense—"It is raining, but I believe it is not raining"—can be said in the past tense—"It was raining, but I didn't believe it was raining." A photograph indexes the past, and is viewed in the present. This means it can be raining in the picture, and not raining when a viewer sees it. A photograph is a fact, an object; but the picture is an experience, not a fact, for a viewer.

I'm no realist, but I live inside a reality, a world that isn't completely mine or consistent, and I share aspects of it with other people. I can delude myself, and also, I like some illusions, they soften hard edges, soft-focus my days. Without illusion, life would be stripped of fantasy's plenitude.

Plus, I wouldn't look at art if it held a mirror to life, especially my life. Kidding. Not.

## LIVING IN A GLUT OF IMAGES IS NOT THE SAME AS BEING A GLUTTON

A 1990s TV camera ad: "Life doesn't stop for you to take a photograph."

One hundred years earlier, "Nabi" painter Pierre Bonnard photographed his lover/partner Marthe, family, and friends—including friend and Nabi painter Édouard Vuillard—in gardens and forests, at play, eating. His photographs of Marthe in her bathtub became studies for his paintings. (I heard that Marthe suffered from psoriasis; took baths for relief, so it has affected how I look at them.) Bonnard liked his figures in movement, to catch the moment as few photographers did then (though Muybridge would, famously). He used his still camera like a cell phone, and by the 1890s when he started photographing, always as an amateur, the shutter speed was there: In 1880, George Eastman had developed a camera whose pose time was 1/50th of a second. Life didn't have to stop.

An arm, leg, a glimpse of torso, Bonnard's framing is unique. People danced across lawns, out of frame, they flew in the frame, two men wrestled in the air. Energy suffuses his pictures, or the dynamic called Life.

One always talks about surrendering to nature. There is also such a thing as surrendering to the picture. —Pierre Bonnard, February 8, 1939

My favorite picture is of Renée, a little girl, hugging a dog. She is bending down, over the dog, her head and face enveloped by a floppy straw bonnet. Three shapes dominate, all centrally framed—a little figure in a white or light-colored and loose smock-like dress; a big straw hat whose brim overwhelms the head and face; and a large, black dog whose head is cradled in one of Renée's arms, the dog's nose and face to the camera. Renée is wearing dark socks or stockings; one of her feet is lifted slightly off the pebbled ground, in movement. Her tiny foot moves the entire picture off the ground and into space.

Bonnard's photographs look as if his camera brushed the surface in fast, loose strokes. Some call them painterly. Bonnard courted flow, or energy, and this correlated to the way he saw in whichever form or genre he used. A broad and complex concept: how we see and what seeing is. It is a mystery, not biologically, but neurologically, culturally, and psychologically. The elements for sight—or vision—depend on culture and society, and remain mysterious because the outcomes are not the same for all people, even when produced within the same structures.

Selective seeing is like selective memory: memory's impositions, derogations, and biases (in favor of the rememberer) situate the psychological, social eye, and confound simple readings of reality: compelling variances of what is seen compete as "Truth." The eye organized by culture, say, compels "seeing." (I look at a dog or a cat and never see food. Rain to me looks like a drizzle or a downpour; other societies have many more words for rain.) People project, mostly unaware of the mechanism, and so reality's constructions conform to already received ideas about it. Contemporary photographers work with that prejudiced, psychological, subjective eye, to play catch with, say, actuality and fiction.

The desire to catch, as Bonnard hoped, the PASSING MOMENT is antithetical to being in the moment. The photographer is an observer to others' moments.

The Picture People have dedicated themselves to this paradox, and consign themselves on either side of the equation.


## FAMILY VALUES WHAT

I was a boy who didn't kill insects or torture small creatures, except Little Sister. She claimed I tortured her, tormented is closer to the truth.

One summer morning I found ecstasy in the garden, our backyard. I was four, and a praying mantis appeared. I didn't know what it was. The creature, I named him Mr. Petey, rocked my world. I watched its little head turning on its neck—the only insect on earth that turns its head. It's a person, like me,

I saw, but even littler. Praying mantises are like dinosaur-age humans. They have a face. They look you in the eyes. Their eyes are in the middle of their tiny heads, and they see the way we do. Totally cool. My PM noticed me and looked right back at me. At me, and I was face-to-face with a god or an alien. The PM got me, he communicated with sympathy and intelligence.

I named him Mr. Petey and wanted him for a pet, a friend. (My parents wouldn't let me bring him indoors.) I could talk to him—he could have been female—he listened to me, and pretty much every day I went into the backyard to find him. Mr. Petey usually showed up.

You can't kill a praying mantis, Mother said, they're a protected species, and if you kill one, we'll have to pay the government a lot of money.

I wasn't ever going to kill Mr. Petey, she was crazy, but I heard about the existence of a protected species, and this thrilled my kid-brain. I wondered if I was one, a special boy with special powers because I knew Mr. Petey. I reveled in talking with Mr. Petey, when I found him on a leaf.

That took some effort. Camouflage is key to a PM's survival, they have many enemies, including birds. (Sad, birds are cool.) Mr. Petey might fear predators but he was a fearsome predator, invisible on a branch.

You can't find a PM stuffed animal, so I made drawings, and Mother sewed me one. Mr. Petey's head flops down after all these years, nearly decapitated.

Mr. Petey—seen it all—Mr. Petey plural. I didn't know then that he/she lives only a year. Still, a PM's short life span fundamentally defies the value of human longevity, its evolutionary merit. The flaws of living long but not living large. Not kidding.

I must've fooled myself—kids don't fool themselves—when a new PM showed up, because their markings and colors vary. I don't know what I actually thought, it's all retro now. But a PM showed up in the spring and stayed through summer, I called him/her Mr. Petey, and one day he went for a vacation in the South. I figured that out for myself. But that was always Mr. Petey in the backyard until I left home.

I was a dreamy kid, I'm a dreamy older dude, but in a totally different way.

My dreaminess gets called "an obstacle to reality."

Looking, observing, I'm never bored. People who get bored are boring, people who don't get bored may not be boring but could be arrogant assholes. I'm not a voyeur, not clinically, according to the tests, but in a way, everyone who's awake is looking somewhat voyeuristically, or voyeur-ing. And, also, what can tests measure except a society's preconceived values, already tainted by its goals. If I am, I'm a pretty passive voyeur.

Landscapes flying by train windows make me sick.

Soberly, I examined objects, close and distant, a star in the sky, Mr. Petey, Mother's face; but I noticed: the elements that seem close may really be distant, your father, your best friend, and what feels distant or remote may be closer than you expect, and sneak up and rock your world. It's facile to say: the terrorist living next door, the serial killer—such a nice guy.

## ART, IMAGES, DEATH

Commercial photography sped up with the advent of the U.S. Civil War: the tech was there, and people could have pictures of the men who left for war, often to die or be maimed.

Before, there weren't remedial visuals or visual transitional objects to survive them. (See D. W. Winnicott.) Hair, nails, other physical remnants and traces were collected and framed, glued in lockets. Fingernail pieces. (Disgusting, sorry.) A rare few had painted portraits on mantelpieces.

First cousins married until after the Civil War, when the Feds made it illegal. In the age of Darwin, Americans worried about their purity, and the government worried about social degeneracy, the birth of idiots. First cousins not marrying doesn't stop that, but may amplify occurrences.

People relied on memory, and also developed mnemonic devices, ever since the Greeks and Romans. The "method of loci" (places) routes memory through visualizations (images), situates a person in a place who then records the site in the mind/brain. Later, the person walks through it mentally, sees everything, and what needs to be remembered appears.

Contemporary artists don't "reflect" objects; artists are IN life, making not "imitating" it, and they also can see objects not as separate from their own lives. Artist Laurie Simmons, in her series *The Love Doll*, photographed a Japanese sex doll, or surrogate female, in domestic scenes, where the Love Doll sits on the living room couch, for instance. Simmons's work pictures social attitudes, sexual fantasies, the regulated poses of femininity. "Attitudinals," I call them.

Artist Rachel Harrison: "People see what they want to see. My art is always loaded. There is too much, on purpose, because I'm not going to give you the thing you want."

What is that "thing"?

A claim was once made: artists make art from chaos. People who say this know nothing about art or chaos.

(1) Chaotic people make chaos, and can't unmake it.

(2) Chaos is not an object.

You're alive, dead. Can people be that different now from when bodies lay dead in front rooms? Consciousness: is it the same process always, and only its contents changed?

Virginia Woolf: "The look of things has a great power over me."

I get comfort from artists' representations of mortality—entrails of the day, autopsies of consumer goods, chunks, slices or mind sets, present-tense approaches.

Where did all the "history paintings" go? Depends on what you think they are. Barbara Kruger's images, words, vertiginous, on walls and floors, remaking space and received ideas. Cindy Sherman's buried phantasms of degradation and decadence; Peter Hujar's black-and-white photographs of catacombs; Renée Green's *Partially Buried*, an unearthing of a Robert Smithson piece and the Kent State killings; Zoe Leonard's ten-year *Analogue* piece, photographs of NYC shop windows, signs, a project of capture; Stephen Prina's reconfiguration of art exhibitions, or the past as an installation; Judith Barry's *Cairo Stories*, film portraits based on interviews with Egyptian women, their histories entwined with their country's; Walid Raad's preservation through images of Lebanon's civil wars; Glenn Ligon's "A Feast of Scraps," in part vernacular photographs of African Americans, an image-history of black America; Jim Hodges's *A Diary of Flowers*, a history of sentiment; An-My Lê's photographs of Vietnam War reenactments staged in North Carolina.

How is the past installed, whose and which history, for public view.

Ilya Kabakov's room-sized installations, Soviet Union dioramas, and fictional picture books of invented characters; Moyra Davey's photograph of dust on a phonograph needle, history as residue; Song Dong's color-coded installation *Waste Not*, 10,000 objects from his hoarder mother's Beijing apartment, nothing could be thrown away; Silvia Kolbowski's "An Inadequate History of Conceptual Art," including photographs of artists' hands, as they talked about an art form that avoided the hand; Adam Pendleton's black-and-white photographs, collages of protest, text, and pictures; Christopher Williams's pictures that question what photography (pro)poses; and Barbara Probst's point-of-view photographs that include her camera, the eye's prothesis, and tripod. The apparatus on show, though no transparency through transparency.

## BLAME EMPIRICISM

Toward the end of the eighteenth and beginning of the nineteenth centuries, there had been rumors of photography, in the days when science and art were near-inseparable, spreading among the elite—educated men and a few women, scientists of all stripes, creatures of the Enlightenment. They heard about the progress of various scientific trials, experiments toward image fixing that had begun in the late eighteenth century: camera obscuras, and attempts to plant ephemeral images on a surface through the effects of light and chemicals.

Photography emerged out of positivism, photo historian Geoffrey Batchen has theorized; photography is like a symptom of positivism, an obsession about proof, for documenting existence. It trusts empirical evidence, it is empirical evidence. Photography's origins can slide into an incessant hope for proof—of anything. It becomes a force in itself, as making images makes us.

Our species needed to fix an image of a house or bridge onto a plate. It did this before finding a way to eliminate the excruciating pain of surgery, say, tooth-pulling. The drive for anesthesia was not higher on the scale of need or wish: to impress a bridge on a plate or piece of paper, that happened first. OK, anesthesia emerged pretty soon after photography, in 1846, when a dentist demonstrated his experiment to physicians who'd sort of given up. Why give up? BECAUSE people believed our species' fate was to suffer, to experience pain, like women in childbirth.

We are all Job; but my biblical namesake Ezekiel was all about curing with herbs, etc.

Attitudes affect revelations, what gets invented, and doesn't, the way society has evolved and continues.

What's important to humans is less important than why.

Empiricism fails, what we see isn't what we get. Love can't be proved. No science to it, no proof in repetitions of it. Certain acts seem, indubitably, love: a mother throwing herself on her child to save its life. Love, instinct, or something else. Fear of future guilt or ostracism from the tribe? Instincts that appear altruistic may not be: the mother's done her reproductive work. Let's move on.

## ANON FAMILY ALBUM THROWAWAY PIX

I hold these pictures in my hands—faces and bodies, dogs and cats flip from one to the other. Pictures, pictures.

Families are tribes, tribes keep relics, pass them on, relics represent ancestral traditions and "purpose the future" (my term). Our relics, these valued objects, "hold" a family, tribe, a people's continuity. "High art"—relics of a kind—creates continuity in value and taste, which is essentially what museums do: hold values continuous. While most of us know, well, some of us, that life is whimsical, temporary, in flux, random

and discontinuous, museums, churches, "culture's placehold-
ers," my term, forge constancy, and though criticized for their
many lacks, these institutionalize traditions, give tribes places
to go to venerate the past and present, together. How else
would people know on what to base their values? Why is the
archive so important? Think about it. The twentieth century
is GONE, so gone, as never to have happened. Buh-bye.

Or the Velvet Underground's "bye-bye."

Societies, without histories, have no value. People without history, also. Values thrive in relation to the excluded, to
the much greater number of objects called obsolete, or unnecessary, ugly, second-rate, third-rate. How else would people, societies, know themselves?

In my hands, I hold these picture-relics, to be family-evident.

In *Forget Me Not: Photography and Remembrance*, Geoffrey Batchen studied a picture *At Rest* (dated 1890, he thinks) of a dead young woman, wax flowers around its frame. The flowers add poignancy and sentimentality. He asks: "Who was this woman? What was her life like? What possible relationship could I, as a viewer of this picture today, have to do with her?"

I ask myself that every day.

## LOVING A PRAYING MANTIS: ON THE ROAD TO ETHNOGRAPHY

I was a morbid kid, but also kind of happy, nothing stood in my way, except Bro Hart and Father. Kidding, not.

I saw us through Mr. Petey's eyes. We/they were fools in clumsy shoes, ugly aprons, eating burned hot dogs, complaining about bugs, while getting loaded and uploading shit on others, people were just stupid. Mr. Petey watched, hunkered down on a leaf, invisible to dull adult eyes.

PMs are carnivorous, so the smell of burgers wasn't disgusting to him. They eat their prey alive, but paralyze them first.

PMs' ability to turn their heads 180 degrees allows them great visibility, also their eyes are sensitive to the slightest movement up to sixty feet away (two-thirds to first base). They have powerful jaws for devouring their prey and ultrasound ears on their meta-thoraxes. They are so aware of their environment, built that way, like some humans who are called overly sensitive.

PMs blend into a plant's leaves and only their movement gives them away, so they fool other insects and us. They can't be fooled because their brains aren't stymied by the problems ours handle, which are bigger than our big brains can actually manage. If a brain is small, dedicated to fewer problems, and those get handled exquisitely, that organism isn't less smart than a human.

His species required no improvement, think about it: he didn't need to evolve, like our imperfect species—heavy skulls sit on top of spindly, multi-parted spines, the body's primary support structure.

Women have narrow pelvises, to winnow out fatheads.

Shoulders are needed for too many functions, too many directions in which they must turn. The knee, by comparison, is more simple, the hip a simpleton.

Mr. Petey was small, efficiently built, and effective.

He cogitated, my thinker-insect. Thought = action.

Go ahead, go play on your own, Mother used to say. I loved that.

So what if I didn't have a "good personality." Mother claimed my personality showed at birth, but my character emerged later. Go figure. My family has strong opinions—principled, stubborn, righteous, judgmental; they're reasonable, smart, assholes, bigots, or nut jobs, depending upon your POV and linguistic code. My father told me I was a brat; Mother might call me sly or rambunctious. Maybe I wasn't cool enough or too cool for school, and so what if Hart beat me up or sat on me and tried to suffocate me or tickle me to death, or Little Sister sometimes ignored me; so what if I wet my bed until I was five or sucked my big toe, not even my thumb like normal kids, or had three cavities at age four because Mother feared government control by fluoride. She was otherwise a pretty rational person.

## NATIVE, NAÏVE NOT

The so-called native informant—a native can be anyone, a member of the Zuni tribe, or an upstate New York gang member, or a DJ—is not an innocent informant. No one's innocent. How should an anthropologist behave with informants? "It entails trust between the ethnographer and subject" (more later). The ethnographer can't trust that he or she knows their subjects' motivations for cooperation. The ethnographer can't entirely know his or her own motives for talking with or choosing subjects. The most obvious stuff wasn't sixty or seventy years ago, and new-style obvious-ness hides in blatant plain sight. Many humanists and social scientists are totally incensed, everyone appears to be incensed about the loss of objectivity and Truth with a cap T. It's not the end of Western Civ. Or it is. Does it matter?

I started with "naïve" images, or I was naïve, the images weren't.

I remember thinking, what's happening inside everyone. I wanted the illusion—a picture talks to me.

I haven't entirely progressed from the vernacular, in all ways. Haha.

See, the naïf or amateur has no cred in our digitized

world. There are no amateurs. Does it mean there is no love in what people do? No, it can mean that those who do it professionally are not as valued, or even themselves value it less, oddly. Or, that everyone feels able to take good photos, and they are—good enough. Yet what is a good photo, and by whose definition?

Some people get paid to take pictures: the professional class, experts, artists, specialists. Often they talk only to each other, a small circle of other picture people. The majority take spontaneous, unplanned pix, especially of family and friends, in which there are what I call "display stances," image-ready attitudes, position-motifs showing status, etc. In the picture-taking and -making age, each generation matures with technologies that "show" them to themselves and others, so everyone can assert self as an image; we are all in image-apprenticeship, and it is through pictures we see ourselves and learn to shape ourselves, to present ourselves.

The pictures don't need to be reflexive. Portraits of selves reside inside or beside portraits of desirable or desired others, too. The other's desired life is a fashion or style, there is no inner to the outer-wear. Fashion and style rule because the shopper assumes the style of the designer and imagines it's his or her own. When in fact he or she is merely branded. (See Erving Goffman's *The Presentation of Self in Everyday Life*.)

Pictures don't tell stories; they match—align with—stories we tell ourselves. In the early 1980s, artists Louise Lawler and Sherrie Levine posted this on a movie theater's marquee: "A picture is not worth a 1,000 words." It isn't, but if it doesn't tell a story, what, if anything, does it tell? Do our lives lean heavily on nothing?

HBO's *Six Feet Under* (2001–2005), a droll series, showed Claire, one of its protagonists, in art school studying photography. In its finale, before leaving her house and home for the unknown, Claire shoots it and her family. Suddenly, Claire's dead brother, Nate, a ghost, looks on, and whispers to her, "That's already gone."

But Claire takes the pictures, because she's alive, and present to remember.

## TELLINGS

Uncle Lionel liked to recite this ditty:

> *Yesterday upon the stair*
> *I saw a man who wasn't there*
> *He wasn't there again today.*
> *Oh, how I wish he'd go away.*

I wished upon the first star that winked at me in a black sky: preserve me, keep me safe, oh little angels in heaven. (No religion practiced at home; angels appeared in museum paintings.) During the Reformation, I might have volunteered to be a castrato and resisted maturation. I heard a recording of the last-known castrato, made in 1904—an eerie boy voice.

I wonder if his face stayed boyish. I wanted to stay a boy. "I'm not going to grow up like you, I won't become an adult." Typical for Americans.

My secret world, once upon a child, included my photo library, definitely a formative, building-block experience, with a system only I knew, because I conceived of it. I hid it. I stored and preserved (thought I did) what I wanted. At age nine, I classified pix, and really did my best to preserve them. Martin Scorsese says preservation is film-making. Think about how much of existence goes into preserving what could instantly disappear, and maybe should, like taking a photo at a wedding. Good or bad? Which is important, the moment or the preservation?

I named my analogue catalogue Zekabet, coding by colors and numbers and symbols I liked—naturally, the praying mantis was significant. It was a kind of me and not-me formulation. My color was dark green, like Mr. Petey's; any home video or Super 8 I appeared in was marked with a dark green Crayola; if I shot it, it was marked with lime green, and any green was number 1. Bro Hart was shit brown. Little Sister violet, Mother gray-blue, Father real red; these accorded with their temperaments. (Mother once wore a mood ring, made an impact.) The code never left my pocket. My biggest conceptual issue was how to show the passage of time, not by dates like the year, say, 1980. Too easily decoded. So, I created a calendar that related to weather, that is, when weather first was recorded in 1870, or Year 1. Simple, but cloud formations and movements were also factored in, because I was entranced by clouds and why they took the shapes they did, that they had volume but were made of air, of space. That killed me.

In the Zekabet, Mr. Petey ranked over all creatures; Little Sister was a special human-creature; also ranking high: outer space, robots, D&D, clouds, rocks, family photos. Kid-time felt eternal, off the charts, and what I felt then was limitless, or more prosaically, if there was time, it was like the waves

I watched breaking far from shore, without end or thought, one after the other. No concern for anything.

An endangered species and I were friends.

Am I an endangered species?

Time stood still when I picked up a smooth gray-blue stone, flat, nothing exotic, but it was in the backyard.

A rock with a crevice, maybe it encased a fossil. Looking, I was outside of time, and as I said, never bored.

Perpetual stillness: still photographs do it for me, not movies, videos. Stopped time is an illusion, OK, is there life without illusion? Delusions, that's different, I know from experience, though experience is a relentless, wicked trickster. Oh wickedness! Yet an ethnographer is encouraged to trust it. See, here's the fault line, there's trouble in paradise.

I was born in the USA, near Boston, MA, June 29, 1978, close to midnight, so I straddled night and day, the 30th, and those numbers mean a lot. To me. When I gamble, I go to them.

"You're emotionally immature," Mother says. Little Sister smiles, faintly, pissing me off.

I know I shouldn't have children.

Parental laws included: "Act like a grown-up." An act. "Why act this way?" I yelled. "'Coz, then it's all fake." A "time out" would get called, I'd skulk to my room, where I calmed down with pictures and games. Everything came to seem fake. I saw that, as you grow up, your true self withers away, though the State doesn't, and you find yourself accepting rules, because that's how it's done until one day you decide: I don't want to walk that walk.

Virtues of backyard = safe space.

I could be alone there.

I learned to embrace aloneness. Big plus for an ethnographer.

Our garden led to the big forest, the unknown, and any stone was a solid thing I could hold in my hand for as long as I wanted that didn't ask me to do anything or be anything, it wasn't for or against anything, it wasn't bad, good, it demanded nothing, like a potential true friend should demand nothing. I learned that true friends were rare, that mostly everyone demands something you can't give them.

When I started school (still being schooled by life, haha), my anxiety launched into outer space. First off, school wasn't home, there were other kids, there was me; I had to be with them, but they could have been other kids, which Mother made a lot of. Was I with the best people, for me? Did I have the best teachers, for me? There was something about me that caused "parental concern," a specific form of tribal concern. The word "gifted" popped up early on the school screen, and meant nothing to me except I was different or special, not the way I felt to myself but to others. Bro Hart wasn't, and that was cool, I wanted to be different from him. Little Sister owned her difference, though it wasn't a gift. To me it kind of was—I didn't get that it was a problem, until later. I thought Little Sister liked her specialness, since it brought privileges. Hart wasn't ever my parents' problem, but the word "track" got thrown around. He was tracking right. I mean, what the hell. I didn't know what was going on with Hart. Gifted kids don't necessarily score high on tests or do equally well on all tasks and responses. My track got skewed. Or, I had a screw loose, depending on who dissed me.

The "gifted" brand rests in a Pandora's box, a grab-bag of mysterious stuff. I heard: How should Zeke be "handled"? Is he overly sensitive? That shit. Ultimately I took the label and ran with it; I sensed I could do with it what I wanted—"let the boy have his head," my namesake Great Uncle Zeke once burbled. I followed my investigations; plunged into what I declared "research," and poked my nose into the family image fog. (Prefigured my becoming a cultural anthropologist.) In high school and mostly in college, I avoided family history, maybe with vehemence. Now, people think it's the subtext, or true undercurrent, of my life.

First off: I hated school.

(1) Didn't understand when learning started or stopped.
(2) Didn't like other kids. Maybe one or two.
(3) Wary of girls, if they talked to me; if they didn't, I fell in love.
(4) Was too aggressive OR not enough—for a boy.
(5) Could boys wear nail polish, like rock guys, and why not? (Possible origins for my work-in-progress MEN IN QUOTES.)

## SACRED PHOTOGRAPHY

I've worked, formally, with family photographs since grad school. People open their doors, let you in, they answer questions about intimate parts of their lives. What's at stake for them is part of my investigation. (For one thing, people want to think their lives are worth talking about. That they mean something. That's totally upfront.)

Then: Why am I interested in this? What's my stake in this?

All "portraits" are also self-portraits.

In the nineteenth century, Thomas Carlyle believed "all that a man does is physiognomical of him." A face revealed a person's character and disposition, if one was skilled in reading it, and physiognomists, natural scientists expert in the field, hoped, like curious people everywhere, to discern from it why human beings acted as they did and to predict what they may do in the future. Criminals especially—they felt certain they could determine them.

The science is archaic, kind of silly, but I understand the belief, even the point: a face lives in the open, naked, except when, for example, women wear veils or are veiled on specific occasions, such as marriage ceremonies. Expressions of happiness and remorse, pleasure and pain etch a mutating portrait. A face changes, none stay the same, except for a girl kept in captivity by her parents from the age of three, and, when she was discovered at the age of sixteen, she appeared to be a child, her face unmarked by experience. She had only known her room, a stunted world. Her growth was also stunted.

Cosmetic surgery manifests a wish for permanent disguises, "to fool" death, which makes life temporary and all acts conditional.

What Carlyle believed isn't far from what portrait photographers or artists do, since their art concerns readings, of faces, stances—e.g., Richard Avedon, Rineke Dijkstra, Roy DeCarava, Collier Schorr, Lyle Ashton Harris, Diane Arbus, Lorna Simpson. Their pictures reveal a tacit belief in physiognomy, that faces should be read and looked at closely, even though faces don't reveal character.

Whistler on his portrait of his mother: "To me it is interesting as a picture of my mother; but what can or ought the public to care about the identity of the portrait?"

The divine face. Divination and divining. The facial divide. Ha.

In the field, we "make" pictures by assembling from and interpreting the images given us. Making sense makes/allows for interpretation.

Are we ethnographers fooled or do we only fool ourselves? Margaret Mead's Samoan girls told her what she wanted to hear, which is instructive, when we know it's going on. Actually, it was a kind of gift to Mead, but I don't do gifts—anthropologically, I mean.

The world is wired. Remote has several meanings.

The shift from analog to digital, for instance, has and will have so many unforeseen consequences. The hand disappears further; tangibility and physicality too. Unmanned drones are just part of the removal, the remoteness, future living has in store.

You are here, you wander there, fear of the Conradian monster within, at home and away. Though "away" can be home.

## FAMILY IMAGES

Hour-long dramas are sustained on TV, but totally losing ground, because of the Internet, which is displacing TV, and theaters; there are far more sitcoms on TV, because the half-hour = more advertising dollars. Thirty minutes is about twenty-two minutes; in that time, a lot must happen to advance the story and keep a viewer's attention; much must be tantalizingly not told, or withheld, secrets to compel viewers to watch next week. Reality TV uses the same narrative devices: who will be the biggest loser, winner, etc., is revealed over time, and time, its extension and duration, is what differentiates narrative from other art forms.

Sitcoms, like families, depend upon consistency of their members/characters, but TV needs comedy in its dramatized horrors, the kind actual families don't experience. Characters must be "themselves" but also develop (the way actual characters don't). Development in TV narratives folds into plots: *Modern Family*'s gay male couple adopt a Vietnamese baby girl and later plan their wedding. Viewers watch their almost-believable, always exaggerated, and bizarre machinations around these events. Psychological changes get embedded, when they do, through the protagonists' relationships to events, not the other way around. Occasionally, both are in sync. Protagonists who go wildly out of character are scripted for actors to leave the show, or their characters die. An audience demands of a TV sitcom or long-running story a commitment to continuity and fidelity, to reasonableness, and a consolatory ending—a contract ensues. *Dallas* blew off the lid of credibility, when one entire season was the dream or fantasy of one of its protagonists. *The Sopranos*'s ambiguous finale infuriated and frustrated some viewers. The show has, for some (me), never ended, just like other tragedies eternally resonate.

The family's contract, though, expected, implicit, or inherent, is to keep its secrets. In *Breaking Bad*, Walter White says his cooking meth and making millions is for the family; his wife, Skyler, hides his secret as long as she can, to protect their children and benefit from the drug money. Secrets are essential to the kinship bond and to husbands and wives, who don't have to testify against each other in court, anyway. What happens in the family stays there: No Silence = No Protection.

I use media to explain certain phenomena and enduring characteristics, as well as new adaptations, of the American family. For example, Mafia movies succeeded after the family was hammered during the sixties, by promoting oaths that, like marriage, were 'til death do us part, while guilt and criminality occurred only by disregarding the family, not the law. Hollywood and indie movies glorified thugs' loyalty to the clan, but *The Sopranos* portrayed mob boss Tony Soprano's sadism so graphically that, Sunday by Sunday, the viewer's sympathy was shredded. Still, violence was enshrined, and, with it and its threat against disloyalty, families were meant to cohere.

The American family sustains itself and mutates along with its movies, TV, reality, comedy, sitcoms, photographs, video, miniseries. Old genres for new ethnicities, types—easy makeovers—fill our many screens. With no end to war and cop stories, big and little monsters for an age of permanent war, and, with the cry for blind patriotism, an American's fidelity to family can be converted into uncritical devotion to country or town.

A family member's self-interest can break a contract, implicit or explicit, in the name of honesty (often a dubious motive, except in the case of the Unabomber's brother and sister-in-law: their disloyalty saved lives), to cure the family or to get just desserts.

## AN ART GALLERY IN LOS ANGELES MODELED ON THE UNABOMBER CABIN

A new space by collector and artist Danny First may just take the weirdness cake.

First has built a 10-by-12-foot gallery in his Hancock Park backyard using the exact shape and dimensions of Unabomber Ted Kaczynski's Montana cabin—down to the plywood patches out front.

. . . First says this isn't out of some weird tribute to Kaczynski and his anti-technology manifestos. It's the shape and the scale of the building that he found compelling. "I've never even seen [Kaczynski's] cabin in person," First says. "It really has nothing to do with the Unabomber. The simplicity of the structure is something that appeals to me—it's like something that a kid would draw. I liked it from the first time I saw it on television."

—*Los Angeles Times*

## GROWING UP IS CRAZY

I totally knew about possessions, and consumption, even obsession, without knowing I knew it, because of John Maurice Stark. Father wanted things, he collected things, because he could. "His things" were his possessions, and a notion developed in me, Zeke Stark, that I was pure of heart, and he was crude and grasping. Later, I learned the word "materialist." He was one—a spirit enemy.

To be possessed, but not possess life. Surrounded by materialists, I partook, resigned, acceding to the pathos of consumables. Pathetic. Working against that. Spirit as substance.

I studied Father taking pix. He set up a shot, camera to eye, pressed the button, pulled the film out, waited like a scientist, and the chemicals acted, or "did its thing," as he liked to say. Then, wow, emergence! The image would appear on the surface, risen! There it was. He showed us "the result," as he called it.

Father = the Polaroid speed of life. A slice of a tiny moment, but then you waited to see that moment, as if it hadn't happened. It was so weird, we watched what we were doing as if we hadn't done it, and now we could see what it was, a magic act that showed how reality might be deceptive—I mean, what would be shown that we hadn't seen or experienced (see spirit photography).

The emerging, part of its happening, happened as we watched. And, every moment you waited for the past to show itself was lost, not present. Like a caterpillar out of a cocoon, the emergence excited me more than the picture. It was a white door he shot, a normal thing, but the magic of its chemistry, way more cool.

In his book *America*, Jean Baudrillard wrote of the Polaroid as a heightened form of photography's uncanniness: "To hold the object and its image almost simultaneously as if the conception of light of ancient physics or metaphysics, in which each object was thought to secrete doubles or negatives of itself that we pick up with our eyes, has become a reality. It is a dream. It is the optical materialization of a magical process. The Polaroid photo is a sort of ecstatic membrane that has come away from the real object."

I learned my way around a darkroom, developing a picture, learning patience—the new magic until that ended, too. Darkroom days ended, mostly for everyone, but some artists keep at it; the preciousness of historical prints will count even more with time.

## SHOOT ME BUT DON'T SHOOT ME

Mother didn't like Father to snap her, as she put it, because he didn't let her snap him. "Don't shoot my face," she'd say. It was a power thing.

Snapshots: an old concept.

Snapshots; snap judgments.

I'll do it in a snap.

OH, SNAP.

Mother never accepted or believed women were inferior to men. It didn't occur to me, either, but Father's undermining her must have contributed to some negative internalizing. Father claimed he was a male feminist, but he was a condescending asshole contented with his bona fides: as he said again and again, he'd PARTIED, smoked it up, did some speed, and when he matured, he got real, studied law, settled down and married a woman better than he was, became an upstanding citizen, or a selfish, middle-class jerk-wad.

Mother explained: many women bought that the home was their rightful place, her mother did, but her mother was very angry and took it out on her and Clarissa, with the silent treatment, white rage, Mother called it. Then, in 1963, when Mother was in college, *The Feminine Mystique* hit the stands, and a lot changed, she said, very fast. Oh, the times they were a changin'. For a radical few of them, there wasn't a need to overcome what they felt was injustice and personal loss; she and her friends felt on track to equality. But people can't lose what they never had, she said. Mother shot me her spooky gravitas look, the mother knows BEST and MORE expression. Ping! Which totally refers to my current story; but I don't want to get ahead of myself, I mean, if that's ever possible. No kidding.

## WE THE PICTURE PEOPLE

Words make images.
People make words, words make people.
People make images. Words and images make people.
How many fallacies fit on the head of a pin.


I'm an image to you, you to me. We create each other in instants of connection, the identity process is interactive, a very fast game. We are The Picture People.

All pictorial depth is illusory, and it may be that all depth is fictional, the mother of all simulacra. We're living behind closed doors, metaphorically, and photographs are not windows; also, whatever an inner thought is considered to be it is carried by language, which is social, and therefore not "inner" at all.

Striking matches, I heard my father yell, Stop. I was five. Could have burned the house down, he said. I was awake, aware then. He gave me the idea. "I could have burned the house down. I could burn the house down." A fantastic image.

Our age began in 1839, with the proclaimed discovery or invention of photography, when the Picture Age or the Age of Images (as in, we live in a glut of images) took its impetus, its nucleus, from the camera and its products. In the modern and post-modern era people have persistently desired to create, remake and pull down images from, of, and off everything. The Stone, Bronze, and Iron Ages, the Industrial Age, the Electronic and Technological Age. No one can argue against calling us the Picture People.

In the eighth century BCE, the poet Hesiod sorted the world of Man into five stages, Golden, Silver, Bronze, Heroic, and Iron, complaining that, with each stage, there was a degradation. He regretted having been born into the fifth age.

But this kind of articulation is OLD, too old to keep repeating. Current prognosticators believe our fall is imminent. Or is already here. Nonsectarian speakers own up to godlessness, but have anyway morphed sin and damnation into civil calumnies. Collapse, apocalypse, extinction, whatever, from our own hands, or our machines. In these predictions, heaven or hell isn't waiting for anyone. Purgatory is here. Reason, probability theories, and statistics do predict the end of something. Oil, say, and water. And it's true, we are incinerating the planet, poisoning and depleting it. Totally. Still, we are alive, we are here now. The earth has been disrupted and disturbed by humans at least since the invention of fire, which must have imitated nature's lightning strikes.

Some have said that our being absorbed in images is the sine qua non for our inevitable self- and other-destruction. Some have said that narcissism, shown by our avidity for images, turned us inward, into inner-bounded psyches, away from the natural order and from a necessary empathy, both underlying our immense species failure and so on. Interiority—an illusion as great as Narcissus found the river/mirror to be.

Narcissism is part of the natural order.

The Picture People are unlike earlier humans only in requiring moment-by-moment proof of the world around them and their position in it. Systems to locate themselves wherever they are. GPS = technological solipsism. When the cell phone arrived, what did people first say on it? "I'm here, I'm walking home." My fave: "I'm waving to you, can you see me?"

Reflections in pools of water might have given rise to the earliest drawings. The Neanderthal or Cro-Magnon or earlier Man noticed an image in a stream, maybe his, probably first an animal's—I can imagine that early man touching his nose, touching the water, the water's slight turbulence contorting his image. Lucille Ball and Harpo Marx mimicked each other, pretending to be mirror images, that's way back, 1950s TV, so if you know the reference, you're doing your media history.

First, I can imagine our ancient ancestor—let's call him Magnon—watching his shadow track him. Shadows attract scrutiny, breed paranoid thoughts, i.e., who's following me, and also provide ocular information and sight-protection when there actually is a stalker.

Modernist and contemporary photography pay attention to the shadow.

An essential immateriality attaches to these tantalizing dark echoes of existence, and what are shadows to this existence, what does their possibility suggest to future *Homo sapiens*? Can the apelike creature make them last? I mean, why did a scratch on a wall ever evolve into a drawing or a painting. That's not really a question.

My script is terrible, like claw marks. Also can't draw, only hit keys, touch and press.

It's not what we know that matters to me, but does knowing it DO anything? What difference does it make to know, when forces within and without move you or even conspire against you?

The need of prehistoric humans and us to make, *homo facere*, and to depict the world is an effort to explain Being. Even to make Being explicable.

It might be a human instinct to leave a mark, to make or manifest an image, to court experience and existence into a cage, to keep it, EXPERIENCE, I mean. Claiming territory, marking it, scratching on walls the objects in our territories, what we capture and kill; animals do it, we are animals. An animal leaves scent on a tree or door, a cat rubs its furry body against a chair leg, darkening it, staining it, oh the stain.

I'm off, off and on. Floating.

What is my subject?

There is nothing outside of images.


## FAMILY DRAMA: GROWING UP MORE CRAZY

What happens first happens indelibly, while the brain is developing. The brain keeps growing, WET and gooey, and early neural pathways plant themselves and thrive. That's childhood, the brain developing into a sweet and sour sticky hive.

What happens in YOUR family first, when you're a little one, is the basic drama of life, and melodrama also starts, shaping the child's bandwidth of vision. I mean, capacity to focus, and understanding of what is seen. A child is beamed to life (and psychic death) by its family; the child magnifies and amplifies that organism, the family, toward all other beings and into all other events.

Attachment issues attachment issues.

Mother feels attached to her ancestors, an invisible mob surrounding her: she doesn't really walk alone, and she still says, if I ask, They animate me. Clearly this is how I became interested in tribes.

Beverly Farms, near our family home, was where Clover Hooper Adams and her historian husband, Henry Adams, had a house, for a time. Hooper is Mother's "maiden" name.

They made her image-obese, and verbose; ancestral images got under her skin, and became incorporated into her self-image. Mother's descendants infused her blood, and she feels their specific inherited traits as effects, which occur by spirit, through character and psychology. Mother explains Little Sister was born an old soul. She laid eyes on her last baby, her only girl, and "I knew who she was. That's why I gave her Clover as a middle name, she's an old soul."

I feel attached to my backhand.

My parents started me on tennis early, because Father wanted me to have a sport I could take into old age. Old age to a kid?

Tennis at day camp, sleep-away camp, I played every minute allowed, high school team for a while, and, from when I was a baby, pretty much, I watched John McEnroe, Johnny Mac, he's screaming at the linesman or umpire, stamping his feet. Wow! He's having a tantrum, Mother dismissed him and his behavior, I was glad, and Father, I don't know, when I started beating him at his game, he withdrew. Didn't matter.

Johnny Mac. His sweat-wet curly hair bounced around his furious face, and I watched him rant, and watched him win. So, weirdly, I was into sports, baseball, football, a nerd, a smart kid, a jock, all emblazoned on my T-shirt, Zeke Starchaser. My tennis aptitude became part of family legend: I wasn't a bully, even too sensitive for a boy, whatever that meant, or would mean to me, but I held the court. Sliced, slammed, spun, confused my opponent—I wanted to win like Johnny Mac.

In Little League, I switched from short-stop to third base. I had good hands, hand/eye coordination, speed, but I wanted the baseline, I liked how the third baseman would leap, glove hand out, for a speeding ball, perpendicular to the field, like a bird in flight. I liked the image.

Bo Jackson was IT, my main man. Breaks my heart thinking about him, his career finished because he actually outran his body, and screwed up his hip. To me, Bo was just like a shooting star. Football ended his baseball career, so I have a declared hatred of football.

To break myself down (didn't know it) I shifted positions in baseball. Also, I ran. I stopped running the mile, stayed with sprints. If you want a change in your life, you have to change position, which is to change your image of yourself. An image is a position, both mental and actual, and vice versa. If you want a different life, outrage your former self-image.

## "SILENT SPEAKING IN PLAIN SIGHT"

I once argued that a family photo album effects a silent conversation (traditionally, men were taught to keep silent about their feelings; these were always secret), one that constitutes an unspoken familial story, which adds to what's reported from sib to sib, generation to generation. The image of the family is built, though, by a combo of words and pix—all media play a big part. For this article, I didn't interview families but grabbed images and read them only as pictures: formal in terms of composition, how the image was constructed, etc., and as interpretation, what they projected. Compared compositions and meanings with earlier family albums. I broke down the photograph: who was placed where, etc. Hierarchies in families determine placement in pictures. I studied their gestures. I'm very interested in facial expressions, especially smiles: they are often duplicitous and deceptive.

For an undergrad paper, I studied an older friend's family album from the fifties and sixties, mainly, in which no one ever smiled. Here, then, since these pix were posed, I considered the role of the photo-taker, the father, who ordered or chose unsmiling subjects. He did not say, SMILE, please. That would not have pleased him.

In the flow between subject and object, between taker and taken, which can incorporate a sadomasochistic element— the actor and the acted-upon—an exceptional development silently declaimed itself. The family dynamic, especially because of the picture taker's POV—he could have chosen to shoot his subjects differently—was manifested: the unseen photographer determined the atmosphere.

It turned out that the man who took these pictures later took his own life.

Both his children, unsurprisingly, grew up without senses of humor, and with fear of others' humor, of jokers. They misunderstood jokes and viewed jokers suspiciously: the joke must always be on them.

I'm looking at whether image has dominated a person or family's sense of itself, themselves or their family, as in, upholding an image of the family.

In the way Mother believes.


## HUMANISM: HOMO SAPIENS AGITPROP

Constellations align in the sky to predict our fate, because we solipsists gaze from and about ourselves. (I was an avid cloud- and star-gazer once upon a moon. Still like clouds.) Stars are not FOR or against me, which doesn't mean I'm not susceptible to superstition, I am, and might conjure solitary stars shooting across the sky for my nighttime pleasure, a stelliferous, heavenly decoration for me, or prophesy.

Humans haven't been on earth long. Stars live infinitely longer but they're hanging in the heavens, ancient reflected light, to spread Nature's glitter over terrace parties, blinking to create atmosphere on date night. Shooting stars serve us the way everything once served humanity, all for us, because solipsism goes a long way as consolation for human limitation.

People could perceive in a cloud any image they desired— God's face, jewels, a dog, a dead lover—while the stars and constellations, with lives infinitely longer than human beings', could predict human fate. Cool, right.

The natural order looks cool, until an animal stalks another's defenseless cub and eats it; floods wash away buildings and thousands drown, and massive craters open and swallow entire villages.

Still, people live on fault lines and in flood zones. I'm not getting into that. Emotions rule, and science can study them, and does, but feelings don't lie down and play dead. They morph faster than we can capture them.

Human narcissism is cultural and psychological. Individuals carry the gene, because it serves survival. Narcissism lies, embedded, in the strands of our DNA, as a coping mechanism for, as just mentioned, survival, species-protection. All the mirrors/screens humans have concocted to gaze at themselves, to record themselves as factual characters or fictional ones—they're for image-grabbing.

There's an overproduction of ego artists jerking the chains of under-nourished narcissists, who don't know how to protect themselves. I know some pretty well.

## FACING FAMILY VALUES

I was the brat, the family's oppositional bugger, enjoying the current of life—buddies, Little Sister's weirdness, Mr. Petey's appearances, pictures and photography. I ignored Hart, mostly ignored parents' battles, because all of that took up my time and energy. I followed, or was led in, a direction from which or where I caught the disease, even as, later, I was writing about it. Not unusual. Check out medievalists who converted to Catholicism. Similar deal.

But with any ideology—cameras: ideological machines, with positivist assumptions—there are holes, and at first, cameras were just holes and boxes, camera obscuras the first images. They left nothing.

"Family" never leaves. Full of holes. Holes full of holes.

OK, photography was invented before anesthesia. What phantom pain was its lack causing?

Human grandiosity needed proof to assure its assumptions about being human and of its superiority in the creature kingdom. Consciousness doomed us to be proof-seekers. The God of religions couldn't assure eternal life, a hereafter, God is dead, right—fundamentally, but often reborn—but a photograph, a picture, offers hope that there is a there—there.

Descartes's assertion, I think blah blah, deified rationality, when people needed to claim immortality by way of human reason, not God's love. But how can I "show" what I think in the world, what I have made?

Later, Descartes's fallacious proof of God's existence came, because he needed to rid himself of doubt. If God no longer needs to think of me, this rids me of some doubt, for instance, about my responsibility to God.

So Empiricism replaced Faith. Or, fostered another Faith—in the positive appearance of things, objects. But Reason didn't promise an after-this-life, and rejecting immortality isn't easy. The search to fix an image also was a quest for an afterworld to soothe the nonbeliever. The rational nonbeliever believes what he or she sees, and relies on proof of existence, which no religion could provide, though miracles once sufficed as evidence, even proof—this character wants a photograph (see spirit photography).

A life span is nothing compared with death's eternity.

Is there life before birth?

Seeing might be believing, if evidence existed that what we saw we saw in common, communally, or in communion. If everyone apprehended the same sense or meaning from a photograph, we might agree on a reality, but that goal for a photograph's purpose, its value, could never be achieved; the phenomenologists made that clear, and the spirit photographers, and the psychoanalysts, and clinical psychologists with the TAT test and the Rorschach, projection. Perception is overdetermined. It also matters who gives the tests and reads them, because this influences the results.

Take a study of rats and grad students: one group were told their rats were brilliant, the other group told theirs were stupid. Same rats, same batch. Which rats did better on the tests, "the smart ones." The handlers' attitudes produced results. Expectations. I've been told by students my expectations for them are too high. Not kidding.

## FAMILY VALUES ITS SECRETS (DOMESTIC TERRORISM)

Secrets swallow families whole.

Suicide. Alcoholism. Murder. Incest. Kidnapping. Disappearance. Adoption. Sperm donor. Individuals spend years searching for people and answers.

Transparency is a cool notion, sure, but it's also an idea-game, or a game idea. Seeing through IT is fantastical, to watch the apparatus at work, the process, whatever, fine, semi-doable, but it's deceptive: other processes lie deeper. The panopticon may once have worked to police prisoners in cells; but observation doesn't stop conspiracies by, say, nonverbal gesture. How we survive is also often a secret. Conspirators barely need to register consent.

I know firsthand.

Prosaically, people in the U.S. rarely reveal their salaries. Even the most socially minded will not reveal theirs. Think about how that works.

Society has its ways to cohere, and prevail.

Sick, quaint secrets thrum subcutaneously on both sides of my family.

Aunt Clarissa doesn't like men as a class, but especially my father and me. Not a family secret. She's not reserved about her feelings. Disdain—no problem expressing it. But she's a recluse and a hoarder.

Ants creep and crawl back and forth to the Queen in the colony, carrying food. Are we not ants?

My brain amps misty, wistful, totally. I see the barbecue pit, my father disdainfully flipping burgers; Little Sister scarce and present, a selectively mute angelic vegetarian taking distance from us way-too-ordinary beings; Bro Hart moaning about some shit; and Mother, reticent, there-not-there. What the hell? MOTHER.

At nine I stared at pictures of Mother when she was nine, so cool, Mother, Ellen, a girl, and only I alone could force a Mother into Being. Mother? I asked the photo. Mother, I demand, still. Catching me out, Mother called me obsessive or a nut job, depending on her mood. I still say to her, "How about, 'My son's impassioned about love, mystery, and loss.'"

We can photograph a life from birth, minute one, to death's last breath.

After-death or post-life is covered by spirit photographers.

Mother says, OK, you're right, you're impassioned, but you have to move on.

That kills me. Mother's beliefs permeated my kid-brain—parental beliefs land hard.

After people die, Mother told me when I was little, what remains are memories and photographs, that's why we take them. Later, she contradicted herself: Your interest in the family photos is morbid, the photos, videos, you're holding on to your childhood, it's almost sick. I ignored her caution and still do. Maybe when she's dead, I'll reconsider.

Often when people die, you reconsider their statements. I stare at their pictures.

I didn't recognize Mother's games playing in my mind. Or in what ways my desires and views began with hers, but then things happened to upset that, and desires settled in another place entirely. A non-place, basically. Or, an anti-place with antimatter. But let's say spirit dominates.

OK, I can't really know Mother, or the other.

The family is other than you, but also the other is in you. You should know yourself, but also you can't know yourself, mostly you can't, because of how you're inhabited by others. Sometimes that other is you.


## FAMILY ABUSE

The worst things happen in families, disgusting, painful, with long legacies, yet the family is idealized, and there's no replacement for its form, not yet. In the 1960s political and social agitation affected social values, and media also remade family: blood ties, no longer necessary, but family cohesion still required loyalty and secrecy.

Communes didn't work, ideal communities—Brook Farm, Millbrook, etc.—and, in whatever form they take, queer or straight, single parent, etc., families remain a tool for survival. An orphan's fate is usually worse.

Child abuse is family abuse. The exceptions, the ones who tell, are temporary sensations—Roseanne; La Toya Jackson, Lindsay Lohan, Patty Hearst, Patti Davis. (The men? Ron Reagan: witty in his indiscretions.) The Kardashians have constructed their own category, a phenomenon of images based only on images. Their celebrity roots lie in O. J. Simpson's relationship to Robert Kardashian, father of Kim, Khloé, Kourtney, and Rob (Jr.), that started in 1971. Father Robert was O.J.'s friend and a lawyer-turned-entrepreneur, let his law license lapse, and renewed it when O.J. murdered Nicole Brown Simpson and her friend Ron Goldman, not criminally "proved," so allegedly murdered. Kardashian was seen carrying O.J.'s duffle bag from O.J.'s house—it was filmed— maybe hiding O.J.'s bloody clothes, a day after the murders, and before O.J. was arrested on June 17, 1994. Robert and Kris Houghton Kardashian divorced in 1991; later, Kris married Olympic decathlete Bruce Jenner, now Caitlyn Jenner. Her Hollywood "reveal" was a *Vanity Fair* cover.

What, if anything, does Kris K. know about her ex's, Robert's, involvement?

What is it we watch when we watch. A family. We watch a family.

## WHERE WAS I?

At puberty, life changed, totally. First, Hart, four years ahead of me, set the stage. I watched him shave, hoping he'd slit his throat, knew when he was jerking off, because his door stayed shut and locked. His voice dropped, stupid Adam's apple grew. His aggression amped. He hit harder. His hair was everywhere. His smell, the products he used. His penis. So it would go for me. And it did, in Zeke's way.

Mother had a vagina. I'd learned the word "vagina" on the playground, or maybe Mother used it, to be anatomically correct. I was already into my penis, pulling on it. But I wanted to see a girl's, for real

At fifteen, I wanted to kill my brother and father. Figuratively, mostly. To be on the safe side, like all teens with bedrooms, I chilled there.

During a siege of parental passive aggression, I'd wait until it blew over or Father drank himself quiet, and imagined another life and another family. Who doesn't, consciously and unconsciously, want to invent a different family story. Obliterate the birth parents, concoct another that fits a wistful, burgeoning image.

I was living a modified second-generation punk life, less violent and into the mix of heavy not death metal, Kurt Cobain. Alt-rock, moaning and groaning. Enraged by everything and everyone. Rage against the machine, dude. The Velvet Underground. Later I got pacified. Loved Pavement.

Rage is normal, Mother said, to pacify me and herself. Progressive parents ruin teen spirit. Seriously, it blows.

Normal is on a continuum between insanity and sanity, but who defines those degrees and what they mean, family to family. Hell. Barely sane, functionally insane, frequently sane, infrequently insane, moderately sane, THIS PERSON COULD GO EITHER WAY, worse than but approximating normal.

I fell into science, first, because of insect-interest and photography, second, because of a super-charged madman high school biology teacher, Mr. Church, Franklin Church, sounds upstanding but seemed kinky. He had a purple scar across his forehead from fighting in Vietnam, hand-to-hand combat is what I pictured. Biology. Math. Chemistry, the warring test tubes.

Mr. Church was cool, at the front of the classroom, tall, bald, his spherical head and bulging forehead, his protruding proboscis, framed by a green board. His scar shone scarlet in the sunlight. Mr. Church wasn't superhuman, he wasn't my hero, but he approximated or had a semblance of uniqueness as he stood in front of us. He appeared indifferent to everyone, removed, distracted, a whack job. Everyone knew that the war had done something to him.

Like Great Uncle Zeke, he will become, in his high school class picture, a yellowed face, just an enigmatic smile, a beefy hand gesturing, goofily spoofing his usual, up against a wall.

What's that expression, what's Uncle Zeke thinking, what's happening in him—interiority. OK, I want that fantasy: mouth opens, shockingly, speaks the Truth. Isn't that the thing we think we want from others—the truth. You don't want the truth, believe me. This little boy wondered: Would the pictures wake up while I slept?

## FAMILY IMAGE, ETC., THE FAMILY MAJESTIC

In my family's photo album, Clarissa's and Mother's great-great-great aunt Matilda stands slightly off-center in the frame, in a longish shot, and central is a leafless tree, tall and straight, bifurcating the picture plane; behind that, a wooden house, whose gable-style roof rises in an inverted V. It's a saltbox house with, it appears, an addition that slopes off the side of the roof. The door is roughly centered behind Tilly's body, just slightly to the right of it. She's a dark shape in a shapeless long dress, her white hair in contrast to her dress. The white frame of the door's window also seems to frame her, partially.

The print is overexposed. (A "self-exposure" in relationship to "exposure time" is a connection I'm working through.) It's set on stiff, gray board. The composition: the long windows in the house mimic the shape of Matilda, or Tilly. She's no Whistler's *Mother*, but the photo's symmetry creates serenity, and drew me to her, Aunt Matilda, there she was. Is. I see her now.

A photograph doesn't speak. If it did it would be just another unreliable narrator.

Everyone is unreliable, except Aunt Clarissa. Ha.

Clarissa has nurtured her highly strung instrument, and believes neurasthenia is a distinction bred of fine minds. Great and small minds think alike.

## YOU ARE NOT ACTUALLY HAVING FUN

Society plays itself out in images: Take picnics.

Now, picture a picnic: a romantic, comforting, and/or familial image. But a picnic won't be as pleasant as its mental picture.

Call it up: Last summer you bought a hamper. It's summer again. Let's have a picnic. Wow. You, mother, sister, lover, brother, father, or buddy spend time buying the food, preparing it, packing it up, etc. You and yours jump into a car, damn, someone's late, wait, wait, then because it's Sunday the roads are jammed, what did you expect, right? Plus, the AC doesn't work. Or someone forgot the blanket. Or the bug spray, and there might be black ants, black flies, mosquitoes. OK, whew, you locate a spot in a park, but it's way more crowded than you imagined; or you decided on going to the beach, and the blanket's down, but there are soda cans and plastic wrappers everywhere. Disgusting. Still, you've arrived. All the food, carefully wrapped and prepared, comes out of the hamper, but the wind gusts and sand sprays over the blanket, the food, people move quickly to save the potato salad, then need to straighten the blanket, more sand lands. OK, the blanket's wrinkled and sandy. Then something spills. Twenty minutes later, you've eaten, everyone's full, and you all sit there, looking at the ocean, lake, a tree or two. After all that effort, an anticlimax. Then? Get drunk. Sleep. Argue. Have sex. Clean up. Drive home.

The word "picnic," meant to be an idyll, signifies an idyllic image; the actual event is mostly hellish.

Our family once picnicked inside the car, as rain poured down.

We can plan them, the way we do weddings, anniversaries, a picnic of delicious eats, sun-joy and togetherness, happiness galore: high expectations for a luxe day to remember, pleasant indolence, blissful relaxation.

Reality disappoints regularly. When people are supposed to have fun, it's likely they won't, because fun can't live up to its image.

Does anything live up to its image?

## SELF, NARRATING

My first pure love was Maisie, the model for all my true loves. Maisie was a tiny, perfect girl. She lived in the neighborhood and we went to nursery school together, my girl next door. We played together, sort of, that is, I acknowledged her presence, even though I didn't like girls. She was in my kindergarten too. I figured I'd marry her, understanding that was the way of it, and I may have asked her.

On the morning after Christmas, barely morning, I awoke because of a weird moaning, a lowing, a freaky cry, never heard before, oh Maisie, Maisie, Maisie, oh no, no. An awful howling, that mother's still crying in my head, Maisie Maisie. Her mother was running or walking on the road, back and forth, shrieking and crying. They lived a long ways down the road.

Maisie passed away in her sleep, Mother told me. Died. She was sick, but no one knew it.

Her parents didn't know? How come they didn't? It's their fault.

No, it's no one's fault. She was sick. She had walking pneumonia.

So, Maisie walked sick in her sleep, walked and walked until she met death, she walked right up to death.

Death kept her perfect in my mind.

The drive for perfection brings suffering.

Maisie was beautiful like Little Sister, who hadn't come into our lives yet.

## CULTURE VALUES LOOKING

"Looking" feels outside of time, call it timeless; but looking is always in time. Looking can make anyone feel out of time, since looking has an ahistorical feel. But when we look at pictures of the past, we look with our history, from inside our time.

Critics, notably Barthes and Sontag, proposed that photography is necessarily about death, because the moment in the photograph is gone, past (even when the person in it isn't, just always younger), the photograph represents the past, and death.

Photographic theory shouldn't ignore the reality of a viewer's presence, who activates a picture. A viewer looks in the present, and brings the past into the present. And context changes, attitudes change, etc., toward the so-called "lost object." Reception, how we read, is also part of the picture.

Roland Barthes birthed reader-response theory, in "The Death of the Author": the rise of the reader was at the expense of the Author.

Humanists went CRAZY. No authors?

A viewer invests in pictures. Projects into them. How far that projection goes, how much "life" the photograph can deliver, sustain, depends on its "art." A vital receiver often sees more than a taker might have intended. Viewers create dimensionality from one dimension.

From nothing to nothing. Nothing more. More nothing. Kidding.

What is inexpressible? What are there no words for? What if you can't experience what there are no words for? So this conundrum is why positivism brought the camera with it. Hypothetically, the invention appears to tell stories and report moments, which themselves can't say what they are but show SOMETHING.

The totally appropriate apparatus for a species that imagines it has more to say than it does.

Plus, the photographic apparatus: one, is an entity proving existence, and its opposite; two, is an entity encouraging projections of the highest and lowest order.

An image is an image is an image is an image. But a rose names something.

## THE PICTURE PEOPLE I: THE FAMILY ALBUM AS TOTEM

In hundreds of albums I haven't found cigarette burns or other defacements of pictures of reviled relatives. It's hard, even when you hate people, to deface their pix. Or burn them, though filmmaker Hollis Frampton did just that in his film *(nostalgia)*. He filmed the burning of photographs he'd taken; it was his entry into film-making, his negation of photography, or of his photographic practice.

Photographs aren't real that way, yet the experience of watching *(nostalgia)* was sad, even devastating at times, because Frampton was burning his history.

I trained myself to spot the empty areas, or what I call "putatively erasable experience," by watching for so-and-so's father disappearing; wife after a divorce, and then I'd gently query the album owner. I hear and register: they divorced then or someone died. No one gets rid of their pets' pictures.

Never pictured, formal failures—no formal announcement

for these events, or "undone-events," those characterizing the "un-bonding family," because those require a spoken narrative, which I designate as "necessary but unreliable voice-overs." With my posse, this necessity hit me hard. Talking over the pictures, because pictures don't talk, they beg for narration. I did that in my first book. But I'm into something different now.

In most albums until recently close-ups are few, mostly medium to long shots: a few portraits in the traditional sense, once done by professional photogs, even until the 1960s, and there are always generic school photos, they continue; but usually in an album, people hang in groups, clustering from short to tall. So, it's hard to see details, features of faces.

Generally, on sidewalks, in restaurants, for group pictures, people stand way back and shoot from far away. I watch tourists getting their pix taken by a stranger who stands too far back. What's up with this? Don't people know where to stand when they shoot? Really, what the hell are they seeing, are they even looking?

"Rational distancing," my term for this peculiar form of inadequacy, is the distance humans believe necessary in order to include everyone fairly. Fairness is a matter of perspective, like the vanishing point in a social setting. But who's in the foreground and in the background, you don't want that, unequal heights, right. Imagine society solely as an image, then imagine its vanishing point. It's abstract but I'm working on theorizing it. People don't recognize that to image a specific event requires a specific kind of eye, a visual inclusion that must entail exclusion, a slice, not the whole pie. It's called framing, and it's not only a photographic or cinematic term but a cultural one too.

(See Erving Goffman, *Frames*.) It's how I can move between the disciplines, by keeping the frame in mind.

"Shifting Frames": to shift them requires mental super-impositions. Like, when people say I'm out of my mind, or You're out of my mind, or You're out of your mind, I think, I'm out of my frame of reference. Not kidding.

Interdisciplinarity is a goal, but few do it, actually can do it. Just like any form of integration—the matter is: what gets absorbed into what, or whom. What's foreground, background, and does the flattening of contrast between the two, or their fusion, prophesy other kinds of blindnesses, say, to differences, or total confusion? (Rhetorical question.) The discovery of perspective, in the Renaissance, brought the vanishing point, backgrounds and foregrounds. The vanishing point may be vanishing, which will have consequences.

When I was about ten, in the family trove I found a loose photo, glued onto cardboard, of four people, three women, one man, all wearing hats. A weird picture: the four are perched at, or in, a long, narrow rectangular opening in the side of a wooden building. All have squeezed into a space small for four adults. The lumber runs vertically, which also seemed strange. The picture was shot at an angle, the rooftop sloping down to the right; above it, framing the top right corner, a triangle of sky. With no bottom or foundation to the building shown, the four might be low to the ground or up high. Impossible to tell. One woman's face is in sunlight, and visible; she's smiling, her arm resting on the sill of the opening. The other three—their faces are shadowed, but the man looks happy. Actually, they appear to be having fun.

Mother and Clarissa didn't know who took it or who was in it. What hit me later about our old family photographs: hardly anyone ever looks like they're having fun. (Fun came later, with Kodak moments.) These characters, they're gleeful as they pose for the camera. Unusual. Maybe they're at a carnival or fair.

## CLOSE-UPS

Faces don't open up, can't read them like a proverbial book, faces aren't prose. We face others with apprehension, in both senses of the word—fearfully and with some idea of comprehension. The mystery of facial expression can't be completely decoded, even the book for Neapolitan gestures, colorful and fun, demarcates social communication, not what people are thinking when they do it.

The heart is deceitful above all things, and desperately sick; who can understand it? —Jeremiah 17:9

Captions can't capture it, they may contain meanings or restrain them. Also, they rely on wily words.

## WHAT ARE WE HUMAN FOR?

With bigger brains, humans are equipped to ask complex questions. Unfortunately, they ask big, sad questions, such as, Is life futile? The wrong questions beget the wrong or no answers; basically, these are unanswerable, because existential, except as matters of faith and belief. I follow Wittgenstein up to a point—that is, when I want more than a discussion about language usage.

If Darwin was right, there are reasons, supposedly beneficial, our species has evolved and developed and keeps going in the way it has, and will. (Even that we are destroying the planet?) Other creatures live integrated lives with other insects and animals, parasitic or symbiotic. They kill each other, mostly for food. They also fight for territory. They steal each other's babies, males kill other males' females' newborns. This is what self-described humans call "Nature." What we call civilized behavior shares some of these facets.

OK, patriarchy had its time and its raison d'être—to track progeny for free labor. New men know that's over, on hold, in suspension, and they are disoriented. They are all men in transition.

## FAMILY VALUES: DOMESTIC DIS-INCLINATIONS

To a kid like me, everything promised freedom, later.

BUT Guess Who's Coming to Dinner: deluded white people.

Father roved freely at night, and fully invaded on weekends. Mother was inner sanctum, the domain, to which Little Sister carried a genetic free pass, always, in every way. When she had something to say, even without knocking, she could walk right into Mother's office. I was pissed off then, I'm still a little pissed off, about her getting special treatment. Little Sister's "selective mutism" had a critical place, established a critical wall, in our house; if she felt moved to open up—total license. She had super-added privileges. Then a child grows up envying the sick and admiring illnesses' dispensations, benefits, not their disadvantages.

## SELECTIVE MUTISM

The Parents researched the syndrome. It's an anxiety disorder. Later, I researched it, and Hart, because he copies me. Selectively talking, a selective talker, otherwise mute at school, in groups. Websites promote a concept: "Ridding the silence."

For a person with selective mutism, it's anguishing, and I get it. But I learned to love her the way she was. I love silence, I mean it.

Little Sister's being, or image of being, and being there,

pleased me, and so did her discretionary silence, which was evidence of a pathology; but I didn't care then, and I'm not sure I care now, my lack of worry doesn't hurt her or anyone, except me, maybe.

One, I need quiet time, space.

Two, lust for a self-possessed, long-distance-running woman.

Three, lean toward peculiar love-troubles.

And, because there's no strict separation between "us" and "them," that's how I came naturally—haha—to observing my posse and me, guys late twenties to forty, and our attitudes toward women, ourselves "as men," etc.

## THE CONTEMPORARY IS TEMPORARY

Ethnography isn't predictive, but explanatory (theoretical).

Story-telling IS an ethnographer's delight. We/they are greedy listeners collecting narratives. Ethnography and fiction both employ narratives, ethnographers hang their hats on lived lives.

Fiction lets imagination happen. We who are not the story-tellers but listeners/readers are taught to restrain our fantasies, and hear what's said, but part of the attack on cultural anthropology derives from the impossibility of turning off psychic processes. Since what's before you isn't stable, an observer can't be, either, in his/her interpretations. Life is a relationship with other life. Humans are entirely dependent upon other humans, right? But you, I, must account for, and expect, disruptions, too. The observer is a temporary entity in relation to other temporary and ultimately inconsistent objects. One object might achieve balance with another, but generally that relationship won't last.

Is inconsistency a symptom or result? It doesn't explain anything, even though it persists. Obviously, it's a paradox, and there's no para-doctor. Just kidding.

Can life feel more temporary? On the verge of disappearing. Still, there are more and more ways to record it.

Nothing stays the same, right. Change isn't good or bad, mostly indifferent, because "life" doesn't care about you living.

A fact on the ground—an observable event, like a battle—is one agreed to have happened, though many interpretations of it follow, say, the massive fire-bombing of Dresden. (See Vonnegut's *Slaughterhouse-Five*.)

A photograph is similar. Cameras don't create pictures. They don't assemble anything; a person places or manipulates objects for it. No wonder an image can't reveal anything: there's no under-image, no substratum, no palimpsest to be erased, no "buried stuff."

I'm digging in the forest for treasure. Feel me?

Now, why shoot what's already there, when a scene can be created, equally true and false, one that's never existed. The mind can decide it's there. In my mind-lab, here's the motto: make what you want to believe.

It's my consciousness, even if it's in the public culture.

Because of the camera and photographs, consciousness changed. Or, put it this way: there could be a consciousness industry, because of photography. There could be pop culture. I am imaged, I can image, and I do not need to be literate about what a photograph is, or about the camera. Everyone can take pictures. Big deal. And, everyone can be made to believe we all see the same way, which we do not.

What does a photograph do for human consciousness? What has photography done? With photography, is one more conscious of the world? Or, only, more self-conscious? We can be shown to others, shown others, other places; but can anyone avoid the projecting of self onto other images? Not mapping, but projecting.

How does subjectivity distort viewing?

The "self" changed with photography, or a new self emerged. That's what some say. Yes, no, I don't totally buy it, but it can't have retarded its growth.

## FAMILY VALUES A BODY BEAUTIFUL

My parents were enlightened, relatively.

But the world happened in me, not them. KEEP OUT OF MY ROOM. I shared it with transformers. Bedazzling realities.

We three kids were dragged to museums in Boston, New York, and other "significant cultural institutions." Our pompous-art father deployed that vocabulary. They didn't really have to drag me, more Bro Hart, who skulked around the vast rooms, not disguising his disdain, welling in his puny secrets. Little Sister drank in art like a wino at a bar, the perfect museum-goer—silent. In front of a Degas dancer, she resembled one; a pre-Raphaelite near a Rossetti, or an innocent child in a Julia Margaret Cameron photograph.

In museums, noisy streets, Little Sister's muteness added depth—her silence amended the need for speech, so I discerned vulgarity in talking just to talk, mouths mouthing sounds, because near this unique creature with her fount of quiet solitude, my mind expanded, and I heard what wasn't being said, since Little Sister communicated beyond language's capacity, and she could always reach something in me. I believed that. The portraits of beatific passivity wounded Mother; she'd stamp one foot, usually her right, and vanish, gone to another picture, unnoticed by me or Little Sister. Little Sister loved them, though, maybe because of their demanding femininity. I can't know. I tried to look at them the way she or Mother might, because I sometimes wanted to be her, a strange envy that caused more family concern.

Mother wasn't masculine in obvious ways—short hair, short nails, mannish suits, not her style; though in the eighties she wore long jackets with boxy shoulders, all the women did. She was pretty, and is, and affected men, heads turned fast, and I saw it as a kid, her potent effect on them. *Then I watched her watching them watching her.*

Way later, learning about the cinematic gaze in a film course that segued into cultural anthro courses, about "fixing" women with the camera's male eye—Father's, basically—I imagined butterflies pinned to a dorm bulletin board. Worse, pinned there, Mr. Petey, an endangered species.

Back then, my parents worried about my normality, because little Zeke felt drawn to age-inappropriate weirdos. And wanted to be a weirdo. But I watched TV. I was captive to the game world, also conforming to trends, D&D and other stuff; I still did my schoolwork, because I'm compulsive and it was easy.

Conforming is the operative concept—talking 'bout my gen-gen-generation; in the end my parents conceded "normal enough."

I tested everyone's limits, that's what they told me; I saw myself as a race car, and they were my track. I don't have tracks, I never did that. I tested them, and me. I still test people, and they always fail. OK, I have my laughs. Yeah. I do whatever, whenever. But also I'm not spontaneous. Highly overrated, anyway, usually just a case of impulsivity or drugging.

An adult or grown-up is an adaptation, a living set of learned behaviors for specific social settings, other contexts. I was coached, verbally, and shown displays of adulthood. I was verbally warned, harshly: Once you're an adult, you will have to . . . If you don't do this . . . It's a natural process, developmental, maturation, the inevitable, natural unfolding of a species, but there's a harshness, savagery, in its execution, its executives. What about the executive function, parenting?

They say: When you're an adult, you'll see. You'll be sorry. Just wait until you're a father or a mother.

I had to keep up appearances, so that when I outgrew my child-self or, colloquially, grew up, I acted like a grown-up.

Some young mammals get dumped in the jungle to fend for themselves. Our species isn't meant to but it does that also.

Does the world happen in them, too?

## PICTURE PEOPLE PICTURE VALUES

Photography developed the way photographs first developed—over time. Many characters influenced its attenuated birth; given its emphasis on reproducibility (see Walter Benjamin), that seems appropriate. Depending upon which historian you read, one innovator will get more play than another: Henry Fox Talbot ("the art of fixing a shadow," he wrote), England; Hippolyte Bayard, France; and John Herschel, who invented the word "photography" as well as the terms "negative" and "positive" for the new medium.

Now, it's a cool medium. Thus would have spake 1960s visionary Marshall McLuhan, if he weren't dead.

At the beginning of the nineteenth century, if you failed at drawing, wanted to produce art, which meant imitating Nature or "capturing" it, the camera machine could do it. Henry Fox Talbot's book of his salt print photographs, his invention of the calotype (talbotype), *The Pencil of Nature*, had a run of seventy copies, but those copies got into the right hands, let's say.

A camera was a bigger pencil, drawing Nature without a human hand. The machine displaced the hand, an art in and for the Industrial Revolution. *The Pencil of Nature* foresaw the coming of Walter Benjamin. Not a felix culpa, like Adam's fall that necessitated Christ's coming. Or maybe it was, if the development of the picture machine actually doomed us. But this we cannot know—Picture People can only surmise about the future, enmeshed in hope or despair about it.

Capturing a scene, face, with the photographic apparatus, frosted an already gooey narcissistic cake. Humanity's birthday cake, say. Pursuit of that capture, the urgency with which scientists and artists sought to stop time, proverbially, or keep it, a snapshot of a moment or scene, is not unlike any adventure or journey, the seeking of spices in India or tea from China. Human beings often get what they want, as a species, even if not as individuals; they strive, invent it. Failures are many, and history records species' successes; these are rewarded. People wanted to fly, they did; reach the Moon; have babies outside the uterus. To some extent, people construct their realities, but unlike other mammals they/individual members are regularly dissatisfied or, worse, miserable, and so humans invented abstract tools—religion, say—to persuade themselves that they might be, will be, or can be happy, if not now, tomorrow. Later, in the invention of an after-life.

## FAMILY DEVALUES

Sad people become artists, mostly sad ones, Aunt Clarissa says, because they can't forget, and they make up worlds to suit their sad memories, but they can't get it right, so they keep creating. That's her version of creativity.

Writers worry about losing what people said, and how it happened; photographers worry about losing how it looked, I tell her.

Clarissa knows it all (she's Mother's only sib, plus older): If you have a happy childhood, you don't become an artist. But what if it's too happy, I ask, so you always want to go back there; and that makes you unhappy, too, because it's totally gone.

That's when you start to write, she says, without a glance, but you start a little late and that creates depression.

In my humblie, artists' explanations are often self-serving, displaying a "self-satisfying sadness" (my term).

Aunt Clarissa is a passivist, takes life lying down, never been on a march, would never go near one, not even a parade, couldn't find the heart or the right shoes. "Public spectacles," Clarissa says, "are hell to us sensitive people."

So, Mother's ancestors were constitutive of her self-image. She inclines toward them, as in anaclisis, or choice of a love or erotic object "on the basis of a resemblance to early childhood protective and parental figures," which might lead you to suspect my mother favored her actual parents, but no. Mother chose her image or constructed it, and "loved" on the basis of dead people. I don't know how Father fit as a love object. Maybe as a disinclination, or recidivist throwback.

My father's genealogy was sketchy, his people wandering to America from different parts of Europe: his mother, English, Scotch; father, Russian-Jewish, Spanish; his grandparents had scattered among nations and religions: Catholics, Protestants, converts from Judaism, arriving in the mid to late 1800s.

Weekdays, my father returned home from Boston, where he performed his corporate lawyering, poured himself a shot of Johnny Walker Black, no rocks, took the newspaper off the coffee table (Noguchi, right), and would walk to one of the plate-glass picture windows.

Did the big view enlarge our sense of the world or just our sense of ourselves?

If nice out, he'd continue to the patio, the adult sec-
tor of the backyard, and sit or lie down, start at the lead
column, drink, and read every page but the women's page.
Bad weather, too cold or hot, he'd lie down indoors, overwhelming the Corbusier lounge chair. You couldn't bother
him, so I'd watch his head moving up and down, side to
side, then it'd wobble. Slug, wobble, slug. He pretty much
held his liquor, pretty much, but when he read, his cheeks
flamed and darkened, and sometimes he fell asleep. I could
look at him then, stare. He looked dead, and it made me
feel peaceful.

Mother thinks she is America. Her family was dis-
tantly related to those who arrived on the *Mayflower*. With
the criminals, religious crackpots, I say. You know, Mother,
we inherited their problems. Wow, she gets pissed. We were
poets, she says. Feminists, abolitionists, politicians, she says.
Her people knew or met the Henry James crowd, etc. When
she came of age, Mother let family privilege go, which was
part of her privilege. The way I'd put it, she practiced a type of
ancestor worship, and it's as if, from birth, she knew herself as
an image; her relatives' images suffused her own. Her family's
house was decorated with ancestral portraits by respectable
English and American painters and, later on, nineteenth-
century photographers.

Mother was constant, with her bad days, sure, but mostly
solid like a pet rock (kidding), plus, she was the Stark family
photographer until I weighed in, sort of. She gave me a cool
little camera for my eighth birthday. In 1982, Kodak launched
disc photography, the easy to use, "decision-free" cameras
built around a rotating disc of film. She bought me one from

that line. It was unfussy, she said. Primitive now but I loved my little guy. I was more interested in bugs and rockets then. Mother owned a Zeiss Ikon, and my father, when he was young, bought himself one of the first Polaroid 100 series cameras. Don't you forget it.

Most of the family portraits hung on the walls at Aunt Clarissa's house—we had fewer walls—and they got fixed in my mind. The ancestors were sometimes mentioned as though hanging out with us. One looked down, when we ate, Henry Adams shot by his wife, Clover, a reproduction of one of her prints. Even Clarissa didn't have any originals by Clover.

Mother's reverence for the dead was manifested in their faces on our walls. These characters couldn't be known, but they were our familiars, their images sacred. So they became models, idols, icons.

The dead have a real presence in my life.

I could say, and will, I was driven INTO pictures. Bro Hart got steered into cutting up dead people, looking for diseased tissue.

Father had inherited few family photographs, so he suffered from major "image-envy." There is a compelling one, though, of his father, my grandfather, Edward (never met him). He married late; in his forties had Father. Grandfather Stark is pictured with an unknown woman. He's not smiling at but challenging the photographer; his stance rakish, an arm around the woman as if she were a possession. He's claiming ownership. His other hand rests on his hip, which juts out, and suggests arrogance, cockiness, or indifference. Maybe impatience. The woman, whoever she is, looks pleased.

This is my father's father.

I admit: my curiosity about others must be partly protective. Sometimes even paranoid. If I know your habits and turn of mind, let's say, I know what to expect, and what might happen, to me. If I can recognize myself in others, I can believe I am safe; if I don't see myself in them, I have less predictive capability, less power, and more vulnerability.

I filter my narrative, along with and through others. I know when to talk the talk, and not. Our species is adaptable.

Mostly, I know when I'm blowing smoke. Some, like

me, use self-denigration as a way to rise up. But when your story goes passive, I mean, when it's changed ON you, that's a whole different condition: then you're not the agent of your story. You may be enslaved to another, and, definitely, not in control.

But if you change your bio, you invent another character. Cool. Then you have to remember what's been added or deleted. Keep those changes in mind all the time, including the consequences—new dates and years for every incident in life—that occur from the switches. (Never do this if you're bad at simple math.) There's a reason great liars are sociopaths, they believe their lies, lie smoothly, lies and truths don't have borders.

You have to be rational about your irrational choices, have second sight, which pertains also to photography.

Call the frustrating effort to document, or "just the facts," "de-fictionalizing"

## THE REALNESS/UNREALNESS OF IMAGES

What you see is what you believe, and what you see may not in actuality be there.

"The aim of anthropology is the enlargement of the universe of human discourse." —Clifford Geertz

Geertz distinguishes between falsehood and fiction: Fiction is NOT falsehood. An image is always fiction, just as a report from an anthropologist in the field—a hut or a bar— always entails fiction, NOT making it up. This is creative interpretation. Interpretation is theoretical explanation, it is

MADE UP, it explains, responds to what a person thinks, perceives, these are also artifacts of the human imagination, because thinking requires imagination. Unless a thought is entirely received and a thoughtless conventional wisecrack, it requires creativity. Thinking IS creativity, it is active, and shows, if their heart rate didn't, that human beings are vitally aware of their environments.

Einstein, asked what a child should read, said, "fairy tales," and, after those, more fairy tales.

Any photograph is a fiction, an artifact, and a social fact, part of and existing IN society.


## REPETITION: PRINTS ARE REPLICANTS

Photographs render worlds.

The original was assaulted by multiples, prints, and by Fordism, and theoretically, seminally, by Walter Benjamin, since to him photography's principal distinguishing, radical element was reproducibility. Uniqueness didn't reside in its one-of-a-kind-ness, but instead its capacity to be reproduced for the many, a collectivity, aligning a theory about art with other theorists in his time like Mikhail Bahktin who emphasized a novel's heterogeneity as compared with a poet's singular voice. Which makes sense when acknowledging a novel's "origins" in Gutenberg's printing press, and reproducibility.

Origins: the ur-moment is not so important in the age of the Picture People. But I happen to like thinking about when humans rose up, stood on two legs, to find they could walk upright, that's cool. Many sit now. An object at rest stays at rest. The restless like me can't rest, even in sleep, where I'm forced to run. In dreams, no one can't escape origins.

Or, origins, such as: The Donner Party and its recourse to cannibalism inflames the fantasies of present-day Americans. The species showed its primal nature, which haunts the contemporary version. I'd never, never do that. But who knows.

Last night, I dreamed I was a fly on the wall. Not in a good way, because I couldn't move or hear anything.

Few want to give up on originality, especially actual origins and their meanings.

Booming ancestry biz. Roots r u.

If it's not one kind of memorializing, it's another. Why do people forget so much, and remember selectively? What does memory do for humans as a species equipped with that capacity. Besides, how hardwired is memory when some have a little, some a lot, and each gen might have to relearn what they should, supposedly, remember.

Various artists make visuals that insist on second sight. Now the viewer sees it again, because of a new context, because it's been lifted, and this move shifts ideas about originality. The original, originality, was a dominant factor in an artwork's value—one of a kind. (Though even God had a son.) Appropriation disrupts the importance of "origin" itself, with consequences far beyond art-making and value. Darwin and artists did it first, I think, questioning origins.

## FAMILY VALUES A PLAY CALLED HOME ON TV

MOTHER: Please turn off the TV. [War footage; violent crimes; weird sex scenes.]

FATHER: Zeke needs to see the real world, Ellen.

MOTHER: Yours or mine?

On TV 24/7: In 1996, "child beauty queen" JonBenét Ramsey was murdered. She was six years old when she "disappeared from her house" in Boulder, CO, but her parents didn't call the cops until she'd been missing twenty-four hours. The day after Christmas, she was found dead, strangled, in the family basement. No sign of forced entry, a handwritten blackmail note. Everyone was a suspect, especially her mother, which really upset my mother. In the photos of JonBenét at beauty pageants, she was dressed like a tiny, perfect princess, costumed and in makeup—a glam, sexy, mini-woman. Mother told Little Sister to leave the room when her face, her mother's, her father's appeared. But for months they did all the time, no escaping this creepy story.

I dreamed I found JonBenét alive, and kept the killer away, until I couldn't anymore, couldn't save her from death, but somehow, before, after, or both, we kissed, I kissed her, undressed her, did something with her, and woke up. Eros wets my bed, because I have sex with a dead girl. When more dreams came, oh man, the shame, I was bad, and, if I'd known the word, I'd have called myself a pervert.

Children can't be protected from much of anything, def not their curiosity; not mine. Youth wants to know.

TV mattered, didn't, wasn't "serious," my parents thought, just seriously detrimental. TV prepared me for life, and I claim membership in the second totally televisual gen: content meaningful/meaningless fused seamlessly. Real-fantasy infused me like Mother's maternal ancestors, who fueled her psyche. I am a TV devotee, a slave to its radiating charms; and, it was all about representation. A weaving and warping made me "myself," and later also, it was any foundation in a storm. TV, definitely, was foundational.

In the 1970s, a TV documentary about the Loud family entranced Americans with its psychological honesty—son Lance came out. There were brazen displays of discord, the parents fought. Divorce was "screened": The Louds fell apart on TV.

After Ellen DeGeneres came out on TV, on her series, *Ellen*, after those shock waves leveled, female hetero/gay men became the new romance, so-called white marriages that could last, or new forms of family. What keeps "family" vital now? The emergence of new ones. Homosexuals, once "banned" from society, defining as gay and/or queer, have built them. First, divorce became common, then single families, led primarily by women/mothers; then an accepted gay community showed its desire for the nuclear family, too. The two-father, two-mother dyad has led the way toward mixed, blended, dyed in the wool—kidding—structures.

Compared with the Louds, reality TV trivializes whatever reality a viewer is invested in, switching all "realities" into sameness, since the programs' form is the same no matter what the reality's content. The form is a blender whose ingredients contain angry slurs, sometimes physical violence, and heavy doses of betrayal. These TV exhibitionists contest with or deform their own credulity, even sanity; and humiliate and shame themselves and others. Exploited and exploiters.

The Eighties, my childhood decade, wallowed in Alice Miller's *Drama of the Gifted Child*. Everyone was "gifted." Miller's parameters were like a fortune-teller's reading, one size fits all. Children were Gifted or Abused—family life under Reagan.

On TV, the McMartin trial in California, a long-running play from 1987 to 1990, and the Little Rascals Day Care Center in North Carolina, with abuse alleged in 1989. The accused were tried individually beginning in 1991, the airwaves filled with lurid accusations of satanic rituals—hysteria and "moral panic," that was the term. The extent of the sexual abuse, number of abusers, was totally incredible, the abusers must have been as fast as NASCAR racers.

The Parents whispered behind our backs, Hart's and mine, then turned off the TV because we were too young. I swallowed big whiffs of sordid disorder and bad words. Later, I caught the documentary, *Innocence Lost*, about the Little Rascals Day Care Center, when, already hooked into cultural studies and anthro, I was totally struck by how a conversation and gestures, and a flawed interpretation of behavior, caused the first accuser to think "something was wrong." It was in a small town, where one mother decided that another, Betsy Kelly, who ran the center and was her good friend, wasn't "really sorry" about the bad behavior at the day care center. The accuser alleged that Robert Kelly had slapped her son. Betsy Kelly apologized to her friend, the boy's mother. It wasn't good enough for the mother. She decided there was "more to it."

On the basis of this conversation, allegations of satanic

rituals spread fast, and soon most of the kids claimed to be victims of sexual abuse. They claimed, or the "experts" did, that it happened between September and December 1988. The therapists had entered the picture, big time, and the children revealed to them "repressed memories." The so-called abusers were convicted, given long sentences. Finally, all of the convictions were overturned, and, by 1997, the prosecution dropped all charges. One hell of a shitty decade.

Those trials, pretty much forgotten, though not O.J.'s or Clarence Thomas's (not yet), were Salem witchcraft redux. Not "the red diaper" scare: it was ANY diaper, all diapers could be suspect, any diaper outside the home was vulnerable, because rituals and rape and sodomy happened a lot in demonic nurseries, even though everyone conscious should know most child abuse is by a child's familiars, not strangers.

Abuse goes on, kids damaged, though the eighties scare is over, but that was my little-boy time

Riots of fear come and go—totally wack. But there's no change in the insular family, and its secret keeping. Much blame.

## CO-INCIDENTALS

During the days I was hanging with Mr. Petey, dwelling on Mother's essence, everything felt simple—not her face, which I couldn't read or find words for in a dictionary. Her wary, subdued glances were coded, and I couldn't KNOW FOR SURE.

Mother wasn't serene, not like Little Sister. Mother

trotted from room to room, brain ON, tight-lipped, but her body wasn't. As part of her boundlessness, she discussed issues with me as if I weren't a kid. I liked that, even if I didn't get it. I got the drift.

Adult stuff seemed sinister—that other world, a forbidden place. I knew I would be forced to go there, eventually.

Mother could play her cards close to her ample bust. It ran in her family, she told me, restraint, reticence, though sometimes she looked stormy. Yeah, and she called herself busty. Usually it was a facial expression that told me more than she said, a powerful image, even when illegible.

In the beginning, since everything was about ME 24/7, everything about her was about me too. I was the Sun, she circled round me. When she didn't want ME to know stuff, it was my fault, my being too sensitive, say, or the opposite. My father teased Mother about her family, especially about Aunt Clarissa, and one afternoon he talked some shit about spinsters and kooks, and Mother went OFF—to her office, locked the door, and didn't come out until the next morning. Dad brought us pizza for dinner. Pizza still tastes bad to me, but along with gagging on it—a huge social limitation.

Mother and her clan: kooks, spinsters, how cool and weird was that, and how did being related to them affect me. It made me special, right.

## FACE VALUES TOO

Americans can't shake their Puritan past. Everyone's still hoping to confess their sins, with TV as the judge, visibility itself giving judgment.

Judge Judy appeals to characters who want public humiliation; those who watch wallow in a common human perversity, sure, insatiable curiosity but also schadenfreude. Also, some enjoy watching others being beaten, verbally. (See Freud's "A Child Is Being Beaten.")

Shame's different now. If shame EVEN exists, it doesn't last long—Pee-wee Herman, Martha Stewart, Richard Nixon, Alex Rodriguez, Tom Brady—they bounced back. Americans forget sinners' flaws and misdeeds, especially if they cry on TV and show remorse. A sinner appears on Barbara wawa Walters, or Diane Sawyer—he/she MUST cry. No crying, no transformation. Without a credible sob-confession, there will be no sympathy for the devil.

## THE BACKYARD (OF THE MIND): AMERICAN IMAGINARY

The American frontier, the backyard: a shrunken mediated space for suburban kids before they hit the mall. Their next frontier.

Barbecue time: men/fathers scored and scarred meat, got sloppy drunk, while the women/mothers ran around, setting the table, bearing homemade potato salad, egg yellow in sturdy glass bowls, maybe Pyrex. Mother bought the fixings from the best shops to show she cared, even though she didn't care enough to prepare food. She had a job, and was asserting her difference, like her heroes: she was not a domestic or domesticated female. Mother had once described herself as domiciled. I was little, and she was on the phone with a friend, and I figured she was saying she was in a kind of jail, which instigated this weird sense of her for me. I looked in pix for that unequivocally revealing THING about her.

I can't explain it, because there hovers an irrational element. Later, I'd squint and look in Mother's eyes for a sign of her obscure confinement: Mom domiciled, Father's bro Uncle Teddy on the inside, upstate. I heard something about his being "a white criminal."

## SHIFT DRESSES, GENDER SHIFTS

Role-playing inhabits family photos, and gender structures relationships in them—pictures are social relations, not just "mirrors" of them. Gender and image, from my POV as an ethnographer, are interactive. Nothing explains better that gender is a performance, which theorists since Sacks and Garfinkel have shown, than that the desire for changing gender must include an image of it. To perform a gender there must be an image to base it upon: this is how a woman sits, this is how a man walks.

Little Zeke once asked Mother: What is your work? She was an editor. She wasn't just a mother or a housewife, she'd told that to Great Uncle Zeke: "No woman in her right mind would be a housewife." Great Uncle Zeke laughed, he always laughed, because he was miserable. It made a big impression on me. I was seven, and I remember, because Father made a big deal about it, how I'd reached the age of reason.

What was reason? How could I tell the difference?

I witnessed my stuffy father doing manual labor, his hands BBQ dirty. He couldn't change a light bulb. Or, wouldn't. But Mother—I noticed how she stared into the space where her backyard must've ended, soft hands in her lap, one gripping the other as if strangling Father, maybe. She festered. I saw the woman she was and also wasn't. I didn't want my true self warped, when I believed in true selves.

## THE PICTURE PEOPLE: SEEING IS BELIEVING WHAT

How far can people stray from constructions that made them "what they are"?

My reasons for studying the effects of images can't be excised from my person, my subjectivity, or neuroses. What I am. Impressive experiences and a procrustean trunk of unconscious images can't be ripped from (my) thoughts and perceptions, also inextricable.

Photography augments society's image of itself, (Or, once upon a time it did.)

In different environments societies have different needs. Some didn't search for a way to capture images. Predictable images conform to appropriate versions of reality.

In the 1970s, when artists re-photographed photographs, appropriated images, and created illusions with photographs, the "truth" of photography, and of art, shifted. Ethnographic work did too. In the past people might photograph a longitudinal series, say, a farm and its workers over a period of time, the town, its inhabitants, etc. Narratives would be written, oral histories recorded.

Can a photograph tell what the written or oral story doesn't? It presents an image. But the person's willful, willing, or involuntary presence—what does that tell?

## UN-DOCUMENTING THE DOCUMENT

In the early 1990s, an exhibition of photographs was curated by Lynn Marshall-Linnemeier, a photographer from North Carolina, an African-American. I saw the catalog when I was in grad school, then researched her work further.

She asked black families in her town to lend her their photo albums, then she selected and printed some of these photographs, snapshots then. So-called ordinary families who were black portrayed themselves. Not as soul-saddened, defeated, as often captured in so-called vérité images, "oppressed Negroes or poor blacks" or "black folk" shot by professionals on assignment in the South. These family albums consisted of individuals, often in groups, happy at graduations, birthday parties, characters playing ball, sleeping in the sun, hanging out, laughing. One photo especially blew me away: A young child, maybe two, standing in a crib on the lawn of a suburban house. The picture was shot from the child's POV, from behind his head, so the shot was low to the ground. The child looked out from his crib, and the view was in a cone shape, of street, houses, a car. It was a child's eye-view, a Christina's world. A new theoretical world, with a new eye wide open.

Documentary photographer Lewis Hine (1874–1940): "There are two things I wanted to do. I wanted to show the things that had to be corrected. I wanted to show the things that had to be appreciated."

Hine's goal for his photographs can't be realized (except in his own eye). The meanings he wants discerned may not be there, because a viewer decides for or against "correction" or "appreciation." Pictures refuse to judge. A photograph records something, sure, SOMETHING gets recorded, is documented, shown, a moment in time, say. But WHO is doing the LOOKING. People glean images the way they think—yes, how they think makes the picture. Projection, right.

Documentary photography performed itself, whatever its subject, since its mission was photographing "others," "image-dooming" (my term) their subjects with set-idea-images or preconceptions, and to an idea of (what I call) "authentic in-authenticity." Marshall-Linnemeier's exhibition absolutely persuaded me, I'd been uncertain, to write my dissertation on family-issued photographs. Without my thesis director, a generous faculty member who follows James Clifford's critique of anthropology, I'd have been in big trouble in my half-hoary department.

Clifford is partial to Stuart Hall's theory of articulation, in which cultural formations are an articulated ensemble, linked, joined, not modeled on an organic living body with an "eternal shape." This theory bypasses or eliminates the question of authenticity or in-authenticity. "It is assumed that cultural forms will be made, unmade and remade." Totally, Clifford.

My article about Marshall-Linnemeier's work appeared

in *Contemporary American Cultural Artifacts*, "Documents of Authentic In-Authenticity." I set in place ideas about the significance of the vernacular, and, through Marshall-Linnemeier's, the uniqueness of self-imaging (before selfies). I raised strong objections to documentary work, I wasn't alone, but included problems in ethnographic practices, with so-called objective findings, and, basically, muddied further the concept of field work, and also compared its problems with those of photography. Surface, depth, what story is being told, by whom, and what for, etc.

I could have disappeared down the rabbit hole then; but my thesis director was totally on board. Sympathetic, with her own agenda, and, already said, the times/the theories were a-changing. Cultural anthropology, a science, art, an approach, or a field of development and knowledge, is part of a nineteenth-century imagination: that human beings could know life objectively, part of the Enlightenment and positivism. People could know reality, separate from themselves. If human beings could know life objectively, arguments would be settled fast.

A viewer now may not be able to tell a doc photo or movie from a photograph on a gallery wall or a narrative film. The doc-genre has embraced its inherent fiction-making, because it had to, after post-structuralism, when makers couldn't claim a lack of bias or POV, objectivity or neutrality.

I'm not saying the loss of presumed objectivity isn't tough: totally consoling when you know what's what, and can illuminate, preach the Truth. Confidence is cool, and indubitably, truth-hunger eats at all of us. When men were men and women were women, the whole enchilada. Sure.

## BACK AND FORTH

Lately, not sure when—time being what it is—I dreamed about Mr. Petey lying in bed beside me, don't know if praying mantises recline, and maybe he was upright on a pillow, telling me what to do.

Mr. Petey had a role—to eat other insects. People have no discernible reason to live, except we're here.

It's weird. After sex some female PMs eat their mates. I didn't know that as a kid. Don't know what I'd have made of it. Petey's life was instinctive, and I can't imagine it, me, acting instinctively, although maybe if someone charged at me with a gun, I'd run without thinking. I hope I wouldn't think I could talk him out of it.

Insomnia comes and goes. I was a sleepless kid, restless to explore the world that lay beyond the big backyard that stretched into state-owned woods, common land or public space, my father called it. Wandering around, on my own, I felt existence had a wholeness and a me-ness it had nowhere else. I lived high in the Ordinary Imaginary, suffering from or supported by backyard light-headedness.

The green expanse transformed into Zeke's wilderness. I started my active imagining there, I mean, knowing I was. I biked there, pretended I was racing in the Grand Prix, sweat running, breezes cooling me. I'd throw my bike to the ground and study the creepy-crawlies and dig for hidden treasure. (Could have suggested field work later.) Things buried deliberately, hidden for someone like me—or just me—to find centuries later.

I can see myself standing with my back to the house,

patio behind me, my short legs solid beneath, but I'm shifting weight from foot to foot, then rocking back and forth on my toes, and I start running as fast as those little legs can carry me all the way to the end of the lawn, and back to the house, then do it again and again until down I flop, gasping, lying there, and breathing, and thinking, this was it, the best, freedom. I want to say, I felt really alive, happy, wanting the feeling to last forever. All alone, content.

Remember, I found Mr. Petey in our backyard—my earthly paradise.

Max Weber wrote, in a traditional society "the world remains a great enchanted garden." Weber was cool.

Call my seminal moments "tradition-bonded."

Oh, man, everything then—without precedent. That's what new is, that's what being a kid is—without precedent, expectation—you don't know what's coming, and you don't know what's hit you, and when it hits again, say, three times, habits form, reactions emerge. A vacuum gets filled.

In a semi-blank slate, I stared skyward, hoping for miracles, and found messages in tree bark, and communicated with consoling animals.

Father had allergies to animals, and I developed allergies to him.

My brief: like other indulged, privileged children from a prosperous middle class, I didn't care what was around me, just knew it was there, therefore mine. OK, sure, lack creates desire, but abundance foments other desires, not only the desire not to desire more, but also the desire to FIND desire when you don't need anything; after all, where does passion come from? The passion to achieve in life? Isn't this why the scions of the super-rich often have no inclinations, nothing they really want to do? The need for renunciation is the source of American Buddhism, spirituality based upon rejecting the abundance of the overindulged, but also the desire that arises—to impede or obstruct even a satisfaction of desire.

Straight up: I wanted what I couldn't have. I wanted a perfect life, a life I made, for me.


## ART VALUES, MY VALUES

In different periods, artists "imitated life" differently, because, duh, life was different.

Turner painted clouds as furious abstractions. Before him, seventeenth-century Dutch artists imitated life, but mostly glommed onto material culture, except for their doing landscapes and cows. Pearly glass windows, crystal goblets— the Dutch mirrored life, and painted mirrors. Visual puns. A mercantile society inspired artists to render trade goods, glass and silver, imitations of their patrons' bounty—their output makes aesthetic sense.

Andy Warhol figuratively lunged at his patron's throat. He painted a dollar sign, a gift for Malcolm Forbes, capitalist tool magazine guy. His portraits of the wealthy are studies like Rembrandt's.

The Dutch spanked their scenes with unnatural light and shadows. Vermeer, totally arresting case, thought to be inimitable but no one knows how many fakes are out there. Rembrandt: introspective portraits. My art history course zeroed in on landscapes, not portraits. The Romantics had an attachment to Nature that contemporary society has lost: Nature as a willful, indifferent enemy, not an ecology or eco-system, but as a symptom of God's power and genius. To naturalists and pantheists, God was Nature. God was in the natural elements.

"God is in the details." —Mies van der Rohe

Craft and skill once were the painter's slam dunk. Along came the spider, photography.

Painter Jack Whitten: "The image is photographic, there-fore I must photograph my thoughts . . . I can see it in my brain, and it's reproduced. I'm using the word 'reproduce' in the same sense that you would use a Xerox copy machine or a computer—any form of a reproduction device."

Gazing at clouds, another diversionary tactic—if an un-wanted prof or student person crossed my path, I looked up.

I found relief, similar to consolation or faith, in clouds, stars, weather shifts, when I acted like a prognosticator in old movies. I took pleasure, pleasure must be taken or had, in subtle shadings, size, shapes, the wind stirring. Night-time: Shooting stars, UFOs.

Here I go, here I go, here I go.

## MAGGIE, SHOT BY PASSION

I met Maggie in college, in Frame, a photo-media group, seconds before digital absconded with a field that once trafficked in positives and negatives, celluloid, tactility, etc., when, figuratively and actually, she and I stood side by side and developed film, printed it, read photo and art theory. The group held intense discussions about aesthetics, and visited New York galleries, museums.

Maggie, she's a New Yorker, with all the image implies, funny, sharp, deep, plus, she has famous parents: Her father is an Internet genius, who cashed in early, her mother a scientist, researching nasty viruses. These people live in and for the present, and for a future they glimpse (unlike my mother's tribe sowing their historical oats). Maggie was adopted when she was an infant. And, yeah, she's beautiful, like Little Sister, but with tawny brown hair. Her father's an alcoholic, so we have that in common.

In college we all discussed photographer Harold Feinstein (1931–2015). He simply loved taking photographs. He was born in Coney Island—I dislike beaches, Maggie loves them—it became his major subject, and he shot there for more than fifty years. Feinstein: "There were so many things to shoot, the question was not how to take a good picture, but how not to miss one." And: "The question is what we don't see, and why don't we see so much."

Frame took its name from Stephen Shore's brief treatise on it: any would-be image-maker could learn how to make a "good" picture. To find the picture, exclusion rules: what remains outside the frame is not the picture, but may become a viewer's fantasy. Feinstein didn't have to leave home or exclude home to make his art. We Frame people argued about this kind of love, and how his way of talking about the field was old-fashioned, but Maggie defended it, him, maybe she was a romantic then, and approved his ingenuousness.

In the 1958 *U.S. Camera Annual*, Feinstein wrote: "You must photograph where you are involved; where you are overwhelmed by what you see before you; where you hold your breath while releasing the shutter, not because you are afraid of jarring the camera, but because you are seeing with your guts wide open to the sweet pain of an image that is part of your life."

No artist would now say "you are seeing with your guts wide open to the sweet pain of an image that is part of your life." Totally corny, right, but also the field has changed: many photog/artists don't look at what's there but construct their realities.

I have an affinity, I'm admitting it, with "the sweet pain of an image." You feel me?

In Frame, I learned you can train your eye to think of the world as a picture, say, in a Wittgensteinian sense—a visual language game.

Artists train their vision—though all vision is trained

involuntarily, since we perceive through cultural eyewear; let's say, artists re-train, or "craft," their vision, "de-culture" it as best they can toward other ways of seeing (see John Berger). Visual tutors can be artists who teach. People learn to see as well as think differently, up to a point (more later). First, people notice details bound up in their group's interpretations, see them through the group's paradigms.

There is no universality in sight, and none in a picture.

"You have a good eye." When? In what context?

Maggie and I framed us, made us by the exclusion of others—lovers as border guards not allowing others entry.

I worried about grades, wanted the best grad school; but I could fuck up, go off the rails, get frustrated, a tendency. Maggie lived unencumbered by grade-worry, she didn't consider failure for herself or me—weird because her parents achieved big. Maybe because she was adopted, didn't get that gene, because she didn't have the anxiety of influence. Failure was my personal terrorist, but she carried a resistant strain of that virus (knew too much about viruses for comfort). Maggie was also doing anthropology, art, and writing, she especially got into Malinowski's diaries, whose "honesty"—ambivalence—caused concern in the field, and Mick Taussig's books.

She denied human failure, which didn't mean she had faith in our species, exactly; she believed in the fight for survival, for fighting for what you wanted. Maggie was all about that, survival. Maybe because she'd been orphaned.

The species had survived, might prevail, etc. (Why or over what wasn't a question.) Successes and failures were fundamental for progress—Maggie followed Karl Popper here—trials and errors necessary to improve the species, in the larger scheme of things. Failures weren't failures, since they produced growth.

No one, I'd counter, kind of kidding, lives in the bigger scheme of things, all life is local. (I once totally believed that.) She'd say, "Failure is not an option"; "Ants can't fail, are we not ants?" I bought it for a long time, until I met failure. Faced it.

I was a cross-disciplinary major, anthropology and visual culture, and my best art guide, my Virgil, was a cool art history prof, handsome in a severe way. She took us around museums and galleries, notably into Philadelphia to see Duchamp's *Étant Donnés*. Maggie and I didn't know what we were seeing, maybe THE inexplicable, similar to when we watched Jack Smith's infamous *Flaming Creatures* in an experimental film history course: we didn't know what we saw. There weren't men and women, there weren't trans men or trans women, there were Smith's characters, who defied any categories.

But from Smith's costumes and party scenes, our costume sex bloomed, with Maggie flowering and coming in many-colored scarves. Fantastic also, the approach of another kind of invisibility. "Invisible" to me—though it was there, I couldn't "see" it. Call it the epicene. No lucidity, and it couldn't be seen through. Some art presents itself uniquely, not rationally, and beyond reason, or based upon other logics, not mine or yours. Maybe against and unavailable to interpretation ("Strictly speaking, one never understands anything from a photograph." —Susan Sontag).

Obstacles grow up to be people, created ignorantly by people.

We can stand in each other's way. Maggie once accused me of that, then said she was sorry.

If I couldn't totally get Jack Smith's film, then I couldn't depend upon my understanding my own culture that much better than the "others" I was studying. See where I'm heading? Significantly, I could shape myself into an ethnographer without a knowing attitude, and could learn as much about my own as "the other," or discover the other inside. That grabbed me most, the other within.

The next rebellion launched itself against earlier rebellions, but this time I raged under the radar. I was chill, driving on cruise control, though in overdrive, and seeking out family albums, talking to the families and writing field notes, annotating the photos, applying ethnographic theory and photo theory to what I found, basically making it up as I went along. It had to be made up.

I was in a discipline, or disciplines, inside an institution where I had to fit, but that in some way urged me not to, also, and I was and also wasn't making my own life. I was adjusting, and maybe I wanted to but couldn't know that yet, but wanted to be choosing why I was bending this way or that.

Maggie's in her office writing her ethnographic novel—I wasn't sure what it would be, but I'd been an influence, she said. She didn't say Good or Bad. Kidding. When Maggie had her mind set, nothing ever stood or stands in her way, and she'd thrown herself into this book, and that let me throw myself into mine.

We worked in silence.

John Cage scored with it. (Haha.) A unique American postwar artist. We studied him together. She loved what he thought, how he wrote it. I felt I'd grown up knowing it without knowing it. Everyone has their illusions, right?

"There is no such thing as silence. Something is always happening that makes a sound. No one can have an idea once he starts really listening."

Silence performs.

Cage's *4'33"*: a composition of those eponymous minutes.

He didn't want to compose music, what happened was music, sound was music. Mother told me that Ezra Pound wrote, "I tried to write Paradise. Let the wind speak. That is paradise." I wanted paradise on earth, and had it with Maggie.

I'd never known this kind of love before, there was only Maisie, and crushes and high school sex, flickers of adolescent love, young lust. Never loved before Maggie—this is an article of faith—I saw the light. She hit me, whoosh, the sound of a concussive tackle, bang. Kidding. See, everything I want to say about love is known, humans know this feeling, mostly they do. And also know it always as a unique experience. You feel me?

Nothing felt the same, feels the same, would ever be the same. Should I make a list? No, but I want to, because I can't stop myself, that's how love is. Love is a Memory of Love. First times for tears, consolation, sitting near her. An ordinary room shifted into paradise, the aroma of her killed me. I liked watching her breathe.

My new life: impassioned, passionate. Passion sounds like an emotion from the nineteenth century. That intensity, the Romantics. My gen is cool, over it, supposedly. It consoles me that the ancients felt the same. In the grip of love madness, you stand in a long line of humanity. Think about it.

Sex, with Maggie: I got it, finally, apprehended, and it wasn't an act. I didn't give her an orgasm, she took it when she wanted it. She did take me in every way, and I took her, and she let me have her, we had each other, totally. I would give her anything, everything. I'd see her and need to touch her, her skin, the flesh on her hips, ass. The fascinating way her breasts moved when she moved, the colors of her labia, heat of her cunt. I realized why Renoir went all garish painting women's bodies, why their flesh had purple and yellow tints, because he saw God in their bodies. Maggie and I—gods together, perfect lovers, soul-to-soul mates, perfect beings being together. If I didn't compare my love for Maggie with a summer's day or a rose, but with playing tennis, I debase romantic love, unless you feel tennis the way I do. So, Maggie was my best partner.

Maggie, always and forever.

Mother says: "You can't ever know about forever, Zeke."

In love we're amateurs. By definition. We do it for love, live for love. In love, I didn't, don't care what anyone thinks.


## FAMILY VALUES

Father showed signs of trouble to come, on a distant horizon, but I'm not sure how much that mattered to me; he was slowing down, that's all, drinking more, coughing more. Before I met Maggie, I basically lived at home, home every weekend, because there were meals, did my laundry. That's when Little Sister and I started to know each other; or, from her POV, I'd stopped being her loud-mouthed older bro.

The closer I came to her world, the closer I came to me, now.

She was making photographs, camera obscuras, a perfect

form for her: the image develops very slowly, and she prefers dark rooms. She gave herself a secret professional name, and indicated she might show work someday. Might not. She never seemed to care about what happened outside her sphere, except that humans were decimating the environment, she had no fear of missing out, no FOMO for her. I hope that acronym stays around. She felt some communication with our ancestors, influenced by Clarissa, because Clarissa took up space in us. Maybe not Bro Hart.

Bro Hart says, "Matilda sees dead people. Yuck." He doesn't know shit. He's selfish, like Father, with a first son complex. So, he sees disease in others, thinks his sibs are lacking, and totally dismisses the baby of the family and her "fruitless endeavors." Right, cutting up dead people is fruitful.

I tell him, "When a pickpocket meets a saint, all he sees are his pockets."

"Up yours, Zeke," he says.

Mother says one day we'll be friends.

Oh, man, no way.

Little Sister: an outsider-insider or vice-versa. Emily Dickinson, Mother says of her; our twenty-first-century Clover, Clarissa says, because Little Sister takes pictures now. (So did Clover Hooper Adams in the nineteenth.) But Matilda . . . Matilda? Can't call Little Sister that.

Aunt Clarissa came around loads to visit Mother and Little Sister. When I was home on weekends and summers, it went OK, within limits—I limited her, gave her less scope, testing my own limits and hers.

Clarissa turned gray, then her hair went white, and she was kookier, maybe a more passive whack job. In the past we'd had some trouble, I mean, she caused me trouble, but later for that. Not in the mood.

Clarissa expands her cocoon, nurses her sicknesses, believing in their truths. She wouldn't want to change, espouses that people should accept their tics, as she calls them. "Embrace your disease." All of her heroes suffered illnesses that helped them be brilliant and more sensitive. And, she unfailingly expects people to come to her—the oracle of Delphi, an hour outside of Boston. Her narcissism swings like that. Many friends have given her up, most anyway can't oblige, even her grammar school friends. But she always has Mother. Little Sister shows her favor, because Little Sister is one of the kindest people I have ever known. I sometimes associate her earlier silences with plain, simple kindness. She didn't want to say hurtful things, but had to be honest, so kept quiet. That's what I suspect happened.

No one prepares a child to be an adult who has to buy toilet paper, a pillow, sheets, towels. You feel me? Malingering was my rebellion against the future unfolding "normally." Things come together. Things fall apart.


## SEEMS LIKE MOVING ON

With Maggie, I learned to structure my days, keep on the paper track, attend classes. Later, Maggie moved with me to grad school; by then she was doing an M.F.A. in writing, working on stories and a novel. I turned compulsive about living up to her estimation of me, because she believed in me, my mind. We scheduled quiet times, and crazy fuck times. I photographed clouds at certain times of day each week, not just loving them the way I did as a kid. I used my love. Which may have been the start of the perniciousness of scholarship. Of becoming an "expert," not just a lover.

Assimilated to Little Sister, her unique discretions, I learned to love Maggie also, as she was, and I liked our quiet, its comforts, and depended on what I believed were Maggie's discretions.

"Maggie, marry me?" It burst out, emotion in those words. Marry me, crazy stuff, but I had to marry her. Impulsive, right, but I trusted all my impulses then. We were young, still in grad school, but hell. Her parents, her mother especially, didn't like me—oh man they were against it: too young, their only child, jewel in the crown, I got that. But how would it change anything, we were already living together.

Maggie would never deny me what I wanted, if that's what would make me happy, she said, Yes, of course. She didn't need a license, but somehow I did. YES. Cool. We had a small wedding, the way we wanted. And life went on. I wore a ring now. New men like to wear rings. (See later, MEN IN QUOTES.)

## FAMILY CONDITION CONDITIONS

My father died a few years after I passed my exams with distinction, and my dissertation was close to written, because I'd totally rushed like a madman. I needed to split, get away from school, into our field of dreams, Maggie and I starting out. Our la dolce vita, our vita nuova.

Uncle Lionel had a one-time muscle-destroying heart attack. When his brother died, something died in my father, and it showed he could feel, and also showed that it's not just married couples who can't live without each other, happily or not. I saw that Father felt deeply. He wasn't a great example of a man—just an example—a good provider, didn't run around, I think—he never doubted his being anything but a red-blooded man, which has something going for it—certainty. He must've been impotent by forty because of the alcohol—he banked on Viagra, sure. Father worked himself up, occasionally, and showed me his way to be a man, but I didn't take him seriously.

His death coincided, kind of, with the death of Polaroid. He'd witnessed the start of the digital revolution, was aware that Polaroid had sold off parts of itself, sputtering to its finish line, he knew it went into bankruptcy in 2002; but wasn't around when it got sold in 2011, and no more Polaroid company. It might've killed him, if esophageal cancer hadn't.

Slugging, cigar-smoking—not in the house, after the surgeon general's report on secondhand smoke—could have irritated his GI tract enough to bring on, combined with his DNA, esophageal cancer. Or, his self-made body environment switched on the genetic marker for C—Bro Hart talks a lot about epigenetics. "It's happening there, little bro," he says, smugly.

Hart's probing dead bodies maybe was fomented by Little Sister's condition. Or, it's a forensic approach to family-ancestor worship.

Through his breathing tube, my father spat out his last words for me. Nothing spiritual from this estate lawyer: "Get your money out of the market."

You're supposed to obey deathbed wishes, and this was doable, and, OK, I'm young-ish, why not. I "obeyed" him, when the market was near 14,000. I took it all out. And then with the naughts' crash, I almost forgave my father for being an asshole. Believe me, I'm as shallow as the next guy. Shallow as a grave. (I'm so running ahead of myself.)

Next came Kodachrome: born 1935, died 2010.

Long Live Kodachrome. Let's all have a Kodak moment.

Goodbye, 1950s saturated colors.

## GRAD SCHOOL BUDDY (BMF)

I shared my intellectual life with Maggie, but also Curtis Woolf. Maybe squandered it. I met him in my first year of grad school, he discovered me, flattered me, telling me I was the smartest guy in our film seminar. Curtis, being English, carried the usual superiority to Americans typical of Europeans, but also was an avid fan of U.S. pop culture. Not unusual. Mother told me that, in the 1980s, people said, usually the Baudrillard crowd: "The French have the theory, Americans the practice."

Curtis was Irish on his mother's side, accounting for his pale skin and blue eyes, but with English guy cool—shaggy, tall, thin, fashion-conscious. English on his father's side. He charmed Mother, extra-super-sweet to her, syrupy wit, and she liked him, though he was such a flatterer.

She insisted: their looks don't last, when they're older, they look very old. Potato sacks, or something like that. Her ancestors, remember, left England for religious freedom, only the gods know what else.

Curtis was really smart—clever, he'd be called in England—and pretended he never did any work. Maybe he didn't. An indolent lad, casual in all things, seemingly, though fierce in debate, but don't call him an intellectual, though he was: the English dislike intellectuals, worse than here in the States. It's about class: Oxbridge = intellectuals. Curtis was from a modest background, as they say, but a teacher discovered this smart kid in his local grammar school, and guided him, then Curtis killed on his A levels, and off he jogged—he was a runner—to Oxbridge, and a life different from his parents', a different class or at least he mixed with the upper classes. Took up tennis, seriously, oh man was he serious, and joined the drama club, less seriously. He didn't have much contact with his parents when I met him; if he did, it was with his mother. An only child, he said. I envied him sometimes. He was going to be a writer, like Maggie.

Little Sister took to him, probably worshiped him, because he teased her gently, and most people didn't dare. Some women distrust super good-looking men. I've been called "great looking," am in good shape, solid features, OK, something to write home about, but Curtis—CW, and I'm Starkie to him—movie star looks. A reverse sexism, I told Maggie, is how some females suspected him, the way beautiful women are assumed to be dumb.

Tennis again, with CW. We played every chance we could and he worked hard to beat me, but he couldn't. Ever. On the court, I killed. He could play with lesser players if winning was what he was after. On other courts, he beat me.

## FAMILY VALUES VALUE

Dignified as ever, when Father died, Mother mourned, Little Sister had Mother's back, and Clarissa hung around the house like a parasite nourished on mourning blood. Father left Mother in good shape, financially, anyway.

Little Sister lived at home, like loads of twenty-somethings, and Mother returned to editing, and also found more "fulfilling work," she says, as a hospice volunteer. Fulfillment? I can see it, in a way, given our family.

Friends ask, "Don't you miss your father?" Nope, it's hard to believe I had one.

When I watch our family videos, with my father at the head of the table, his contempt is evident, or maybe it should be read as discontent or plain drunkenness. I don't miss him. Not a fun drunk, like Great Uncle Zeke and his bro Lionel, just a sullen one, on the brink—anger. He hadn't achieved what he wanted, maybe to be an artist, he hadn't had the courage to try, and he resented us for holding him down. Mother stayed with him anyway. The few photographs I shot of him he decided made him "look bad," and he tore one up in front of me. That's primal aggression.

OK, Maggie and I had our groove on. By the end of coursework at grad school, together six years, our life didn't run on thrill, totally normal, and we were absorbed in our work and supported each other's projects. Her parents supported her financially, and though we married, our bank accounts stayed separate. She had more than I, that way, but I had fellowships, and Mother helped me sometimes; after

Father died, I inherited some money, which was held in a trust for when I turned thirty-five. Bro Hart, same deal. Most of it was left for Mother, and a big share for Little Sister. She was getting better, not exactly in the real world, say, not employable yet. She talked more easily, but wasn't destined to be wordy. Kidding. Went to art school for a bit, found friends.

We were cruising along, eating three solids, Maggie vegan for a time, drinking to chill at the end of the day. Writing, she turned more quiet, concentrating, and reminded me again of Little Sister, which was cool. I felt I really understood Maggie, and her need to be in her own head, the mental space inside her novel, her thesis. CW and she were both writing novels, and I listened to their writer issues, credibility was one, and the problem of working with or against coincidence. Cred is always a problem, in whatever field you're in, right. How to gain it. When you lose it, and why. In life, I said, there are so many coincidences. Maggie said, But not in fiction, it's very hard to make it work. Too bad, I thought, because it happens, my life's full of them. But it confirmed: art is not like life, and life is not an art form, except for aesthetes. People can buy almost anything, including "taste."

Sometimes I took pictures of her when she was absorbed, at her desk, a woman reading or writing, like the Vermeer I worshipped. Maggie wondered about my photographing her, maybe a little invasive, or showed my insecurity about her. Did I worry I'd lose her, that she'd disappear? Also, she felt self-conscious, she said. She hadn't; then she did. Weird.

## LOST AND FOUND OBJECTS

Oh, man, it hit me: you're way too concerned with photographs dutifully taken, saved, and treasured, "kept images." Super-fixated maybe, because of my childhood, or on an hysterical mission, in the sense Freud wrote about hysteria. And, apart from everything else, like mental illnesses, my project didn't feel ethnographically clean. Logically, my mind shifted to the other side, the rejectamenta. What isn't kept and why not?

It was late for the morning, and I lay in bed like a drugged person, and that's when the idea aced me. It flashed. It hit me, I'd look after the lost, care for the unwanted. Image detritus. I'd turn into a finder of the unwanted. Homeless photographs, the exilic.

I hunted the streets, sidewalks, under tables in restaurants (in winter, found gloves everywhere); the floors in clubs and bars; now in digital time, there's way less. What people throw out tells an untold story. (I'm not a garbologist.) There's still purging among overinflated consumers of tech. Get rid of stuff and buy the new, so material shows up, photos left in a book, books tossed out everywhere; I've found thumb drives too. Meanwhile, garbage trucks drop cartons and garbage collectors run wild in the streets. The streets overflow with rejection.

Get up early, get home late, find stuff. I fall asleep when people awaken, because I like the night. Or I'm just up, sleepless. Maggie learned to sleep through it.

•

I call the streets a field, and "going into the street" is going into the field, both a concept and an activity. If journalists can talk about "the Arab street," an ethnographer can employ it: what begins, happens, and ends in the street, it's all an object for study.

Humans become runaways and homeless—on the street, you're nobody's child. The denizens of the street, their skin roughens from exposure, they walk, their eyes down or listless, straight ahead, some must wonder why no one cares, or are themselves beyond caring. Their lives are junk, they are expendable and called "eyesores." Other people don't want to "see" them, they walk with their heads down, right.

The eyesore characterization meshes with humans as images to themselves and each other.

"You don't want to make a bad image, do you?"

Eyesores irritate another's eyes. The image-condemned, at the least, should be relegated to invisibility, they should relegate themselves, they should live under bridges or in urban caves, because they're ugly to the eye—not murderers, but the ugly can expect no pity. They should fucking disappear, right?

Previously "wanted material," even cherished goods, turns into stuff, crap, junk. Broken furniture, sagging, tic-ridden mattresses, worn clothes and their lives on sidewalks and in streets, useless. Abandonment makes objects ugly.

Americans waste more food than any other people/nation in the world.

In my circles, in a year, people throw out more than most people in the world own in a lifetime. They coveted, bought, once loved that chair or teapot, but, fickle consumer-characters, they toss it out, not looking back, no regrets. Hoarders are Extreme Materialists.

Right, everyone's talking 'bout "first world problems." I say, Lipstick on a pig.

What's called a "bad picture" ends up on streets. Half a head, blurs, generic tourist shots—no face can be discerned—and views of innocuous buildings by anonymous rivers no one remembers or even the country they were taken in.

The concept of "a bad picture" intrigues me. (A "bad relationship" also.) Like the beautiful, which relies on symmetry and balance, a "good picture" is produced by accepted ideas about framing and composition, though these can change.

What are the errors in seeing?

"You have a good eye." Right.

Ordinary citizens might hope to take "good pictures." For artists, good can be bad, bad good—artists say Fuck You to the beautiful; while standards of beauty shift every few years, anyway.

Take the "behind." Rear end. Bottom. Ass. Booty. It's taken years, but the big butt is again an object of overt desire. Ass enhancements in New Jersey.

Flat, white asses, they are so over. Thank you, J.Lo, Beyoncé, Kim Kardashian, Nicki Minaj. Your bounty is our bounty.

The sublime, a wily notion about awe-inspiring terror and impossible beauty, found favor again in the late twentieth century; some art critics regularly applied the concept, especially to Caspar David Friedrich, an exemplar, also Gerhard Richter.

From the sublime, to the unwanted, to the ridiculous: thrown-out framed wedding pictures and candids of Christmas trees—holiday parties, happy scenes—stain the streets, lie in gutters, cascade from garbage cans. Generic, but each meant something specific or even important to people in them. On the street, nothing, detritus. Object-death.

Divorced people tear up their wedding pictures, take

them off their walls, throw them in the trash, discard the guilty, painfully irrelevant in their new lives. The discarded, or dead love-mementos, if all were collected, would make mountain ranges as big and high as the Rockies. Picture it.

If you can, and you're an artist, hey, man, here's a project. Ha.

Some of the found wedding pix were shot at New York's City Hall. So I went there, another field, and spent days watching people waiting to be married, in the most democratic institution anywhere, seriously, except for a public library; everyone's included, no one's denied, pretty much. Wedding parties range from simple, bride, groom, and one witness, to large families sitting and standing in shapeless groups, to women dressed in floor-length white gowns, men in tuxes or dinner jackets, to jokey costumes, and bride and groom wearing flip-flops and jeans. Bridesmaids and groomsmen follow their leaders, clucking after them, children racing, screaming or hanging onto their mothers and fathers. Lots of drama, weeping. Giggles. Anger. I was especially surprised by the number of sullen grooms, pregnant brides, and enraged mothers-in-law. They were noteworthy.

The weirdest throwaways: a nuclear family's albums, its history in photographs, to be incinerated. For just twenty bucks, I bought a large cardboard box at a thrift store in upstate New York: hundreds of loose photos, two albums, and many little photo books from a camera store, depicting at least four generations. Their anonymity becomes stranger as you look at them—-this is an anonymous family, an anonymous man, woman, son, daughter, maybe an aunt, a grandmother and grandfather, mother and father to whom? Here's a boy graduating from grade school. In one I've been studying, the portraits of their pets, animal companions, dominate. Here's a family that didn't have anyone to keep these photographs. Studying them, I see them aging. One person always absent—the family photographer. A man, probably. A husband, a father. But whose?

The greatest violation I ever committed? Buying this carton of photos. I a stranger now possessed them, and it felt creepy, as though I'd stolen the Elgin Marbles all over again. First, I looked at pictures of this family with a cold eye, a stranger's eye that didn't care about this anon family, had no connection to it. But who was that family, and why had the line ended, if it had? The stories came to me: when the last X died, the house was sold, because no one was around to keep it, typical family diaspora, or everyone was dead, and one day the new owner discovered in the back of a closet—in the attic, always the attic—a big carton. The new owner opened it, wasn't curious, barely curious, and tossed it. Maybe the garbage collector brought it to the thrift store where I found it and paid my twenty bucks. I left the store like a thief Legal thievery is ubiquitous in a material world, and I'm a material boy.

I became familiar with the family, and had the urge to name each person, each character in this silent album. I felt each deserved a name, was a character in this unwritten novel. James Clifford and others talk about ethnography as writing, even as fiction. I'd call this novel *Anon*.

The Bible started like this. A, B, C, D noticing, in their different lifetimes, all the strange shit, incredible rumors and tales reaching future religiosos in far-off villages, about a lamp that didn't stop burning for eight days, about an infant in an anonymous manger, and the stories and the characters— too strange not to record. Right? The tales made the rounds, so there must be something to them, right, why else would we be hearing them. Like all urban tall tales.

Through this anonymous family, I apprehended my anonymity, to others like and not like me. Through these throwaways, I observed myself as a stranger. Our, and your, family pictures are nothing to a stranger.

Uncle Zeke, a happy guy with a flag behind him, or a nothing, a no one. Mother, Little Sister, Father, Clarissa, faces, bodies, bone and flesh, voices that don't speak . . .

So, perceiving culture and society entirely in visuals, and before my eyes, I am up against my limits. I narrate through images, what they appear to represent, with my thoughts working as subtitles. But it's false, in a sense, because all are essentially UNTITLED, OHNE TITEL, incapable of being captioned—or captured. The uncaptioned (photograph) suggests that an object can't be named.

I see their common rites and rituals: birthdays, weddings, graduations. Cooking is done in a large kitchen or a cramped one, with an island or a rectangular table in the center of it, people always prepare food. Usually a female. People eat food on a table in that kitchen or at the island, or in a dining room. People take pictures of their meals.

I could be any one of them, and anyone could be anyone, you might be in one of these, I might.

When I was a child, whatever happened was special, ours, mine. Now nothing is. There's no weird when all weird is expected.

Sometimes I think about Mother and Father, how it might have been between them, what their love was like when it was young. I can't feel it.

## THROWAWAYS

My attachment to throwaways became peculiar to Maggie; sometimes even I felt insane caring about a family that had no one to care for their pictures and stories. No one cared but me. But I kept going. Right, impulsive, also compulsive. My course work was done, and my thesis, Maggie closing in also, and, when we did finish, we'd take our fancy break, fly to London, no obvious language barrier or problem, though life is language problems, easier because CW would show us around. I planned to scout in London, studying "others (supposedly) like me" in their various images, social media, selfies, graffiti. Our stay would be temporary.

Temporariness is temporary and constant, too.

I hold these truths to be selfie evident.

Instant capture belongs in the tradition of positivist photography. But proof doesn't prove anything except its own apparatus.

I sometimes wonder if kids feel about it the way my father did Polaroid. Or the way I did, when I saw the magic in it.

When the cry goes out at a party, in a bar, "Let's take a selfie," people gather fast, one holds the camera, shoots. Then another, or ten. Everyone laughs at the result, sometimes surprised by a crazy angle, how good or bad the pix are. The picture produces an image of vivaciousness that may not have been felt in the party or bar: the image itself bumps up the spirit, retroactively and presently.

Selfies conjure instant togetherness in a way that Polaroids never did; they amazed because of their instant confirmation of presence. Working theory: in this (con)temporary life, lived virtually, often alone, teleporting, etc., people look for physical intimacy and closeness, constructing rituals for it, maybe reminders of intimacy. Selfies confirm physical closeness, proximity, they don't document the way photographs did in the past. The selfie is ONLY about the moment, is eminently disposable, like moments themselves.

Things aren't meant to be kept.

I like throwaways and can't do it.

I'm thinking about what's disposable and why, dead love. Ex-lovers.

"Let's take a selfie": a call for social cohesion is worthy of ethnographic study.

What anyone paying attention gets: The thrill is gone, it goes fast. It won't do what it did yesterday. Thrill needs to be amped. Needs create their own needs, then others, and more, alongside business's creating demand. Steve Jobs knew the thrill of the new, and how design lived in the mind as the current of the new, that was his object and he made it.

Then the cry is heard throughout the land: "How did we ever get along without this?"

You could say, This is a funny time. You could, but then you wouldn't be me.

The only way of knowing a person is to love them without hope.

—Walter Benjamin

## EPISTEMOLOGICAL (AND FUTURE) BREAKS

Time is a human construction, the twenty-four-hour day invented by the Egyptians, and divided into two twelve-hour partitions. A twenty-four-hour clock was first constructed in the late 1300s, mostly for astronomical uses.

Einstein wrote, or maybe he didn't, if he didn't, he should have: "The only reason for time is so that everything doesn't happen at once."

I've imagined not having clocks or calendar, the chaos then. Nothing could go forward, no one could know past from present. And there may not be any difference. Really.

I suppose that's why belief systems function, to give us conceptual ruts to run, to dig deeper troughs each time. Animals use their instincts in ways we can't, and I suppose they don't have pasts like humans have, though elephants walk toward a burial ground to die. Animals have emotions, a sense of time; birds migrate, all creatures procreate. But our sense of time, our clocks, our duty to clocking in and out, that's not a fair sense of time. That's a fear of time, because we know we will die. We're such time-sensitive creatures. Time-stamped, haha, but we can't find the stamp.

Time passes; otherwise, you did. Sacred films and tapes of weddings and communions, anniversaries, get boxed and tucked on a shelf in closets, to rest in obscurity. Sure, everyone wants them; no one looks at them again.

The virtual album is a double negation, there/always not there.

The virtual fosters ephemeral, nonphysical attachments and formations, fast and fleeting so-called communities.

Throwaway cameras briefly decorated celebratory tables and mandated everyone to shoot the party pix, but albums are now atavistic.

The institution of marriage was helped by the legalization of gay marriage at the start of the twenty-first century. Stimulated the wedding industry.

I foresee a You Are Not Invited card. Just kidding.

The matte or glossy snapshots, in a drawer or album, represent images of a past event, but is it a memory, when stored away against time, and forgotten, then only recalled seeing it? Is that memory? Even if in time you recognize no one and nothing by them, even if you have the memory only because the photo exists. The photograph is only an elegy to a reality, or "elegiac reality": a fact or document, and a memento mori.

I call these "kept images," they're rarely revisited. Sometimes I refer to them as "sad mistresses."

Kept images bear "image-heaviness," carrying the burdens from the past, as well as of present imaginings, which become concretized as fact—this happened—or metaphorical, and both figure powerfully in consciousness and unconscious behavior. To be "image heavy" might make you look in the mirror frequently, or shop all the time, uncontrollable manias toward looking fashionable, to mimic your fave star, that is, to project a not-you to maintain a sense of self by finding an image that protects you and projects you into the world; or, you might begin collecting objects that agree with your hoped-for image, things you might not even like, oddly enough, but which you believe others treasure and that align with a hidden, aspirational being. Image heaviness entails due diligence, maintenance of any tendency or habit. Keeping up, in all its connotations, is another way to think of it. Plastic surgery, new cars, fresh tech. My term is "image sickness," for which there's no doctor.

## TIME: ARTIFICIAL AND PRACTICAL

Mr. Petey, sturdy, surviving "all of history" (phrase tossed around at home), was perfect, I idolized him, but couldn't sidle up to him or pet him, though he let me touch his back sometimes, gently.

The more mosquitoes there were, the more PMs showed up, but I didn't know the cause, then.

An insect was definitely not-me, but one loved me, at a distance, with hands-off love, which I came to maintain and promote. There are so many more kinds of love than "let's live together and have kids." Forever.

Mr. Petey says nothing about me. His cool was at odds with my jumped-up boy life, except when I was near him, communing with him, quieting down, and then he saw ME. I hoped I was like him, only bigger. I felt he knew that, and me. To be known, solid feeling.

Love is not a thing or a possession. It's immaterial, evanescence itself.

Loving YOU gives ME no security, is not safe, you are not safe, I am not safe.

Can YOU love without the object "saying" something about you? Is there a love without dependence or necessity?

People want love to make them feel safer, and select partners to "support" them; but they also want passion, which is not safe. Everything done, aware or unaware, promotes or debilitates chances for survival. Loving a creature indifferent to you wraps you in a blanket that doesn't keep you warm.

I once was happy to be a malcontent.


I LEARN FROM ANIMALS.

I LEARN I AM AN ANIMAL.

I LEARN I AM DIFFERENT FROM OTHER ANIMALS.

I LEARN I AM A HUMAN BEING WITH A BIG BRAIN.

Use your brain constructively, Mother instructed, which means zip to a kid.

## SEEING IS BELIEVING WHAT YOU SEE

Objects now are so small, terabytes of data, a sliver of silicone; simultaneously there's bigness in the Koolhaas sense, bigness for itself. Two divergent tendencies and practices, two sides of the blah blah. Then there's volume, which, like the camera's eye, does what its organic other can't. And also can't handle. Going blind, blow it up big. Going deaf, volume up, up. Hearing gone, tiny, invisible ear-helpers have arrived, so be cool. Faster, lighter digital cameras, phones, computers. The third millennium is war, terrorism, surveillance (anyone can do it), and swell tech toys. Divert and subvert, subvert and divert.

Humans enabled themselves to see what is not humanly accessible, the invisible becomes visible. Except there's this obstacle: not comprehending what can be seen by the naked eye, or even when seeing artificially.

Special effects, the speed of cameras: these manufactured objects show what the eye can't see by itself. Down the long evolutionary line special effects might become necessary for survival—when the species lives in total darkness, say.

So, no, art doesn't emerge from Nature.

Also, to behold what the human eye by itself can't proves the power of objects, tech, doing what limited humans can design. But where does the emphasis lie? Not on the being's capacity—on the machine's. Humans create machines that, in a way, diminish themselves, contributing to our species self-image-destruction, while the species destroys its environment. Relationship?

There are ways civilizations died that we don't know.

Stephen Hawking has warned the world about Artificial Intelligence: soon, he cautions, humans will be controlled by their own intelligent machines and devices, doing it faster and better. Hawking doesn't strike me as an alarmist. It might be where our intelligence has been heading, to the ultimate metaphysical authoritarianism.

## DO OUR ANIMALS LOVE US?

A cultural anthropologist can't know but only assay reasons for behavior or activities. We investigate, listen, have informers. But, as Geertz wrote, "The ethnographer does not, and, in my opinion, largely cannot, perceive what his informants perceive." Ethnographers surmise or "perceive," as Geertz puts it, "with, through, or by means of."

I want to know about a society's attitudes toward pets, say, through photographs of them. Usually dogs and cats show up in family albums, parakeets, parrots, turtles, fish. (Not in the Stark family's. Sigh.)

Humans recognize big and little, maybe big can protect little, we imagine. But how do dogs account for their size: in dog parks, big and little sniff each other's genitals. What's happening there? Humans are not meant to act strictly on instincts; they are there, though, but a maternal instinct in some human females might not have a chance.

Regularly, the family dog is pictured seated on a chair, apparently looking at the camera, smiling or straight-faced. Often it will be seated, on a chair or couch, next to the dog's human companion. Cats rarely are shot this way, that is, posed, since cats don't usually do what they are asked to do; dogs are eager to please and will obey commands such as "stay." Often, a dog is shot risen on its hind legs, as if standing, humanly, at the sink, or with its paws on the kitchen table. Rarely are pets, now animal companions, shot in action, because the picture would be out of focus.

Most frequently, a pet is pictured in its owner's or some other person's arms or lap. This pose, the embraced dog or cat, marks ownership, of course, but as an "image" it is similar to landscape paintings that first showed a lord/owner's territory, he having commissioned the painting; later, the landscape became a treasured common or accessible view—for example, the Hudson River Valley School artists' endless representations of that river. With photography, artists such as Ansel Adams shot pristine pictures of the mountains and valleys in the West. Carleton Watkins's photographs, for the majority of Americans, were the first pictures of the West. The first time people saw images of it, what was out there.

Imagine, what is prosaic now was once like, in our time, pictures sent back from the moon.

When a person and pet are photographed together, sometimes they look at the camera or at each other; alternatively, the pet might look at the camera, the person at the pet, and vice versa. Not unlike pictures of human friends together. Cats are mostly shot on their own; again they don't sit still, unless well trained or nearly dead.

The anthropomorphizing of animals is clear in pictures with dogs. A double portrait shows the relationship between the two species; but, as codified images, they also construct that relationship.

Dogs and cats shot on their own represent the ultimate humanizing of them.

These are vernacular pet portraits.

The dog looks at or toward the camera—at the person behind the camera. The cat does not. These behaviors for or against (kidding) the camera figure as "display stances and position-motifs." Pets, I've noted, signify for humans: they are image-status bearers, especially for those people I call "breed worshipers." Breed worshipers are unconscious or conscious purists, who hope, by being represented by a pure breed, their own mixed or mutt-like flaws will be significantly muted or ignored. These same people are often the hounds of style.

## NATIONAL, ICONIC IMAGES

I found this pic in a bag of throwaways.

Handwritten on back: "June 15, 1949: Ernest + Dusty. 'Look at my dogs ears. Ernest is mad. Notice Oddie.'"

A cryptic message, "Ernest is mad," frames an otherwise iconic image of an American boy and his dog. Sun shining.

Maybe a farm, or a house in the countryside. Anyone seeing this pic sees a version or typology, an image of "America." There are several, but this notion of the West and prairie and farm remain most "symbolic." The State Fairs, and all that stuff, so different from what's actually going on in those places: meth, heroin, opioids.

Wild animals, undomesticated, under-domesticated, increasingly show up in people's habitats and photographs. Many reasons for keeping lions and tigers at home: I prefer to think that, as human beings become more dissatisfied with their own over-domestication and conformity, a wild animal substitutes for the losses that civilization has brought. Civilization, so-called. The many wars now, everywhere (in 2014, forty-one active ones), and the West's participation, starting or aiding them, also suits this interpretation, augmenting other more rational "irrational" reasons—economic, territorial, sectarian, etc., human beings are bellicose, and have not stopped being territorial, in small and large ways. Small ways: the academic community, where fights over subjects, claims to have been there first and to own the subject abound, ad nauseam; these claims are not so different, only in degree, from dogs pissing on trees (which humans do, at times; certainly men still spit from rooftops) or going to war for land, oil, diamonds.

## LITTLE AND/OR BIG INHERITANCES

Dumb and dumber times in the nineties, when I came of age, whatever that means, with a super-smart president, Bill

Clinton, impeached for lying to Congress. During his trial, his emphasis on the verb "is" turned tense dinner-table conversations into discussions about tenses. And blow jobs. So, BJs became the sex act de rigueur for high schoolers. We boys got lucky.

In high school, I acted "regular," a boys-gone-wild character, haha, good with my crew—checking out bands, downing multiple shots and vomiting, going to raves, clubs, a little stealing and mischief, nothing felonious, and girls, and yeah, drugs—weed and what was in our parents' medicine cabinets. Predictable. I drove too fast until I stopped driving completely, I freaked out, blind drunk driving.

Later I was stunned with regret, because I knew I'd forgotten important things, lodged maybe deep inside a strange brain zone. Hormones, too, chemicals = voodoo and magic. Those days and years, walking in the halls, going to one dopey class after another, thinking about my hair, my skin, my penis, their penises, her breasts, their vaginas, maybe I'd wear eyeliner for a week, holing up in my bedroom, taking tokes out a window, I felt me was also not-me, this me might be me or, conceivably, a traitor. Could I decide that, or anything?

I quit the tennis team end of my junior year, because it wasn't cool, and I was smoking a lot of weed, and on the court had thoughts like, Why am I doing this? But much worse I lost sight of Mr. Petey.

I DJed in high school, LOUD, a kind of counterphobic acting out to renounce loving Little Sister's quiet. Didn't last too long, because it encouraged my control issues. Actually, now I'm supersensitive to sound, probably because of my early predilections.

But in bars and clubs, doing field work, I blend in, wearing tiny ear buds, disappearing into a scene the way Mr. Petey taught me, and the way an ethnographer should be. (See later, MEN IN QUOTES: To stay on course, and, with monastic deliberateness, even at loose ends and at odds with myself, but my self needed something to be myself, I found a new field, New Men.)

If I were hired as a history DJ, of cultural and psychological sounds, I'd underlay a hiss on every track to signify what you can't really hear anymore but that resounds, and gets submerged by current noises, or might be totally repressed or somehow erased from consciousness, and the hiss would remind everyone that life-stuff is disappearing, involuntarily.

I'm near the fence in the backyard. Mr. Petey is hiding. A breeze wafts and causes a slight movement, a leaf rises in the air, and he is revealed.

A praying mantis is so cleverly and naturally hidden, I had to learn it.

I see him, he notes me. Mr. Petey doesn't lift even one elegant leg to run. No, he turns his tiny head, and faces me, and looks closely at me. His protruding eye beads stare at mine, or me. Mr. Petey cocks his particular head to get a better view of this large, clumsy, fatheaded creature staring at him. Intelligent Mr. Petey. I want to stroke his slender back.

I hold this image in my mind, vivid as it was then, maybe. I don't want it to tarnish. What if I can't, and this never returns. HISS.

When I freeze in place like Mr. Petey, I make myself

invisible, and people walk right past me, or forget I'm there. In London, where I went, in part, to study "others like me," I practiced invisibility. I wanted to be able to disappear.

Some tell me stories as though they're talking to an empty room. I know how to turn into an ear; then, nothing stops them from revealing private episodes. I give them no resistance, sure, like a shrink.

I know, the capacity for invisibility sounds crazy, but I'm sure I have it, since I've performed it frequently.

I'm an image of a member of the human race who revisits the past in images, like Mr. Petey, he's an image now. I think this, and wonder, "What is a thought?" An image is one, maybe. As an image I'm thinking of an image.

## APPEARANCE IS REALITY

A character can be redeemed especially when the "actor" is televisual. Then they can escape the stigma of being "ugly as sin" with plastic surgery (see Paula Jones, who said she had an affair with Prez Clinton—soon her "witchy" honker disappears; Linda Tripp, Republican operative spy in the Clinton White House—she ratted out Monica Lewinsky—face totally done). People believe the "even-featured." A straight face tells it straight, right, Beauty is Truth, Truth Beauty blah, "Ugly" False and Evil. The bad guys have scaggy skin, banged-up noses, ruddy scars, etc. Literally, marked (up) men.

A proposition: people shed ignorance by gaining

knowledge and changing attitudes, change can create forward movement in one group or arena, stasis in another. There is backward movement too, which some might call differential progress on an economic model. There's also nullification and cancellation: famine here, plenty there; floods here, droughts there.

I'm in my time, a knowing ignorant or an ignorant knowing. What I know is a bit of something that's not whole, and it's all about disconnectedness, I'm in the drift. Then there's drag. Drift, Drag, Drift, plus the Goertler effect: turbulence in everything.

Change changes change. Many get shortchanged.

OK, there's reliability in DNA, the latest omniscient narrator in our lives. Still, O.J. got off: one of his dream-team lawyers, Alan Dershowitz, said of the L.A. police, "In their minds O.J. was guilty, and therefore it was OK to frame him."

I met Barry Scheck, another of his dream-team, in a restaurant, I'd had a few, and went up to him. "Alan shouldn't say things like that," he said. So, I pressed him, because who didn't watch that trial, I was sixteen: "O.J. never said he did it."

People get off even with masses of DNA evidence indicting them, because human beings' minds form in sync with prejudice; prejudiced witnessing does not evince credible "evidence." Vision is free of culture, society, never. The video of Rodney King, in slo-mo, a black man clubbed, kicked, beaten, "proved" only that seeing is believing what you want to believe. Cops get off. LA riots.

Slo-mo—"invisible to the human eye" movements made visible. Eadweard Muybridge: his magical series of a galloping horse's four legs in the air. He wanted to know if all four legs went airborne. Great inventions come from curiosity. Prosthetic limbs developed, with the help of slo-mo, and helped also by Iraq and Afghanistan war veterans, the brain makes a fake arm move. Watching motion, suspended, helped make machines become airborne; with animation, Pixar, etc., bodies can be re-made, wholesale plastic surgery.

Slowed-down dream scenes serve "past-ness," and slo-mo beautifies "reality," sex, for one. Drug experiences, say, in Darren Aronofsky's *Requiem for a Dream*, slowly turn bodies into plastic, elastic forms, slithering and flowing like molasses. The characters have sex, sleep, walk in druggy dreams, so slowly. The mechanics of bodies encounter the effects of entropy, bodies not in motion remain immobilized, static. Slo-mo's a downer for eyes, evanescence without a pulse.

Bodies can resemble their own ghosts in this sluggish limbo-land, a tech purgatorio.

The camera tweaked Walter Benjamin's imagination. With a machine, no-hands, anyone can make art, it was social, democratic. The eye isn't the hand, it's mechanical, the hand in art is trained, though the hand "feels," and a bass player, say, has a touch and a feel. People feel music, also. But skill is involved in seeing, also. Benjamin wasn't considering an educated or educable eye, "eye-education," selective vision, and subjectivity. "The Work of Art in the Age of Mechanical Reproduction" is brilliant, seminal. Just saying.

All inventions are either for us or against us, and sold that way, even washing machines.

Designs for prosthetics, etc., slo-mo's benefits when

stoned, are damn cool. Technology can also distract: human claims for its successes inculcate passivity in users. Humans can come to believe too much in their tools, and depend on them for happiness.

Something is always trending.

## A BOY, A SHUTTERBUG

With my starter-guy, I shot trees, flowers, clouds, cloudless skies where Great Uncle Ezekiel and Uncle Lionel might be rocking. The little disc camera did everything automatically, but I shot out of focus, because I moved the camera, liked blurs, unformed things like me. I wasn't into the mechanics of cameras—lenses, focal length, speed—just the imagination behind the camera—me. I was engaged in me, what was before me, which became a strange ownership, probably symptomatic or evidence of a little person's pride in what he believes he controls. Silly tot.

Later, when Father allowed it, I fooled around with his Polaroid cameras. Dad knew Land, its inventor, personally, or I thought he had to, the way he talked about him and his camera. John Maurice Stark bought every Polaroid camera that came to market. Top of the line. Each time, the newest version was sleeker, flatter, faster.

Polaroid collapsed past, present, future, and started me up, collapsing past, present, future (waiting for it). I LIVE that. We live unaccountably with time. Time does damage. I can't account for my time, no one can. Time just goes on, and humans are left alone, wondering what the fuck they're doing in the here and now.

## ACADOOMIA

Scholars fall for their objects of study and nurture them, their childhood dreams. When I'm grown up, I'm gonna be . . .

Few of them know why their interest becomes a passion, a purpose, a mania.

Biographers relinquish their own lives, absorbed in another's for years.

I might want to analyze a person who does that. Wonder if they're a class or type, discernible.

Necro-image-love (my term) has its advocates—Edgar Allan Poe, for one.

English profs and historians et al. profess a love for their period, "their person," usually dead, my him's or her's, they say, and these enunciations reek of scholarly necrophilia. Professors may also closely mimic, in style, their self proclaimed soulmates. When listening to them at conferences, as they talk about their subjects—Marilyn Monroe, Lincoln, Tupac Shakur, Marx, Sappho, Emerson, Whitman, Virginia Woolf, Steve Jobs—I hear their urgent claims for their idols, scholarship a facade for image worship and identification.

Image worship thrives, because of distance and lack of actual contact; a pseudo-intimacy relies on DISTANCE, because to be close while far, intimate but remote, makes any relationship possible. The "other" has no way out. (In his bio of Jean Genet, Edmund White admitted that his subject would not like him.) Like operating a zoom lens, people at a distance own the ability to be close, maybe to what shouldn't be allowed near, which again exalts and exaggerates people's position in the universe, to themselves. Runs the grandiosity engine, big time.

In my field, I didn't have that kind of love. True, I was all about Geertz, say, Jean Rouch's anthro movies, cool stuff. Cultural anthropologists do have favorite tribes, clubs, gangs, thriving on multiples is dope, and years and years ago, one of them might have extolled "his pygmies." Pathology is where so-called sanity also is.

## INHERITANCE, A VALUE?

Clarissa talked way too much about our sterling ancestors, and turned me off. Mother's family was "image-saturated," my term. Many pix were taken or painted by amateurs in the family and artists, such as salty Great Aunt Dot. Clover Adams had earned a few lines in history books, because of her marriage to an Adams, and she was Mother's and Clarissa's very special claim to fame, to their family's importance. I was kind of, well, underwhelmed. But Clover Adams's birth was coincident with the birth of photography: the historical Clover was born into the same age as mine, and she was a picture person. That's solid. Plus, she took photographs, sort of a professional. But her husband, Henry, believed that the medium couldn't "catch the spirit" compared with painting, say. A brilliant historian/writer, but not a visionary.

Clover was a hero to my feminist mother and aunt.

Photography was also the family's vice, in some sense, by fostering life as images, especially of the past.

What's a vice? Never personal. Usually compulsive behavior, bad behavior, according to society's dicta.

Love photography, live it, and life is behind the eye of a viewfinder.

Aunt Clarissa was not about being in the moment, but about finding IT, transcending base society, aka Transcendentalism, by meditating on life's bounty and breathing in, breathing out poetry. Possessed by family history and the literary arts, she mostly did her present in the past, a fusion she made work, or, let's say, in her mind she did, and maybe that's all that counts when you're an egomaniac.

Spiritualism had a doctrine: there was an interplay between the living and the dead.

She said Little Sister had linked souls with souls of the past. Clarissa believed human spirit, energy, was transmitted from the dead to us, also that spirit settled in us to send on to the next generation; spirit communicated, good and bad. (See "trans-communication.") Photography was about spirit catching, for good and bad. Nonsensically, our vice was carried on in the open, everywhere.

Clarissa reveres Joan of Arc, Margaret Sanger, Emma Goldman, Gertrude Stein, the last two lapsed Jews; Father's eclectic ethnic and religious ancestry made him a quarter Jewish or an eighth— a macaroon, he'd wag at Clarissa. Ask her, she'll tell you Gertrude invented the twentieth century. Hey, I rag, Stein was no feminist. Better not tease Aunt Clarissa, she's beyond earnest. Almost humorless. Worst kind of person, in my book.

Straight up, Aunt Clarissa's in love with—not admires or cherishes—she is in love with Stein, and her famous and obscure ancestors. She's in love with their images, she has no idea what they're like, so Auntie is my model for an "image-lover." Everything I knew about images, in a way, derived from her, first; I mean, Clarissa set me off, set me up, inflamed my imagination, even though I wasn't aware of it. So, of course, it's powerful, and I was powerless, when these attitudes, loves, entered into me. Boundless, what you're not aware of, boundless in effects.


## FOR THE LOVE OF IMAGES

Addicts' brain pathways narrow and deepen, pathways or furrows polluted, their brain chemistry transformed to light up pleasure-neurons, like Times Square LEDs. (Neon troughs.) The Picture People are addicted to images, in all their varieties.

We fall in love with an image, images; a notional picture of an ideal, the loved one, instills itself in the psyche. Quickly, people feel disappointed in actual living love objects: actuality doesn't jibe with ideal images. But an image can be forever (like mind-perfume).

Love is a superimposition—no, love is layers of transference and projections that thicken, and thicken, obscuring the ground; love's too gooey to have a discernible bottom or top. Passion and lust are untaught feelings, always unschooled, and have been, since humans appeared as homo erectus, or before them, feelings detonated the species, and, with ravishing energy, caused upheavals in behavior with unexpected, uncontrollable consequences.

Once upon a time, the Western concept of romantic love was started with a grammar for lovers, or a kind of map to the heart. No one follows Andreas Capellanus's *The Art of Courtly Love* anymore, supplanted by advice columns, talk shows, astrology, apps.

It's not what women/men want, it's what DON'T they fucking want. Human insatiability. Capitalism fits it, not the other way around. That desire-machine ain't all that bad, right; but maybe that mountain shouldn't have been climbed. Maybe "civilizations" shouldn't have expanded. Look at the loss.

In sixth grade, I danced with a girl I liked and had my first public boner. The girl moved as far from me as she could, without actually dancing on the other side of the room, and everyone with half a brain knew. My penis humiliated me, desire overran me, my mind couldn't shut it down. My penis did it, not me. Did I tell her that? I don't know.

## LOVE FACES LOVE

One-dimensional love, and thinking, compares with simple mental pictures and their simple-minded makers. People seek resemblances, most don't think pictorially in an exciting way. Face it, most people don't have interesting thoughts. Flat thoughts from flat-lining flat-footed flat-heads. The world is flat.

The Roundheads took their name from the Puritans' unadorned haircuts; they were not Cavalier.

Sex before romantic love, before passion had a name, what did early humans imagine hit them? Lust like a need for food. Gimme gimme. Temporary coupling, the female was pregnant, the male didn't know who did it. When did he figure it out, or was it she? Matriarchies depended on males not knowing. Did the female know how she got pregnant but keep it to herself and that way maintain power? But when the males went out hunting, the females might have stirred up trouble sitting in circles, laughing at the males, and also creating language. Females never had to be silent to do their work.

Poet and critic Eric Mottram theorized that monasteries were the first factories. No women there.

The need for workers turned families into factories.

Royalty required heirs with a provenance, so aristocratic ladies hid errant pregnancies from husbands by racing off to Italy to bear children. Their ladies-in-waiting returned, carrying infants in their arms, raised them as their own. Royal bastards.

Romantic image-love is a transference so complete it competes with so-called "real life," more real to the image-lover than an actual object. Nothing interferes with this purer love. I told Mother, during a crisis—she was urging me to examine my new love—"I know what I'm doing, some of it. Anyway, I chose it." "You didn't choose it," she said. Can't argue with that. I tell her a crisis can be a moment for opportunity. She shoots me her look.


## FAMILY MATTERS: THE MATTER

Mother probably knows if Clarissa has or ever had sexual feelings. She registers as several gender identities. But I can't imagine her lusting after anyone. My imagination is limited.

She has always lived near her adored baby sister, and also is close to Little Sister. Clarissa doesn't disdain Bro Hart, because he, though male, became a medical doctor. A hypochondriac tolerates doctors while despising their expertise.

After *You're a Picture, You're Not a Picture* was pubbed, Bro Hart turned uglier, more brutal in his attempts at one-upmanship. "Hot shot academic," he sneered—I mean, like Snidely Whiplash. Totally ridiculous, Hart, a constitutionally weak sadist, no cojones.

The story goes: Hart was four, I was a newborn, he entered Mother's bedroom, she was breastfeeding me, and the little boy, like a storm, raged, leaped at me, and I needed defense from his tiny fists. He has hated me since. That's the skinny. Those primitive furies: instincts or good judgment? It could be a real high messing up Hart's pictorial face. A borderline personality could do it. But why bother.

I used to believe, really believe: Clarissa represented a dying breed, spinster who stayed home, close to kin; I don't think that now. Her kind just morphed: no more spinsters but another type of female. She prefers to live alone, not to be encumbered by a mate, male or female. Doesn't want it, that, domesticity, wants love, sometimes, but doesn't want someone else around.

Blood tells, as a fact. Aunt Clarissa carries many of her line's recessive traits. She's a trickster, or she's her own person, either way.

## THE GLUT OF IMAGES, BORING

To generalize, and I do, and why not—I grew up surrounded by images. But I also grew up not believing in the reality of images. That is, they were first established as "only pictures." Meaningless. That's totally wrong. But it's how they were culturally embedded. They do have a reality, in spite of their "illusory nature"—just an image, two-dimensional, a window, so-called, into the world. Dependent on illusion, and insubstantial space, but that's not how it really looked, or how I look; or a picture only intimates the past, as Sontag and Barthes suggested long ago, and is never corporeal.

Illusion! People believe in God, they own that illusion. But pictures exist, we can actually see them, factoids, whose effects contribute to "real" illusions. They have actual places in our lives—in a cell, say, on a screen or a wall—though they are not the thing, just a thing. The thing that makes its thing-ness is its quiddity, its whatness.

Creating an image is an achievement, culture. Early humans carved, scratched, images on cave walls. They depicted the animals they hunted and ate, or who killed and ate them. (See Werner Herzog's *Cave of Forgotten Dreams*.) With newer carbon dating, some scientists think Neanderthals might have made them also. The fear of and love for Nature resulted in new needs, for icons to protect them, gods, goddesses, saints. Yahweh didn't allow graven images, which explains Christ's entry onto the scene, half-man, all god, eminently picturable.

God encouraged representation, that's a conundrum. Why would a perfect being have lacks—especially in imaging, especially an omnipotent, omniscient protean God. Why did people abandon pantheism, and arbitrary, even erratic, gods, who are more like humans, for just one God. One God = the origin of the original and its claims.

Humans don't want God to be like them, they want a perfect image.

## UNCLE LIONEL IS A STORY

I dreamed about being a medical doctor because of Father's bro Lionel. Uncle Lionel told me people wore green uniforms at his hospital; I pictured him jumping around in the halls like a big insect, because of the way he lurched drunkenly in our house. But Bro Hart went into medicine.

When Uncle Lionel was drunk, he leaped on the couch, collapsed, slept, drool on his lips and chin, disgusting but kind of cool. My father held his gin better, for a while. An estate lawyer and his own state: he knew how to consume, until it consumed him. Uncle Lionel was two years younger than Father, so close they really didn't need to talk, but they caught up every day in a kind of code. Somehow, Lionel loved my father a lot. Also, Lionel was easy-going, and took after Great Uncle Ezekiel, who was his generation's family clown, roly-poly, wearing a fat man's smiley face. Lionel's sense of the ridiculous aided my dour father.

Father believed in himself: he was way more than a connoisseur, he was an artist manqué, and proud of it—a little self-deprecation showed how manly he was. Occasionally he shot a family picture; but his output—art. Mother earned her B.A. in English from one of the sister schools, but her super education didn't count. The primary family photographer was in a classic no-win situation: my father considered that pretty much everything lay beneath him—including taking snapshots. He self-described as hip, because he had college buddies with funny names, Fluke, Bottle, shit like that. Sometimes they visited us, weirdos he was proud to know and not to be.

Mother's shooting the family pinched the cheek of

gendered behavior. Being Christian, she'd learned to turn both cheeks, a lot, like a revolving door. Kidding.

Great Uncle Ezekiel: when he and his brothers were kids, they formed their own basketball team in the Not-So-Tall League, they were all under five feet nine inches. They even had shirts made up; there are six photos of the team. I'm named after him, right, and the word handed down is, "Great Uncle Ezekiel guarded like a wild dog." (My killer gene plays tennis.) Father's generation is taller, mine even taller, except for Little Sister. She's a throwback to long-gone shorter relatives, who stood in doorways that would decapitate me.

When I visualize my namesake, I see a shortish, round and robust man, smiling. He goes off half-cocked.

He wore comical ties, cracked stupid jokes, he was a raw guy. In a family photo, he's a young guy, lean, a lad, an all-American, wearing a boater, his arms crossed at his waist, one of his legs forward, making him dynamic; his shadow looks long, probably it's close to noon, but the wind is blowing, so maybe it's not that hot. He's standing on a boat named *Sunshine* (written on the back of the photograph), sailing on the Monongahela River. He calls it a "boat excursion," somewhere between West Virginia and Pennsylvania. Behind him and facing the river, a woman has raised her arms and appears to be taking a picture or looking through a telescope. (To the side and front of her, there's a large tourist telescope.) The American flag waves behind Uncle Zeke, seeming to touch his shoulder, creating a perfect photograph, the image of America on the Fourth. Can't tell tie's color, this is b/w.

Uncle Zeke looks like Mr. Independence himself, a

spirited, red-blooded American fellow, exuberant about his future and country. That haughty, bad-boy smile: looks like nothing bothers this guy. When he visited us, he transformed my sardonic father, got him giggling, but I don't think there's one picture of my father laughing. Fake smiling, sure.

Great Uncle Ezekiel lived with two secrets: he was born an androgyne (intersex, we say now) and changed surgically to a male, a fact hidden from the family for a while. Great

Uncle Zeke's parents made the decision, urged by their doctors and followed. De rigueur, then.

(Bro Hart's second wife has a secret—she was CIA, maybe still is.)

The family, and outside-others, mostly knew about Great Uncle Zeke's first secret but not his second secret, which finally came out, much later. Madge knew about his being an androgyne, though not when they were dating, when he thought women didn't go to the toilet. His other secret, that one landed heavy on her.

CIA biz remains a guarded family secret.

Nowadays there are no secrets.

Photographs DEPICT secrets; or they can have no secrets, being just what's there; or photographs intimate secrets, and anything else you imagine might be there. Contemporary artists, in very different ways, play that hand: An-My Lê; John Divola; R. H. Quaytman; Anne Collier; Barbara Bloom; Stephen Barker; Gregory Crewdsen; Sarah Charlesworth; Roni Horn; Bill Jacobsen; Justine Kurland; Jack Pierson; Arthur Ou; Seton Smith; Barbara Ess. Actually, this list could be endless; photographs tell nothing of themselves.

I stare at old Zeke, in photos ranging from when he was three, posing for a professional in town, sticking his finger up his nose in a high school graduation photograph, his eyes bugging out at a party after his college graduation, looking boisterous with the Not-So-Tall basketball team, or beaming as he cuts the cake with his bride, Madge, and on and on. Three years before he died, an arresting one of him with his head drooping to the side, a melancholy expression on his face. I want to peel away the emulsion, get under that sad sack image.

It's a primitive urge, or just silly, but no matter what I might seem to know about fiction and the illusion of images, I'm a small boy rushing around, curious to learn what's what, riveted by who's who, like Great Uncle Ezekiel, and still shocked at what I see that no one told me would be there. I want other pictures to rub away what I do know, and bare a braver, newer world, something exciting—for a change.

A family resemblance shares tragedy's attribute—it can't be avoided. You can't escape what it says about you. Genes have predictive power; epigenetics depends upon both environment and the genome, because a gene's protection against cancer, say, can be switched off. They've done studies with identical twins, one smokes, gets cancer, the other doesn't and doesn't. Some people can't handle how much the genes affect outcomes, sure, environment is important, probably it's 60/40 genes vs. environment, or maybe 50/50. Consider family resemblances: your parents' genes show in your body type, your facial features, so genes must have similar effects upon raw intelligence, proclivities. Some accept one part of this equation, physical resemblance, but reject the other. Not logical, but that's human beings, picking and choosing.

Few want to believe how much is predetermined. I find it reassuring. Free will, maybe THE contentious issue, anyway, definitely limited, and I prefer relinquishing power to my genome, and its taking some responsibility for my predilections and tendencies.

I've wondered since I was a teenager: could Great Uncle

Ezekiel have had any kind of a sex life? He and Margaret didn't have children, if that means anything. I don't know why they named me after him, I'm not like him, according to Mother, but l feel implicated in his ignorance.

Families do that, *implicate* you in them. When I think about Great Uncle Ezekiel's shock at seeing his blushing bride, Margaret, on the can for the first time, I immediately see a pic that could never be pasted in our family album—the unrecorded image, one of the awkward notes of life, always unpictured. Or sad occurrences are shot, they're not in family albums, they're obscene, or they're in art galleries, blown up bigger and bigger.

On the left: Great Uncle Ezekiel age four, with his mother, Rose née Turner, holding him, and anon woman. On the right: Great Uncle Zeke at eleven or twelve, carrying what might be presents. Are they his, for a birthday, or is he giving them to someone?

Everyone saw him as a clown, at least acting like one. But what does comedy tell, and does it reveal as tragedy does? Say, about Great Uncle Ezekiel.

Was his life really a tragedy? With inevitability to it? A comedy's only inevitability is surprise, an unforeseen punch line. You guess it, it's not funny. Uncle Ezekiel—his life's a toss-up, he was funny, everyone said, but his life wasn't funny, only surprising—but no joke.

Tragedy builds to a foreseeable inevitability—consciousness of it rising like the sun—the end is inescapable.

I can't see that in photographs—fate. Clowns terrify some children. Clowns look like sad figures, dressed in funny clothes, and they make weird faces. They could easily morph into tragic characters, never heroic ones. A clown rescuing a child from a fire would look funny, wack. *Capturing the Friedmans* was a documentary about an ordinary suburban family, father, mother, three sons, until the father was accused and convicted of multiple counts of child molestation. One son, Jesse, was convicted, also, then paroled from prison after serving thirteen years. Inside, the father committed suicide, or just gave up the ghost. Another son, who was not involved and never accused, became a professional clown. In the movie, you watch him arrive at a child's birthday party, in his clown outfit, bursting with fake joy. This guy chose to entertain children. You have to wonder. It's a crazy irony.

Bernie Madoff's sons, they didn't know, I just know it; one was a suicide, the other died of cancer. It had been in remission, and returned, he said, because of the tragedy in his life, the accusations against him. He argued for his innocence, to his death.

I bought it, buy it. They were all duped.

Madoff's wife, the boys' mother, was interviewed on *60 Minutes*. A sad character, she was alive like an afterthought, and slumped in a chair way too big for her small frame. She looked shrunken, a terrified little doll. Defeat and trauma braided her face; she is hated and considered a monster, because her husband destroyed people's lives. She says she didn't know. Wives can be entirely out of it that way, and I don't think she had a clue, or her sons. She won't have anything to do with her husband, but she's already on the fade, while Bernie Madoff goes on, coaching inmates about money, etc.; they respect him, he said in another *60 Minutes* interview. He shows no remorse. Worse, he doesn't appear miserable. The other prisoners don't mess him up—no biggie if the wealthy get robbed.

## THE PICTURE PEOPLE FACE VALUES

Most of us live on the skin of existence, it's where we are situated; it's where photographs collide with lived life.

Skin of existence: a thin skein covers us, concealing deepdish discontent.

If I can explain this: much of private life, so-called, is silent, a silent conversation with ourselves, we tell ourselves things we don't tell anyone else, except therapists and psychics. We imagine acts that appear on the surface will be taken at face value, unexamined, unanalyzed. People don't see themselves as superficial, but sometimes call their behavior transparent. Or know they're difficult and admit it (often with perverse pleasure). People see pictures in both ways, as transparent and difficult to read.

We act based on an image: "I can't see myself doing that." DO YOU GET THE PICTURE? DOES THE PICTURE GET YOU? (Bears repeating.)

Illusion shapes and shelters us, as necessary as oxygen and water. Illusions won't die, they are not delusions, and seem part of a human being's hard-wiring. The illusion, say, that life will continue as it was yesterday or an hour ago, could be genetic.

## FAMILY, FAMILY

Little Sister's youthful discretions and silences didn't stop me from talking to her, but she could put a freeze on, paralyze people the way Mr. Petey did his prey before gorging on them. She composed, in my eyes, an ideal picture, but in three dimensions; when I discovered an otherworldliness in her, or another dimension, I believed her linked to our ancestors in more ways than blood.

I accept the return of the repressed, though also have rational urges against it. But resemblances, not physical, temperamental, flowed between Clover Adams and Little Sister. Together, the metaphysical couple made my maternal family uncanny. Actual twins separated in life by 1,500 miles were often alike. But their separation was 150 years.

It was written, notably by her fiancé, Henry Adams, that Clover wasn't beautiful.

Little Sister is. She owns symmetrical features, hazel eyes, porcelain skin, straight blond hair to mid-back, and is always referred to as pretty or beautiful. Her appearance, the surface, is unmarked by the inner turbulence that results in her not speaking. She speaks more, but still not much in public.

I'm creating her word-picture. Describing people—with adjectives I call "non-specific descriptors" or "neutered language"—turns them into clichés, generics, brands. Millions of women fit her profile. In your mind's eye there's a version of her. Then add: selectively mute, left-handed—these aren't immediately obvious, no instant visual (vis-factoid)—and what is imagined?

Words create images, right; but controlling them is trickily elusive, and visual images may be still more elusive, since there's no dictionary for images, and always a diffuse etymology.

I prefer, maybe weirdly, the obliquity of pictures.

In photographs, Little Sister is never central in the frame but to the right or left, a stealth figure; even in a corner of a room or frame, she assumes space and volume, her physical presence displacing more than her small body. In my eyes.

When Bro Hart and I stood next to each other in pix Mother took, he loomed over me until I turned thirteen; I shot up ten inches, became the taller boy, which he hated. You can see it. I know his expressions. The power shift shows especially in later photos, after the family dispersal or common nuclear diaspora, when there are scant photos of us together, except at weddings, where we stand far apart. Totally obvious, because it was also physical that gaping distance between us, at his second wedding. It was plain as the noses on our faces. Ha.


Thoughts for today: efficacy of the word "plain."
    Plain observation. I love that. There is none, but I love it.
    Plain talk. Pain talk. Haha.


## ANTI AUNTIE

Self-historicizing, selfie-narration: Clarissa dumped me when I became a "man." I came of age, she lost interest, the boy had vanished, and this cruel exclusion struck at the dawn and curse of adulthood. She excluded me, ignored me as much as she could.

Who was the family symptom carrier: Little Sister, Clarissa, me? A family board game, spot the problem child.

OK, Clarissa had downed many potent combos of drugs, tons of natural remedies, and had doctors' scrips to undo the damage. Her biological, neurological grid had already electrified her: she was like nobody I ever knew or would come to know. An object for study. Gertrude Stein stopped speaking to her nephew, Allan, when he was eighteen. From what I can figure, that was the deal.

"Men and girls, men and girls: Artificial swine and pearls." —Gertrude Stein

Clarissa's nasty move provoked intense and close-encounter familial shocks, especially for Mother, who'd beg her, "What is wrong with you? Be kind to him." Clarissa adapted, the way our species does, and simulated gestures of civility. To be kind doesn't require a lot. Kindness is a behavior; a kind person does no harm, and can be enough in a cruel world; but a kind person doesn't necessarily have to sacrifice anything. Like: Kind people contribute to charities and don't get their hands dirty.

To give Mother cred, she felt "grossly disappointed in Clarissa," but "Ezekiel, we're sisters." Clarissa believes and has said, "I created your mother," but it's well-known lore that she tried to smother Mother five days after her birth. Not unlike Hart with me.

Aunt Clarissa sprouted from a poisoned branch of the family tree.

Self-admission, and here comes the dope (haha): I collaborated, was Clarissa's puppet for a long while, and did her bidding. She fed me stereoscopic slides, family lore, and while I hated the mysticism of blood ties, etc., I ate it also, maybe I was force-fed, but it osmosed inside me, my system. When she dropped me, splat, I've come to understand, my puppet self yearned for a puppet-master, and was led in a direction where I caught a disease I was investigating.

Not unusual.

She never could make it up, dropping me, no way. I'm not the forgive-and-forget kind of guy, also not a love-'em-and-leave-'em guy. To the max.

## MISCREANTS / HOMEMADE FAILURES

Bro Hart's bad enough, but several assholes have married into the family, and there's nothing to do about in-laws but despise and ignore them. I wonder if blood-kin marry idiots and bring them into the family with intention, to destroy it from within. In-law disasters occur regularly in families, where, and nowhere else, things happen that should get people jailed because of how dangerous they really are. Psychological outlaws.

My father's brothers' spouses and their children—and even Mother's sister Clarissa—they didn't spill their shit all over us. OK, Clarissa did work my nerves, and Father—he didn't give a damn about anyone, really. Bro Hart and his first wife—a damaged duo—got divorced, but he kept the dog. Cool. Then Hart carted in his second wife, a creep like him, and, because she seethed about her wretched family and its traumas, and stuff no Stark had anything to do with, we were slammed anyway. In-law shit. Oughta be a law. CIA, as noted, or was.

Father stopped speaking to his older bro, Theodore, Teddy, an ordinary criminal, Mother said, a thief. Another family secret, another scarlet letter, and nothing to the world at large, but sinister in ours. Reason for the break, still reverberating. Weddings? How does the tribe meet, on whose territory? The schism started before I was brought mewling into the world, which I entered through Mother's vagina, her birth canal, and when I see her, I'm like, How, and Wow. You feel me?

Teddy: a social outcast, a stigmatic, in Goffman's sense, and our only "legit-illegit" relative in the family, intriguing to me. He did what is invariably called a "stint," or four years, in the whimsical slammer.

He was an outsider.

There are outsiders in families, the colloquial black sheep, or they are in-laws, step- and half-sibs, etc., who are psychological outlaws.

There are very few outsider artists in photography, just semi-sophisticated weirdos.

The Godfather said: "Keep your friends close, your enemies closer." In families, there's no difference between friends and enemies, and there is no choice.

All in the family. No kidding.


## LIFE AFTER DEATH: LIVED BY THE LIVING

So, Great Uncle Zeke, had two secrets, right. He lived his other secret deeper, more hidden, and no one knew but the other secret-sharers: he was a cross-dressing heterosexual. Great Aunt Madge found out, after he died, going through his clothes, saw bras and girdles, dresses and slips, high heels

in a size II, neatly piled, she said, in a small trunk he'd squir-
reled away behind other, large boxes, on a shelf higher than
she could reach. (She was even shorter than Zeke.) There
were photographs, too.

I'm assuming that seeing him in drag was her last,
grievous shock, because even though a picture can't tell
"the truth," since it can't narrate itself, along with the other
breath-stopping evidence she discovered, the photograph of
Great Uncle Zeke wearing a string of pearls, a long black
wig—looks like the fifties or early sixties—holding a big doll
close to his chest, blew her away, literally.

Notions flood my head, while I project into hers. It's not
their house, but where was he? Clutching a doll? They didn't
or couldn't have children. He's gazing at the camera, the photographer, sexily, giving a low, sultry look that Margaret . . . I
never saw that look, she's thinking. Look at me, I'm a woman,
a made-up, lipsticked, sheath-wearing man. I'm happy like
this, and you never even guessed, Margaret.

It's reported she fainted, or collapsed, survived a near-
fatal heart attack, and died ten months later, just about a year
after Zeke (both pretty old, in their late eighties). Married
people often die within a year of each other (should discour-
age marriage). Couple mortality is a real phenomenon, but
people who register it think it's just a coincidence. Humans
are related to other creatures that mate, from big to little,
mammals to birds, and die when the mate dies. Lovebirds
drop dead in their cages soon after their partners do.

People might recognize how the loss mattered to their
friends' health. So, I'm not saying humans don't realize it, but
they shake their heads, bemused, and toss it off. They don't

prepare for that eventuality: grieving people can will themselves to die. A broken heart, say, becomes a bad heart.

Margaret's death came as a total shock. I heard how it
happened, and it stunned me, really, and taught me about
good and bad secrets, and trust, which was a big reason, later,
I saw a shrink, to trust someone, not unique. Great Uncle
Zeke's being a cross-dresser wasn't meaningless, but it wasn't
such a big deal. I mean, my gen and younger think of gender
issues differently, and, after 9/11, some of us expect terrorist
attacks, etc. Not in a paranoid way, just part of the zeitgeist.
But Uncle Zeke's secrecy was scary to me: personal secrets
could have tragic consequences.

I began pondering consequences, which I never had, not
as a child, for sure nothing felt consequential then, although
everything actually lands in a profound way. The consequences
of bad stuff caused time-outs, punishments, criticism of my
behavior. Maybe I'd made Little Sister cry because I grabbed
her toy. At four, you wouldn't care; by nine, you would, if you
had a heart at all. A child feels free, unhampered by consequences. This child did.

Besides, timing matters. You don't necessarily find out
when you need to know, to act, to avert disaster, say: a message arrives, post-dated. OK, it arrives, but if it's not timely,
temporality affects its meaning. People say, "If I knew that
then..."

Steve Locke, an artist, told me, after he'd figured out a
problem, "Like most discoveries, mine came too late." (He
contributed to a panel I organized as a grad student, on painting's and photography's relationship to time.)

Location, location, location.

Position, position, position.

Time's not on your side.


## IN A FOREIGN FIELD

Things were going along OK, with some changes and hitches, but Maggie and I were good.

The first week of 2005, we traveled to London for our big break, our time against and escape from the usual, and no school. Etc.

Foreign field work: delving into unfamiliar zones, becoming unsettled in my being, happily disoriented, happily observing other attitudes, behaviors.

I noticed ordinary details, walking speed, dress styles, voice volume on streets, in the Tube, in cafés. Male vs. female differences in all of these, also.

Listening to people speak, paying close attention to understand what they were saying, upper, middle, and lower class accents, was hard at first. I watched their mouths. Everyone seemed to eat faster than Bostonians. Noticed more halitosis, maybe because of speed of ingestion and poor digestion.

Pub life differed from bar life, unless they were destination hot spots, then pretty much the same, crowded, louder music. Wine bars, classier, less raucous everywhere. Local pubs had a vocal, even vociferous cheeriness that bars don't foster. Bars, in Cambridge, Boston, New York, felt mute compared with pub bonhomie, until much later in the night, near closing, when drunkenness ruled. More vomiting in the streets in London.

Maggie and I visited the usual places, some of them. She

opted for the literary: Keats's house, Dr. Johnson's, Dickens's, Woolf's, Bram Stoker's.

I saw the Queen's residence in Richmond; the peacocks in Holland Park wandering the grounds, sometimes unfurling their tail feathers, an obscure thing or two; Maggie and I visited the crazy architect John Soane's house together, and we also did a lot with CW. He squired us.

By the end of the second week, restless, I found some people to talk to about their family photographs—CW put me in touch.

On the street I wrote notes and took pictures as aide-mémoire, and felt touristy but I behaved the same way at home. My perceptions of self changed in another context, as if foreignness was itself second sight. Really, I fit right in, but that sense of being a curiosity remained, and later registered more.

I wanted to investigate, experience solo days and nights, and the night life. Maggie was cool, we never stopped each other. I continued to practice invisibility, a skill I'd worked on forever, Mr. Petey as my guide, and, as an outsider, I practiced blending into the crowd, a necessary job description for an ethnographer.

I went to a club, where I'd heard people were scoring drugs, easy to spot with the bathrooms busy, heavy pockets, furtive hands clasping, unclasping, hands in pockets again, and then I noticed two guys enter, they were dead wrong for the place. The men stood there for a while, looking around. I knew they were undercover, and instantly, but very calmly, I stood up, quiet as Mr. Petey on a branch, and left the guys I was sitting with, all mates, they said they were, and walked like a ghost past the undercovers, who didn't notice me, because they were looking ahead. They had an object in view, and I wasn't it, not yet. I sidled by them.

I was often living in my head, even with Maggie beside me, so it was easy to act like a ghost. I returned the next night, or the night after, can't remember now. The mates didn't know I'd split, and there had been some arrests, and then they noticed I was gone. They were cool, though.

I'd go into cafés, workers' ones, so-called, and have a poached egg on toast. Or, I'd go to a fancy hotel and have tea. I could move in and out, not having a classification in London, except American or foreigner. I'd watch people. I wanted to be a fly on the wall. People's conversations depend on their day, news, weather, mishaps, and often a crisis. I'd listen in. The English are famously more circumspect than Americans, they even fear Americans' rage for informality and blurts of intimacy.

Often CW was showing us around, the city's huge, and he knew it pretty well, he took us to the V & A, and often we were riding the Tube, traversing the city below more than above.

Our sublet was big, a London flat with many rooms and solid walls. Maggie and I had a huge bedroom at one end of the apartment. CW, when not taking us around, was often out all night with friends and he often slept on the couch in the living room, down the hall. Maggie could be super-energetic, editing her novel, optimistic, sometimes I thought frantic, and by the third week she was losing weight, and I worried she might be sick. She felt fine, absolutely brilliant, she said, adopting the coin of the realm. Her mother phoned more than usual and sent emails, her daughter far away, OK.

On some days, her enthusiasm waned, but her work was work. Mine too. Can't be high all the time.

Sometimes, Maggie seemed more concerned about appearances than usual, what people thought of her and me, or how I looked. What I wore. She seemed more unsettled than I was. Either I was realizing it more, as we knew each other better, or I was finally seeing it, what had always been there. Living together is weird, a marriage of true minds means you can deal with the untruths, also.

Right, we're out and about, walking a lot, eating well, getting drunk, sleeping late, keeping up with the English Joneses, and we're both doing our work.

The fifth week we're there, a chilly morning in early February, I'm on a double-decker bus with CW. Maggie had decided to sleep in. CW and I were heading to the Tate (Turner Whistler Monet exhibition). I like staring out of windows, ever since I was a kid, from our house or from the car, or the school bus. Life goes along, and keeps going, and this was sadly comforting, that constant movement.

CW is beside me, and then I hear something from him, he says something, eyes down, face obscured in shadow, so I turn to look at him. His face has a startling expression, trouble smeared over it.

Wassup, man, I ask. Or something.

"Starkie, man, I'm sorry, man, I don't know how . . ." Then he lifts his head, I will always see that head rise, his twinkly blue eyes darting like a snake's.

"Starkie, Maggie and I are in love."

"What?" I think I said, What. I said, I think, "What? You're kidding me."

No, he says, and I go blank, and he tells me how it started more than a year ago, they didn't want to hurt me, it just happened.

They they they . . .

I stood, glared at him, about to strike his pretty face, because I wanted to kill him, I would murder him. I had no words, I had nothing. I ran down the stairs, we were on the top deck, hit the platform, and leaped off the bus. Blindly. Didn't even know I was doing it. Had to get away from his sick words. Him. I'm not sure if the bus was moving. I fell down, anyway, sat there on the sidewalk, near the bus stop, stunned, all those ugly words on me, and I couldn't move. Maybe I'd hurt myself, but I didn't feel it. I felt nothing.

I had to find Maggie, because she'd tell me he was lying, that it was all a sick joke.

I should've seen it coming, the writing on the wall, recognized the patterns, right.

Looking outside, I wasn't looking inside, and I could avoid things right before my eyes, and not know it, like psychologists studying rats and believing they understand themselves. I was extrospective. Kidding. Clueless dumb asshole me.

You're not aware you're in another narrative. Someone's changed the story, right. You don't know, because you're playing your usual part, when nothing's usual, your script doesn't have the new lines.

I got up off the street or sidewalk, don't know how long I'd been there, dizzy, I felt like throwing up, I thought I'd been hit on the head, my head hurt, the bus must've passed by, Curtis didn't jump off to help me, I would've killed him if he'd touched me, I swear I would have. I picked myself up, people stared, simultaneously staring, looking off, and ignoring me, the foreigner, that American, because it was embarrassing, and I hailed a taxi, I'm pretty sure, but my memory is scrambled, the shock of being sucker punched, and somehow I got back there, and when I walked into the apartment, Maggie was there, waiting—it had all been fucking planned—white as a ghost or a sheet, but Maggie wasn't a clean sheet, she was dirty, filthy. I hated her for loving her. I couldn't see her face, I couldn't believe it was her face. She repeated what the Shithead told me, what what what, I shouted, or screamed inside my head, what what what, she wasn't in love with me anymore, she said. Don't say that, you have to love me, you have to, I said, and she was very sorry, she really was, I was great, she said, she said all the right things, and I hated her, "blah blah brilliant, handsome, wonderful," and I wanted to strangle her. "Fuck you," I said, and threw something. "It didn't happen all at once," she actually said shit like that. "It wasn't Curtis . . . something was wrong, we didn't talk, you at your computer . . . it just happened." One day she knew she didn't love me anymore. Words, no blame, no fault, dead words, believe me, you'll see it will be . . .

Slimy worms crawled from her mouth.

NOTHING SCREAMING NOTHING.

I hurt her, fuck her, get her back, make her mine, murder her. Even now I still don't remember most of it. I moved into a hotel, or they did. I did. It had cable, I watched porn, jerked off until my dick bled, drank, cried, drank, cried, didn't eat, thought I'd die, and prayed I would. Stuffed a wool scarf in my mouth to scream.

Maggie worried about me; in the beginning she said she did. I didn't believe any utterance from that treacherous mouth. She moved out, and so did the shithead, but she would call me, and I'd hang up. No, I was in a hotel, and they were still in the flat. She knocked on my door, and I wouldn't let her in.

I was a dead man walking. Rage balled me up. I didn't know anything or that I was storming around London, around and around, riding the Tube from one end of the city, riding back, days and nights went by, I rode all the lines as far as they would go. Sometimes I jumped off at a station because its name struck me, and I wandered somewhere, wherever. I don't remember. Foreign streets lay outside me.

Out of their mouths, shit and vomit all over me, me mewling and sick. They wouldn't stop, sensations, I couldn't make my brain stop, I didn't know what IT was, and I couldn't. Treading in place. Dreading waking. Lost my heart. Lost everything. I couldn't keep my eyes open. I slept, wanted to sleep, wanted to wake up dead.

Love isn't a science, relationships don't yield repeatable results.

Why did she stop loving me?

Sometimes I could visualize scenes between us, little acts of kindness, lust, I reheard conversations. Incomplete, always.

Is that when she stopped loving me? That moment, and what was that look in her eyes, on her face? How her mouth pursed then . . . I didn't say anything then, I let that moment go, I was stupid. Was that when . . .

I practiced invisibility, right, when it suited me, like with her, when I needed to. I told Maggie, after I super-reluctantly agreed to meet her in person because I didn't know what I was capable of doing, I told her she was an evil bitch. I could see right into her, that she had no heart, no love. She had killed my heart and hope.

Maggie, get your fucking divorce, I told her I wouldn't fight it, and she said she didn't want anything, didn't need anything, she wished . . . Fuck you, I said. Get your fucking divorce, I hope you both die. I warned her that shithead should stay away from me, I wasn't kidding, and fuck you both, I said.

Then I made myself invisible and walked out of the café.

I left the café and kept walking, grabbed my bag from the hotel, and fled, took flight. I jumped on a train to Paris, checked into a hotel, walked around, stopped in cafés, saw nothing, watched without seeing, slept without sleeping, lived without living, then on an impulse, I had many, jumped a train to Amsterdam, walked around and around, the canals, had a prostitute in the district, they sit in the windows, like fleshy mannequins, like men go shopping, I was a creep creeping along, buying sex, how low could I go, did we do it, I mean, did I stick my dick in her, or did she suck me off, I can't even remember, so fast, and kept walking, feeling sick of myself, everything. Then, sometime, to Centraal Station, and hopped a train to Bruges, then Maastricht. I suppose I ate, but don't remember food. I didn't want food, everything coming into me was poison.

If I had thoughts, if I was thinking, it was only that I didn't believe anything, I believed only I could never feel again, or be the same, because I'd been touched by the loveless hand of dead love, no love anymore, I was unloved.

What is a day, a night, to the half-dead? Half dark, half light.

Dull, duller, I was the puniest of dopes in the pathetic blah blah blah. Or, I was one of the saints, and no one else would ever touch me. I moved through, passing by vacantly, naked, clothed, on the streets, inviolable.

I took another train, into Germany, and jumped off at Freiburg. Heidegger's city. Free city. This is one of those strange things that happen to people on the loose and ready to do anything. Life took a turn I couldn't expect, but when you break ties with reality, or anyway the reality you had lived in, events occur; on my own, things, people, came to me. I was suspended in time, and slow, and could be caught and caught up in others.

I was hanging around. I was a stranger among strangers, and I didn't know what I was doing.

A painter took me into his home, because he liked Americans, that's how I recollect it, and told me I'd been around Freiburg's museum for contemporary art, maybe for two days, I can't remember where I slept, and he noticed, a curious man, a kind teacher, he noticed me, so he talked to me, and invited me for a pilsner. I must have told him stuff, maybe about how I was going to study men like me, and more stuff, and he heard me, and made an offer. He took me in, because he saw a guy, me, on the loose, not a dangerous character except to himself—I was my only enemy, he said, but he was wrong; I had enemies. He offered me a room, his empty attic. I could stay there, if I wanted. It wasn't good to sleep in parks, he said.

The painter was a true gentleman, old school, seventy-five years old, and he didn't expect anything from me. He'd been born in 1930, a youth decimated by terror, no control of anything. He had an ex-wife and a girlfriend. He drove me to his house, on the outskirts of the city, and showed me the attic, where there was a bed and a chest of drawers, he gave me towels, and showed me where my bathroom was, it was small, but mine only, and left me alone. I lay down on the bed, the comforter overwhelmed me with its soft, warm embrace, and I slept and slept. I don't know how long I slept.

One day I woke up and walked into town. Then I walked into town every day, and sat in cafés, strolled around the old city, where Stars of David were embedded in cobblestone streets, names of dead Jews carved into stone. This was, I saw, guilt lying in the streets, glittering. Maybe I thought of my father's Jewish great-grandfather.

I was dead, walking on the dead. I played out an internal drama, a single character drama, invisible, the way I wanted it.

In cafés I observed people and imagined that: either they were watching me or they weren't. I noticed that, when I believed one or the other, I felt my way of observing them changed. If people were noticing me, also, they might be doing it malevolently or benevolently. I kept my notebook on the table. Every action or behavior had another behind it, every attitude another behind it, and then I could sometimes feel the weight of existence and interpretations, as physical, these many layers, and then I realized that any notion I had of seeing through people's behavior, comprehending it, or of its having some transparency, was absurd. Heavy lay the layers, I ostentatiously wrote in my notes.

If the layers added up, as beneficence, I could drink a beer, quiet, calm. If the layers, one resting on the other, complex human "being" fusing together, seemed threatening, I left the café. Some afternoons brought peace, others chaos.

At the house I contributed money to food, and the painter mostly left me alone, his home my sanctuary. Maggie didn't know where I was. No one did. I told the painter my name was Henry Adams. Adams, he repeated in his German accent, and nodded. He accepted me.

I watched him paint, sitting on a chair, I was quiet like Little Sister. He'd placed white skulls on black blankets, on his studio floor, and he would look at them, eyes steady on the inert objects, and maybe he saw them move, or he could move them. I kept very still and practiced invisibility because if I moved, the skulls might pierce my own. I didn't feel my skin protected me, a raw blob.

It was spring, the growing time, and I watched plants growing in his garden. I watched bees suckle from blossoms, birds talk in trees. I waited for Mr. Petey, he never showed up. Bamboo trees brushed against the house, whoosh whoosh whoosh, the wind breezed by, whoosh whoosh whoosh. I took walks with him, maybe we walked a few miles, side by side, or he walked in front of me. I followed him, my guide. He was, then.

I hold these memory-truths to be possible: I saw strangeness, a girl and her dog disappeared suddenly, as if kidnapped, I still don't understand that. Shooting stars were common, and faces in clouds talked to me. Sometimes, Mother.

I loped along and occasionally took pictures. Or made notes. Young men and women didn't interest me. Also, I didn't know German, and realized that people interested me when they spoke, and I could understand them. So, my being an ethnographer was a total joke. I didn't watch people as if they were in a zoo, though, that felt too weird. Somehow I decided it was comforting, realizing that talking in a language I knew made people interesting. It made me believe I might be human. People stared, I stared back, and one raised his fist, I think he did, but I couldn't know if that was real, a threat or a greeting; or these events, these people, if they were real. I embraced all of it, as normal and as true to what I was, who I was. Who I was saw what he saw and heard.

The painter had a passion for eggplant, not cooked, just the shape of it and its gleaming purple skin. He dedicated days to studying one and making drawings of it. I didn't get it. I tried to look at it, but each time I did, I got bored fast. It was just an eggplant.

One night, at dusk, in the distance, near the trees, eight children ran around, probably playing, shouting, running back and forth. It didn't look like play. I knew I should see it that way. Young animals, wolves, lion cubs, play with their brothers and sisters, but they're actually learning how to hunt, to kill, eventually. I couldn't see anything but these children, young animals, learning the same skills as other young animals. I turned away, walked home, into the house. I knew I would never look at children the same way again. It seemed inconceivable to turn back.

The painter had a sauna, and every day he took one and came out bright red. That alarmed me, and I told him it might not be good for his heart. He patted his heart, then me, on my back, and opened a bottle of red wine.

At night, the painter wore a monk's robe, listened to Bach or watched the news on TV. The phone rang once in a while, the children he rarely mentioned, but seemed to love, his dealer, an old friend, a former student. He was glad to hear from them but didn't seem to depend upon it, or them. It was his life, he had his life, and lived it with a consistency, a constancy that he liked. He didn't seem bored by the sameness of things. Actually, he was turned on by it, and painted it.

I understood that, later, when I watched things, and went my own way too, in my head.

His girlfriend spent most days away, working as a teacher for disturbed children, and hung out on weekends, mostly. She painted also. I don't know what she thought of me and my living in his house. She seemed cool. I liked that she wore Yohji Yamamoto only. I liked her dedication to one designer. She kept quiet, and sometimes told the painter his breath stank. The painter would go, Oh no, and pop some mints into his mouth. He appreciated her telling him. He loved raw onions. I thought that was probably very German.

One morning, the sky looked ominous, and kept me inside; the next day, I awoke to a blue, cloudless sky, and walked into the garden. The noise in my head had dulled to a lowish stutter, no banging, no loud ticking time bomb, time is not the bomb. Ha.

More flowers were coming along, sprouting blooming, more colors and natural brilliance, and the buzzing in the air—sounds of life—sounded harmless, so I decided to leave. I wanted to. It was an impulse. The painter wasn't sure it was wise, and his round face turned solemn.

We took a long walk, later, when the sun was going down, the days were longer heading toward summer. We didn't speak much. He saw that I wasn't the way I'd been, though I didn't know what I'd been.

That night I packed what I had, not much, and the next day he drove me to the train station. He was calm, I was resolute, also nervous. I mean, whoever I was, I had to leave. He watched me buy a ticket to Paris, and then stood on the platform with me. The train pulled in, right on time, crazily on time, and then he watched me board the train, and before I left the platform, and walked to my seat, he called out, "Henry," and I stopped at the top of the stairs, and looked at him. He looked small from the train platform. He handed me a flat package that I knew must be a small painting or a drawing, and wished me great luck. Then he said, gravely, "I love you like a son." My father never said he loved me, and he was actually my father, actually I was his son, his second.

I can picture the painter and the scene now. It's very reassuring.

I traveled through Germany, Holland, Belgium, jumped off in Paris, and then bought a ticket for the train to London. I couldn't return home, return was impossible, I wasn't wanted, and couldn't be there, there was nothing to return to, and no home without her. I had failed at what I wanted most, Maggie, though she didn't believe in it, failure.


## ASSOCIATION, DISSOCIATION

I found a generic hotel room in London, in the East End, and walked around during the day. At night, within my limits, I caroused at a pub. I hung with a loose group, two artists, female, male, a financial writer, computer software nerd-genius, art critic and historian, a multi-faceted posse like London's new face, though it was also two-faced, everything was, and one face hid the other, the way the sun hides the moon.

We collided in a pub. Just ordinary, my temporary local.

I mean, it resembled ordinary life, with some order: I shifted from my hotel bed to my local and back, and sometimes I caught a big American movie in central London, where crowds of tourists wandered, and, like me, looked up and down. I visited galleries and museums, I didn't focus, couldn't see anything. The contacts I'd made before, I didn't want to connect with; I knew them through that fucking shithead creep.

They call it a fugue state, what happened to me. It's not at all musical (kidding). I was escaping reality, in flight, suffering dissociation and a dissociative amnesia, a kind of selective amnesia like Little Sister's selective mutism, so the memories were still there, unlike regular amnesia when they're gone forever. Mine were buried very deep and most will return, the docs say. I don't know about that.

I didn't want to remember, didn't want to know.

I transformed, to myself, into an incomplete, imperfect stranger. Rage would come, I'd feel something, not blank, but nothing subdued my mind's febrile activity. I wished hard I were home, a boy protected, again, but no protection existed for me, I was an adult, and madness was my only sensation, and pain. I crushed my homely thoughts to powder. Which I snorted. My memory is holes and spots, and turned who I was or became into daily guesswork.

Every night, the end of day, had a destination, and I talked to these people, one or two would be hanging out, Guinness or wine in hand, a whiskey—looking back now, I believe pub life could be the virtual world's flesh-oasis. I listened to them. They used words I knew, did things I did, or had done, or hadn't done, but I followed along.

An artist took me to a club where a conceptual poet stood

on his head and lectured, I can't remember what he said, he
spoke from memory and very fast, but by the way he stood on
his head, or that he was standing on his head and speaking at
the same time, I knew he and I could be friends, and that he
understood the world the way I did.

I talked the talk, did the walk, but Zeke was gone, I
wasn't myself, or whoever he was, and no one knew, or if
they did, they were too polite to say. They let me in, whoever
I was, maybe their pet, their bitch. Kidding. I was American
in some way that amused them, within our various differences, and cool, because I was an other to others, eccentric
like them. My name to them, also, was Henry Adams, and
no one took it as a joke, a simple old Anglo name. It wasn't
a joke, I was Henry Adams, in some way. It might be true, I
didn't know Zeke, the name in my passport. I couldn't identify with it or his face. I didn't want to be that failure, the
man Maggie didn't love, she had been so much of who I was
to myself. Maggie loves me, so I'm the guy she loves. Then
she didn't, and I wasn't.

Also, I convinced myself I could be Henry Adams, if he'd
lived a very long time into the twenty-first century. I told
one of the women, an artist photographer, that my wife had
committed suicide. It wasn't my fault, I said. The woman was
totally sympathetic.

That pub bonhomie masked my sad nights. A bloke called
Anthony, a critic from the Caribbean, thought I was wry. I
probably talked about American anti-heroes and gangsters, and
men born under the sign of feminism. I could spout theories,
and had recall of quotations from Geertz, say, as if they were
song lyrics. I had a mild form of dementia. Ranbir, a historian
focusing on the Empire and its colonies, a skeptic, asked me if

I was related to the Adams family; sure, I said, he's an in-law; and the sympathetic artist, Benita, an Argentinian, toasted me warmly. Sometimes we kissed drunkenly, or snogged, the English say, harmless mammals getting warm. Miranda, a Marxist economist, a Nigerian Igbo, spoke French, and we talked about money and the market. She knew I had some money, to her I was a rich American, even if I wasn't, I was for her, and, for sure, I had some, because I wasn't living on air, even if my head held an empty space.

The English National Health Service is pretty cool, and I scored tranquilizers and sleeping pills, and anything I couldn't get that way, I could from a private doctor. I don't think I remembered my family for a while, and didn't contact them; but I think Maggie let Mother know that I'd be staying longer than we'd planned, because life was good, she lied to her, easy for Maggie, and then I had flashes of being Zeke, or myself, and when I did, I contacted Mother, and, basically, I lied to everyone back home. I didn't know what was the truth, or I knew the truth could lie. Betrayal was so dramatic, it counted as unreal. I'd been betrayed. Deceived. I'd been lied to by my fucking best friends. Feel me? I had a hard time saying Betrayed. Everything was on fire. Aunt Clarissa had betrayed me, but I didn't consider it like that, because she was my old aunt and a little crazy. Maggie. "You betrayed me," I said to a mirror. Believe that? I'm that cliché, *Taxi Driver* De Niro to his mirror, "You talkin' to me?" but I went, "Maggie, I'm talking to you. You betrayed me. Betrayed. BETRAYED." I wanted to make it feel real. Like, looking in a mirror, looking at myself saying those words, could make me experience it. Make it real. What a fucking joke, oh man, totally ironic.

I didn't know what hit me, and it kept hitting me.

•

July 7, 2005, 8:50 a.m.

Suicide bombers set off explosives on three Underground trains in Central London.

An hour later, a London bus gets blown up at Tavistock Square.

Fifty-two people were murdered, over 700 people injured.

Four suicide bombers dead.

Two weeks later, several attempted terrorist attacks were thwarted or failed.

Four attackers were jailed for a minimum of forty years.

Their 9/11 was 7/7.

No one I knew had been hurt, but they knew some people who'd been injured, not killed. Terrible.

My head hurt a lot. Flashes, scenes, faces, corpses erupted in front of me. More and more horror and memories returned, a few, some very bad ones, in fragments. My life. It was too much. I decided to go home, I would, I couldn't stay, and didn't think I was fleeing, not London. The bombings had rocked me, everyone had been, everyone, shocked, I was no different, but it wasn't home, and for me, straight up, it worked like shock treatment. That's how I see it, now.

When 9/11 happened, I was twenty-three, with Maggie, and we were good, the world outside us turned to shit, and with 7/7, that returned, not the trauma but it awakened one, it was more like a reality external to me, internal only insofar as everything, back then in the good ole USA, had changed. Hope sank with Cheney, Rumsfeld, W, their criminal, vindictive war.

I read about a guy who heard that some people hadn't

died on 9/11, because they had changed their plane reserva-
tions at the last minute, and they were saved. So now this guy
makes a res and always changes it at the last minute.

Fate-cheaters and fare-beaters get caught.

Told my pub posse I was splitting for home, and sobbed,
heaving, piss-faced, but it was time, the great cover story, so
abstract: it's time, right. I felt moved toward something, the
crimes and consequences of home. I am this home boy who
flies home. I'm not a refugee, I'm not a DP, I can fly away.
Privilege, yes. I don't know what they thought. I didn't know,
and in a way didn't care, since it was all temporary. The next
days or week are blurry, blurrier, still.

Anyway.

I returned with dread, with some small hope for re-
spite, relief from anguish, a hope to get it back, my memory,
Maggie, my mind.

Home to Mother. Really.

The unavailable woman, ur-woman: Mother didn't reject
me, ever. No joke.

At home, no one talked about the English 9/11. 9/11 over-
shadowed their 7/7, it existed in the shadow of the towers,
right. The English won the war to lose it, that kind of thing
all over again.

I started treatment, talk and drugs, the story came back,
or stories, I related various versions, and was able to finish
my dissertation, OK, like a zombie. I was already in the last
chapter, and could rouse myself to write a paragraph, check
footnotes; I contacted my committee, efficient or catatonic,
because I wanted it done I told my chair, and doing it kept
me going, at first.

At first I wanted to live, to murder shithead and hurt Maggie. Or, win her back. I flowed both ways. Retrospection, when it came, kept killing me: I saw us together.

Retrospection about the weight of non-response, which oppresses differently from loud, violent speech. A silent partner can drive you mad.

I took non-response for love, unqualified.

A silent partner can murder your heart. For the uninitiated, silence can be unusually terrifying. I should never have believed in her.

My dreams were ugly, pills helped me sleep, shoved my unconscious down, and when it did rise up enough to penetrate the brain drug-fog, shit everywhere, rooms and rooms of shit. Life was shit, my life was shit, an easy association.

Delete all. Right?

## IMAGE CROSSINGS

Jesus explained to Lazarus's sister, Martha: "I am the resurrection, and the life, he that believeth in me, though were he dead, yet shall he live: And whosoever liveth and believeth in me shall never die."

I'm Lazarus, risen from the dead. OK.

After Jesus raised him from the dead, Lazarus lived another thirty years. He had to flee Judea because of threats against his life—Christ's miracle man endangered the state. Tradition also says Lazarus never smiled again except once, when he saw a man stealing a clay pot. Lazarus smiled at him, and said, "The clay steals the clay." Pretty good. A man's life is a tautology. I suppose Lazarus's was redundant too.

I look away from people's prying eyes, I watch people running in the street, wonder who's chasing them, I want to find pictures and not see illness, I wake up and go back to sleep, I do what I have to do, and get a day, a night, and etc.

One may surely give oneself up to a line of thought, and follow it up as far as it leads, simply out of scientific curiosity, or—if you prefer—as advocatus diaboli, without, however, making a pact with the devil about it.

—Freud

On Freud's desk, in the room where he saw patients, he kept figurines, his collection of antiquities, including a statue of Asklepios, the god who loved human beings most, and maybe Freud loved people most, or more than most, or most likely he was one of the most curious people about other beings. Probably he was. Freud was an idolatrous Jew, a classicist, and in some ways he lived a life antithetical to Jewish belief, which reviled idol worship and proscribed graven images.

TO ANALYST: I'm going to make a pact with the devil.

She doesn't think that's funny.

Maybe Geertz, who had no time for Freud, maybe Geertz never had a total meltdown.

Analyst says I'm delaying life, that I want to stay a child, return to childhood, blah blah.

Maggie loved me as an image. She fell out of love with it.

## SEEING PROVES NOTHING

Ansel Adams: "Not everyone trusts paintings, but people believe photographs."

Gone like the rotten wind.

First, a photograph confirmed "reality," proof of a bridge, a person's existence, while, almost simultaneously, spirit photography burgeoned, the antithesis of so-called reality, and an inherent rebuke.

Photographic truth contained its antithesis.

Many early spirit photographers were women, many women mediums. New fields open up to all comers, since necessarily they're non-traditional; but spirits and irrationality weren't, they were analogues to, and stereotypes of, femininity—no big leap to accept a female medium or spirit photographer.

People believed ghosts spooked pictures, not photography's chemicals. Those mistakes, splotches and blotches, like Rorschach inkblots, coincided with a wish to see the dead alive and hear from them, again. Especially, in the U.S., with the Civil War's decimations.

Photographs documented ghosts (still now, as late as 1960, groups formed around spirit photography), and exhibitions, such as *The Blur of the Otherworldly*, at UMBC, curated by Mark Alice Durant and Jane D. Marsching, and one at the Metropolitan Museum in New York, confirmed continued excitement in them and what we can't know and want.

Oh no, we don't believe in it, but wait, there's life on Mars, potentially, right, they've found flowing water, and no one ever expected that. "Following the water is a good idea," a scientist said. Mars had been believed to be arid.

Mostly they were fakes, those pictures.

The field, bifurcated from the start, split. Like others of Western civ's products, a binary evolved, fiction/fact. Christ: a man and God. First, a picture of an actual tree, or house; a little later, dead babies, like dimpled clouds, at their mothers' breasts, husbands' faces sprouting from their widows' eyes.

To mix it up more, take the imagination—not fact, not fiction. Imagination is the mind's psychic product. The mind is an abstraction, right, and there's no physical entity for "mind" or "imagination." Both abstractions that allow for abstractions.

Lately, an interest: What is it that people of different cultures imagine, and why? Why do people want what they want, what is the fantasy in their minds, and why?

Back in the day, photographic chemicals, the fluids, were likened to vital fluids, human fluids. In a sense, they flowed into each other.

Facts flowed into fictions or fused with them, and the other way around.

True is not Truth, but also what is untrue or, let's say, unprovable, is not a lie, not fallacious.

Spirit writing is the mysterious appearance of words on photographs, and it fascinates me, in the same way that scientists fascinate non-scientists who ask, How did you know to do this; or, writers are asked, Where do your ideas come from? And, children want to know why is the sky blue, or how do voices go through telephone wires, and pictures arrive on screens.

Sometimes, mediums heard the dead speak, and acted as conduits for messages from them, and wrote them down.

Moses heard God (not dead yet) and wrote the Ten Commandments. Spirit writing?

Ted Serios (as in, seriously?) photographed himself "thinking," "stuff" emerging from his head, usually his forehead. Imagine a photograph of Einstein thinking. Ideas might produce a kind of thought-sweat or halo of energy.

Are we not fields of energy, matter?

Aura photographs, from Duchamp to the present: the light or halo around a head, and its colors, describe or report a person's state of being, or affect. People do see auras. Is every one of them crazy?

Contemporary artists also work with auras. Artist Susan Hiller, from her book *Auras and Levitations*:

> Walter Benjamin described loss of aura as symptomatic of the artwork in modern times. He knew that the word "aura" would be widely understood, either as a visible reality described by mediums and clairvoyants and researched by certain scientists, or as an imaginative paradigm familiar from images of halos in traditional religious paintings . . .
>
> Digitally montaged photographs . . . , presented to us as visible traces of the phantasmal, they are the most recent manifestation of a desire to experience, record and classify spectral phenomena, a desire that coincides with the history of science as well as the history of art, with complicated connections to both.

Augmenting Hiller's claim that science displays a "desire" to know about auras, and other manifestations: in the 1970s Ralph Abraham, a mathematician, wrote a proof showing that vibrations exist. When the Polaroid SX-70 Land Camera debuted in 1972, it was called a "wonder." Some groups thought it could photograph "miracles."

ANALYST: What miracle are you waiting for?
ME: Funny. I'm not waiting. I feel her.
Silence.
ME: She's around.

## THE INENARRABLE

Before 1802, cirrus, cumulus, and altostratus clouds hadn't been given names. Untitled before 1802, the shapes were present in the sky, ethereal or ephemeral, presumably since the big bang, but un-designated, until they needed to be. Why then?

The world hasn't been fully seen, until it is named. Different cultures will have many names for an object that another doesn't even have one for. But there are specific words for nonspecificity, or non-states: the word "nonexistence"; names for states that presumably can't be described or defined adequately but that can be experienced, the "in" and "un" words: inexpressible, indescribable, ineffable, inchoate, unreal. Some conditions can't be translated—a transmission or flash of insight when a problem is solved, as the brain leaps, neurologically.

Certain states of mind, our species decided, can't be described but we still have words for them. Wittgenstein would object: "What we cannot speak about we must pass over in silence."

People are rarely silent.

All naming is a form of translation, and the written translates events, impressions, etc., into a representation, and often misses its mark. WHY?

The inenarrable—incapable of being narrated.

Spirit photography courted the inenarrable.

Paradox: this word names the un-tellable.

Inenarrable, a strange word, was needed, right. It actually defines the paradox of ethnography: it's assumed, by the field, that everything can be narrated. Ethnography is, at its core, because of its emphasis on field work, trusting of various translations, say, languages and facial movements, based in storytelling.

A straightforward, uncomplicated transmission? No, there's always mediation, which accounts for Geertz's emphasis on "thick description." Non-ethnographers often use this term, which Geertz took from Gilbert Ryle, and out of context. (Ironically.) Geertz called ethnography an elaborate exercise in thick description. "Thin" description doesn't get at context, and doesn't pay attention to the significance of actions. The classic example: one boy's eye involuntarily twitches, while another boy winks. In appearance they look the same, but a wink is part of culture, a twitch is involuntary. The ethnographer must record the winks, not the twitches.

So, ethnography, first, is an activity; second, it's exploration and interpretation. Third, writing, and writing narratives.

All accounts must account for it, the unaccountable.

Human nature isn't natural, it's an invention of human beings, totally reflexive.

To account for the new, people find new words, and with these new products, come apprehensions, experiences. Take sexting.

Take the noun od, \äd\. It was a hypothetical force formerly held to pervade all nature and to manifest itself in magnetism, mesmerism, chemical action, etc. Od was coined by chemist and philosopher Karl Ludwig von Reichenbach as a name for his hypothetical force. He proposed od because he thought a short word starting with a vowel would be more easily combined in compound.

I studied mind-cure, or metaphysical healing, which
strikes at the root of disease; I went into hypnotism,
mesmerism, and phreno-magnetism, and the od
force—I don't suppose you know about the od which
Reichenbach discovered.

—Edward Eggleston, *The Faith Doctor:*
*A Story of New York*, 1891

In 1784, Mesmer's name was applied to a technique for
inducing hypnosis. I could not have felt mesmerized before
Dr. Mesmer appeared on the scene.

Words don't betray us, we do.

Words insinuate. Pictures doubt.


## HOME TURF (THE DOMESTIC FIELD)

Being more or less "regular," or functioning, by 2008 I began
work at the Library of Congress, researching family albums
of the celebrated or famous—in comparison with the volk,
and my found families. I came upon material about Henry
and Clover Adams, especially Henry, because the Adamses
may be the most written-about family in American history or
the family that wrote the most.

Clover Adams was known for her wit, charm. Henry
Adams and she married in 1872, and had no children. Clover's
salon was famous in D.C., and she and Henry entertained
only the best D.C. had or who visited there. In the last
three years of her life, she took photographs, seriously, and
published some. Clover's life was full—of books, art, talk,

purpose of a kind, let's put it, "for a woman of that time." No one knows exactly why, in 1885, she took her life: there's conjecture and supposition. She appears to have been clinically depressed after her father's death, and to this day her suicide is considered a mystery. That's the skinny. Also the family lore that I knew, repeated by generations of hagiographers, but now I got into it my way.

In 1843, a girl, Clover Hooper, was born to a Boston Brahmin family. Her mother, Ellen Sturgis, was a woman of unusual, formidable character, a poet, transcendentalist, a feminist.

Her poem, "I Slept, and Dreamed That Life Was Beauty," appeared in the first issue of *The Dial*.

I slept, and dreamed that life was Beauty;
I woke, and found that life was Duty.
Was thy dream then a shadowy lie?
Toil on, sad heart, courageously,
And thou shalt find thy dream to be
A noonday light and truth to thee.

Margaret Fuller said of Ellen Sturgis, writing from Rome in 1849, "I have seen in Europe no woman more gifted by nature than she."

Ellen Sturgis married Robert Hooper, of similar provenance. He was an eminent ophthalmologist, but Ellen's sister, Susan, thought Robert wasn't interesting enough for her. But they appeared to have made a good marriage, and produced three bright children, the two girls, Clover and Ellen (after her mother), and a boy, Edward (Ned).

Clover's first and formative tragedy was the death of her poet/feminist mother, Ellen Sturgis Hooper, of TB, when Clover was five. Her mother was buried in Mount Auburn Cemetery, where Clover's aunt Susan was also buried. (Aunt Susan was a suicide.) Clover was old enough to remember her mother. The trauma of her mother's early death was one of many, though, in a family of suicides and depressives, not unlike that of Virginia Woolf's, whom Clover did not resemble (as far as this inadequate, nonobjective biographer can tell). Her brother, Ned, and their sister, Ellen, were also suicides. Ned stayed alive after his beloved wife, Fanny, died of TB, because he had five daughters, whom he raised solo, but then he did himself in.

Clover and her sister, Ellen, and brother, Ned, were raised by their benevolent father. Dr. Hooper educated his daughters best as he could, against accepted fashion, and Clover studied at Louis and Elizabeth Agassiz's eponymous school in Cambridge, where she was taught Latin and Greek. On her own, she learned German, French, Spanish. I haven't found out much about Clover's relationship with her sister, Ellen. (The only sisters I've seen in action are Mother and Clarissa.) They kept in touch, weren't close, it appears, and maybe they didn't get along, took separate paths, basically, or stayed out of each other's way.

Clover and her crowd lived through (or died during) the Civil War, her generation overwhelmed, scarred, and shaped by the war's devastations. (See Louis Menand's *The Metaphysical Club*.) More trauma. They all watched sons, husbands, fathers, brothers march off, many returned wounded, physically and psychologically, many died.

NOUVELLE ICONOGRAPHIE                    T. II. PL. X.

CLICHÉ A. LONDE                    PHOTOTYPIE BERTHAUD

MÉLANCOLIE CATALEPTIQUE
(ÉTAT CATALEPTOÏDE)

Two of Henry and William James's brothers, Garth (Wilky) and Robertson (Bob) James, served, and survived. All his life, William James suffered from emotional and psychological problems, including depression. When he was a student, William studied the photographic portraits Charcot took of "mad people," especially women. "Hysteria" distorted their faces and bodies. Not surprising that William James took an interest in mental anguish.

Among the soldiers who never returned, there was Clover's cousin Robert Shaw, who led the famous Massachusetts

Fifty-fourth Regiment of African-American volunteers, and died with his men at Fort Wagner, near Charleston. Clover had watched the parade, when Shaw and his Union soldiers marched out, from Boston, to join the fighting. She was probably living at 44 Summer Street then, the family home. (See 1989 movie, *Glory*, about Shaw and the regiment.)

A year after the War ended, in 1866, Clover traveled abroad, as it was called then, with her father, another part of her liberal education. She didn't marry until she was twenty-eight. Henry and she became engaged on February 27, 1872. For their honeymoon, they traveled to Europe, a grand tour kind of thing, and, most significant, to Egypt, where they sailed down the Nile, and where Clover had what might have been her first breakdown, or break from reality. She wrote her father, "Life is such a jumble of impressions just now that I cannot unravel the skein in practical, quiet fashion."

There isn't much to go on, but before they sailed, they met up with friends from Boston, the financier Samuel Gray Ward and his wife, Anna Barker Ward, who'd been close with Clover's mother. Mrs. Ward apparently helped Clover, or ministered to her. Clover wrote of herself to her father, "for a long time past I have found it impossible to get my ideas straightened out at all." She found it hard to write even him, and didn't want him to show her letters to anyone else.

Dr. Hooper was more enlightened about females than Henry. On March 26, 1872, one month after their engagement, Henry wrote, "She is certainly not handsome; nor would she be called plain, I think . . . She talks garrulously, but on the whole pretty sensibly. She is very open to instruction. *We* shall improve her. She dresses badly . . . She rules me as only American women rule men, and I cower before her. Lord! how she would lash me if she read the above description of her!"

Two months later, on May 30, Henry wrote another friend, from Clover's father's home: "In fact it is rather droll to examine women's minds. They are a queer mixture of odds and ends, poorly mastered and utterly unconnected . . . She commissions me to tell you that she would like to add a few lines to this letter but unfortunately she is not able to spell. I think you will like her, not for beauty, for she is certainly not beautiful . . . but for intelligence and sympathy, which are what hold me . . . I do not fear her separating me from my friends."

"Clover wants to add that she can't spell."

She can't spell, hot damn, that's a totally familiar "joke" in minority terrain. She laughs at her own expense, which may be why Henry James found her "conversational, critical, ironical," her wit "distinguished by . . . genius." The Master thought Adams "a trifle dry."

James thought she was "a Voltaire in petticoats." Clover and Henry James were lifelong friends, and, in addition to their early lives in Boston, they spent time together in D.C. and in London. In 1880, when Henry and Clover saw the Scottish Highlands, touring around, they visited London, and spent time with both William and Henry James. She called husband Henry and herself "the wandering Americans" and divined differences between Brits and Americans: "Our land is gayer-lighter-quicker and more full of life."

Their first home together was at 91 Marlborough Street

in Boston. Their second in Washington, D.C., was opposite the White House.

Like Henry James, Clover was discriminating; she was also judgmental, a moralist, sometimes moralistic, while adamant about not espousing or having any religious beliefs. She refused to socialize with Oscar Wilde, when he was in Washington at the same time as James in 1882. "I have asked Henry James not to bring his friend Oscar Wilde when he comes; I must keep out thieves and noodles or else take down my sign and go West." James was visiting the States, because his mother was dying, but was still in Washington, when she died, and rushed to Boston for her funeral.

Clover was very critical of James for abandoning America. "It will be a heavy blow to him, the more so perhaps that he has been away for six years from her and it's the first time death has struck his family."

"Dear Pater," October 30, 1881: Clover wrote about an American friend's annoyance with an English woman, an aristocrat, and went on to add, the friend "can't forgive Henry James for his *Daisy Miller*, and, when I said he was on his way home, maliciously asked if he was coming for 'raw material.'"

Clover wrote her father every week on Sundays, often more frequently. Her letters to him (published in *The Letters of Mrs. Henry Adams*) are beautifully written, acute, descriptive of her time, its politics and personalities, newsy, gossipy, insightful, and wry. She spells perfectly, but is self-conscious about her writing, even or especially to her father, and writes: "Oh, for the pen of Abigail Adams!"

Her commentary on the English, for one, shows her wit and sharp tongue. (The Brits were the colonists' bane for years,

right.) "For sordid niggardliness no one can beat a Britisher ...
They save on table linen, towels, candles and fires, flowers
and underclothes, to put monkey-jackets on their servants."
She could be sardonic, also sarcastic and often caustic.

The earliest letter in the volume, to her friend Mary
Louisa Shaw, describes the grand review of Grant's and
Sherman's armies, May 23 and 24, 1865, in D.C., not long af-
ter the Civil War ended. Lincoln had been assassinated, and
Grant was president. The letter is a detailed account, fresh in
feeling, and remarkable for its observations and writing:

> About nine-thirty the band struck up "John Brown,"
> and by came Meade with his staff, splendidly mounted.
> Almost all the officers in the army had their hands
> filled with roses, and many had wreaths around their
> horses' necks. After Meade passed there was a pause.
> Suddenly a horse dashed by with a hatless rider,
> whose long golden curls were streaming in the wind;
> his arms hung with a wreath, and his horse's neck
> with one, too. It was General Custer, who stands as a
> cavalry officer next to Sheridan. He soon got control
> of his horse and came back at a more sober pace, put
> himself at the head of his division, and they came
> riding by, 10,000 men. Sheridan's cavalry, Custer's
> Division, are called cutthroats, and each officer and
> man wears a scarlet scarf around his neck with ends
> hanging half a yard long. Among the cavalry came
> the dear old Second, Caspar Crowninshield looking
> splendidly on his war horse—then came artillery,
> pontoon bridges, ambulances, army wagons, negro

and white pioneers with axes and spaces, Zouave
regiments, some so picturesque with red bag trousers,
pale sea-green sashes, and dark blue jackets braided
with red, red fezzes on their heads with yellow tas-
sels. Other Zouave regiments came with entirely different uniforms, gay and Arablike. And so it came,
this glorious old army of the Potomac, for six hours
marching past, eighteen or twenty miles long, their
colours telling their sad history. Some regiments with
nothing but a bare pole, a little bit of rag only, hanging a few inches, to show where their flag had been.
Others that had been Stars and Stripes, with one or
two stripes hanging, all the rest shot away. It was a
strange feeling to be so intensely happy and trium-
phant, and yet to feel like crying. As each corps com-
mander and division general rode by, the President
and secretaries and generals stood up, and down
went the swords as salute, and the colours dipped.
Between the different corps there was often a delay
of five minutes or so. Then the crowd rushed to the
front of the stand, cheering the different generals,
who had to stand and acknowledge it. Grant looked
so bashful and modest with his little boy sitting on
his lap—it was touching to see him. Sherman was
nervous and looked bored—talked fast all the time,
his hands gesticulating. I like the President's face—it
looked strong and manly.

She was persistent from the start, and found ways to do
what she wanted. No one wanted her, a girl, to travel that long

way to D.C. to watch the military review, but she wouldn't be stopped. "I vowed to myself that go I would."

The married Clover (Mother drummed into me: a marriage contract turned women into their husbands' property, like sheep) followed wherever Henry went—whither thou goest—he took her places, though, great cities, Paris, Rome, Venice, where the couple shopped 'til they dropped, art and furnishings, and shipped the precious stuff home from Europe. (They built a grand one in D.C.) I'd call Clover and Henry connoisseurs, and also low-grade conspicuous consumers.

The term "conspicuous consumption" is conspicuously absent from contemporary discourse, because the people who contribute to the discourse about aesthetics are themselves conspicuous consumers.

In 1879, the couple again traveled to Europe for Henry's work. Her letters home about Europeans, her observations of these others, show Clover's distinctively American POV and her distinctive writing style. To her father, she writes, after having spent some time in Spain: "The Spaniards are the most kindly, sympathetic, childlike, unpractical, incapable, despondent people I ever saw, with a magnificent country which they are utterly unable to develop, a rotten old church in which they don't believe, a king whom they know and declare to be a mere puppet, a longing for a republic which they can't manage, and a lurking conviction, which [the couple's friend] Don Leopoldo frankly avows, that the Anglo-Saxon race is going to crush them out."

It's said Clover and Henry knew everyone who was interesting.

When she and Henry moved to D.C. in 1877 for Henry's work, Clover served daily teas for the Five of Hearts, their close circle. She was named the first heart by others who included John Hay and his wife, Clara, who didn't say much. But John Hay, and this was a matter of distinction, when he was a young man, his first job in D.C. was as the unofficial private secretary to Abraham Lincoln, right after Lincoln's first inauguration. He lived in the White House, and when Lincoln couldn't sleep, the War disturbing him, he'd walk in his sleeping gown to Hay's room and spend the night talking and joking with him.

The fifth heart: Clarence King. After some wandering, King studied to be a geologist. He was a very religious man, and, it's said, sexually driven. His first claim to fame was that, while he was director of the Fortieth Parallel Survey, he revealed a major mining fraud, a company duping its shareholders with false claims of precious gems. Plus, he broke social norms: King, who was white, married a woman—it wasn't a legal marriage but a ceremony—who was black, had children with her, told her he was black, and all of this, his domestic life, was kept hidden from his crowd. He went about "in society" as a single man. Even the Hearts didn't know, supposedly. Maybe Hay did. They were very close. King, a wild man, totally.

I'd have tea with these characters. I don't know about every day. But Adams couldn't have been such a prim stuffed shirt, the way Henry James thought, if he hung with King. Plus, Clover didn't do ladies' lunches, didn't go to them in D.C. She had her Hearts.

A regular or regulated life includes daily rituals. Even three meals a day ties you to a routine.

The couple looked at contemporary art, including going to the Philadelphia Centennial Exhibition of 1876. Clover also went to galleries on her own, or with a woman friend. Viewing pictures in New York in 1881, she might have been "inspired" to begin photographing. (See bio by Natalie Dykstra.) Clover bought or was given—acquired—her first camera in 1882.

Clover must have used Henry's on their honeymoon in 1872. Sailing down the Nile, she took a stateroom picture of him, he's reading. It was his camera. Why did he get the equipment, and when did he stop making pix? Did she inherit his camera?

HENRY ADAMS IN THE CABIN OF THE "ISIS"
*Photographed by Mrs. Adams*

Mathew Brady was an inspiration to her. His Civil War battlefield photographs, especially, affected Clover powerfully. In a way, to her, they may have been from a photo album, an American family album, because the War was a devastating family affair. Interesting that, in 1878 in D.C., Mathew Brady photographed Thomas Alva Edison, making Brady seem closer in time, to me.

With her own camera, Clover photographed friends, visitors, family, grandees, those important in their day. Also, Henry, and their dogs. Clover loved their dog Boojum the way I loved, and love, Mr. Petey.

Funny, by the time I took pictures, I wasn't playing with Mr. Petey so much, and I don't know where I put the ones I did take. My classification system must have broken down, before I did. Ha.

Clover kept a journal documenting shutter speeds and development results for each of her photographs. She took her endeavor totally seriously. A few of her pictures were shot to be published in journals, though Henry didn't like Clover's doing "public" photography. Poor Clover must have suffered from his attitude toward her sex, though her letters never show that. To the end, she describes him as tender and kind.

She made professional portraits, working when her class of women didn't: they were hostesses, mothers, charity-ball-givers, etc. No photographs show Clover's face clearly. In one, she's on her horse—she loved riding—and half-faces the camera but coyly, and shot from a distance, she's hiding her face, which is ironic, because she took portraits.

But she was the model of a new kind of woman, and, in that sense, was portrayed by Henry Adams, who wrote two novels, both anon, *Democracy: An American Novel* (1880)

MARIAN HOOPER

*From a tintype taken at Beverly Farms in 1869*

and *Esther* (1884), both based on Clover. It's a little weird and contradictory that he, who denigrated women's minds, wrote from a woman's POV, and with sympathy. They're not great novels, but I liked them OK. The books served as an insider's view of D.C.

Also, Henry James's 1884 story, "Pandora," not his best, was based, I first read, on Clover. But in Henry James's notebook (page twenty-five), he writes that his "Pandora"—she doesn't come from an upper-class American family—meets and socializes with a woman, Mrs. Bonnycastle, based on Clover. (Good castle, good home, James had liked spending time with Clover, in D.C.) Pandora is making her way, moving "up," in this society.

The gist: On a ship from Europe to America, a young German diplomat and aristocrat, Count Otto, meets Pandora, from Utica, and later sees her in D.C., much changed, belle of the ball kind of thing, and he sees that she even has the president's ear. Otto becomes very curious about this young American woman, because he doesn't know her "type." What type is she, he asks again and again of two older women, who know the American scene. She's "self-made," he's told. Maybe, also, James saw Clover as self-made, without a recognizable model, for how she thought, what she did and didn't do, who she became.

James appropriated the New Woman for his novels and needs (and I'm appropriating the New Man, for MEN IN QUOTES, not kidding). James knew some independent American women, American expatriates, his Boston feminists (see *The Bostonians*), in action, at tea, on walks. He dined with them, knew their conversation. Famously, he befriended the much younger Edith Wharton, who had the means and the fortitude, the brilliance, to create herself as a creator. He knew Margaret Fuller, the Peabody sisters, but James, like Hawthorne and most of those high-born, intellectual men, mocked Fuller, the exception, Emerson. The new women traveled outside not only their circles but also their native land, and Margaret Fuller found love in Italy. Also Henry's sister, Alice, who died in England, found a female companion who was with her until her death.

Alice James might have been a new woman, but she was independent only in her spirited, sharp mind. Her neuroses did her in, early, her father hadn't educated her like her older brothers, he wasn't like Clover's. Alice believed she was dying most of her life, and then of course she died. (See her diary, introduction by Jean Strouse.)

James identified, ambivalently, with these females, and made them his characters, protagonists, tainted and maimed, idealistic and pure of heart, representing aspects of himself, and his conflicts. They struggled, he did. (See Colm Tóibín's novel *The Master*.) Many didn't marry, and he played with a few of their hearts, dallying, even disastrously, with some, Constance Fenimore Woolson, especially. In Florence, she and Henry James had lived together, secretly, in the same house, sharing it but not a bed. James couldn't be a husband, like the men who falsely wooed his female characters. He left Venice, and some time later Woolson took her life. He visited her grave, later.

The number of suicides seems disproportionate in their subculture, but I don't know. These sad nineteenth-century characters lived before the drugs that make life bearable for present-day depressives, manic depressives, etc.

I could have done myself in, I'm a Hooper, with some sad genes, along with intelligence, creativity—I mean, for depression and suicide. Suicide is a tragic inheritance. It may be genetic and, also, psychologically inherited. There's research from the Emory University School of Medicine that shows it's possible for some information to be inherited biologically through chemical changes that occur in DNA. The scientists discovered that mice can pass on learned information about traumatic experiences to the next generation, which somehow transfer from the brain into the genome.

Oh, man, bad genetic inheritance never came up at the Hooper-Stark dinner table. No way. Mother's ancestors permeated, but their sicknesses were ignored in favor of their promise for us, the inheritors. Selective inheritance, totally.

Mother looks to her dead relatives for juice, what she calls inspiration. Different from what Clarissa does, but still there's thriving from the permanence of the dead.

A college prof told me: came a time he couldn't commit suicide, because he'd brought a child into the world. He felt an ethical responsibility not to burden his child with hopelessness.

Freedom, limited the way it is, allows some choices: to have or not to have; to have and to hold, then not to hold; to gorge or purge. Ha.

## CLOVER'S LAST TRAGEDY: HER OWN

Her touchstone, best friend, closest, oldest friend, nominal mother—her father died in April 1885.

Her sister and brother didn't tell her, though, until it was too late for her to attend his funeral. Even if it was because her sibs were concerned about her mental health, this must have hurt Clover. Was it malice, an act of revenge against the sib the father might have loved most? Oh, man, that must have killed her.

After his death, Clover's depression turned acute and dangerous, and Henry and their friends were worried. Adams did what he thought best. He took Clover away from home, out of her element, to the Allegheny Mountains. She was exhausted: she'd been her father's devoted caretaker in his last months. Adams believed a change of scene would restore her. He also wanted to take her to Yellowstone, but the trip had to be canceled, he wrote their heart-friend, John Hay, because "we broke down." He and Clover returned home at the end of July 1885. They went to their Beverly Farms home, then to their D.C. house at 1607 H Street, where Clover became even more withdrawn, staying in her bedroom, not seeing anyone, and her friends worried even more.

One morning, Henry left the house for a dentist appointment, and, after he was gone, Clover swallowed photographic chemicals, an excruciating way to die. He returned, and found her. She probably left a note for Henry, she wrote letters, right, but it was never found, if there was one. Adams destroyed all of Clover's letters to him. A fastidious historian destroying primary material inspires astonishment and horror in me; it's even crazier, for an eminent historian, that, in *The Education of Henry Adams*, he never mentions Clover or their marriage, their years together erased.

If Adams had kept a photo album, he would be one of those guys who'd have torn out her picture. Worse, the ones she took, the negatives, etc., kept in their home, he destroyed.

Scholars believed that Henry Adams never wrote or spoke Clover's name again, the accepted view for a long time until letters turned up, which he had written to Clover's friend Anne Palmer Fell.

"During the last 18 months, I have not had the good luck to attend my own funeral, but with that exception I have buried pretty nearly everything I lived for." The letter is dated December 5, 1886; she'd died on December 6, 1885, a year before.

For her memorial, Adams commissioned Augustus Saint-Gaudens to make a sculpture. Saint-Gaudens (1848–1907) was considered the greatest American sculptor, whose work includes the *Sherman Monument* in Manhattan and the *Shaw Memorial* in Boston, honoring Clover's cousin, Col. Robert Gould Shaw, and the men of the 54th Massachusetts Regiment.

Henry chose Saint-Gaudens, only the best for Clover. The bronze sculpture's full title is *The Mystery of the Hereafter and the Peace of God that Passeth Understanding*. The memorial and grounds, in Rock Creek Cemetery, were designed by Stanford White, also the best, which Clover would have expected, no, demanded—the celebrated couple were known for their exquisite taste. And independent thinking. When she and Henry were asked what they thought of George Eliot's marriage to a younger man, Clover famously said: "We declare a woman of genius is above criticism."

Saint-Gaudens's statue, usually called "Grief," allegorized Clover Adams as a serene, hooded figure, in black cast bronze, her head draped in stone folds curving around her face and torso. The figure appears to be hiding or withdrawn, as Clover once had hidden in the few photos that survive. White's granite block stands behind the seated sculpture. Clover/she appears to be resting against it, the body's pose might also suggest resignation, to God, I suppose. She is leaning (nb: anaclisis), and maybe she is being cradled, by the mother who died when the girl was five.

Tragedy's tragic muse.

Adams kept up his long-running romantic friendship with Elizabeth (Lizzie) Cameron, the wife of Senator Don Cameron, an alcoholic. If their intimacy had affected Clover's state of mind, no one knows. Clover was friends with Lizzie, also. It wasn't a usual ménage à trois; if it was, it was sublimated. Henry wrote Lizzie more than affectionate letters. No secret to Clover, and Clover also wrote them to Lizzie. Whether Clover believed that Henry was in love with Lizzie Cameron, again, no record, just supposition.

An ethnographer isn't equipped to truck in unsupported supposition, unless it's based in culture, society, that is, somehow routinized behavior, an expected wheel turning a social system to keep it going, stable. Maybe a romantic friendship did that then, kept society singing. I don't and didn't feel equipped to say it was merely a social pattern, in their case. Maybe Clover didn't see it, that theirs was romantic love, or Henry's was. Or maybe what she saw was within the bounds of decorum.

I didn't "see" Maggie and that fucking creep, had no clue, and it happened before my eyes, seeing can't be trusted, because eyes are the windows to the mind, right, and the mind sees what it wants to see, and I did (which affects how we see photos and how we make images). Adams didn't fuck Lizzie. Later, she had a child with her husband, and Henry adored the baby.

## NOW IS, ISN'T

I'm in D.C., and get down into this stuff, and stall. I didn't know what I was looking for, really, but told myself, It's the time to visit Clover Adams's memorial, everyone else in my family has already, even Little Sister, or maybe especially Little Sister.

Little Sister relates to what she calls her sentries, or guardians. For a long time she's been aligned with Mother and Clarissa on their psychic trail.

Do it, man, I exhorted myself, it's now or never, but what an idiotic way to think, right.

Only a representation, Clover's statue, and it didn't look

like her, though no one knows now what she looked like. It mesmerized me, I was mesmerized, and I can't say what happened as I stood there. Adams's effort to immortalize her spirit through Saint-Gaudens's statue and Stanford White's setting, this monument, maybe it was his grief touching me—I communicated with it, his remorse, and such weird sensations flitted in me, affected me. Haunted would be the conventional term.

I stayed way longer at Clover's memorial than planned.

During that time, I still planned—or got lost. My reluctance to leave, both mental and physical, surprised me. My mind said, do this, my body, do that, and I couldn't move: in stall mode.

This might be sacred ground, I speculated, I might have been touched by the sacred, which is what church-going is meant to evoke, but never did for me. And suddenly, crazy as this sounds, I became intent upon a mission. I mean, as if there were a mission to accomplish, maybe a mission impossible—kidding—but a kind of return of the repressed I had to come to terms with, my past, my family's. I felt freakily alive, energized, even full or fulfilled. It was magnificent being there, on the top of my very own mountain, with a mission. This feeling-experience was novel, not even what I had felt with Maggie. But Maggie must have been with me. She was always with me, because she was not with me. I thought a thought that couldn't be thought: maybe it's not Maggie, it's Clover, she's with me. I wanted it not to be Maggie, right, and took it as logical, at least reasonable, because since the divorce, I hungered for a connection to life, and Clover could be the way, a way, to love. Simple.

Lots of religions encourage ancestor worship: you keep faith with ancestors, and believe their spirits want to comfort and help you, and that they want you to come to them. They will stay with you, be IN you.

In Vietnam, people leave food at the graves of their ancestors.

It wasn't crazy, it was cultural. Aunt Clarissa's speeches about Clover, well, finally I heard them, paid attention. Let them in. Teachers say students don't use it until they need it, and now Clarissa's encomiums and tributes to our long-dead relative sounded like revelation.

I COULDN'T TEAR MYSELF AWAY. I couldn't stop looking, the way I couldn't stop anything. I couldn't explain it or explain it away.

I didn't tell a living soul.

Can belief be rational? Is having faith in something a belief? Faith in a person, or a feeling.

Science was started by quacks and geniuses.

## RELATIVE ABSORPTION

My visit to Rock Creek turned out to be the second exception I took to my basic rule, Be a doubter, a skeptic, especially of the irrational, or emotions (threw that rule away with Maggie) But I couldn't distrust what I felt. I/it was shifting, unconsciously. I've come to realize that.

Entrancement—at that moment it was logical mind-balm—I was entranced and also it was natural, I told myself: Clover was a blood relative. Right. See, "natural" is misleading, but I used it. There was nothing wrong if I found nurture in the faith of Mother and Clarissa, their psychic connection, because at last it connected me also. This empathy came to help me, to guide me.

Clover and I had both been hung out to dry by our spouses.

My family didn't own any of her original prints—there aren't many, and what there is lives in the Massachusetts Historical Society.

I went there, later.

After filling out forms, I was allowed to ask for and handle precious materials. I wrote on the call cards what photographs and letters I wanted to see—everything. The librarian delivered these to me where I sat, a wooden desk.

Clover's hands touched these, there was a direct contact now, her DNA had to be on these, and even though my hands were gloved, it's what I felt about the prints. She'd labored to make them, with her hands, they were close to her. Relics. Being related to Clover Adams helped me, I thought, maybe she could help me, I believed that. Rational, irrational, it didn't matter. The most important things were: Love, for instance. And, hope. And here were both.

I kept returning to her honeymoon, and her picture of Henry in their stateroom. That deluxe, romantic honeymoon, and Clover, like Cleopatra, and Henry, no Marc Antony, I can't see that. No, they're floating down the Nile on a boat called *Isis*. They're in their stateroom. Or they're on deck. And suddenly Clover's world is dark.

I'm wondering, speculating, about her breakdown.

Maybe not coincidentally: Clover's last letter to her father before the Nile trip was dated November 17, and the next, when she landed, December 5, 1872. This also means, during more than two weeks, she didn't hear from him, her steady heartbeat, life support.

There is an oblique mention, in a letter to him, of her suffering on the Nile, and to a friend, but no cause is specified. Her father had to have been aware of her depressions. They might have started after her mother's death.

Depression: there is much speculation about Clover's

breakdown; I suppose it's historian decorum that says, No documents, we can't claim it, not even speculate.

I will: SEX. I'm just a low-down ethnographer.

My speculations: Henry and Clover didn't have children. But Henry appeared to love children, at least he doted on his nieces. Henry had probably wanted children, with Clover, and she couldn't have them. Or, he didn't have the sperm count. Anyway, no children.

In an 1883 letter to Henry's romantic friend Lizzie Cameron, Clover implored: "go to the Louvre . . . find a portrait of a lady in black, young child standing by her, by Van Dyck and tell her how she haunts me." It must have been *Portrait of a Lady with Her Daughter* (1635–40).

Maybe she'd wanted a daughter.

She also longed for a mother, her mother.

Seeing that painting, Clover remembered her mother, how she had once stood by her skirts, how she had adored her, and the painting of a woman and child weighed heavy, never left her, that "ideal" image, which could never be hers.

OK, all circumstantial evidence, but from it, here goes: on their honeymoon, their attempts at sex, a disaster. I picture fear on Clover's face, seeing a penis for the first time, and then it became erect. Henry tried to enter her, and couldn't; or, his erection failed, or she fainted, or intercourse was painful, too much for her. No blood, she rode horseback. She loved riding.

Their attempts at lovemaking/sex might compare with Virginia and Leonard's thwarted attempts.

Whatever happened in that stateroom, or in a hotel before they sailed, and in a beautiful setting, sex was not beautiful.

Not for her, not for him, not with her, or not ever. Clover's depression had been coming on since their honeymoon began, then finally a break from reality, and a blackout in letters to her father and from him. Not a word. So, the boat ride along the Nile was nothing like Cleopatra's, nothing like Shakespeare's vision of these lovers clinging to each other with pyramidal lust.

ME: Clover and Henry's union was a white marriage.
ANALYST: Maybe.
ME: Mariage blanc. I like French better, blanc. I could find out.
ANALYST: Why is it important to you?

I kept seeing Maggie and me, after our no-frills ceremony, basically an event that said this was a wedding that wasn't, and no dedicated honeymoon, just a fuck-fest, we didn't pay attention to the niceties. Nothing issued from us, either, except misery.

Maybe there are a few non-wedding wedding pictures extant, if she had any and didn't destroy them. Anyway, I'd been dead set against them, told her how no one ever looks at them later, they go into a drawer, become kept images, blah blah blah. I interrogate myself: Could Maggie have been the person I was in love with? I must have made her up, this soul partner, what a concept. Maggie wasn't Maggie. She wasn't real then, she didn't exist, she's not real now.

It occurred to me: I'd never considered Clover to have ever been an actual person. Her life and fate, sure, the family god, I knew about her, but looking at the statue, I felt this unbidden sadness and a flow of negative energy. Totally weird. Some-thing shot into me, like I was mainlining electricity, maybe Henry's pain, I thought, first, I'd been using his name in vain. Ha. The longer I stood there, the pain softened or lightened, hard to describe that, but it was more like a melancholy tune playing inside me than a drum machine drilling into me. It wasn't Henry, so it must be her, her sadness, and she had let me feel it. Or, I just did. I'm not saying the dead have volition. But then do any of us? I felt as if the sadness, which felt wistful, might also be mine, and maybe had joined with hers, but it was mine, because I was feeling it. You feel me?

I kept on.

## REMOTE CONTROL, REMOTE CHANCES

Is remote control inherently alienating?

One afternoon, after hogging a tennis court in Central Park by taking on all comers, I checked my voicemail and heard this:

"My name's Valerie I was a patient there and last time I was discharged was maybe uhm uhm two years ago, and very important that Dr. Wilson the head psychiatrist gets in touch with me, I was supposed to get surgery, I was discharged to get surgery, on my knee, uhm, Dr. Diane, uhm, New York NYU for drug blood diseases, they discharged me, but I couldn't get it because I had nowhere to live after I had the surgery. I know Maureen. If possible could you get the head psychiatrist, I think it's Dr. Mars, I need the medical records of that if possible. It is very important . . . 'cause I'm seeing a judge that I can't do any more rehab, and they're denying me, I had enough rehab, and I need my surgery, and I'm in a wheelchair. I can't walk no more. Get back to me, please, please help me out. This is very important. Bye-bye."

I thought about calling her back. I could tell her, Look, you have the wrong number. I wasn't the right number. Or, I could mess with her mind, be a sadist or a Svengali; but her mind was a mess. Or, I might be the right number, in a way. I could talk to her, maybe save her from her terrible addiction, be a hero. I tried that on. I try on many coats and hats, seeing what fits. I can picture Valerie, how she looks, young, scrawny, beaten up, scared. I deliberated: Am I her keeper, or my own keeper? Is this a New Man or Old Man question?

What can any of us keep.

I decided to be quiet.

Silence can be like thunder.

Hello, silence, my old friend.

I see a cloudless sky, an open field rolling, and within its stillness and quiet, and from a plain bedroom, young John Cage hears sounds in a sweet breeze, bird songs, and the boy feels a rush. Sufficient unto himself, he knows that, and his ingenuity, his awareness, completes him. Silence gathers energy the longer it lasts; with duration, chance happens, life's full of what's not expected, he gets that. He wants that.

Cage, in glorious solitude, listened to life as it happened. And, I could feel him: a lanky boy, in a plain bedroom, his large, pink ears sticking out, a skinny, long face. He's grinning like a fool. He played the fool.

Little Sister prepared me for the silence required in thinking, writing, reading. I don't blame her for what happened between me and Maggie. Silence became an intangible obstacle. She has to deal with it, hers, all the time. Don't know how she does it.

Student silences sucker-punched me. An education major explained: a teacher needs to allow thirty seconds for a question to be answered, the prof can't jump in until thirty secs. A student will respond, then. I tried it. How long is thirty seconds? One one hundred, two one hundred, three . . . four . . . five . . .

Abandoned sounds of suppressed anger, repressed thoughts, tremble in the ear. No one wants to hear them.

I landed in a family obeisant to history's silent murmurs.

Maggie's placid expression—and beautiful smile—I took

for acceptance and pleasure, in me. I never imagined she wore a mask, and don't know why I didn't. The stare: her slate wasn't blank, prejudice had been written on it, by her mother whose bilious complaints about me were inscribed at the top. Daily, Maggie saw, with her own eyes, my flaws, and took invisible notes, and the slate filled up with my failures. The man she'd chosen to call hers disappointed her. In sickness and in health. Oh, man, meant zip to her.

I need to listen, to hear, without ideas; without them I might have heard Maggie's discontent.

Silence can be dishonest, and violent speech threatens. The other's silence might be stuffed with rebukes, even hatred. Mother told me about her best college friend, the person she trusted most in the world, who actually had so much contempt for her, and never said a word, and then a letter full of hate to her. No love, Zeke, not a word.

Shithead's multiplex head-nodding affirmations. Fuck him.

Listening harder, I might've heard what was there that hadn't caught my other senses. Might have heard what I didn't want to hear.

Yogi Berra: You can observe a lot by just watching.

An image: Cage and Berra in a room, roaring together.

Inchoate sounds are interpretations of loneliness.

With no ideas, I could become an adept.

The power of clairaudience: hearing sounds beyond the reach of ordinary experience or capacity, like the voices of the dead. Clairaudience entered the English language in the 1860s, a portmanteau of clairvoyance and audience.

Where do the voices of the dead go, and old languages, endangered species, many dying daily. Life keeps dying.

Consciousness of time, duration, sensing that IT ends, charges experience with finitude. That is, reality. That is, death.

In silence, spirits roam.

Cage looked to Kant: Kant wrote that there are two things that don't have to mean anything—music and laughter. No meaning but to give deep pleasure.

Explaining Clifford Geertz, Raymond Benton Jr. writes: Culture is not a force or causal agent in the world, but a context in which people live out their lives.

Which means, culture vultures, back off! People can't seek out culture, and, if they try, they do it within the context in which they exist.

Cage: "The sound experience which I prefer to all others is the experience of silence. And the silence almost everywhere now is traffic."

I compare traffic with images.

Everywhere, everything, everywhere, traffic. We walk, sit, think, drink, have sex, eat, etc., in traffic.

Cage, sound, silence, chance: on photography's compass. Photographs: silent. In need of explanation, response, facts don't provide interpretation. A definitive moment comes by, with chance.

Chance massively affects field work. It should, anyway. Things should be unpredictable, right. You shouldn't know what's what; who will say what, you can't know—it's about discovering who, what, how, why, while there; who knows why. (Who's on first, ha.) You read about your subject, place, religion, customs, foods, rites. Still, researchers, theorists, and critics travel with their preconceptions—why else would they go? They have IDEAS about something, right? An ethnographer tries to dissuade herself from preconceived ideas.

Chance must have a chance at rearranging the so-called mindset.

It's chance, meeting the one you love. It's chance meeting the second or third or fourth one you love. We're not mourning doves who mate for life, OK, some humans do. With a bird's small brain, maybe there's no monotony.

Even with humans' bigger brains, monotony—bad sex, boring days, bad jokes—is tolerated. Monogamy arose along with or after monotheism. Many gods could wreak their terrible wrath, and monotheism simplified existence, and made it safer (more boring).

Monotheism gets high grades for progress, but there's no logic there. Without proof of one god or many, what difference does it make? Any valid argument for why worshiping one god trumps worshiping many, or why mono-anything implies sophisticated thinking? Don't think so.

Monogamy enabled males to track their progeny, protect the gene pool. Same deal with lions, etc., in the animal kingdom.

Monogamy brought monotony, Fordism and the factory line, repetitive labor, and tendinitis.

The aleatoric is denied in a factory line and marriage.

Mother had a close friend whose husband bored Mother to death, he said dumb, obvious stuff, no sense of humor. I saw, when I was a kid, that he bored his wife. But she never left him. Takes all kinds, people say. Actually, there aren't that many kinds.

Longevity isn't a matter of chance, genes, sure, and environment. The well-off live longer than the poor-off. Rich men find it easier to marry again than poor ones. Old men draw younger women, with power and money. Anthropologists note the sense of these arrangements, then reserve judgment. Western women don't like to acknowledge their attraction to and dependence on earners, successful men who keep them in the style they want to become accustomed to, and believe in love, holding to an illusion of their purity.

Some people take advantage of chance, most don't. The ones who do are called lucky. "Luck" means a person who takes chances others don't (out of fear of change, lack of foresight, stunted psyches), finds opportunity in a random event, say. If things work out, the person is called lucky. "Lucky" people have less fear of failure.

People find what they want to find, because they look for it (how stereotypes work; see Goffman's *Stigma*), and don't see what they don't want to know.

I need to finesse chance into dailiness, to rearrange my brain and sever those entangled neurons that keep me on the wrong "neuronic" tracks. Ha.

## IMAGES: TRUE AND FALSE

Inevitably, a ghost haunts pictures. A ghost is also an image, the word ghost gets used variously. I might say, a ghost in a picture is the amorphous shape of wishful thinking, or the "spirit" of hope. The interpretive ghost haunts people who try, as ethnographers do, to understand what may be indifferent to human understanding and the idea of sense.

No person alive lives without wishes that might morph into ideas and beliefs.

Some illusions are held to be true.

Not an illusion but: what if there were one right way to do it? I'm haunted by that idea, and that I will never find it.

Time passes, and what is "true" or "false" changes, which makes absolutes tricky. Convincing nonbelievers to believe a theory, or believers not to accept it, is near impossible.

An atheist, like me, takes an absolutist position, and probably I shouldn't, still I do, because I don't believe in a god or many, but also paradoxically believe there are things I can't know, like a god, or spirits, or ways the dead inhabit the living.

If I were to believe in God, I would test my ability to be free from a habit.

So-called "reality" contains many contentious, enthralling realities, or belief systems, in which people believe in life after death. What does that mean? The Lazarus story is a model, right.

Realities transpire, one after another, emerging from, while also binding to, predecessors.

## ON "THE PERSISTENCE OF AN IDEAL IMAGE"

In the beginning there is nothing, and then nothing becomes something, and something becomes everything, and you're fucked.

I own an old photograph—not a mental image—of a little girl in a garden. I don't remember where I found this stray. Can't see her face (not unlike the Bonnard in this way). The girl wears a white, long-sleeved cotton dress, like a smock, and is smelling peonies. It's an antique, creased photograph

backed by cardboard. In white, she—I call her Alice— and
the white blossoms share center space. Around her, leafy trees
and bushes create dark shadows, so negative space encircles
and frames her. To me, an idyllic image. I like to think she's
being embraced by her garden.

That picture foments wordlessness, if that's possible, because I've just used many words describing it. I'm not without
words, but only believe I am. How can that be a feeling? Now,
that little girl dies at thirty-one, say, but the love doesn't die. It
exists, somewhere, in its own field. It's immaterial, right.

I hold the love and her in my mind like in a locket or my
garden. I tend my garden, it's what I have.

Now, hypothetically, you enter a garden.

You are entering a garden. Do you see an English or
French garden, wild grasses? A rosebush. Flower pots. How
is it you, or I, imagine this or that, first? Then other images

intrude, and a scene fills out. Other views, mental pictures, manifest. Or maybe your garden is cacti in a sullen desert—daunting, stark shapes, nature's gravestones.

Take a stroll in your image garden. Where are you? Is it around you? Maybe you're at a desk or on a train or in a bathtub or sitting before a screen, or staring breathlessly at an indifferent, glorious horizon, or, walking on a city street, where buildings rise, taxis run by, horns hitting dissonant notes, and last night's ravers lope along the streets, ravished.

You want to be ravished, you were, once. That garden. That playground. That forest. That ocean.

Look at the roses, tulips, crocus, peonies, lavender, myrtle.

You experience memories as olfactory sensation, and yes, you can smell the flowers. In that garden, baby love wanders, first love, love at first sight, all those wishes, those hopes.

Treasured images.

Fading images.

Revive them!

In mine, she stands beside a sunflower and screams joyfully at a passing butterfly.

In mine, Mr. Petey appears on the side of a wood fence, and only his movement shows him, because he blends in. He turns his head, his magnificently detailed head, and looks at me. Where have you been, Zeke? he asks, silent and still. Why have you forsaken me?

I haven't, I haven't, I say. I'm crying now.

There's too much loss.

The endurance of specific memories, and only those, mystifies me. Scenes return, seemingly haphazard, repeat and repeat, and, later, lose their distinctive edges and blur into others, become one more loss, just another question: did it happen? Or was it a video? Or, memories find other color-ations from the current flow of new interpretations.

Let me go against type (mine)—let me recognize proph-esies, salutary unknowns, and please let me embellish my time here with unusual possibilities.

The brain WANTS memory, must need it, because it's part of the evolution of the species, though it's imperfect and imperfect-able, so far. Am thinking that will change.

Why does memory outwit us?

Much of mine is painful. How does that help evolution. Or, anything.

## SHOOT ME

By 2011 I had owned a BlackBerry, two iPhones, two digital cameras; by 2013 I had an iPad mini, Android, another iPhone, another camera. I'd round a corner, send a text, see something (say nothing), click. I'd look at it, upload. Or delete it, it didn't matter in so many ways, let me count them. Can't. Lots more where it came from, like piss.

It's all about you and your reality, life is your personalized stationery.

I felt no urge to be an artist, just to keep up and happy with novelty, the tech snap-ons, la vita nuova. But I became occupied with things, collected objects and held on to stuff. I couldn't throw anything out and it was dismal. I'd lost Maggie, and everything I thought I knew I didn't. My analyst suggested I couldn't throw anything out because I'd been thrown out. I identified with everything, lost and found. Not kidding.

I was further from my image of perfection, whatever that might be, not that I had ever been near perfect.

I noticed what I framed and didn't, a central metaphor, "What do you, Zeke, let in, or leave out?" Asked myself: does this picture show how I see the world, or is the world always already there? Or, why is it I see this way, not that way? Do I have the chops to make a picture that matches how I see the things before me? Or, can I change the way I see the world before me, and make others see it the way I do? Unlikely.

Information isn't knowledge, information is data in need of interpretation.

> What do images do? Do they illustrate? . . . But do we not already have too much to look at? (Generosity.) Left to myself, I would be perfectly contented with black pictures, providing Rauschenberg had painted them.
>
> —Cage

Selfies, Instagrams, gifs, etc., here now, gone when, change changes, people want change to feel new when they're not, because when you are new, you don't think about it. We're born heathen, promiscuous, polymorphous perverse, and then gimme gimme, and headlong, bound to betray first, second, third loves. Is there a rationale behind the change, does it lead to something? Oh, sure, commerce, but is that ever all there is.

Disassembled, dissembling in pix that r us.

Picture people unite! Fight images! Deny images! No? Love 'em, love our voluntary servitude, or leave 'em.

Vilém Flusser: people LOVE being functionaries of the camera.

DO WE KNOW WHY WE TAKE PIX? Is it a "PERSONAL" or "SOCIAL" DECISION? WHAT IS THE IMPULSE?

## IN MY BACKYARD

Where was I then? Looking at the sky. Mother, totally present. I led a supercharged-child-existence, unhampered by reality, mostly.

Self-narrating, self-history-building.

It was a bright afternoon and school was out. The school bus driver, Chubby Lola, dropped me at the top of the road leading to our house down a long lane, I guess I was eight or nine, but on an impulse, I suppose, I turned in the opposite direction, because I didn't want to go home. As far as I can recall, it was the first time I didn't want to go home. I'm not sure why it occurred then, this feeling. I don't think Father had punished me or something like that. I walked until I reached a little post office that served the area. I knew it was there, but didn't know I was heading to it. Walking in alone surprised me, opening the door by myself, I hadn't done it there before. By myself. I liked that.

The postmistress, Cassie, knew me. Hello, she said. I mumbled, Hi, and looked at the stamps in the glass cases, lingering, because I really liked the pictures, especially of animals, and then read a WANTED poster, a fuzzy picture of a girl and a boy, teenagers. They had robbed some houses in the area, and the poster said anyone who sees them shouldn't approach them because they were armed and dangerous. I stood there. These strangers looked very mean, they weren't acting like criminals, this wasn't TV, and they might rob our house. What if Mother was killed. I'd hear the shots. Her screams. I'd hide under my bed, but they'd find me, they do on TV. Or, they wouldn't see me, but I'd be forced to do a line-up, then I'd have to testify, and the killers would put a hit out on me. I couldn't identify them, I'd plead to the cops, they'll kill me. No way, I wouldn't be able to escape, they'd find me under my bed. The girl would yell, "He's just a kid!" "But he saw us," the guy would say. "He can identify us." And there's no Bruce Willis or Liam Neeson, no fanatic to kill them and save me. I scream, "I won't tell I won't tell don't kill me." Boom, boom. I'm dead.

I'm kid-sobbing. Cassie runs out from behind her cage, but as she did I raced out of the door, and ran all the way home. Mother wasn't back. Nobody was around to know I was late. Little Sister was two or three, her nanny in the kitchen making dinner, which she did when Mother drove to Boston. Bro Hart was probably in his room, jerking off. He was about twelve or thirteen. I avoided him, stayed out of his way, he could beat me up.

I didn't know what to do about what happened, talk or bury it. That seems crucial, how a kid handles a bad event. I felt humiliated, totally freaked, and I was still scared in the house, because the crazed criminals might invade it any time, armed and dangerous. I'd never taken those words seriously. Just TV talk.

I walked into the garden, it was late spring, maybe that's why I didn't want to go home, and I looked for Mr. Petey, but he wasn't around.

The only people I worried about being murdered were Mother and Little Sister, not Bro Hart and Father. I don't remember feeling guilty. I don't know how I got over it, either, and maybe I didn't, maybe it's soiled my psyche forever.

I'm sick of love; I wish I'd never met you
I'm sick of love; I'm trying to forget you.
—Bob Dylan


## IN REAL TIME

I'm on the street, at a corner, nice day. Suddenly the corner's busy, many people jostling against me, and I'm saying I'm sorry for something I did—I bumped against a small woman, dark eyes, dark curly hair, dark skin—then the swarm moves on. But the little woman looks back at me, because I'm apologizing, and her face . . . her expression . . . you know, a little weird. She's definitely surprised. I don't know why, I smiled big. I know why, stupid Zeke, I was feeling good.

She had just picked my pocket. Right. I'm saying sorry to her, no wonder she's surprised, she's met the nicest mark.

The weird thing is I'd been thinking about my wallet all morning, that I should move it from my jacket pocket to my pants pocket, but I didn't. I was feeling good, and shifting the wallet meant doing something that felt bad, I mean, it showed I was skeptical or paranoid. I don't get it. I just didn't switch it, when I knew I should, and kept thinking about it. You know, you do it or you don't. I do and also don't. That's the abulia. My Hamlet shit.

It was a late October day. I'd just worked out, and didn't want to move my wallet. Those sharp-eyed cons spotted me and swarmed, a plague of human locusts.

I'm sorry, I say to her.

Fuck me. Thirty minutes later, I reach for my wallet to

buy something. No wallet. ATM, credit cards. **$$**. Gone. It's an empty feeling, really bad. So, I replay the scene in my brain, I'm approaching that corner, I'm feeling good, and there's a sudden swarm around me, a woman's close, I take a bump, and, because I was goofin', daydreaming, I figure it was my fault, I bumped her.

I got mugged.

I launched into action, canceled my ATM card, phoned Amex, found out from them it'd been used—they did it fast, they were fast, pros, and Amex told me at what store, which location, and when—exact time, it was minutes after it happened—and then I walked fast to the store. I almost flew, and located the manager and learned they had video, they gave me the time that the bozo with my card used it. They keep the video for a week, the manager said, and with all this info— oh yeah, the thieves bought over $200 of cosmetics and baby things—I ran to the police station. I tried to report it. Tried is the operative concept. It wasn't like the precinct was busy, but the cop who wrote up the report was almost asleep, though not actually asleep. Technically, awake, but mentally nowhere. I must have explained and repeated the scene and the info in the same way, same words, five times, and each time he read it back to me he'd got it fucking wrong. I thought I'd lose it. I said, finally, hoping to seem nonjudgmental, OK, I'll come back tomorrow. He said, Yeah, see Detective Sanchez, she'll be in. Ask for her. Sure, I said, thanks, and hurried out the door and to a bar where I have a tab and laughed in my beer.

I had everything the cops could want. That's what I'm thinking. I returned the next day. Detective Sanchez was a genius compared with the first cop. She asked good questions, she repeated my answers correctly. She wrote it all down, and I left feeling there would definitely be some action. She said she'd call me soon. I felt renewed, there's a case going. CASE number blah blah.

I tell no one about the crime, no one, because being mugged feels girly. I admit it, victim-hood makes putative men feel the way they imagine women feel all the time. Defenseless. Weak. I know, this is ridiculous.

Two full days went by, and where's Detective Sanchez? I knew the video in that store would be kept a week, so I phoned the precinct, but no one was available because there'd been a murder in the neighborhood, and everyone was out there. The entire precinct except the person answering the phone, who was probably in New Delhi, everyone's out there, like it's a picnic. Detective Sanchez, OK, she's the lead detective, she should be at a crime scene.

Another day, another no call, and I phoned again. Detective Sanchez says they're working on it. What can I say? OK. Then I look at my bank statement; according to it, I had taken out $2,800 of my savings, in cash, which about wiped my savings. One of them had used my stolen ATM card before I canceled it. It was an inside job. Obvious.

I reported to my branch, in person, and filled out another report, or reports, one certified by a notary in the bank. I spoke to three different bank managers, who told me different things, on two different days, a few days apart. Bottom line: my money would be returned. No problem, they'd cover it. Cool. But my theory that it was an inside job went no where. How else did the cons know exactly how much to take out, just under the amount I had? Blank eyes from a dead chorus. Why didn't the teller think about it, flag it? An unusual withdrawal. Almost closing the account. Why didn't she say, Are you sure you want to close the account? They always do that.

Did the first bank manager raise an eyebrow? The next? Or next? Nope, because they don't give a shit, the insurance company pays the bank for these petty losses, why bother, man? OK, that's the private sector, but the cops, they work in civic space, they're on the public tit. We pay them. This gets worse. Detective Sanchez? She played me. I called, she didn't call back, she called back once, said she was still working on it. Finally, I went to the precinct again.

Me: I got you all this info, you could nail those cons.

She says nothing, just looks at me.

Me (twitchy): Look, you had video on those characters. You could have nailed them . . . You'll forgive me, Detective Sanchez, and I know this may sound funny, but you could have made a good collar.

She just breaks up. She's laughing so hard now, I'm looking around at who else is watching. Then she stops—and her smile looks as if it could break her face.

She says: You know, you watch too much *Law & Order.* (Hahahaha.) But I'll tell you something. Call me any time you want. I'll always be happy to hear from you.

I bet she's still laughing.

I didn't tell anyone.

Is this accountable or unaccountable? An account means it adds up, this doesn't.

I have replayed these scenes, reread them, my futile attempts at catching the wrongdoers, the thieves, and, though they used my credit card to buy baby food and Pampers, and I had some sympathy for their baby's needs, I couldn't just say, OK, they're poor, damaged by society's inequities, and blah blah, because they also cleaned out my bank account, or tried to. How does that merit sympathy. OK, I'm privileged, and have no right to have more than anyone else, and I'm cool with that. But those people didn't know what I had or didn't have. I could have been saving all my life, and that money represented IT. They couldn't know, unless they'd been tracking me and were doing their own kind of Robin Hood–like social justice, and stealing from the rich(er), which is highly unlikely, because they wouldn't have the organization to have had someone checking me out for weeks before, and then following me until the perfect moment came for their swoop and lift. No way.

Ambiguity up, security down, vagaries in my face.

They're called "challenges." Oh, man, yes.

I figured it was also a part of my field work. Life, I told myself, is my field. I'm in it, studying it, interpreting it, actions, reactions. Right, I do watch and have watched too many police shows. I'm an American, I love crime. Mother watched the O.J. trial, if work didn't interfere. Crime not the way it used to be written, say, in the 1930s, by Raymond Chandler. Or, in the 1940s, crime as portrayed in noir movies. I grew up watching it, in the eighties and nineties: *Hill Street Blues*; *Miami Vice* (crime as style); *Law & Order*; *Kojak*; *Columbo*; *Homicide*; *NYPD Blue*. The list goes on. The vérité stuff, Errol Morris's *The Thin Blue Line* got a convicted man released from prison. Watching crime, I'm not a criminal or committing a crime, or being murdered.

Let's face it, bad things don't happen to people who watch TV, except their asses spread, they die earlier from heart disease, etc., because they don't move, except to go to the refrigerator. If Americans didn't watch TV, more of them might get killed. If they didn't see ads exhorting them to go to their refrigerators, they'd be a lot healthier. But what's health until you're sick.

I concentrated on tennis, tearing up the courts, until I got tendinitis, then I became obsessed with Roger Federer, tennis's Mikhail Baryshnikov, imperturbable and graceful; when down a match, even two, he rose like a phoenix, not kidding, but he wasn't a machine like Pete Sampras, but so intelligently organized and super-confident. To raise his game, Fed's choreography turned tighter, he ran the balls down quicker, part of his dance. When he began losing more regularly, my heart felt sick, but I was trying to learn from him how a Master loses, and keeps going. For one thing, he was fading but still brilliant, and he brought out the Tap, a forehand takeback. He used it, and no one could return it.

When Agassi retired from the game, another blow. He was a magnificent wild man, and something about him, though he wasn't a consistent player like Fed, compelled my sympathy, even when I learned, along with the tennis world, that he hated playing. That killed me. I switched my passion to Djokovic, when Fed lost in a quarter-final, but when Fed raised his game higher, and the two played against each other, conflict.

My animus was directed at Andy Murray. From the moment I watched him play, he annoyed me. I disliked him. He's a better player, now, bigger, physically, but he reminds me of an animal mildly tamed by holding a racquet, and not a hatchet.

It took me a while to get used to how much the serve dominated the game, it never used to. It was serve and volley, rallying. Andy Roddick, for one, came along, serving aces one after the other. Aces, speed, massive shots and power, now all the men, and some women, notably Serena, hit 125-mile-per-hour serves and return them, they're all physically powerful. And that means tennis metamorphosed from a game of finesse to power. You still need mental prowess, because tennis is an existential sport, mental like chess, and great players beat themselves as often as they are beaten. Maybe more.

Power underscores everything, everywhere, but I hadn't included it in my game, or in life, say. I didn't get it, except as an abstraction. It's not.

ANALYST: Being betrayed by a friend is terrible. It is disturbing.
ME: Pathetic. I had no idea. I thought everything was cool.
ANALYST: You trusted them.
ME: Because of trust I was powerless. I beat myself. Never again.

I took lessons to master the two-handed backhand. Very hard, mentally and physically, going against your training. And, two-handed doesn't look as good. But it's about power.

Changing even one habit is mentally awkward; a habit

appends a personality. We are our habits. What isn't a habit, every thought could be, every habit can stunt the mind and body. After Father died, I phoned home, expecting him to answer, he used to, at night, and of course Mother picked up, and for about a year I felt surprise. I was calling her, I always said. It was out of a habit.

Without a habit, the emperor has no clothes (haha). I'm not naked yet. I decided to try one new behavior each day, drink my coffee ten minutes later, then later. A gradualist's approach.

I'm alternating realities, not finding an alternative.

Here's a certainty: most things can never be proved.

Doubt casts shadows, but doubt appears when the sun is out. I mean, when you're in love. When you feel loved. In life even a tiny alteration can be effective.


## THEORY OF ATEMPORAL LOVE

People fall in love with images, that's obvious, all those movie and pop-star and celebrity-personality posters on bedroom walls. Dead, alive. Marilyn Monroe sells more dead than she did alive.

In my role or pose as a social scientist, let me call this phenomenon "image-necrophilia." I view family pictures, criticize and comment on contemporary photography, but I am also a studied imbiber or guzzler of images. I myself am an image to others and myself, for example, I am a youngish man, who wears black slim jeans and sometimes a brimless hat, sometimes not. Get the image. It wears me.

Love can be out of time. It can reject age, race, nation, etc. It can go against time, it can be without time. This is "atemporal longing" or "atemporal love."

People fall hard for an image. The image never has to die, unless something comes along to destroy it. The love object dies. Body gone. Grief. But then all love's disappointments end. Physical body death doesn't make love die, right. There may be no death of love, ever, in life. Or, any relational dynamic. The beloved can't change, the image doesn't, and the living lover never needs to change.

That which doesn't change can also be narrated, I want to narrate that. I want to tell the ordinary story of stasis, of being stuck.

Pictures of the dead don't change death into life. Pictures are reminders. Stuck in the mind.

No one can take the dead from us, their images, and "necro-photo-philes," my term, refer to them with unedited wistfulness.

Spirit photographers used gauze to create the illusion of ghostly spirit oozing from the dead's mouth or eyes.

New mourners devour pictures of the deceased. Time stops for the dead, and in a way the mourner, who is suspended in time. Time collapses, like the grief-stricken who fall into a timeless abyss; time's suspension makes space for implausible wishes. Impossible to explain this.

Let's say there's safety in image worship, in adoration from afar, which thrives with distance. No one can stalk the dead.

DISTANCE and the zoom lens: it makes the photographer close while far, it allows for a seeming intimacy, which is remote and perfectly anesthetic, and perfectly deceptive. Created by close-ups and zooms, intimacy, poignancy, is a primary effect, and "revealing," its greatest illusion.

## A MAN OF INACTION

I'm an oxymoron, moron ox, dumb pun. Who cares.

Theoretical border crossings, shifting fields of inquiry, morph into self-made mind wars. I renounced and claimed and accepted and denied what I once held dear.

Total hedonism, total boredom. OK, pathetic, not cool. I can spend lots of time massaging my fantasies, and thinking about what wastes my life.

Mistakes come to be patterns. Societies have ill-made "patterns."

Medical researchers and scientists search for one cause, for a patient suffering with various symptoms, or "diagnostic parsimony," its colloquial handle: "Occam's razor," the one-size-fits-all solution. For extremely difficult cases, long-term undiagnosed diseases, ones they can't find a cure for or even relief, that elude correction, they continue to seek one underlying cause. They haven't found it yet for cancer, and, compared with some very rare diseases, cancer is simple. And, physicists hope for a unified theory of the universe.

I used to be a patternista. When I was little, with Mother beside me, I solemnly followed the hands of a tailor pinning cloth to the dotted blue lines on a translucent pattern, then cutting away the material, with a large, serrated scissors, and I thought that was so cool, she was cool, also the way she dressed in asymmetrical clothes. Uneven lengths. One shoulder bare. I thought it was because she was Asian. No one said that, but here I was, making cultural (racist) assumptions. Later, I distrusted my assumptions, and now I don't want to follow patterns.

But I watch some movies again and again, because they don't change. The movies run on, I can stop them now, I don't want to. Second and third times, I notice more, or focus on details I hadn't, because I know the story or, anyway, I know what happens, and don't need to follow it. By the tenth time, none of this matters. I just watch, calmly soaking up sameness, no matter if it's *The Godfather: Part II* or any of the Bourne movies, their violence domesticated by the screen, and familiarity. Almost nothing on view, except a murder or accident in real time, can be completely undomesticated. Twenty-four-hour news cycles make tragedy repetitive, the spectacular familiar.

9/11 was an abstraction for many Americans, it may have happened in real time on TV but it didn't actually hit them. Oh, yeah, they could hate Arabs more, or Muslims, if they knew the difference, but the experience was remote, repeated and repeated on TV, and fodder for bellicose politicians eager for war.

The war on terror begins there.

Many people in uptown Manhattan didn't feel 9/11 the way people downtown, downwind did. No one uptown got covered in ash and soot. A Brooklyn guy whose open windows let in fragments of paper, and who knows what else, split the next day. Everyone in NYC says the day was so beautiful, the sky so blue, and days like that have become a

"9/11 kind of day." Maggie and I were in Boston, and watched on TV. Horror at a distance.

TV, my familiar, and the American family's biggest picture album, with recognizable characters; some not so much, at first, then they become regulars. Doesn't matter what's on it, except for a bulletin or news alert, and then, well, it's a tragedy that didn't happen to me. Not yet.

I can watch a screen 24/7—name it, whatever flows and streams. Ethnographers observe, I watch, I spy. Ha.

Moving pictures relax me, a photograph doesn't let me rest, exactly because it doesn't move or narrate, and I have to make it into something, this surface, whose "depth" is all question, no answer.

Walking around by day and night, pounding my brain with necessary un-thinking, I returned in spirit to Rock Creek, those feelings, and Clover, and, I swear, she was totally real. It didn't matter if it seemed crazy. She was real to me. I'm not alone in these feelings, but I thought I had protected myself from this stuff with my "professional outlook." We who are jaded, we're the worst, because we deny a need in ourselves for the illusions we work hard to shatter. Super-vulnerable.

I was aware of, even attuned to, psychic phenomena; in my family, it happens, there are many occurrences. I don't profess the virtues of either the phenomena or my family, but admit the presence, when years ago I didn't, when I was just a three-dimensional guy who lived in two dimensions. Bandwidths. Love, for one, streamed narrowly.

Can love, as we talk about it, be an instinct? Or is it fear of loss of survivors, or of future guilt? Fear of ostracism by the tribe? Instincts appear altruistic, and may not be: the mother's done her reproductive work and wants it to prosper.

Some mothers throw their babies out of windows, or hand them over to lovers who beat them to death.

Timing. It wasn't the right time for you and Maggie, they said, you were too young, etc. But why should love be fixed by time, because like time, love is a human invention. (See earlier.) How does one invention get determined by another? Love doesn't have a repeatable formula—but falling in love always feels the same.

Disaster shall fall upon you, which you will not be able to expiate. —Isaiah 47:11

Expiate once meant confronting evil, plus, assuaging guilt. I need to expiate or ward off evil, but to do that I need sacred rites for purification, and I have none, and no, becoming a vegan wouldn't hack it, and purging and cutting and all of that won't cut it. Ha

I need rites, know wrongs. Impossible to enumerate all of my wrongs. And being wronged. Repent, atone, all you who did me wrong. Seriously.

In a modest way, probably as an outgrowth of my field work, which required me to abandon my home, and I don't mean home in the ordinary sense, I left my self-place, also an image of place. Home is prosaic, always. And I grew closer to what I couldn't see but only feel. With a better grip, or not driving myself so hard that my head was banging, maybe I wouldn't have left this safe place, this self-place. I could say, I went into an out-field, into the image-stratosphere. But I was observing myself, too. Maybe it was fated, a sad notion, especially for a cultural anthropologist, who doesn't believe in fate, and who follows, dispassionately, culture's flow.

That's about when I hit my internal pause button.

I've been stopped more than twice, and have been reset by coincidence and the inenarrable.

A time-stretch came when, in my own lost-and-found depot, I assumed various guises, acting like different "men"—pretending—since the one I'd been or become hadn't satisfied HER. I duly remade myself into the best friend who betrayed me, and wore the costume of a Don Juan.

I was a biological male transitioning into a different kind of man. (See later, MEN IN QUOTES.)

Curtis the shithead could seduce women, he tuned in to what they wanted and turned them on like lamps, that was his power.

I sat in front of a computer, in parks, I hiked on avenues, I sat in movie theaters, traveling from one screen to another until I'd seen all nine or twelve or until the theater closed. I raced bikes, I played pick-up basketball on city courts. Anything could lead me anywhere, by selecting irrationality from a rational position, hating my own routines, when I used to depend on them, so I ate food I never liked—I wanted another kind of taste in my mouth, I wanted to feel comfortable. You're sick, in a sickbed, and there's no position that's comfortable, that's how it was. You will try anything, right?

When anyone spoke to me on the street, in a park, bar, café, you name it, I took the bait and joined into any conversation. In the park, a religious man, a devout Christian, as he told it, learned my name was Zeke, and cried, Ezekiel, and, I said, Yes, answering him, and he practically fell down at my feet. Almost on them. Told me God had sent Ezekiel a vision. Ezekiel saw a valley of dry bones, which foretold the first coming of Christ (I didn't say, Wow, more than one?), and the first resurrection from death unto life, if you believe the Lord's word.

I said nada, but he stared meatily at me, a blood-lust gaze.

God said to Ezekiel, "Son of man, can these bones live?" So, Ezekiel (who's no fool) says, "O Lord God, thou knowest."

Clever, right. Then he wanted to sell me a Bible. I said no, and told him I was a confirmed atheist, though I respected his beliefs. He fled.

Seeing dry bones—a terrific metaphor, and I can't escape the fact that it suits everything I feel now. Can these dry bones live?

## THE STRANGER WITHIN (GFTS STRANGER)

Goffman, in *Stigma: Notes on the Management of Spoiled Identity* (1963): the central feature for a stigmatized individual's situation is "acceptance." How to get and keep it. To fit in. To hide the impairment, virtual or actual.

Spoiled identity. How cool is that characterization.

In the U.S., it's high school. No one feels accepted, popular crowd rules, and almost no American gets over it. People feel excluded, always and forever after. They learn to need a crowd, they learn that being a stranger has few compensations, when the slide is downward. In all animal groups, exclusion rules; among males, there are fights unto death for dominance—who gets to mate and procreate, who owns the territory. Human men fight in bars, play war games on boards, become legitimated soldier/killers.

Max Weber said a nation-state was defined by one aspect only: it is legitimated to kill.

Nation-state: is exclusion a survival trait? Is there an instinct, starting with the formation of the family, to expand into tribes and groups, to separate kinds from other kinds arbitrarily, to assure loyalty? Many mammals require it for survival.

People bet on winners and losers, in every sense.

Goffman: "Now turn from the normal to the person he is normal against."

Normal is against, and there is no baseline normal.

I'm tired of doing normal, if I ever did, and of being that kind of person who attempts it.

In *Madness and Civilization*, Foucault explained that leprosy disappeared by the end of the Middle Ages, but the leper houses remained, everywhere in Europe, structures ready for the sick. And, once that space opened, it stayed open, that is, "the values and images attached to the figure of the leper as well as the meaning of his exclusion" remained. By the Age of Reason, madness is unreason and danger. "The 17th century created enormous houses of confinement," Foucault says, because of the fear of scandal. By confining the mad, scandal could be avoided.

I can totally see that. If you get put away, do you tell people, does your family blurt it, not usually, unless you're a reality TV star who flaunts his addiction to get back in the public eye. Black eye.

Under a cloud of suspicion I rambled around, but I wasn't

totally out of it, I mean, I knew when to check in enough so that I could be left alone.

I like clouds.

You can imagine being an intriguing character, even though mired in self-hate, while un-friends stay at a remove, uncluttering your little life—fewer to keep out, fewer who reek of the incendiary past. Old friends, without them, I am calmer. No one can hold up the past, and the future doesn't have a past then, also.

Being suspicious, being a suspect, fascinated me. I projected an attitude unlike Zeke's: I looked too long at someone, then turned away. I doubled back, when I didn't have to. I stared at a woman, she looked back, I dropped my eyes and strolled off. Now, this kind of behavior can be a game changer. Fomenting doubt in others about yourself/me. I formed what I call "accidental connections," hanging at cool bars, talking up the ladies, haha, and sometimes I was a cad, bad, a lad, or sometimes I was had. I disguised myself to myself, and sometimes I fooled myself, and thought I believed what I said and did. Repetition helps that along, belief needs sustenance. Faith is continuous belief. But that was hard for me, and I dropped many poses, sometimes in the middle, because I couldn't keep the faith. Like, one time I was with a woman, and I'd told her I was a psychiatrist, and I discussed me and my case as if it weren't mine. She got hooked on this interesting man, I could see it, because I embellished him/me. The betrayal by the wife and the best friend, wow, she almost gushed. People, OK, women, just love this shit. In my role as his shrink, I was all-knowing and generous, sensitive to the max. Seeing that it worked so well on her, I couldn't go on. I began to feel awful, absolutely insincere even if I was talking about me, sort of. I looked at my phone and said, Jeez, I have to go, and basically lurched out the door. Threw money on the bar.

Friends with benefits (once in college, before Maggie) and hookups: in place of commitment, sure; to satisfy needs, sure; in obeisance to lust, yes. From the naughts on, the unconventional turned conventional, examples abound like sorority girls with tattoos, these shifts show new mating orders. How do we make ourselves available, and for what, and how long? The divorce rate has declined since 1980. It's the economy, stupid.

I got into staying home, weeks on end, except for analysis. I searched online for anything tasty, diversionary. Welcome home, distractions! I searched for news of my betrayer and spied on his academic activities. I thought I might put a hit out on him, or do it myself.

Meanwhile, I discovered that the FBI had spied on Warhol.

In 1968, the FBI sent agents to Oracle, Arizona, to report on some dangerous and subversive activities. They were tracking Andy Warhol, who was shooting a porn film. The agents delivered a deadpan description and interviewed locals who also witnessed the revelry when the Factory came to town:

> _____ advise that he lives Oracle, Arizona. He owns a horse. On January 27 or 28, 1968, he received a phone call from _____ in Oracle Arizona, asking if he had a horse that could be used in a film that was being made at the Rancho Linda Vista Guest Ranch at Oracle, Arizona . . . A blond, curly headed male then unzipped and pulled down his pants. This same man

then performed an unnatural sex act of Cunnilingus on the female. The other male individuals held the girl down. She did very little struggling. She and the male actors continued to use profane and vulgar words during their sexual activity. The spontaneous conversation was recorded and their acts filmed. After about one minute the female got up and sat in the wash. She folded her arms over her bare chest. Somebody later threw her blouse and trousers over her back. She then put her trousers and blouse back on . . . The man continued to wear her panties over his hat _____ stated that "his horse broke loose about the time the unnatural sex acts took place . . . The men played with each other's rear ends. One had flowers sewed on the seat of his trousers in the shape of a diamond." One fellow was hanging by the knees, face down, out of a tree, and kissing on the lips one of the other men on the horse. All the men looked like hippies and were very vulgar in their conversations. The men were trying to kiss each other. The men were trying to kiss each other. The owner of the ranch told the FBI also that "There was a total of 14 men and one girl, VIVA, who stayed at the Guest Ranch. But did not have a complete list of all 15 people but had a partial list furnished." In cabin no. 33 were two men: Warhol, and _____ who she "believed to be lovers . . . they both slept in the same bed." _____ acted as the right-hand man for Warhol. He did most of the talking to and for the group. He had his address as _____, New York, NY. "_____, who slept with Andy Warhol, acted like a big sissy and did not take part in the movie. He wore ankle-strap thongs."

The agents weren't just sightseeing. The investigation continued as the FBI tried to gather enough evidence to prosecute Warhol for interstate transportation of obscene material for taking the film, *Lonesome Cowboys*, from New Mexico to a film festival in California. Two dutiful [G] men actually went to the festival to watch the movie and deliver their own reviews.

On November 1, 1968, SAs _____ and _____ attended the midnight showing of the motion picture, *Lonesome Cowboys*, at the San Francisco International Film Festival . . .

The movie opened with the woman and her male nurse on a street in the town. Five or six cowboys then entered the town and there was evidence of hostility between the two groups. One of the cowboys practiced his ballet and a conversation ensued regarding the misuse of mascara by one of the other cowboys . . .

There are other parts in the film in which the private parts of the woman were visible on the screen and there were also scenes in which men were revealed in total nudity. The sheriff in one scene was shown dressing in woman's clothing and later being held on the lap of another cowboy. Also the male nurse was pictured in the arms of the sheriff. In one scene where VIVA was attempting to persuade one of the cowboys to take off his clothes and join her in her nudity, the discussion was centered around the Catholic Church's liturgical songs . . .

Another scene depicted a cowboy fondling the nipples of another cowboy . . .

There were suggestive dances done by the male actors with each other. These dances were conducted while they were clothed and suggested lovemaking between two males . . .

There was no plot to the film and no development of characters throughout. It was rather a remotely connected series of scenes which depicted situations of sexual relationships of homosexual and heterosexual nature.

The FBI actually followed Warhol and described his work. They filed a report on him. In a sick way it was kind of scarily cool.

## CAN YOU SPARE TIME

Cut out doors and windows to make a room; it is on its non-being that the utility of the room depends. Therefore turn being into advantage, and turn non-being into utility.

—Lao Tzu

I clutched at straws and took "non-being as utility" to heart, not only my non-being, but loving non-being.

Time's what I had, an illusion.

In the not-distant past, everything fit me, every act apposite to Zeke, but I disowned that, after breaking apart, seeing only darkness, forced to move invisibly.

The invention of God, in my legend, falls under "species

grandiosity." "God" achingly suggests people's desire for perfection, rooting idealism in mysticism, the supernatural, spiritual. But even God felt lonely and created humans in his image, which is the way humans brought themselves into the picture. (God must be more than human and also human, if we are in his image.) He brought forth his only son. A human God, the Christ (Pharaohs were also considered gods): people could identify with Him; be resigned to a mortal life of suffering, since they could see themselves in Him, who suffered, also, and for them, which made them Christ-like; even life's end or punishment, death, might be bearable, because He had died for them, and they would join Him, sit beside their Lord in heaven. No narrative has a better ending.

Who would die for me? Kidding.

Few want to die, though people also take their own lives, rather than being taken, destroyed psychically, and suicide becomes a singular ambition, whose successful completion alleviates pain, and everything else. Something to live for.

"To my dear friends and chums," a man called Michael wrote, "it has been wonderful and at times it had been grand and for me, now, it has been enough." This was his obit for a *New York Times* listing. He took his life and, obviously in advance, paid for it to be announced.

> Your picture hangs in a forest. Where you are is
> a fine place. Take me. Of psychic occurrences,
>     imperfect knowledge.
> My pleasures, unseen, silent.
>                                         —Ezekiel H. Stark, for Clover

## BEWILDERING, BLISTERING

You imagine other people have it together. Wrong. Oh, man, totally wrong.

Living is a bewilderment. Maybe I can't explain this. But doubt isn't anthropology's subject. Conflict, maybe. How do societies live with doubt, how do we and they manage uncertainty. It's a subject I could study, why not, aren't I my best subject, I doubt myself, not meaning to, life handed it to me on a platter—kidding—feel it constantly—doubt— and people doubt me. Rational people who want to succeed in life do not show doubt to others, and mostly don't apologize.

I'm ready to apologize for things I haven't done or said.

ANALYST: Who would you apologize to, first?
ME: I haven't got a list.
ANALYST: (silent)
ME: You know.
MORE SILENCE.
ME: Maggie.
ANALYST: Why?
ME: I probably pushed her away by things I said. Or didn't . . .

ANALYST: You think you could have changed how things
   went.
ME: I could have changed me. Early on. I wasn't . . . I wasn't
   something. Enough.
SILENCE.
ME: I failed her.


Some people have always doubted me, or been wary. First, I
was a brainy nerd a little before it turned cool or nearly cool.
I found a way not to doubt myself, not to double think, until
a floor dropped out of me. My bottom, ha. No basis, no foundation. No woman, no cry. (Father played that LP a lot.) That
realization about the ubiquity of uncertainty—can't explain
it, exactly—it forced me to consider the absurdity of learning
about others, I mean, anyone, and going "into the field" to
study them. Any field, no field has a level playing field.

   I mean, what do "I" expect of "them"?


## CO-INCIDENT

I received a phone call, and heard two men talking to each
other. There were other voices, fuzzy, in the background. It
was an old-timey party line or a crossed line.

   I said, "I'm on the line, did you phone me?" They kept
talking. I called out, "I can hear you. Can you hear me?"
Nothing, they kept talking. Muttering. I heard, "Asshole."
Then, "He should have buried it." They were talking some
strange shit. If it had been ordinary, I would have hung up.

One said, She didn't do it. Another said, Hell, you mean she still has it. The first one, Yeah, she has it. OK, the second voice said, we'll get it from her. Then, several more "asshole"s. Something about "produces mold."

The line went fuzzy, and I heard several clicks. Mutterings. In the past, I would have ignored it, but now everything that happened fit into a growing trouble set. A growth industry. Doubt Writ Large.

To disguise my old self from my new self—see, if I didn't, I'd be tempted to return to the rut—I deliberately embraced erroneous ideas, fleetingly, then dropped them, to traipse after ephemera and wishes. I didn't believe in stuff like the world is flat or deny climate change. I wore the ephemeral. We're ephemeral, right. I'm worn out. Ha. OK, this stuff doesn't lead me anywhere, but I don't need a direction, a goal. I choose the irrational from a rational position. I'm positioning myself on Undo, undo even undoing. Un-think, because routines dull the mind, and you don't see what's in front of you. Familiarity breeds contempt, and also lack of in-sight and out-sight.

Same old. Same old. Imagine if every time you entered into something, experience actually counted.

The second time around in love: I don't buy it. But I want love with a different result from the first time. Love as an experiment with a pure result.

I'm a picture to myself, a mental image; but when I look in the mirror, I don't know that person. Analyst says that's dissociation. I don't know him.

I could love anyone, anything. I love an image, big deal. Who cares, really, who gives a fuck.

It wasn't just, whatever you think it is, I said to my

analyst, I feel Clover, I didn't just "project" her into being. Sure, transference, that was on the table, and the couch, and it's what love is, anyway. I fell in love with an essentially always unavailable woman, the image of a beloved.

ANALYST: Does Clover love you? Can she?
ME: It doesn't matter.
SILENCE.
ME: She makes me happy.
ANALYST: It doesn't matter that you can't hold her in your arms.
ME: Is that a question or comment?
ANALYST: A question.
ME: In my dreams.
ANALYST: Those are dreams.
ME: So what. That's what we analyze. There's truth there. Right?

It was a mind game, and it wasn't.

I had time, right, I had it, and didn't have it. I discovered how to leave love and find it again, we find what we need. I found someone who is not actually there, I saw her right in front of me. OK, I'm in love with an image.

Mother says, when you're yourself again, you won't think this way.

I don't buy that there's a self waiting for me to return to or become, that is some old-timey shit. They split the atom, right?

I don't know. Love has an object, it is something, it has quiddity, totally, but the more I felt myself or feel myself not Maggie's other, the less I believe in romantic love or that it is or was the only way to love, the only way of passion. I'm not talking about robots, dummie-substitutes, cybersex. It's here, that love also, and this society is in transitions of all kinds. Everyone's creeped out by this, but I don't know. I don't see obvious, conclusive harm. People can come together to have babies, shop them out, get them from donors or from machines. Life is brought into life, artificially. And, love doesn't have to play or be gamed the way it's been for the last 500 years. Romantic love grew into wanting to be with someone forever, all of that. That could be over. It didn't start out "romantic." Except, will people ever be secure enough to live without a net? Probably not. Drugs might help that along, offer a false sense of security—is there any other kind?—singing lullabies to the brain. To feel content, to have it all pleasant, in the maniacal face of loss.

Zeke's new MO: All love is substitution.

In ethnography, as in life, I now believe we find what we look for, not in a good way.

Accept all substitutions.


## I BECOME A DOMESTIC SPY

Oh, man, even if I explained my motives for becoming an ultra-low-level domestic spy, I'd be skimming the surface. I won't say when I did this gig, act as an agent for the U.S. Post Office, or why. It came from somewhere in me, this need,

OK. I was stale, and pissed about everything—including lost mail, like Florida grapefruits sent to me for Xmas that vanished inside the post office—line-standing, the incompetence and stupidity of my post office station, I could go off at any time about anything.

It began innocuously, but I was inoculated. Ha. I received an official letter from the USPS in D.C., asking me to cooperate in a study "about making the postal system better." To help in their "collection efforts" (domestic spying). My duty involved telephoning a special # to record the mail I received, using their code numbers; the # of pieces in any day, and the exact date I received the test mail, as the USPS called it. If I didn't know the date it had arrived—let's say, I had been away for two days—there was a problem: that particular test mail wouldn't count. I couldn't approximate, I had to know for sure, and be honest, honesty is usually wasted effort; so I was, because I wanted to nail the USPS and I wouldn't need to lie to do it. Mail came almost every day, all kinds of envelopes. I had to phone a telemarketing firm, with my agent number, punching it in or speaking it into the machine; I'd get a recorded message and answer the simple questions, pressing #1 or #2; but sometimes there were additional problems, like my having been away for more than two days, when I was supposed to have let them know two weeks in advance if I were going away. I didn't live that way, I often didn't know my comings and goings until I went and returned. Then my uncertainty about a letter's actual delivery date forced me to speak with an actual person, because there was a problem, and it wasn't straightforward. If I called after midnight, when I came home from a club or bar, it was more complicated.

The mail had by then actually arrived the day before, so instead of pressing #1 for Today, I had to hit the keys for yesterday's date, which meant I had to know the date. I didn't sometimes, or it was physically hard to press the keys, it was a long night, maybe my eyes weren't focusing right. It was easier just to press the #1 key for Today. But that meant every night I needed to get home before midnight; often I couldn't or forgot, and then there was that annoying end-of-day duty I'd voluntarily pledged to do. It was a simple job anyone who could read, hear, and count could do, but after two years I'd had it; being civic-minded and responsible was a drag. Civil servility, for zip. The post office will never get better. It's over. Old technology. It can't compete, and it wasn't built to compete. And, it's not environmentally friendly. But the loss of post office stations can destroy neighborhoods.

Agents had to return the test mail every few weeks, which required going through piles of mail and finding the right pieces to check off from the list, and place those pieces in the envelope. Bad mail waited to be purged, and I needed to shred irrelevant documents, or disguise them. Shredding takes too much time, so I'd spill ketchup and mustard all over the mail. I don't think Richie or any other of the mail carriers surveilled the garbage cans (maybe suspicious supers); but if someone was checking the cans, he/she wouldn't want to get messed up. That's what I counted on, propriety, staying clean, but I didn't really appreciate desperate acts then. Also I couldn't return the test mail from my own zip code. They'd already mailed us agents self-addressed stamped manila envelopes, folded inside smaller ones, so everything was disguised, people's names, mailing addresses from FL, MN, England, all fakes; but they were uniform, same names and addresses every time. I could tell exactly what was what, so the demented civil servants in our mail-disaster station could too.

I'm not a suspicious-looking character, trained by my status-wary parents to blend in, and also I learned how from Mr. Petey. T-shirt or long sleeve shirt, black jeans, dark jacket, voluntary uniform. When I was required to carry mail into another zip code zone, I became aware, one, of how many mail carriers there are; and, two, that any border crossing, inner or outer, is a fragile divide, invested with power or not. And intentions are no cover story. I became sensitive to how I might appear to others; crossing over, I slowed down, like, this is hyperbolic, walking through Nothing to Declare at customs, and wondering What is Something to Declare? Then in that second, that delay, I knew I was betraying what I did feel guilty about that could get me stopped, like in a shrink's office when you stop, hitting right zap on the nexus of the hang-up. I haven't been stopped at customs recently, not since I was twenty and had no knowledge about the treachery of border crossings.

Often, no agents are standing around Nothing or Something to Declare, because FBI or Interpol have done their work before: you're on a list, and would have been stopped earlier. Supposedly. Ends up: no one's there. Still, I'm guilty about something, and get shaken. Not stirred. Ha. Right, I'm expecting to be caught for something, whether my name registers on their screens or not. I'm expecting to be taken away for something I haven't done, something that is not on my person, no plants, meat, drugs, nothing but my burden of guilt.

Totally ready to confess.

Get past customs, and all these strangers are standing, eager, anxious, waiting. Boom, fluorescent lights, expectant faces—could it be YOU after twenty years?—you're parading on a catwalk in a human being fashion show. I'll take that one; no, that one's not right. Nope, that's more like him.

Reporting on the USPS, its failures: I wanted this urban adventure, not about sex, drugs, rock and roll, etc. Done and done again. Overdone. Being an agent felt clean and dirty, but I was undercover. I wanted to feel worthy about something. I'd started watching spy movies incessantly, after the betrayal, so that was going on also. Media assists! I'd been set up to be crushed, because there had been such an emphasis on loyalty in my clan, but Clarissa betrayed me, and Father—he wasn't a loyal man. He was selfish, loyal only to himself.

In my mind, now I was acting like a "man." I wasn't terrified of anthrax on my mail. My post office had been shit way before I moved into the zip code, maybe before the WTC was built, that far back, and those times were better, Father said, the sixties, the parents told me stories about their time, and they told me I would have mine. Maybe their time was better, but it was also worse, four major assassinations in five years: JFK, Malcolm X, Martin Luther King, Jr., RFK. And others, right. Fred Hampton.

Long live rock and roll, rock on.

I'm living in my time with their time's traumas. Those murders are all mixed up in American minds, mushy minds contracted into dumb knots, numb nuts from Hell. Oh, snap, the feminists caused it! Black power! The pill! You don't feel the trauma, it hits again with new terrible events, the shock returns, but it's wearing a mask, and you don't know what has hit you.

Oh, man, the contradictions, the paralysis.

I was bothered, worried, that Richie, my sharp mail carrier, might find out. Richie: a put-upon black guy whose wife left him with their baby boy. Richie could find out what's up, because he cared about delivering the mail, not dropping it on the street, then trashing it. He might scope out the situation, figure I wanted to nail him: my intention was never to rat Richie out, whatever he may think now. It was and is the system. OK, this volunteer spy job, ridiculous. My buddies dismiss volunteer work. They didn't know about this project. And other stuff I was doing. Am doing. I bet their secrets would repulse me.

I am frolicking in failures other than my own. I'm no visionary. I like ruins. I am a ruin. I'm experimenting with un-reality, and I like it.

No matter what, I performed my agent tasks: report the number of pieces of mail received and the dates they appeared in my mailbox. Phone a number and answer an automated voice's queries. Walk outside, wearing what I wear, to return the appropriate test mail in an alien zip code.

On a particular day, though nothing weird about it, late fall, sunny with a chill, I came home from teaching, and opened one of the coded USPS envelopes, with a familiar address, a small city of Massachusetts I knew well. As I said, nothing was supposed to be in it except the codes I needed to report, how many pieces, and the date. Occasionally a postcard arrived. This day, about a year after doing undercover work, I opened a square, greeting card–like envelope, and there were words inside and not a code and numbers. In plain handwriting: "The way to heaven."

I was expecting something like this, this kind of message, and naturally, or natural to me, I wondered what was the way to heaven. I mean, not exactly a celestial wherever, but could it be that I was closer to heaven, or happiness. Or that it was coming toward me. I'm not ashamed of my interpretations. Was I knock knock knocking on heaven's door, was my luck about to change, big time.

Nothing happened in my mailbox for a while, but I gave hard looks, hopefully inscrutable, to the mail carriers. Seriously, they know where I live. Except our street doesn't have a regular carrier anymore, since Richie retired, and now the carriers and their routes vary, constantly. The post office doesn't want us to get close to our civil servants; it objects to our having a relationship with them. But UPS, that's different. That company, staffed by people in brown who often are, chooses friendly characters, who know our names, and they're a private company. OK, they want to make a profit. Right. But I think this is weird—we citizens aren't encouraged to feel close to a government worker. I mean, if the government wants its people to "trust it," wouldn't it make sure that we knew our mail carriers' names and we had a friendly vibe, a relationship? This won't ever happen. In the meantime, capitalists understand the uses of trust better. In God we trust not. Really.

Sometimes I needed to go to the post office, which I don't like to do anymore, I used to like it, because of the crazy convos happening on line, but now—who knows what might break out. The civil servants don't serve. Mostly there's no one at the windows. Institutional sloth, and madness.

One time the line was moving, oh, man, it was moving,

whoosh, and I spotted the manager on the floor, a fake-friendly type, and said to her, "Wow, the line's really moving today." She looked toward the cage where a guy was working, then at me, and said, purposefully, "Oh, him, yeah, he likes to work fast."

He LIKES to work fast.

She said it as a challenge, to me. A jaw-dropping interaction right there.

I never saw that dude again, never, not even once behind the cage. They got rid of him, because he made them all look bad. That's not civil service. That's uncivil service.

ANAYLST: You once told me about a frightening experience in a post office.

ME: Yeah. I was a kid, I freaked out about a poster of teenage robbers.

ANAYLST: Yes.

ME: That's ridiculous.

Identity theft and hoaxes, that wasn't happening in Mother's day. If Father was alive, he'd probably say, It's your time now, Zeke. Oh, man, say it ain't so.

Hoaxers now devise sophisticated traps to dupe old, fragile, lonely, needy people, or people who lack thrill and want to feel special. A celebrity writes you an email, and says you are known to her or him, Wow, a star knows you! They know you will understand that they require secrecy and privacy, and then this mega-star reveals her- him-self, and the bait is dropped, the hook sinks into a vulnerable psyche. Oh, I want to be noticed by a star, because that means I'm a star too. Oh, we the people are fucked. Thousands of suckers are baited every second. And those robo calls, no end to deception, no end to deceivers.

Remember that saying, It takes all types. Does it?

Another kind of viral hoax is benign, jokes or urban tales. The first I remember landing in my inbox was about a man who went to a hotel and was staying for a while:

Dear Maid,

Please do not leave any more of those little bars of soap in my bathroom since I have brought my own bath-sized Dial. Please remove the six unopened little bars from the shelf under the medicine chest and another three in the shower soap dish. They are in my way.

Thank you,

S. Berman

Dear Room 635,

I am not your regular maid. She will be back tomorrow, Thursday, from her day off. I took the 3 hotel soaps out of the shower soap dish as you requested. The 6 bars on your shelf I took out of your way and put on top of your Kleenex dispenser in case you should change your mind. This leaves only the 3 bars I left today which my instructions from the management is to leave 3 soaps daily.

I hope this is satisfactory.

Kathy, Relief Maid

Dear Maid—I hope you are my regular maid.

Apparently Kathy did not tell you about my note to her concerning the little bars of soap. When I got back to my room this evening I found you had added 3 little Camays to the shelf under my medicine cabinet. I am going to be here in the hotel for two weeks and have brought my own bath-size Dial so I won't need those 6 little Camays which are on the shelf. They are in my way when shaving, brushing teeth, etc.

Please remove them.

S. Berman

Dear Mr. Berman,

My day off was last Wed. so the relief maid left 3 hotel soaps which we are instructed by the management. I took the 6 soaps which were in your way on the shelf and put them in the soap dish where your Dial was. I put the Dial in the medicine cabinet for your convenience. I didn't remove the 3 complimentary soaps which are always placed inside the medicine cabinet for all new check-ins and which you did not object to when you checked in last Monday. Please let me know if I can be of further assistance.

Your regular maid,

Dotty

Dear Mr. Berman,

The assistant manager, Mr. Kensedder, informed me this a.m. that you called him last evening and said

you were unhappy with your maid service. I have as-
signed a new girl to your room. I hope you will accept
my apologies for any past inconvenience. If you have
any future complaints please contact me so I can give
it my personal attention. Call extension 1108 between
8 a.m. and 5 p.m. Thank you.

    Elaine Carmen

    Housekeeper


Dear Miss Carmen,

    It is impossible to contact you by phone since I
leave the hotel for business at 745 a.m. and don't get
back before 530 or 6 p.m. That's the reason I called
Mr. Kensedder last night. You were already off duty.
I only asked Mr. Kensedder if he could do anything
about those little bars of soap. The new maid you as-
signed me must have thought I was a new check-in
today, since she left another 3 bars of hotel soap in my
medicine cabinet along with her regular delivery of 3
bars on the bathroom shelf. In just 5 days here I have
accumulated 24 little bars of soap. Why are you doing
this to me?

    S. Berman


That's cool, right, no one hurt, but the one about Richard
Gere and the gerbil up his ass, pre-Internet, persisted, an ugly
urban legend. Even one of my friends called and said, "My
friend's mother works at Cedars-Sinai in LA, she's in ad
min, and it's true, because Gere came in for . . ." Overnight,
the joke disappeared. Maybe that's when Gere became a

Buddhist. But you can't say "gerbil" to a certain population without Gere being remembered.

You don't know wassup. You can't be sure. Symbiosis awry, human parasitism, unembarrassed narcissism, this is an arena ripe for ethnographers: study the hoax, hoaxers, hoaxees, understand the reasons societies develop them. Their purposes, how they serve, for example, is it anything like the purposes jokes serve?

Some long scams nurture weak egos, then take them down. Others, the kind I was subjected to, worked off greed, and, with variations, all used the long con that is performed by big-concept grifters.

For example, I received a business letter. An actual letter. It provided a company name and London telephone number, but no address.

Dear Ezekiel Stark,

I am Martin Toynbee, the managing partner of Toynbee & Toynbee, my subject David Stark died in testate, his wife and children with him in the tsunami of 2003. He has left $6,860,000, and I decided to contact you on the personal conviction of trust and confidence to assist in distribution of the money left behind by my late subject. My proposition to you is to seek your consent and cooperation to present you as a relative/next-of-kin and beneficiary of my late subject. This will be executed under a legitimate arrangement that will protect you from any breach of law. If this business proposition offends your moral values, do accept my apology. I hereby use this opportunity, asking you to exercise Utmost indulgence to keep this matter/proposal private.

I received another request a month later, from a different "solicitor," both in 2010, both from London. Of course, I thought back to my time in London, when I was like a dead man walking, and thought back to the people I hung with, and wondered, but then I decided it was worse: it was a random attack.

The second letter had no letterhead, no company name. In its "proposal," my putative dead relative, should I like to claim him, had lived in China.

That wasn't the end.

I received a handwritten letter from a London address, about someone searching for me, a relation of mine, the letter said, but who was no longer of this world. That intrigued me. I kept myself from answering it, for a while, anyway.

"No longer of this world." Someone did have my number. Would I go for it? It might be true.

The stuff got progressively more hardcore. This was addressed to me:

I am working in a detective agency. My name is not important now. I want to warn you that I'm going to watch you and monitor your telephone line. Do you want to know who paid for shadowing you? Expect my next letter. Probably, you don't believe me. But I think that the attached record of your telephone conversation will assure you that everything is real. The record is in archive.

The password is 123qwe

We have a tape of your conversation
- important for your life
- Your phone is monitored
- attention
- You're being watched
- important
- We monitor your privacy
- I'm monitoring you
- important information
- We're watching you
- Danger

This seemed like a practical joke, a silly scam in the age of scams. But added to the other letters, this accumulation, man, might be important evidence, or evidence of a societal shift, or even evidence of no evidence. I mean, it might be nothing, or it might be something. It's got my name on it, literally, and, personally, this IT or NOTHING came for me and added to the significance of the unaccountable variety.

"Your phone is monitored." Right, that crossed line, weird phone call, I'd heard clicks. But why me. Still, why not me. I mean, why anything is anything or anyone, and there's an entire novel range and variety of cruelty. People will do anything for a stupid high. People do the same old with new toys dressed up in new rags, OK, and work the same routines. Artists are people who hope not to do what everyone else is doing, and usually end up doing it. That first human-like character, that eternal question mark, the one who made the first mark, who first scratched on a wall: What was its origin in the early human brain, that impulse? Mark-making, painters call it. Evidence of life in front of a canvas. Photography, not that way, only about other-ing, marking that others are there, or a place, I am here, looking at it, or you, and I'm not you. I can't be you, see, I'm holding a camera.

Make a mark, or be one

I held on to the communication. You never know. White House intern Monica Lewinsky kept the blue dress with President Clinton's sperm stain on it. You never know when you'll need backup.

I was being bamboozled, targeted, and, one day, I quit spying for the USPS. Bad juju. I kind of believed they'd try to keep me on, and coax me to stay, but my handler ho-hummed, and yeah-yeahed, after I explained I needed to stop—for health reasons—which he didn't even question. Pissed me off, my insignificance obvious.

As compensation, they sent me a USPS T-shirt, and thanked me for my service to the government. Wear it, and blow my cover. Half-kidding.

No one knew about my gig, and never would, even though I received a Certificate of Appreciation, with a government seal, for being a "valuable federal agent," no revealing even that honor. Kidding. Plus, the USPS sent me first class and airmail stamps, two one-hour telephone cards, which can come in handy if your phone crashes, and a plastic letter opener with a motto just above its razor-edged blade: HELP-ING THE USPS GET BETTER EVERY DAY. The letter opener enticed the opening of letters, but mine are mostly bills or charity requests, and don't contain secrets. Getting a letter in an envelope, especially handwritten, not asking for $$, is a souvenir of antiquity, a fragment of a Greek vase in your mailbox.

My image of being a secret agent made me feel a bigger me, but more, the image I composed for me from this secrecy, this actual, bona fide ridiculousness, made me feel better. I know it's really idiotic.

What do you want? I know I want things, something, not material things, but I have been living around materialists, who accumulate, and they seek status, and don't know it. It can rub off, it can begin to affect you, you need to get away. I did. Hide away in a cave, with wifi. Haha.

I live a private life. But what is private.

## LOOK IN A REARVIEW MIRROR, THE END IS CLOSER THAN IT APPEARS

> O my soul, do not aspire to immortal life, but exhaust the limits of the possible.
> —Camus, quoting Pindar, in *The Myth of Sisyphus*

The world turns, returns, damaged, renewed, and, say, art is what some people do before death, its own thing. Life happens unconsciously, then imperceptibly, incrementally, consciously, it begins to add up, seems to be something, something of your own, and then there are circumstances producing consequences, and they show up, subtly, or blow up in sudden, horrifying ways: Hiroshima and Nagasaki. Your mother is murdered. Your husband has left you.

Few recognize what's happening, as it occurs. Except visionaries.

It's a new day that dawns long after it's new. To feel surprise is surprising to me. The unexpected can't be expected, but it's coming.

My memory is a little messed up. I phoned home because that's what I do. I have always kept in touch with Mother, even when I cracked up in London, I let her know I was alive—I think the German painter called her also—she championed me in her unique way. The last time I called her, or the time before last, Little Sister answered.

I'm Tilda, Zeke. Don't call me Little Sister.

OK, I said. Hi, Tilda.

She'd been reading Virginia Woolf's diaries. Mother had all of them. Tilda quoted: "Madness is the least of my sensations."

Madness was a family thing. Nothing unusual.

That's cool, I think I said. What are your most sensations?

I was kidding around, not expecting anything.

She said, You guys just see patterns. My feelings are mine. Secret.

I go something like, Very funny, you know I keep your secrets.

She changed the subject or handed the phone to Mother. I can't remember exactly.

Two weeks passed, I think, anyway, sometime later, Mother phoned. "Little Sister took her life."

I flew to Boston, rented a car, drove home, a familiar now unfamiliar ride, and all of us were gathered there. Bro Hart, his CIA wife. Clarissa. Family friends. Mother said she was glad Father wasn't alive. This was the second time I heard Mother cry.

Mother found her in her bedroom with the many windows.

I often speculated about the maternal line, suicide, and mental illness, it was abstract.

Little Sister was a mystery, from when she was small, but she was our mystery, we were used to her, nothing about her seemed strange, to us. She was just quiet.

I returned to that "Way to Heaven" letter. Maybe Little Sister had been telling me, warning me: she was going to leave this world for the next. Maybe she was doing what artist Ray Johnson did. For a year, he sent odd, cautionary, and oblique postcards to friends, but he was a "correspondence artist." His death cards may have been stranger, but they fit a pattern. Even anathemas align when evidence shows a pattern.

She said I saw patterns. She didn't like that. Why?

Not saying I don't sometimes cut along the dotted line. I liked big scissors cutting fabric pinned to a translucent pattern, following blue lines. I liked our butcher's cutting meat, neatly. I suppose that makes me a horrible person.

The other's suicide causes an eruption of DULL HUGE EMPTINESS, a pneumatic drill of dumb thoughts: Unbelievable. Unacceptable. Unanswerable. Futile, rhetorical. When did she decide. Why. How could we have not seen it. Mother aged overnight, totally I thought she could die of heartbreak.

ME: I talk too much, like Little Sister said. You let me talk. You encourage the worst in me. I'm kidding.

ANALYST: I don't think so.

ME: Don't think I talk too much?

ANALYST: Don't think you're kidding.

Sick weeks passed, months, time, time again, until I watched myself in a dream, writing on a piece of paper, I didn't know what I wrote down. I stopped and looked. is/was is/was is/was is/was is/was is/was is/was is/was is/was is/was . . . Mother was nearby, and I shouted, "Mother, life is a verb. First, Is; then, Was." You're here; then you're not, that's the deal. Life is the in-between, that's it.

The dream felt so cold.

Little Sister's dead. I shake my head, forget, lose it, then IT would rise against my wish to return to the past before it. I relived her life through mine, going through the photo albums. I didn't look through her things, I didn't allow myself, not yet. Mother kept her room as it was. Life stopped in that room. I was afraid to see it. That's true.

Her life ended, mine looped backward. "Madness is the least of my sensations." I felt mad once, after Maggie, a buzz, a scrambling in the brain, mind-implosions, not able to control thoughts crashing into each other, a terrible sound inside I couldn't stop, not any of it.

Friends called her suicide a tragedy. In my demented academic brain, I'm thinking, Not in the classical sense. Where's the hubris and fall? The inevitability? In her mother's genes? Me too, I've got them.

Tragic accident, a grave mistake, she lost her way, went off the track. Little Sister left a letter—a suicide note, they're called—for Mother, and she wrote it was better this way, she blamed no one. She even thanked her. I can't believe it, no blame, good to the end, but her end was bad, and no good comes from bad. Someone said that.

I repeat, repeat, a death is repetitive in its effects, though it happens differently, it's always the same, and those who are left behind tell the same stories until memory fails. No one gets out alive.

A leap into the abyss, people say almost as an obligation, especially if the suicide is a jumper. The abyss.

## DEATH CUSTOMS

People don't live death or experience the oncoming of death, in the same way, with the same intensity; if we did, we couldn't go on, right. We don't feel the same about everyone who dies, even someone we were tight with years before, he dies, you've been out of touch, and hear about the death, and usually it's a "That's sad," a memory or two, and you're out of there. Otherwise, we'd be continually wailing and mourning. Life would be all mourning, all the time. An idealist might say: war would come to an end. Anyway, imagine: you FEEL more for the anonymous. You'd FEEL the same for others you feel for those you love. "Those you love" makes me sick. Your life becomes greater than your little plot (pun intended).

I'd believed: Little Sister was contained. What she contained destroyed her. I never thought she was unreasonable. I try to be conscious of her, but she's gone. Still, my activity is consciousness, compared with Little Sister's; that is, it's how I am different, but it doesn't matter. Her death should make my life different. I should become accountable for something. That's what I told myself. Those words became a drive, I was engulfed, inevitably, though, by me being who I was, anyway. I couldn't mean anything different, not after a while.

Many very early societies believed, and there must be some that still do, that death is unnatural, that dying was not in the original order of things. Just like in the Western tradition, people wrote myths about the beginning, genesis, when we lived in a garden, in a bounty of life without death, and then fucked it up. People were meant, in some cultures, to shed their skin like a snake, and stay young and alive, and, if they didn't shed it, they would die. Death began for one culture when a woman didn't shed hers. This could relate to facial surgeries and procedures. In many ancient, early societies, they believed in the renewal of life through the renewal of skin. This society does, though supposedly we realize facelifts and derma-peels don't prolong life. But that's just reason, which is nada.

I shaved my head, as a sign of mourning. But I looked like any balding or completely bald guy. I thought of marking my face, like the Sioux, but that seemed too obscure or post-punk. I wanted to display for the public, I'M MOURNING, I'M IN GRIEF. Couldn't use an obscure language, another society's codes would be misunderstood, what with tattoos prevalent. I settled on a black armband. I suppose I don't have to explain how that got misread.

Intellectuals and academics read for assurance: of the worthiness of reading, for one thing, and thinking, ideas, life of the mind (see Coen brothers' *Barton Fink*). I reread Freud's "Mourning and Melancholia," *Civilization and Its Discontents*, "Thoughts for the Times on War and Death." The death drive: an unconscious wish for stillness, entropy. Consciously, suicide to end anguish. I read about a suicidal person's moment of decision, when, people who are living say, she makes her decision, feels calm, relieved, even happy. People who really want to die find a way. I watched *The Big Lebowski* again and again and again. I reread *Madness and Civilization*.

Mother told me about a psychoanalyst who hated Freud,

and he seduced his patients. When he was found out, he killed himself. Clarissa's friend took her own life because she was in debt, and shamed by it.

I read that suicide is homicide, the other way around.

I totally see that. Because depression is anger turned inward, my analyst said. So suicide is homicide turned inward, homicide is suicide turned outward. In the past, if you were mad, you were put away and the family shut down to the public. No one cares now. I mean, some people don't want other people to know there's a breakdown, or suicide in the family. But it's ordinary. Secrecy is becoming an antique constraint. Victims and survivors often do tell-alls.

Dishonor, defeat, failure: people expect to be exculpated, or they don't care, and public appearances satisfy the public's gaping maw.

From the burning Twin Towers, men and women jumped out of windows to escape death by fire, to another kind of death, but did any have hope for survival, to be caught, somehow? That God might intervene.

There are survivors of everything, each survival is different. Surviving what, and surviving for what, that's something else. When does the survival gene get switched off? A trauma can do that.

The ordinary is as much an accident as the extraordinary.

> Out beyond ideas of wrongdoing and rightdoing,
> there is a field. I'll meet you there.
> When the soul lies down in that grass,
> The world is too full to talk about.
>
> —Rumi

This poem was painted, in block letters, on a wall at the hospice unit where Mother volunteered.

Hospice people put it this way: when people start leaving this world, they're "actively dying."

Mother says if I spent time caring for a person who's facing death, it might help me. Get out of this, feel differently, become a different person. She's serious. I'm thinking, hospitals breed disease.

She's been volunteering, for perspective, she told me.

I didn't want to know.

She bore Father's death well, that's what Clarissa kept saying then, she's bearing up, doing as well as can be expected, etc., palliative phrases, bromides.

Like a new project, Mother became very interesting to me. Who she was, if I could find out. Also, in analysis, she played a huge role. Of course, right.

I depend on or need a project, I include myself. I am one. Mother became one. The existence of Mother and Clarissa, the gen before me, had kept me from being the next to die. While they are alive, I wouldn't die. Mother would die sooner. An accident. Cancer. The natural order of things. But then Little Sister took her life, and the order of things wasn't natural.

It wasn't too long after Maggie split, and I split apart, that Mother wanted dying strangers to surround her. That's how I saw it. Their eyes recede, she told me, they stare at you, out of little death-pockets, and to comfort them, she sings to them, does what she can. They die, one after the other.

Mother wrapped herself in loss and soldiered on. She wouldn't kill herself, but further immersed herself in death, as if she'd meet her baby and only daughter on that plane, if she stayed on it. I think she blamed herself, but never said it.

Mother needs to feel useful, part of that Puritan thing. Keep busy, do good works. I guess I favor her. Death's part of life, she tells me, patiently. Hell, yes, I think. She tells me Buddhists believe you die twice. Your death, first, and then the second one comes after everyone who knew you dies. Then, it's as if you never existed.

You never existed.

Mother tells me it's her calling, Little Sister is calling her. We both live with ghosts.

If I let myself, if I let go of time or of the present tense in which I live, tensely, ha, I see Little Sister with Clover. Clover welcomes her into the truth of life after death. Corny, oh man, yes, they're inhabiting the spirit world, a special unembodied place, because they were suicides. Not Hell, where Dante would have put them, I wouldn't. Their hell was life, after a while, hell for Clover. I suppose Little Sister too. But I can barely let myself imagine hers. I knew her, alive. I never knew Clover as a living person.

Little Sister had a goth period, serious goth, black lipstick, blackened eyes, the look fit with her silences. Ironically funny now.

I contemplated a memorial for Little Sister, but I'd be walking Henry Adams's path, his memorial work for Clover. I found that a big problem.

Ultimately, or penultimately, I became curious about actual dying. Mother hooked me up with some hospice people.

The hospice nurse wasn't morbid like a funeral director:

You can take someone who's got cancer from top to

bottom, but then as soon as they're kind of dying from their cancer, you can still stick a tube down their throat and kind of put them on a ventilator and try to resuscitate them. The question is, just because you have the tools at your disposal, is it reasonable to apply them? And that's the only reason why a hospice referral is ever considered, sort of—what's the word I'm looking for? That's the only reason why we have to sort of think about this at all, is because there's always something you can do, and when is it smarter to actually shift the goals of care away from life prolongation and toward maximizing quality? Because most people, if you just talk to them kind of in the abstract, or even concretely, if you had a choice between living a shorter period of time with better quality of life versus a longer period of time in a life sustained by this and that treatment, and this and that hospitalization, most people will choose quality over quantity. But not everybody.

Death's door, in a hospice unit, isn't a metaphor, since once you walk through that door, or are wheeled in, though you might be kept going longer, usually you are.

At death's door, what would I want to know.

A nurse practitioner, who leads her hospice unit, talked to me about pain, psychic and physical, about who wants to die in pain, and why, and the misunderstandings about pain itself and the methods used to relieve it. Options play out differently for patients, the people around them, and professionals. Some patients view pain as a test of their personal strength. The beginning of the end of it: childbirth. Pregnant women bite the bullet to feel the pain, you know, natural childbirth. This authenticity shit has no limits.

Pass me the morphine. Please.

People can die quietly, with atropine, if their families let them. Atropine dries up their saliva, and then there's no death rattling, no discomfort for the dying.

There's psychic pain and physical pain.

The nurse told me: there's a huge fear of addiction, dying people are afraid of getting addicted, or their families are, for them. Your mom, an addict? Addiction is a question of brain chemistry, and the brain chemistry of addiction and the brain chemistry of pain relief are completely different things.

It's nuts, I say to Mother, later on, and she nods, calmly. Zeke, she says, why do you think people will be any smarter about dying than they are about living? But think about this, will you, just one hundred years ago, all medical care was basically palliative. Back in the day, there wasn't really anything anyone could do for anyone.

> The truth of an idea is not a stagnant property inherent in it. Truth *happens* to an idea. It *becomes* true, is *made* true by events. Its verity *is* in fact an event, a process, the process namely of its verifying itself, its veri*fication*. Its validity is the process of its vali*dation*.
> —William James

Things fell apart for me in several ways, and I won't count them, trust me.

Family photos in physical albums, gone, zip. No hidden treasures, only files on desktops, apps, and everything is deletable. Could be good, deleting all. Could be a positive change that so much possibility—possible possibility—makes hanging on to the past less important. Because a photograph proves nothing, it's incoherent, uninformative, inconsistent, undependable, though it is more than nothing, or "proof" of nothing. If a "document," it confirms movement toward the undecidable and inconclusive. As a form, you could say, actually, I'm saying, a photograph recognizes its own INCOHERENCE. In two centuries, the medium has evolved from claiming to be evidence, to representing a circumstance in life, to "being" no reality and only a perception or a condition from a subjective POV, to extinction of its humanist and enlightenment past. With digitization, possibilities multiply for what humanity can imagine itself as, which it might one day be or fulfill.

A photograph infers, doesn't confer.

Humans split the atom, but can't split themselves from their images.

"I love the activity of sound . . . sound that doesn't mean anything." —Cage

Pictures don't have to mean anything. Life doesn't have to. Deal with it. Face values. Time's an abstraction, but reality makes it mean.

Ezekiel Stark, former image investigator.

## MOVING FORWARD BACKWARD

I want never to forget forgetfulness, and then maybe I'll remember.

Mother is a spiritual atheist and I'm pretty sympathetic. She's even more committed to her ancestors, because Little Sister's with them, and feels closer to Little Sister, which comforts her.

Mother and I—"Mother and I" is a new construction—have become closer. Maybe I am different from any Zeke I've ever been, or maybe she didn't care to keep a maternal distance. Who was left, anyway. Me, Clarissa, Bro Hart.

She hardly ever talked about Father, hardly ever mentioned him, no telling of any little stories. That became weirder to me. She didn't remarry, so I assumed she still felt married to him, loved him, somehow. I asked her one night, when she was visiting my place, she visited me more, Little Sister gone, a bonus that made me feel guilty, actually, because it made me happy. I was a middle child, displaced by both ends.

I took Mother out to a great restaurant. I asked her. Did you love Father? No. I asked why she married him in the first place, why she stayed with him. She said something about the heart being a mystery, some shit like that. She changed the subject, somehow. I let her. I was sort of stunned, anyway. Then, she told me more, over time, things I didn't want to know, but that made sense in a way that I couldn't stand.

I knew she had lived in Frankfurt, Germany, for a year, when she went to study abroad, and she wanted to learn German, to read German philosophy, and she didn't want to go to Paris, which to her seemed like a cliché. She wanted to find herself. She'd always been a good girl. JFK's assassination shook her hard, but she didn't become a hippie.

The Vietnam War was building up, exploding. I didn't know that she had met an American guy, an enlistee. He felt it was his duty, he had dropped out of college. There they were in Frankfurt, fell in love, she was madly in love with him. They were together for six months, but he was going to Nam. He wasn't there long when he was killed. She never could love anyone again, after him, she couldn't.

OK, I didn't love my father, but Mother's not loving him seemed dishonest, hypocritical, unworthy. Right, I was being moralistic. She'd promised herself to him, so she thought I should understand that, given my feelings about Maggie, and my weird thing for Clover (as she put it, indelicately).

There's a nun-like thing about Mother.

She returned to the States, finished college, met Father during college, he was finishing law school, married him, because she wanted a family, children, and to work and get on with life. She never left that dead soldier. John. That was his name, she told me. His best friend, Rick, went to Nam with him, but Rick came back in 1968, headed straight to Amsterdam, to hang out and smoke hash, the way everyone did. Rick became a hippie ex-soldier, and some people hated him because he'd gone to Nam, some were OK, he was in a lot of pain, and no one understood. Rick moved on to heroin. He couldn't get enough, became homeless, then finally he couldn't get high. No one could put up with him anymore. He hanged himself in a park there.

Mother thought it could have happened to Johnny, if he'd made it out alive. She might never have gotten him back, anyway. She assured me my father never knew.

Mother said they had a good sex life. She said something

like he was affectionate. She admitted maybe he knew some-where, deep inside, but because of his drinking, it didn't mat-ter. "He was married to his Dewar's. But I tried to be a good wife."

I'm not angry and I am.

Mother's "trying to be a good wife" killed me, that the concept of goodness and a level of deception merged with self-abnegation. Her loneliness from pretense, and my father's not being loved, even though he was a shit, seriously depressed me. I don't know, it brought me back to whether Maggie ever loved me. All unhappiness is local. Even if Maggie did love me once, even if she returned and apologized, apologies come too late, brought by a misguided mail carrier. The letter's too late to count. No one enjoys reparations.

ME: Sex and love aren't the same, she said.
ANALYST: You've said that.
ME: OK. My mother shouldn't.

Listening to me talk was awful; I felt like an idiot, the gifted child failure. Feelings can be stupid. I was Mother's "adult child," which is what it's called these days, so I have to make the transition. People really believe they can move out of what they were and felt. Move it all, transition from grief to normal life, from one body to another, and most trivial, it's said: transition from one job to another.

In hospice, it is the big T, and, after T, NADA.

There's volunteering, believing you're a good person;

there's volunteering, knowing you're not. I'm in the second group. My conscience is transient, or relative, I hold a thought, an opposing thought, weigh them, and, even in a context it's hard to know what's right, ethically. I used to think Mother was more ethical than I could ever be.

People think they care; often, it's selfish, so that they can like themselves, or because they want to be cared for; religious maniacs care about what they care about, and go to hell if you don't. How do we talk to ourselves about our lack of caring? Blah blah, and we walk on by a slumped body on the sidewalk. Have to do it. Survival of the fittest. Otherwise, we won't get to our therapy appointment. OK, all too human and inhuman.

Caring gets produced by a system that makes caring what it is. Caring could have another form, shape. Trying to imagine another kind of caring . . .

No one wants to face death, though, except Mother and hospice people. They want to, all the time.

Mother hooked me up with the hospice's spiritual care counselor, Ralph. Our meeting was totally serious, humorless, so I couldn't be my usual self. Kidding. I wanted to know what was expected of a spiritual care counselor. I had absolutely no faith in any of that, so I was curious, maybe morbidly curious. Not kidding.

Mother wanted me to know Ralph, and I think I know why. He was much more grave than the nurse practitioner.

"A counselor is neutral in terms of different religions. Near death, there's the medical side, social side, the other dimension is the suffering of the patient, which is not amenable to their treatments. It's not precisely psychological, it's more transcendent than that. A person's relationships, with family, themselves, and with the transcendent, with God."

I didn't rebut God. Why bother when there is no God.

"The counselor helps the dying person to discern what suffering derives from their relationships. Because the dying have got more important things to do than die or think about their dying. How do you live what's left of your life to meet your needs and to meet your expectations?"

I said, But most people are afraid of dying. I am.

Ralph nodded with compassionate understanding, and I nearly lost it.

"Most people who are WELL are afraid of dying. There's an old saying, I think it's Plato, who had put it that young men fear death; old men fear dying. People near death tend to be much more focused on what happens before death and the process of dying than on what comes afterward. Somebody's dying of terminal cancer, say. The profession won't be surprised if they die within six months, sort of a negative definition. A near horizon for most people."

Near horizon, not vanishing point. Western Civ had reasons for its development. The unachievable became desirable: a vanishing point encourages viewers to seek what's always out of sight and beyond reach. It encourages ambition, and came about with the Renaissance, when artists got out of the religious business. A near horizon—a concept for a photographic effect.

Ralph told me that dying people often don't want their families to see them die.

"There was a young man under fifty, dying of cancer. He and his family were from Brazil, and we were finally able to find them. They came, and all gathered around his bed, for several hours. They left to make the final arrangements. He died before they got back. He waited until they were there, so he could say goodbye, or they could say goodbye. People are trying to make peace with themselves."

Mother wanted me to make peace with myself. Little Sister didn't give us a warning, though maybe she did, and none of us picked up on it. I need to be more forensic in my approach.

Doctors keep people alive, I say to Ralph, when they can't cure them, when they won't recover, but why can't they just die without pain. Just put them out of their pain.

"For doctors, death is the enemy, it's a failure. So, they're hostile to it. Hospice workers believe death is a normal part of human existence. But we suffer in different ways. Absolutely the key denial of a healthy society, a society of people who medically are healthy, is to deny death and deny suffering. We think suffering has no right to exist. But it has."

I stopped recording Ralph then, and sat in an empty lounge or waiting room, I was there a long time, after Ralph walked away, wondering about "suffering having rights." A promise to a dead person is weird, Mother's to Johnny, mine to Clover, OK, I get that. But it's how things operate. Present behavior is based on the wishes of the dead, or what we imagine they want. Nothing concrete, but something like an inborn version of legacy, a reason to continue, that incorporation. I owed Little Sister, I'd never given her anything, and I never promised anything. But we, or maybe I, had never allowed her a right to her suffering, to own it. Whatever that is, I mean, I can't exactly put a face to it, that right. We have a right to happiness, why not to suffering. The eleventh right.

Maybe the family tried too hard to erase Little Sister's pain, anguish, difference. Maybe if we dismissed it, she could. And that way we could alleviate our own suffering. I wish I could speak to her about it.

They cramp our style, rain on our parade. Don't want to bother too much with unhappy people. They don't want to help themselves, right. There are professionals to deal with them, oh yeah, and, if you volunteer, what's your problem, right, you must not have enough going on in your own glorious existence. Etc.

After Little Sister died, maybe six months later, Aunt Clarissa wrote me a letter, and I opened it with a kind of crazy pleasure, using my second USPS letter opener—THANKS! YOUR DAILY REPORTS KEEP US ON THE CUTTING EDGE. They sent it on the first anniversary of my retiring from domestic spy work, another gift. Ain't life grand.

I didn't actually want to read her letter, she'd always been so weird to me.

Dear Ezekiel,

I hope you know which wars are worth fighting. All your ancestors got you to this point and I thank them (gratitude) Allow your soul to heal (as you know every illness has an image). Examine the burdens you carry and try to get rid of what is unnecessary.

Your mother needs you. Yours, Clarissa

That was it. Her missive was at least a communication. Or at most. I wondered if she was telling me my life wasn't a total mistake, because that's how I wanted it to read. Or that it was, and now it was the time for me to get in line. Get with the family program. I wondered if it was her kind of apology.

I thought to send her some of my flawed, capsule narratives:

Ezekiel Stark, a skeptic in his field, was promising. He studied small groups or areas of cultural concern—family photographs, the basis of images, men. His dissertation pubbed by a university press, his gig in acadoomia was upped to associate professor. He walked the halls of academe, walked the line, talked the talk, and went by the book. He was a good enough colleague, if sometimes too aggressive when he thought he was right. He always seemed preoccupied. Sometimes he partied. Sometimes he was a hermit. He did his version of field work. He wrote papers, articles, books, he made a splash, and then he floated.

Or, Ezekiel Stark married young and loved his wife passionately, and she left him for his best friend (typical, right?) and he went mad. He fell under a spell, one way to put it, and broke down like an old car. He took a break, then carried on, unhappily, but functioning, as they say. When his baby sister took her life, this was the "peripeteia" he'd only read about, a sudden turn of events, the unexpected is never expected—her suicide. He thought: was it meaningful, could he make her life mean something, was it a wake-up call (more triteness). Nothing worked. So he took another longer leave.

Or, Stark entered psychoanalysis long ago, but he

occasionally opts out, and escapes self-reflection. He might say he is now dedicating his time to the god who heals, Asklepios. Also, he continues to investigate what can't be known, because the irrational is more powerful than the rational. Stark believes: It was her unconscious that took Little Sister, so it wasn't intended. He's more interested in the unknown realm of unreason than the world of reason.

Clarissa would like that, though more and more, as she ages, she doesn't recognize the boundaries between those realms.

In Little Sister's bedroom, Tilda's bedroom, in her walk-in closet Mother found some artwork, unsigned. Photographs of the family, of herself, some friends, male, female, other, and also pictures of words. Words singled out, cut from magazines, reshot and blown up. Words she liked or didn't. Used or didn't.

I didn't want to see her portraits of me, myself as she saw me. I didn't know she was shooting them. Plus, she never showed me any of her work. And I had never asked, a bridge I didn't want to cross or a question I didn't want answered, because YES or NO had its problems. Responsibility and rejection, in that order.

If I ever attempt more family image work, I might approach Tilda's art by broaching treacherous ground. Specifically, a photographer's disposition—the subject behind the camera toward the object—though this subject matter reeks of intentionality, almost an art crime.

I'm wondering about the effects of family resemblance: when an artist pictures a family member, what's the psychological impact of that family resemblance? What is resonant?

Is the image always a self-image/portrait, when the shooter resembles the poser, and projects into it?


## IMPROBABLE LIFE

After Uncle Lionel gave up the ghost, and I don't know who got his—kidding—on the way to the cemetery in a town about thirty miles from our family home, in a limo following the hearse, I had a weird sensation. I smelled an aroma associated with my kid-hood, I saw myself running in our backyard, Mr. Petey on the fence, and I lost myself for a while. Some town cars were following, snaking behind, headlights on. I'd never been in a funeral procession. Father said nothing. He wore dark glasses, so I guess he'd cried. Mother and Little Sister talked a little—Little Sister was crying. Closer to the open gates of the cemetery, the sensation intensified. Our car crawled to a stop at Lionel's grave site. The coffin was poised over the dark, empty rectangle, and two grave diggers, one old, one young, stood, both smoking, in the distance. Uncle Lionel had lots of friends, he was a cool guy, not like his younger brother; everyone gathered around, a minister stood up, began to read, and I wanted to bolt. Mother, sensing my restlessness, took my hand, and I couldn't. As soon as people had thrown flowers on his coffin, I wandered off, because I knew I would see Maisie's grave, I knew it would be near Lionel's, and I walked about thirty feet, and there it was. OUR DEAREST MAISIE. TAKEN TOO SOON. 1979–1985.

I touched the engraving, her name, the numbers, six years of life. I hadn't thought about her in a very long time. But I knew I'd meet her again, find her somehow. Then I walked back to Uncle Lionel's grave, sadder. The grave diggers were hovering. I stared at them, and wondered about how they came to be grave diggers, death's maintenance men. They looked glum, then they didn't, expressionless, or they were just workers. I kept watching them until my curiosity got to me. So I told them I was studying cultural anthropology, and was curious about how they'd become grave diggers. The younger one, who wasn't that young, said, "Joe Strummer, you know, the Clash, he did it in seventy-three, so I thought, why not try it." He turned away, laughing.

The older man told me his father did it. It was steady. He said, you get used to it. "I like it when families come back and put flowers on their graves." Then the two began shoveling soil over the coffin, and I looked down at what was Uncle Lionel in a wood box.

No alas poor Yoricks, no bonehead skull in hands, but I knew those guys would have some stories.

And, there came a time when I did, when I volunteered as a grave digger, for the hospice. I could attend funeral after funeral, and observe the bereaved, their behavior, the rituals. I thought I'd understand death better, death rituals, anyway.

Some people attending were distracted, some weeping, some couldn't stand up, some stalwart, the young wives and husbands stricken, very young children ignorant, playing; older ones looked confused, and often were crying. Some people couldn't leave the grave site, some couldn't get away fast enough.

When people threw themselves on the coffin, jumped into the grave beside the coffin, I hated it. It unsettled me in ways I couldn't understand, which is what's most unsettling.

Some hold religious services, with ministers of different

types. Most do something. A minority do nothing, some family members argue about who should speak, right over the coffin. Some carry flowers or pictures, which get buried with the dear departed. Pictures going with them is what—poignant, pathetic?

I wait along with the other grave digger until everyone splits, then we fill the grave with what's called backfill, pat down the fresh earth down until it's flat. A few people stay behind and watch a long time. That makes the job harder, their watchful eyes, whose meanings I can't know. They can't leave, the sobbing ones, slump over and need to be carried or held up. Next year, the bereaved spouse might remarry. Move on, or never move on. Mostly people do, though.

Being a gravedigger turned into routine work, fast, the way the old guy said. The thrill was gone. Half-kidding. Not exactly just like clocking in, but I adapted to it, became inured to it, the process, the grieving families. It must be like what a medical doctor feels, watching sick people and knowing the end is coming, that there's no hope. They step back. They adapt.

I became too detached, and felt it was unsafe to continue. But what is safe for someone like me. Unsafe at any speed.


## PEOPLE DO THEIR LIVES

Some people want to forget, just go on. Not me.

My speculation is that "never having to remember" will be an add-on for future brains. Memory implants will also be available, seem natural. The synthetic knowledge/memory servers or providers will first be expensive, then cheap. The ante will always go up. The lobe/region of the brain for memory will wither, turn into an atavism. (Like the appendix, it might erupt with infection—killer memories?) Learning will be moot. Chip in, chip out. Could be a good thing, but depends on who makes the chips and on their uses.

Security is the biggest problem, the way Etta James sang it, "I want some security . . . / Without it I'm at a great loss."

But why trust companies that promise security. "Are we not men?" Not kidding.

Without accrued memory, people won't have a conscience, remorse, or guilt, all of which depend upon memory-work. If it's not remembered, no one regrets a past bad, or good, act. Forget about it. Memorials and monuments will be built for a while, to assuage or prick conscience. But they'll be more instances of public hypocrisy, since, in the future, the dead won't be owed anything.

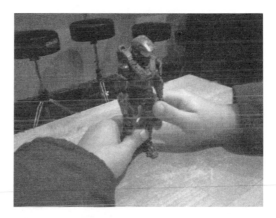

Me At The Magic House

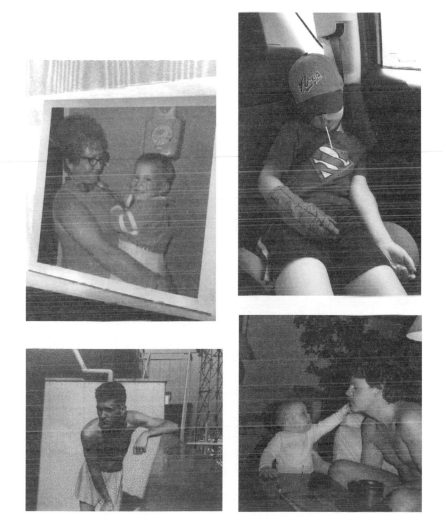

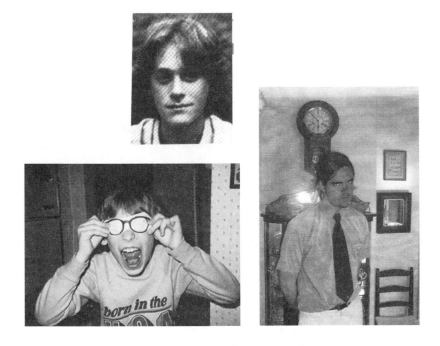

# MEN IN QUOTES

A Field Study

Ezekiel H. Stark

When I was a child, I spake as a child, I understood as a child, I thought as a child: but when I became a man, I put away childish things.

—1 Corinthians 13.11

Not where I live.

—EHS

Mick Taussig describes ethnographers as strangers. I'm a pro at strangeness and estranged-ness. And, E strangeness. Taussig doesn't see "us" as estranged, but as outsiders whose position helps us see what insiders can't. Best case version, in my view, Geertz, in *After the Fact*:

> To convey . . . what it is to be an anthropologist not off somewhere beyond the reach of headlines but on some sort of fault line between the large and the little, photographs are quite inadequate. There is nothing to picture . . . They marginalize what is central. What is needed, or anyway must serve, is tableaus, anecdotes, parables, tales: mini-narratives with the narrator in them.

So, I wanted to collect those, some of which Goffman would call "atrocity tales" or "circles of lament."

I began my project, MEN IN QUOTES, earnestly, knowing my department wouldn't go for it, which added a thrill, probably inspirational, and also I was close to taking the pause, or in their terms, a leave. Bye-bye!

Plus, the field work didn't require me to go off the reservation, since I was already living on it. Or off it.

## MAN UP / MANY DOWN

Ethnographers research the usual and unusual, normal and abhorrent, on the prowl for material, subjects, the true enchilada. With my tribe, sample, or posse, I'm a native informant as well as a researcher. I watch myself and similar beasts. I was a new man among new women, and we new men needed help, and Zeke to the rescue.

I was a privileged, educated fuck-up, semi-successful, part-demi-new man, a suitable subject for treatment. I wasn't looking for myself, not mirror images, either, but maybe to learn more about who this guy was, or thought he was, beside and with other New Men. Without presuming objectivity, I can remain inquisitive, skeptical, open, naïve, sophisticated, or D. W. Winnicott's "good-enough" observer.

To do my field work, which was among people I knew, I developed a survey with open-ended questions, and emailed it to my sample group. For the purposes of this report, I ganged together responses to questions, as if each of the guys was in the same room talking, say, at a local bar. They weren't. (But, in a larger sense, aren't we all in the same room talking, usually not listening?) I did one-on-one interviews, and taped them, also (as I did with hospice nurses and counselor).

My thrust: to observe and engage with my male peers as if studying an ethnic group or a tribe, a sub-subculture that also selected me, in which I'm also a member, and this in itself upends the subject/object dichotomy. I don't pretend I'm "just" an observer. In the field, ethnographers become engaged, entranced, involved, even entangled—to the extent they know where they stand and where the "other" stands; they can draw a perimeter, a boundary. They have a chance of maintaining distance, to "see" as outsiders the way Taussig has proposed, but . . .

My informants have anonymity, and, without naming them, they agreed to let me quote their stories and comments. To protect the innocent and guilty, I shift characteristics, and paraphrase remarks. Subjects will be identified by a number, which denotes nothing, not their place in an alphabetical list, etc. Pure randomness is impossible. I won't provide the usual categories—race, age, religion, etc.—alongside the number, because these tend, even subliminally, toward prejudicing reactions. Unfortunately and ineluctably, everyone bears internalized, imbibed culture, and society lives within and brings these to every thought, response, everything read, heard, seen, etc., filters reactions. Expectations about others are waiting, like the herpes virus, to strike.

My sample is comprised of indigenous (no exogenous) urban, self-identified men between the ages of twenty-eight and forty-five. All classes, putatively; class in U.S. is self-defined and labile. Various races, ethnicities, all major religions (plus Baha'i, pantheist, atheist, agnostic): ancestry and origin ranging from Vietnam, China, Africa, Europe, Latin and South America—majority, hyphenated Americans: all U.S. citizens, one naturalized. Mostly heterosexual men, since my interest has also to do with attraction between men and women. Two divorced, many married, or living with, dating, or single. One gay/queer man, two trans men. All daters use or have used dating apps, hookup apps, social sites, for sex, in one way or the other. (Lust is single-minded.) All have watched porn, some are regular users. Many grew up suburban like me, or in farmland/country, but each considers himself a city-dweller, urban. None expresses longing for the plains and wide-open spaces.

My native informants (and I) do not represent a cross section of U.S. males. This is a self-selected subset, a minuscule percentage of the male population. Still, they represent "something."

I intend to explore: what are "men" now, after the women's movement of the 1960s and 1970s, feminism, generally, how has that changed us, in what ways, and the women we know and love or hate, and what do we want from women, not what do they want. What about our fathers? (What about mine?) How did our feminist mothers and sisters and aunts and the women and girls affect us? New rules?


Subject 10: I would say having an older sister helped me. She was of my generation, and I saw what she would go through, and how she would handle things. I think simply having a sister caused an ingrained understanding of a female view of the world—one which was quite different than mine and my brothers'. It's true, though, that we felt there was quite a bit of favoritism bestowed on her from our parents, and this caused resentment. She had her own room, for instance, while all three of us were housed in one room. This was a childish resentment, though felt, but I see now that this was simply based on economics, as my parents are not wealthy, and it costs to build separate rooms.

## MAN QUA MAN (TOWARD AN ETHNOGRAPHY OF THE NEW MAN)

Not leaving home, I could strip field work to basics, a minimalist's approach, say, the way structural filmmakers and certain photographers, such as James Welling, Marco Breuer, Liz Deschenes, Vik Muniz, Shannon Ebner, bare the elements and materials of a photograph—to shoot "for" the illusion, to shoot light, say, not to deny its essential presence (pre-digital photography, especially). As a participant observer I don't sojourn in foreignness, in otherness, place, language, customs. Sure, I still make interpretations, I'm not totally against them, just not through layers of a language that's not my mother tongue, plus, I can sleep in my own bed. I don't have to be any more disoriented than I am.

A participant observer can "thickly describe" better, understanding where he's coming from, and the other's idioms, gestures, intonations, etc. Geertz cautions ethnographers about digging in our own field. (Digging your own grave.)

I get that. I also look to James Clifford for intellectual guidance, a free-thinking spirit with an agenda, in part to take down the old guard, which he has.

My interest in Freud and respect for psychoanalysis aren't usual in ethnography. Geertz has been vicious about it. (I read Freud in college, and have been in psychoanalysis. That's a bias.)

The New Man, a construction—or fiction—observed in the 1990s, designated, inadequately and vaguely, characteristics of boys born under the sign of feminism. The term has explanatory power. There's irony in its use, because new gets old so fast. There is irony, everywhere.

My sample humor me or partly agree about resuscitating the term New Man, and I'm hoping that, as we go along, it'll become useful to them.

Subject 18: One characteristic of the New Man? Prone to getting kinda overwhelmed. Will develop a certain degree of self-righteousness as a defense against guilt, though won't voice it—will just rub and warm up that gland every so often when confronted with his lack of productivity. There's a certain self-consciousness that comes from being in that position: New Man, New Dad, New Husband. So you kinda talk about what you do. You notice how you conduct yourself. And, because, if you're me, you're spending more time engaged as a parent, you're juggling work more and that produces this amped-up thing. And you refer to yourself as you all the fuckin' time. At least I do.

Subject 1: It's funny. When you ask if I'm interested in these issues, and I really am, but I hardly ever spend concerted effort thinking about them. I wish I did. I don't know if I needed feminist theory to understand, but then again I don't know a world where I didn't feel its effects on my conception of myself as a man. I feel like feminism is so deep in the men of my generation that it's elemental, invisible and ingrained. With some men I know, though, yes—it's just invisible.

As an ethnographer, I understand there will be exaggerations, half-truths, and lies. I lie or reshape my narrative, also, and, also like other people, I don't always know when I'm lying or mis-remembering, or if I'm reshaping my tale because of, say, trauma or sadness. Lies have their own truths, if you catch them, and I listen closely for omissions.

When taking notes, I have to find the words that'll fit, while maintaining meaning. Tone is something else— harder to represent. Email works: lets the subjects present themselves; their answers tend to be lengthier and, usually, clearer. (This might be the first of a series of studies on NEW MEN.)

## NOTATION, INTERPRETATION, TRANSLATION: WHEN NOT BY EMAIL

Trouble reporting a speaker is demonstrated when, say, a U.S. subject speaks the word "really." Really? Really! Really, with low voice, meaning some irony. Really—with no specific emotional demarcation, flat, more subtle—it may demand an as-yet undesigned emoticon. (Hieroglyphs: expanding or limiting expression?)

Or, take "fuck." Sometimes the F-word repeats several times in a sentence: That dumb fuckhead, he totally fucked up our fucking deal. Nuances.

Again, this is a start, far from perfect or definitive, suggestive, yes, and it's not a longitudinal study, I'm not hanging with these guys for their lifetimes or mine. At least I don't think so. Men die younger than women, though New Women increasingly have stress-related coronary disease. Heart disease is underreported in women, and heart attacks come on differently for women.

I'm into a view of the New Man, focusing on specific traits and attitudes, here and now. For instance, during my posse's lifetime, abortion has always been legal, the pill available, which delineated or encouraged men's changed attitudes.

I had met most of these people by going to a neighborhood bar. One actually went to my college but I never knew him. Being a participant observer can be dicey: while noting subjects' comments, I need to add to the conversation, never dominate, and let it go where it wants but also not be passive, not just an observer. An uneasy, indefinite status.

Here's a story I wrote them to display my openness:

My mother took a man down with her "acute return of gaze" [they liked tennis terminology], so she was called "challenging." When I was a boy, I became totally self-conscious about looking at females; I mean, I was noticing Mother's sexiness before I even knew I was, and then I'm absorbing her ambivalent responses, which made me conscious of what might have felt or become a "natural" response, socially approved, or whatever. I got stymied. I got stunted: how was I supposed to look at females without being a creep.

I have theorized: it appears instinctual for males to tag females as their sperm carriers. But cultural behavior is also class-related: grunts, lip-smacking, whistling, shouting obscenities occur among some men and not others.

I can't say that story elicited much.

My subjects recognize their differences from their fathers, especially in relation to women and masculinity, but are, in varying degrees, wary of making claims for themselves, very skeptical. Some talk more confidently of having progressed from their fathers' "older" positions. Some feel they have inherited more attitudes from their fathers, mostly unwanted, occasionally not. Others deny any inheritances.

Subject 22: My father didn't relate to women. Didn't understand them. Wasn't able to seduce them. Didn't know how to make them feel like, you know, a woman. He distrusted them. A man's job was to run the house, make the money, make the decisions. Be like iron, pound your fist. Things like that. Very antiquated. Almost medieval.

Subject 7: My generation learned to accept women's sexual freedom, ultimately their bodies were their own to do with as they pleased and that as a man I had to earn their fidelity and, or, respect for my pride. My father's generation took women's sexual freedom as a given, or at least they wanted to. He's just twenty-five years older. For me, my attitude toward women's sex lives is sort of a concession rather than a real address. The more human, or rather the more engaged with women as equals I become, the less mysterious they've become. In some ways it makes it easier to remain emotionally distant, and wary of women, in the same way that perhaps I distrust other men. I'm not sure if that's a healthy perspective to have. My father and his peers still wallow in the "mystery of women" in a way that no longer interests me (though it did when I was a teenager or in my twenties). It may not be a generational thing. It might be more individual. I think that my dad and his peers were/are more wholly reliant on women than I am . . . I probably see women as more wholly individuals than my dad and his group of friends are capable, and that says more about the times, the difference between our prime and his prime, than about the morals or ethics of my dad's generation. In part, my attitude is different because I have three daughters by three different women. I'm forty-three and I've had to deal with an army of ladies in my life—grandmothers, would-be mothers-in-law (if I were to ever marry), close first cousins, a slew of women friends and lovers, my mother and her friends.

Subject 2: In college, there were a lot of politics for the sake of politics, a lot of young people trying on various postures, ideologies, a lot of PC enforcement both direct and indirect. What I'm trying to say is that, having had my political upbringing there, it's impossible for me to know whether my gender politics are generational or situational. When I get offended at a sexist comment my father's friend made, do I find this "objectively" (as if there were such a thing) offensive, or is it simply activating my programming from college's hypervigilant culture?

Subject 23: I'm not sure I know what feminism has affected in me. I do know my first serious girlfriend was a brilliant feminist and we always argued about the ups and downs of equality. My gen tends to accept women as peers. If I had to guess, I'd say my father's generation would have trouble doing so. I also think my generation may understand women less than my father's.

## I, A MAN; I, AN IMAGE

Guyville in jeopardy: The New Man is analogous to Henry James's New Woman, but change for him isn't about his greater independence; it's about recognizing his interdependence, with a partner, in my study, usually female, even dependence upon her. (This produces ironic situations.) He must recognize different demands and roles for him, and for her. A New Man must investigate the codes that make him masculine, and the models for heteronormative behavior. And make him who he is or was, make him what he never believed had been "made." Right, a made man.

Subject 23: We think we can be whatever we want to be. My father's generation, they all went into the army or sold drugs.

Subject 1: The burden of living up to a very good father's example, or not repeating a very bad father's mistakes, is always a pressure on my generation's psyche, if I had to generalize. The difference, as I see it, has to do more with expectations of child-rearing—the whole "when I'm a dad, I'll do things differently, i.e. better" idea. My dad's idea of raising my brother and me was limited to material well-being: fed, clothed, educated, then at twenty-one: father gig over. I expect more from myself were I to have kids one day.

Subject 9: My father had, and still has, no confidence in himself. He imparted that to me, and I've been trying to overcome it for most of my life.

In the 1960s, when many of our mothers came of age, long-haired men were seen as more feminine but hip; the short-haired macho men were soldiers/warriors in Vietnam. Feminine men and masculine women have probably always existed. Styles change. Masculine women, especially notable, in the mid to late nineteenth century, early twentieth: George

Sand, Natalie Barney, Vita Sackville-West, et al. Plus, female explorers and adventurers . . .

A single, white heterosexual thirtyish man in Prada or the Gap on a date; a fortyish married, black, two-child father, in Levi's, watering his lawn. From the possible panoply of images, on what do men base/select their appearances and behavior? (Clothes don't make men, they augment images of them.) What goes into their choices? How does each perceive the woman across the table from him, in a club? At breakfast? What image, what female, does he want to see there? Why? How does he think she sees him?

The charge or vibe is interactive.


Subject 20: I remember being in the first grade and I had a male teacher. I remember the parents talking about how unusual it was for a man to be teaching the first grade. It was just so shocking to them. If a male elementary school teacher was shocking, a stay-at-home dad would have been outright absurd!


My subjects are not diehard dandies; some veer that way. Most wear male uniforms, T-shirts, jeans, skinny or loose, black jackets. Style-affected, not afflicted, from my POV (the Gap; Armani; Timberland/hip-hop; boy band/waif; post-punk; new mod). The younger, the slimmer: After twenty-five, chests widen, stomachs bulge, asses spread. Most of the posse visually reads "male." A New Man doesn't deny choosing an image, he is conscious of it. Many believe women choose them based on their image.

The New Man's mother or sister probably had read *The Feminine Mystique*, which, like Rachel Carson's *Silent Spring*, had immediate impact. Generally, 1960s feminists arose, eager to throw off their gendered chains: housework, child work, cooking, all unpaid labor. There were the college-educated housewives, internalized second-class characters. (See the AMC series *Mad Men*.) They would march under the banner of second-wave feminism. They opened employment doors, got Roe v. Wade passed. Many lesbians and people of color didn't find a home in the movement; some lesbians faced outright hostility from Betty Friedan and other middle-class, white, heterosexual women worried about charges of man-hating, or worse.

Now, with gay marriage legal, hetero-norm rules.


Subject 9: My relationship to women may not have been the most typical. Until my twenties, my dad was a closeted homosexual. He and my mother still have a good relationship.


Subject 16: When I was in my early teens, maybe 13, my dad explained to me how men can and should be feminists. And my best friends in high school were all women. Any respect I received from my male peers seemed based on my ability to shut out the regular harassment I received for those relationships, as if I knew some secret about women that my peers didn't. My father's suggestion stuck with me, and also his self-deprecating sense of humor, particularly as it relates to women, to seek endearment from women with strong character.

## WHAT DO NEW MEN WANT?

Subject 23: The biggest difference between our generations would be this self-referential element. Now, you can create your image without doing actual work. That's a strange kind of man.

Subject 24: On the one hand I am who I am. Feminism has definitely affected my attitude to women (for the better) but to myself? I occasionally catch myself making rote assumptions or taking ancient attitudes that I shouldn't, that belong with my father, or another pre-feminist generation, and that are sadly ingrained from my upbringing/culture/time. Does it make me feel less pressure to "provide" as a man—yes, some. Does it make me respect women who are strong, intelligent feminists—yes—and conversely, does it make me disrespect those who are not, who just want a ring on their finger, babies and a husband to take care of them—certainly. That is the cost to women who choose to ignore their sisters' gains— some men, like me, will think less of them. They ignore such gains, and stay with the classic tropes. Is that judgmental of me and (sometimes) wrong? Maybe so. My girlfriend wants those things, and I love her a lot, so there's the conundrum I have to live with.

Subject 11: Ah the feminists of old! How I miss them. They were my teachers and mentors. Where are the Emma Goldmans, the Lucy Parsons, the Gertrude Steins. [NB: I

didn't interrupt Subject 11 to tell him Stein was NO feminist.]
The greatest influence they have had on me is directly through
philosophy and politics and indirectly through my most free
and powerful female friends and acquaintances who enrich
my life with their independent spirit and immunity to the
prevailing social architecture. My mother, quite a feminist
in her own right, was perhaps my biggest influence. It's just
too bad she was so emotionally abused by her husbands to
ever see what my needs as a man might have been. To her, all
men were not to be trusted. In a way, then, I don't trust them
either. Including myself.

By the late 1970s, the budding New Man was born into an
atmosphere that simmered, not steamed or boiled, with ideas
of advancing women's rights, equality under law; the demand
for women's rights around the globe, equal or similar to men's.
But the Equal Rights Amendment losing, and the insistence
on this one issue, once it lost, created a political vacuum, and
feminist ennui, I believe.

(There is some discussion about what "equal" means, also
in sex. Orgasms, or who's on first.)

I mean, we boys breathed the aroma of freer lives for
women, but in actuality what was happening on the ground
wasn't so sweet. Still, their/our mothers and aunts espoused
women's rights, and we/they learned them, early. Our fathers
(some who art in heaven) squirmed, resisted, supported, ignored, or asked for divorce. Or, she did.

Subject 17: I noticed that a friend of mine seemed, in his relationships to women, particularly his wife, like a throwback.
He works a lot, and seems to not make time for his wife,
trained as a teacher, but who watched their child full-time.
Surprising to none of their friends, they are now separated,
pretty much because of his not being around at all. The
breakup in itself also reminded me of an earlier generation,
when people would break up more readily—my parents separated after forty-nine years, but many of my older relatives
are on third or fourth marriages, with kids from scattered
spouses.

Subject 7: Truth be told, my father taught us, and many of
my friends' dads taught them, how to philander. They all did
that, and most of my generation fell in line with that to some
degree, and intensely in certain periods of our lives.

Subject 4: I grew up in a house full of women, my father and
I and my mother and my three sisters. So I always put the
toilet seat down—and I do this at home, still, even though I
live alone. I understand menstruation. I have a lot of female
friends, though I have a lot of male ones too. I like people not
because of their sex but because of who they are. And even
though I generally "identify" as gay (I don't really believe in
"identity"), I have had desires for women, one in particular,
and I still desire her when I think about her.

## DEFAULT SETTINGS: RACE, SEX, ETC.

People arrive in the world with default positions for sex, class, race, maybe intelligence and sexuality, constructing early, essential environments; let's say, they're preordained—what I'll call "unoriginal sin platforms." These positions generally stay set—like marries like—though positions can be reset with effort or by chance—father beats the market, class shifts; sister becomes brother, gender shifts (sexual attraction is very complicated); white marries Asian or black marries white, their children affect "visual race" shifts.

A person can now consciously immolate default positions, bodily ones too.

Historically, gendered roles went unquestioned: gendered behavior was attached to physical bodies, which designated roles in families, for one, making roles more than just acceptable but expected and natural—natural for women to do X, men Y.

While I was doing this project, I had dinner with a gender-queer friend, born female, and not in my sample. We met in grad school and stayed in touch, through all her changes, and mine. She calls herself "she," and sometime after we got together she wrote me this (abridged):

"But because I think the shift is toward interrogating 'roles' entirely, I don't take testosterone but I have a 5 o'clock mustache and no tits. I often use the men's bathrooms because the women's are so tightly patrolled. I'm an outsider in both. Or an insider but at risk, staring at gender's seams. I'm often implicated in deception by people's assumptions about my gender. A checkout clerk says 'he' to me. I unconsciously puff up my chest and perform 'he.' In the women's bathroom I chat in line to my friend and make my voice higher and more gentle to calm everyone down/earn my passage. But what if/when they find out? And what is it exactly that they find out when they do?

"I'm also confused about my attitudes towards women because I'm also confused if I am a woman. Genderqueer. I'm certain I haven't had 'women's' experiences ... like walking down the street being catcalled, like sex with men, like straight female bonding . . . I have been called a feminazi though, I have been reviled as dyke and dyke is especially bad because it falls outside of male sexual use."

Since the traditional behaviors that once aligned bodies with roles have been shattered, attributes of femininity and masculinity lie in pharmacies, surgeries, and at makeup counters. Trans men and women demonstrate gender fluidity. Gender isn't role-reliable, and no one should be complacent (most are). The feminists began this push, to unyoke gender/roles from the body, to make it an unsettled proposition.

(I know my mother and her friends did, tried.)

Bodies—and roles—moot.


Subject 13: Men are now expected to understand women and not to see them as mysterious or inexplicable. While this is of course very good, it flies a bit in conflict with the facts: that men and women are rather mysterious to themselves and all the more so at this pace of societal change. I think that men are now expected to be able to balance two conflicting directions. They're expected to consciously absorb and adopt an ever-growing intimacy within a family but still provide a sense of the exciting, of bringing home (and sharing), a bigger world. Even if, and perhaps especially if, the woman is also very active in the world of work or other activities.

Subject 21: Some friends claimed there had to be an element of evil, you know, like conquest was never egalitarian, and that women AND men secretly want to be dominated. One acquaintance, he advocated for what he called "the caveman approach": a demand, straight up, to a stranger at the bar at closing time. Look, I have been happily married for ten years. The "mating game" mentality is a distant memory for me. But anyway, looking back, I wonder if the two approaches are so far apart: perhaps the convincingly sensitive routine was just a Trojan horse to conceal a caveman.

Gender bending was more style than substance, but also helped, incrementally, foster gender-rights movements: David Bowie, Prince, even Jagger, became models of difference, though with less discernible political effects, until recently, with the trans movement. It has produced dramatic results, in relatively few years, and, compared with other rights movements, has been accommodated very quickly. The reasons why should be studied: What about its claims appealed more? For one, my theory is: it has spread and been adopted quickly, because the academy for over forty years has taught

courses on race, gender, and women's and gay rights, and has
been educating generations about it, preparing the way for
acceptance.

Caitlyn Jenner's 2015 transformation from Olympic ath-
lete Bruce Jenner, assisted by Hollywood cosmeticians, dress
designers, et al., caused attention and controversy: Jenner's
"choice" to look glam and femme; her telling Diane Sawyer
she felt she had a woman's brain. But on November 12, 2015,
because Caitlyn's a learner, she was quoted as saying: Being a
woman "is more than hair and makeup; it's more than clothes.
If I have a platform, it's not just for trans issues. It's also for
women's issues" (*New York Times*, Style section, D11). She's a
Republican, her politics not transformed at all.


Subject 21: I'm not a good example. When I was growing up,
my concept of gender was a little fuzzy. Probably still is: I
don't really have an idea of what masculinity is. And maybe
it's not just me, maybe it is generational. I don't measure up to
what I imagine other people's concept of masculinity is, so I
don't pay much attention to the concept. It'd be nicer to measure up on some general standards for humanity, not some set
of gender-specific benchmarks.


Subject 3: In the context of parenthood, many groups I encounter (most of them heterosexual, though not all) split
down the lines of gender: the women hang out together.
The men hang out together. It drives me a little bit bon-
kers, because I find most of the women better friendship

material than the men. But in the parenthood context, it's more difficult becoming friends with women than at the office or elsewhere. And the fathers can be weird about homosexuality, gender roles, all that (though my non-parent friends, gay or straight, tend not to be this way, at least not so impulsively). I've seen some of those fathers burn out—shut down, not open up to their spouses, families. This happens with women, too, obviously, but men, I've noticed, tend to be more frequently exhausted by their slightly evolved roles as more involved parents. Women have been exhausted by parenting for years.

Subject 5: Me, I grew up in the church, I was excited to get married, have kids, and possibly be in the ministry, continue the lifestyle I was bred into, the only lifestyle really, Jesus is Lord, and that is the way shit goes. I taught Sunday school, went to Europe to a Bible school for my first year of college and wanted to save the world. There were no women pastors, no real positions of leadership for women, they cook and are great at getting the social side of things going. I can't wait to find one of my own! Fast forward a little, to art school. I had come there never drinking, never doing drugs, a virgin, and generally an innocent child of twenty. I wanted to witness and share the love of Christ with all of these people "living in darkness." I soon found that these people, the gays, the freaks, the hippies—all seemed to be doing pretty well. In fact, I was the one that lived with guilt and shame and sorrow, and this constant feeling of someone watching me. They were comfortable in their own skin, way more than me in mine. I found the women to be incredibly aggressive. I

will never forget a girl walking away from me in her apartment, dropping her clothes, and *begging* for my virginity. All
the heroic bullshit male braggadocio AND dreaming, and I
couldn't do it. It wasn't special, it was . . . crass. Kind of gross
even. And it started happening with a lot of girls at art school
and realizing a lot of the guys around me found women who
were really aggressive, who slept around. It turned a lot of us
off. Super free with their bodies, less interested in men for the
traditional needs but also really fun to be around.

Subject 10: Some of your questions, Zeke, make sense for
someone from New York City or a big city background—
with the many forms and expressions of what it means to
be female. It's good to remember that where I lived, feminism didn't exactly penetrate. Typically, the females did the
housework, did the cooking and cleaning, and the males
went off to work. I certainly have this way inscribed in me,
and certainly there is this nostalgic and sexist desire to have
meals, and so on. I don't express that ever, because it's not
right, but it is swirling in there, and my upbringing played a
big role in this.

In 1991, the cultural studies visionary Stuart Hall announced,
"The time for essentialism is over."

A lot of people still haven't gotten the message.

DNA appears to be unprejudiced evidence or fact, objective scientific data; but humans will use science the way they
use everything—imperfectly and with prior assumptions.
Objectivity also eludes scientists, because they are looking for

something, to prove an idea or hunch. Colloquially, they have a lot to prove.

Needing to be right at all costs is a great human and societal cost.

## MASCULINITY AND ITS VICISSITUDES

In *Gender Advertisements*, Erving Goffman analyzed ads in mags and TV: a man's head is always higher than a woman's, so he looks down, and she looks up to meet his manly gaze. Obvious now, but in the 1960s people weren't reading images like that, except Mad Ave., that was its power. Ad agencies in the 1950s and '60s were where Ivy League men who didn't go into the CIA, and English majors who would never write the Great American Novel, landed, to pen brilliant copy inspired by Edward Bernays. (Freud's nephew. Psychology gone amok.)

In the late twentieth century, into the twenty-first, images of Men as Men became subjects for interrogation, in the academy, in movies, art.

In Clint Eastwood movies, his character often protects women from other men. Clint Eastwood could do that, side with women, because his masculinity would never be questioned. That is, men can be "men" only after they have acted like men, and been totally accepted as manly.

In art, in the late 1970s Richard Prince's appropriation of the Marlboro Man on a horse, smoking, was considered an early critique of masculinity, the Western male image.

Subject 23: We're less masculine than my father's generation. We don't value it so much. We're greedy about women. We want them all. But, once we find what we want, we can chill.


Subject 2: The actor Michael Cera? He was the boyfriend in *Juno*, and Jonah Hill's opposite in *Superbad*. He is a sweet, slightly befuddled, skinny, thoroughly de-masculinized character, completely unthreatening in any physical or sexual way, and he would seem to be the role model for this new generation of males, and is much beloved of this new generation of females, thought of as the ideal boyfriend, etc. This doesn't sit well with me. When I watch Michael Cera I'm struck by the absence of a sexual energy, the denial of the risk or danger that is always inherent to sexual energy . . . as if this generation's answer to the problem of physical and sexual dominance/brutality on the part of some (too many) men of all generations is to get rid of not only the dominance/brutality but of all physicality and sexuality.


Several subjects thought their fathers understood women better.

Though a generality, this belief needs further exploration (in my next study). It's conceivable that "father's understanding women better" derives from the New Man's witnessing his parents playing more fixed or settled gendered roles. Life's uncertain with transitions, with more "we'll make it up as we go along."

## MEDIATED MEN

Subject 1: Masculinity is dead, at least my father's generation's idea of it. I think they came of age during a time when men, even if they dressed in tight-fitting pants and dandyish collars, were still very un-ironically macho in that seventies kind of way. I think men nowadays take a more ironic approach to masculinity—especially hyper-macho posturing. Though I'm not sure how to contextualize the whole tongue-in-chic lumberjack thing that's been going on around Brooklyn.

Subject 7: Masculinity is a far more complex phenomenon than most care to admit. Men can, and women who perceive men as omnipotent protectors and standard-bearers can, lean too hard on rationality as a predominantly male psychological feature. That pervasive attitude has done men a disservice socially. That perception has proven unreliable if not dangerous in the range of human endeavor—from the institution of marriage to global politics. I think self-reflexive attitudes about masculinity are undergoing an evolution, a shift from a lonely rational space to an emotionally complex, socially richer understanding of how the so-called masculine and the feminine operate in whatever ratio simultaneously from one human being to another.

Subject 19: When I was quite young I had an argument with my little sister. I was angry for some reason, probably she was mocking me. We wrestled, and she punched me, not hard, and suddenly I got angry, and there was a moment when I realized I could kill her. I could actually take her life. I was so much bigger and stronger. And I realized I had to stay in control, so I would not hurt her. And since then I've always felt it critical that I maintain control. I've never wanted to use my strength as some kind of weapon. I think that's become something of a life anxiety.

Subject 13: Masculinity is an odd thing, it seems to be something where our society has split radically along class lines: the middle class and liberal upper class now expect men to have a much more "respectful" masculinity, but apparently this is less the case in the working class and the conservative wealthy classes where they still seem to be expected to display flamboyantly their outward masculinity. Myself I don't know much about this at all from a personal level; in my background masculinity was perhaps seen as a very dark thing, something that led to secrets, molestation, for example, back many generations, but that's not typical (though too common). The main thing that I can say is that it seems that ideas of masculinity have expanded in such a way that men who can be sympathetic in affect are more accepted. But it still shocks me that the simple idea of men being close, intimate (confidant-type) friends is seen as questionable.

The weak geek has always been around and sometimes gets the girl (the meek Ashley in *Gone With the Wind*). With the omnipotence and omniscience of virtual life, nerds and geeks get laid more easily. Bill Gates and Steve Jobs didn't play rock and roll in their garages, and became superheroes. The computer affected masculinity, and with it a new masculinity, if it exists, came along on the heels of the 1960s women's movement.

Subject 4: I feel sorry for women who pinch themselves into really uncomfortable clothes and shoes so they can be attractive to men, because the men they will attract are not "liberated" men. But perhaps all women don't want to be liberated, either. Or, they don't know that they do. Margaret Atwood's *Handmaid's Tale* discusses this phenomenon and takes it to its extreme. In any case, I also feel sorry for men who think that being a man is all about being an asshole, acting macho, having power over others, competing in sports or competing in general. At a very young age—and perhaps this leads into questions about whether being gay is something one is born with, developed in early childhood object relations, or whatever, it doesn't really matter to me "why"—I decided I didn't want to grow up and be the type of man who played sports or did math. I didn't want to compete, I didn't want to sell anything to anyone unless they wanted it. I still don't. (I think advertising should be banned.) I think this was a conscious rebellion against my father, even though my father always insisted I could be whatever I wanted to be. He tried to make me interested in sports, but it never took hold.

Subject 11: By the way, I'm not trying to be funny. I'm taking your project seriously. But as T. E. Lawrence said to Allenby when the latter called him a clown, "We all can't be lion tamers." The race of Homo Artisticus has high expectations of the world and low expectations of himself. His wife-friend and bulldog-baby must accommodate (his favorite word) his bouts with "bipolar disorder," his favorite disease. "I'm feeling bipolar," he says when she asks him to look for a Real Job . . . One night stands are cool. It's called "hooking up," so never say, "Let's hook up tonight" to your nonsexual partners. The problem is that he doesn't want to use a condom. "What, you don't trust me? By the way, what's your name again?" The wife-friend, though, must wear long vintage Laura Ashley dresses even when riding the communal bicycle to Whole Foods. If she looks too sexy they have another fight. "I thought you stopped dressing like a slut when you graduated!" On the other hand, he wants her to stop smoking so much and getting shit-faced drunk with her old college buddies. "You're never going to be a famous poet if you drink all the time."

## MAN (HOOD) UP / DOWN

In 2014: less upward mobility in U.S. than in any other Western nation.

The image world is relational, inter-relational, vertiginous. The New Man developed AS images, since masculinity and femininity exist primarily as images and behaviors (which can and do change) in relation to each other.

Subject 2: I'm comfortable with my politics, with my certainty of equality between the genders, with my commitment to supporting that equality and speaking out against inequality and discrimination. I think much of our culture has come with me. But when I look at men of the next generation, I wonder if it has gone "too far"—from an ideal of equality to something more like the erasure of all difference and the suppression of all sexuality. Which is probably what my father thinks when he looks at my generation.

## AMERICAN MALE ACTORS, OR, MEN WHO PLAY MEN

Richard Gere plays a gigolo; he also plays a wealthy businessman who hires a call girl for a week (and falls for her). Dustin Hoffman plays a man whose wife leaves him, he gets custody of the child; the low-life street character, Ratso, in *Midnight Cowboy*, and a man who dresses as a woman to get a TV part. Robin Williams plays a man who dresses as a woman to be the nanny to his own children and win back the wife who left him, and, in *One Hour Photo*, a demonic stalker. Eddie Murphy plays everyone, but not a romantic hero (racism). Ryan Gosling plays a romantic New Man who never gives up getting his first great love back (and does, because he's Ryan Gosling); he does great oral sex, too. Gosling also plays killers. James Gandolfini plays a sadistic, troubled mob boss in psychotherapy; in his last role opposite Julia Louis-Dreyfus in *Enough Said*, he played a man who can love. Joaquin Phoenix plays everyone, from a mad Roman emperor, to a gangster, to a New Man in love with a cyber-woman's voice in *Her*. (Is a movie like *Her* preparing humans for robots; is body changing also preparing us for robots?) Matt Damon plays a soldier hero in *Saving Private Ryan* and a psychopathic killer in *The Talented Mr. Ripley*.

Read the name, see the image: Robert Redford; Leonardo DiCaprio; Johnny Depp; Jamie Foxx; Tom Hanks; Jeff Bridges; Robert Downey Jr.; Denzel Washington; Kevin Kline; Steve Carell; Will Smith; Matthew McConaughey; Michael J. Fox (before Parkinson's, *Back to the Future*); Jeffrey Wright; Patrick Wilson; Nicolas Cage.

RIP: Gregory Peck, sexy, bad guy in *Duel in the Sun*; good guy lawyer in *To Kill a Mockingbird*. Jimmy Stewart, in *Rear Window*, takes off his T-shirt, no muscles. In the 1930s and 1940s, being buff didn't make the man. But after World War II, soon there were Charles Bronson; Steve McQueen; tough/sensitive guys, Marlon Brando; James Dean. Future identities will be based upon what and whom? Or, is "identity" about to become redundant, ruptured forever? Irreverence for origins likely segued into irreverence for gendered behaviors.


Discomfort and anguish about the body of origin can be deep, starting very early in a child's life. The pain, though, may not be assuaged by body modification, since it doesn't restructure a psyche. Psyches are comprised of wishes and fantasies, with their own independence, while formed in tandem with the environment, culture, and society.

No one knows where it will go, how far, what the results will be years from now—the effects of hormone treatments, irreversible operations—no one knows, and if disappointment at transitioning will be great or small, or not at all. No one knows, long-term, how psyches will react, whether the fantasy (expectations) of body change will be satisfying, or if the psyche won't be placated. Other issues come forward then. Or gender realities sit somewhere in between. This cultural and social phenomenon is not an individual experience, may be an evolutionary moment, or revolutionary one, hard to say.

If both gender and identity become fluid and situational, life will be a much faster game.

Subject 3: One thing I've thought about lately is the workplace. I've been working for magazines, and under the assumption that people working around me were sort of post-gender, or close. But that's extremely naïve (duh). I've seen women fired clearly because they've exerted too much power over men (who retaliate), and I've seen women passed over because, for instance, an editor thinks magazines are supposed to have "arguments," and then casts that term to somehow exclude women writers. Especially men a decade younger than me, I'm forty, act like the requirement to find something close to gender balance is a thing of the eighties and nineties, though not everyone's like that.

Subject 8: Though the men I know may not always think of women as equals, or treat them as equals, they're certainly aware that they're supposed to; when they don't, it's often symptomatic of the fact that, being very privileged or coddled or self-involved or whatever (insert other negative attributes), they tend to find ways of treating many different people as not equal to them, and doing so could mean demeaning women or emasculating men or anything in between. Actually, my most regular and aggravating experience of this has been men talking over and shutting down women in groups. Which goes to show that how one relates to women, or anyone, is situational; or, at least, the situational oftentimes trumps or undermines how one feels abstractly. And this is true with me, too, of course if only very occasionally!

I queried my subjects about friendships, with women, attitudes their fathers had toward women, and femininity. (Father thought it was almost impossible. "Really, son, you always want to have sex with them.")

Subject 1: Many had mistresses, and it wasn't possible for them to have women friends. That's one huge division between us . . . In one of my father's books, I found an old photo of a pretty European girl, and asked who she was. My father ripped the photo up in front of me. I bet even if she were a friend, the reaction might have been the same, because being friends with women, that didn't exist after marriage and kids.

His father's rash act, ripping up a photograph, made me think about the former evidentiary "nature" of photography. Also, that the photograph, as a preserve of memory, even a bad memory, is often shoved inside a drawer and hidden, rarely ripped up, that is, even when it's legible. Sometimes a person who doesn't like the way she or he looks will deface her own face or a body part that "looks bad"; usually people don't destroy pictures. Now with digitization, it is entirely changed. Erasure is meaningless since abundance assures us of an eternity of images, allowing for infinite deletion. But the photo was, for the subject's father, evidence of an indiscretion, which, his son imagines, might have been only a friendship.

Subject 2: My father and his friends still occasionally use the word "broad" or make offhanded comments about how women are terrible drivers. Their wives, generally speaking, aren't bothered by this, or at the most will roll their eyes. It's hard for me to watch.

Subject 24: Masculinity, in the nurturing home-building way, changed for my generation, which was essentially the indie-punk one, we rejected that, so that is a huge difference, with real repercussions. We have moved beyond that now, though, and today's men seem to be happy with family lifestyle. Good for them. The pendulum swings back and forth as life makes its merry dance.

Subject 20: I think that men in my generation don't care as much about upholding a specific image of masculinity.

Most of the time we don't project our masculinity to prove ourselves as men, or for that matter to prove ourselves to be straight men. Men from my generation have come to acknowledge and respect that women can compete with men, of course in intellect and academics, but also in physical labor and sport. I remember my mother telling me about her college experience, and the only sports available to women were cheerleading and basketball. I remember thinking about how unfair that was. Men in my generation have higher expectations of themselves for being engaged in family matters and lower expectations about being just the provider. Even though our egos are still there and we still feel responsible for taking care of our families financially, I feel like it's easier to set our ego aside and be equal partners with women in work and at home. I think that because of this, men and women engage more with each other in relationships. They figure things out together, whether it's about finances or how to discipline or motivate children, rather than making those decisions on their own, without the input of each other.

## MEN SHOW THEIR FEELINGS(?)

New men fear being vulnerable but more, they fear showing it, and fear what could be excess(ive) vulnerability.

Subject 4: My father likes to shake my hand, but I insist on a hug.

Subject 7: Men are emotionally weak, however dressed in a kind of "I don't give a damn" type of costume. For most guys, violence and anger are easier to handle than sadness, grief, the powerlessness of death or profound loss.

Subject 10: Emotions are very difficult for me. I intellectualize a lot. I understand things intellectually. Which is not the same thing as emotionally. If feminism has taught me anything, it's taught me to speak to the mechanisms of being male, the disorders and orders of it, how masculinity is formed, why, and what society needs from boys to make them into men, in the very narrow and concentrated ways they do.

Ironic boasting helps us "men"; irony allows for "just saying," or not saying, lessening or diluting embarrassment. Studying male vulnerability, I observe various forms of irony used by all kinds of men.

I'm also aware of how ironic it is that I am doing this.

Male boasts can be a survival tactic, a display to enhance invulnerability and attract females or other males. Florid displays, in nature, can enhance good outcomes for mating and breeding, to attract females or other males.

Then there are the quieter men, the modest ones—the Mild Ones, not the wild ones, I forget which subject said this. But he's a mild one. And understated.

New men have retro impulses, which find their way into our conversations (and suits).

Hookups aren't for everyone.

Subject 15: Friday night my new friend invited me out to a bar where a woman he was pursuing was having a birthday party. He's handsome, thirty-nine years old, single, and, basically, acts like a seventeen-year-old in regard to women. We went to the wrong bar. While we were having a drink, my friend started talking with a beautiful young woman (probably thirty to thirty four years old) sitting adjacent to us. She immediately took to him. She and a friend were obviously out to meet men. When she told him that she and her friend were in town for the weekend (she was from Iowa, her friend was from Portland), he jokingly said, "So, are you looking for guys to party with or what?" She immediately, and in all seriousness said, "Yeah!" and pressed her body up against his. He didn't know what to do. He knew how to pretend to be a man, but he didn't know how to actually be one—at forty!?! I see this so much. Men in their thirties and early forties who still have all the same sexual insecurities of a high school student. I find this unbelievably depressing. I don't see anything positive or cute or remotely interesting about this. Never mind the fact that this kind of adolescent paralysis could only come about due to a total misunderstanding of what sex is—the act itself—but imagine the larger cultural repercussions of who-knows-how-many-forty-year-old-men stuck in a state of psycho-sexual suspension/regression! What potential is there for living a good, meaningful life, when the failure to take responsibility for one's own thoughts, desires, and actions is so heavily, and so deeply mediated, and when, paradoxically, so much of our social life revolves around the indulgence in, and the never-to-be-completed, perfection of the self?

•

New men often want new women to make the first move. One guy in my sample says he won't ever make the first move, not anymore. Women have to call it, and he's ready, if they are.

One of my gay male friends explained, "That's why being gay is easier. Men always want sex."

My group is often confused. Many feel, if a woman wants it, she can and should make the first move. But can a guy tell when she's being subtle, because she doesn't want to look uncool? Or, if the guy makes a move, and he's trying to be subtle, same deal, it might not work out. Too much ambiguity on both sides. Sometimes ambiguity is necessary, because emotions generate ambivalence, and hesitation, the need to feel out the situation. Uncertainty creates troubled waters.

One subject insists, No is no. She says it once, it's over. I'm over it.

None of my sample has raped a woman. They all say they'd never do it. I can't be positive, have no proof, and want to believe them. OK, that's totally non-objective, especially because rape stats in the U.S. are off the rails. So, someone's lying. Or, someone believes he didn't force her.

Boys born under the sign of feminism and the women's movement should have learned respect for No. The new man learned: When a woman says No, she means it. If the new man is "civilized," he gets it. But, actually, not using force might be the first sign of a male being civilized. It's always called "brute force," like a Bruce Willis movie.

Another case: she wants the guy to show more aggression. That he desires her, wants her, which can get tricky.

Still, male aggression, fear of the other, including females, and psychological problems about their mothers and fathers—neuroses—can vanquish "educated feelings," emotions resist "education." Irrationality trumps civilized behavior.

Most people have no idea why they feel what they do.

At Yale University, in 2014, signs were posted: "No means Yes, and Yes means anal."

Then there's the hookup. Straight-up sex. No strings, no commitment, once called a one-night stand.

The difference now is that young, new women are agreeing to and setting up sex dates.

The one-night stand, Mother told me, in her crowd, might have been a beginning of a relationship. That was the 1960s and '70s, she said, women had sex, chose it, this was the Sexual Revolution, we felt freer, and also got fucked. And felt fucked over. (My translation.)

New behaviors are unsettled, and unsettling, without agreed-upon codes. (Colleges struggle to make them up, rules, adjustments, dumb as they sometimes seem.)


Subject 8: Your question about how we new men act toward women seems a little academic to me. Or maybe it's just difficult to step out of my experience of something so broad and complicated, yet mundane and for the most part automatic, in order to describe and assess it. For the most part the men I know relate to women in what seems to be a very conventionally progressive and healthy manner. Their fathers probably do, too, though I'm sure rough patches have been smoothed over and the progressiveness has been ramped up, barring any backlash against feminism.

Subject 22: I see in my close male friends a tremendous patience and respect for women. Maybe I just picked good friends. I also see men addicted to fucking. I was a man addicted to fucking for a long time. And that isn't always a mutually nourishing thing. Sometimes it can be but it's easy to become a micro Genghis Khan. I've seen men fall into that. I remember a broken male friend of mine—truly broken, lost, scared—telling me how all he did now was pick up women and ejaculate in them and leave them in hotels. Told me that with a straight face like it wasn't horrifying. Maybe he's the most evolved of all of us?

## IN AND OUT OF THE CLOSET

Human females and males can both be the colorful sex; that goes in and out of fashion. The two-piece suit hangs in closets, worn by all types of men, not necessarily for work: it works for hipsters, queers, straights, trans men, mad men.

Why the two-piece suit's persistence? Easy, economical, unfussy, lets "men" just be "men." Designers have pushed sari-like long skirts. Good for hot summers, not for cold winters. Also women adopted the suit, they adopted trousers widely in the 1920s, the trouser suit in the 1970s.

Subject 19: Anyway, when men of my gen get together—I should qualify this as when heterosexual men get together, and most of these opinions are really from a hetero perspective—there are numerous conversations and jokes about sex. Often men appear to be in competition for who has had the most, or craziest, sexual experiences. Or who is the most depraved/salacious. Women are still highly objectified in these huddles, and it's something that I've observed ever since middle school. Men show restraint when women are in the group. Today women would never accept that kind of behavior from men, and I think men have learned it's not acceptable, not pragmatic, and it would also be fairly disingenuous because I don't think it's how most men really feel. Most of the sex/objectification is about men relating to each other as men, sexually, tribally, the dog battle for alpha status, supremacy, etc. It's a lot of posturing and acting, it's about male insecurity and confusion with sexuality and our place in the world. Possibly it is because men feel threatened by women, but I don't quite relate to that personally.

## ARE THE NEW WOMAN AND NEW MAN IN SYNC?

Subject 3: I also feel burdened by fatherhood, and it's strange. My father, for instance, never had to take care of children while my mom left for a week, never had to rush home from work to pick up sick children, never had to pack a lunch or change a diaper.

Subject 8: My parents married very young, so they basically grew up together. She became a feminist and he learned to relate to her as that. But at the same time, she became a mother, and he became a doctor, she had a part-time job doing something that was never quite as satisfying as it should have been, and he spent the majority of his time immersed in a career that was increasingly satisfying (and well paid). And they learned to relate to each other in those ways, too.

The majority of U.S. females are earners, sometimes the only one in their families, single mothers, et al. They are graduated from college in greater numbers than males. And with the economic downturn of 2008, many jobless women used that period, and their savings, took loans, or got grants, to return to college and earned degrees to help them find better jobs. Most men did not, and the gap between the sexes grew wider.

Men are still expected to carry heavy suitcases up three flights of stairs, to satisfy or help women. Unless the woman objects, he will, usually. On the other hand, with more girls doing sports in school, they are becoming physically stronger. Might not need any help. On the other hand, if you are stronger, isn't it the gracious thing to do?

Subject 14: I didn't have much of a father. And when he was around, he didn't father much. And this is more or less the norm for the friends I grew up with (in high school and beyond). So I suppose the first difference is that I found myself having to draw an image of masculinity to imitate from women (and children). I don't think he had to do that.

A guy can agree, and want, to be a house husband, watch the kids, do the home biz. Does it affect his sex life?

Subject 3: The idea that women were made/not born—same for men, or at least that was the idea—fascinated me, because I didn't have much interest in being a man, at least the kind of man my father was, though my father's masculinity is, I've realized, a little hobbled, which already brings up a question: Is failed masculinity better or worse than successful masculinity? . . . There's still some benefit to "being a man," I think, and I think you can do it without being a creep to women. But it's a subtlety. Some are better at it than others. I guess what I'm getting at is: How do you throw out the bath water without the baby?

Subject 7: Virility is a coveted aspect of human life. In and of itself male vigor is positive. Women want it in men, and women who feel they have no use at all for men admire it, emulate it, and respond to it. The can-do attitude projected from and onto maleness is still very present in American society. But it's a kind of, or rather can be a kind of "drag," a performance of sorts, any man can play the role. It's easy to see and only the simplest of us appreciate the one dimensionality of that subject position.

## TIME OUT WITH MOTHER

I visited my mother. She's a good listener, and I was explaining how young women are different from her generation, how they're redefining femininity and equality in relationships. Women now don't want to be man-haters. (Mother shoots me the big look.) They want their way, independence, but paradoxically they also want men to be powerful—even independent women are like that. Plus, they're dissatisfied. "Disillusioned," Mother said. They're conflicted, I went on, like the new man is [Agreement here]. So I laid my concept on her—"post-feminist malaise."

"Oh, jeez, Ezekiel."

Not an unexpected response.

I challenged her to table tennis and blew her out of the water. (She beats me at Scrabble, mostly.)

She supports my doing this field work. She probably would support my doing anything.

## MASCULINITY: OBJECT OF STUDY

Theoretical work on masculinity (and whiteness, though not my field) began in earnest in the 1980s: Klaus Theweleit's *Male Fantasies*, seminal. Many academics, mostly male, got into it, Women's studies offered courses, cultural studies too. Social scientists were already there, but looking at differences between men and women from their angle of vision.

Subject 24: I am one of those men who is more at ease with women, for whatever reason. Some of them are decent reasons, but it's just a comfort thing, and I'm OK with that.

Subject 12: Femininity and masculinity, at least their social expression, are interdependent—gallantry arose in association with the idea that women (at least chaste, noble women) could serve as objects of desire in a divine sense—that there was something godlike about womanhood that men should be willing to die trying to protect. That notion of masculinity was dependent upon an opposite notion of femininity, and as the feminist movement has prompted a shift in the latter I do think many men are now completely confused about their role in society—some abandon any idea of masculinity altogether, some hold on to it in aggressive, thoughtless ways with no consideration for other people.

Right, no femininity without masculinity, and vice versa, terms in relation, always, and sensibly, from my POV, women's studies has expanded its field of vision, to include masculinity. (If you build it, they will come.)

Women in the academy worry that men (biological; trans) will dominate, the way men have always, in everything: e.g., they talk more in class, on panels, shut women down. Will trans women be more assertive? Anecdotal: Two trans women have told me how hard it is to give up "male privilege."

How far can people move from the constructions that made them "what they are"?

And in opposing also betray their origins?

"Whether 'tis nobler in the mind to suffer / the slings and arrows of outrageous fortune, / Or to take arms against a sea of troubles, / And, by opposing, end them." —Hamlet

Time will tell, and, throughout it, people have told lies.

Will the newly independent woman lust for and mate with a less ambitious, nice guy who doesn't care about career, doesn't shoot deer, likes to bake?

Subject 19: There seemed to me a moment when being a feminist was a culturally exciting thing, but now it is often used as a slur. I hear people accusing others of being a feminist, rather than individuals seizing the term. Often people go on the defensive, as if being a feminist is a bad thing. I think in the last ten years we've suffered some kind of regression. There is an obvious nostalgia for older repressed generations. I think both men and women feel this nostalgia. In many of my friends' relationships, women are breadwinners. In my own relationship, my wife makes significantly more than I do and is more ambitious than me. My wife resents this to some degree, and wants me to be more of a breadwinner. I think it's a nostalgia for our parents' era. We're in a subconscious dialogue with our parents as we become the age they were when they raised us. Forgive me if that makes no sense.

Subject 11: Lack of muscular development from fear of manual labor. Skin white as Boar's Head–brand sliced chicken. Skinny capri pants that looked better on the woman who donated them to Goodwill. Yellow plaid shirt with pearlescent cowboy buttons. Rat Pack hat. Ironic baby-step walk with shoulders hunched up as if the world were filled with refrigerators falling from the sky.

Subject 17: The dignity of women is important to me and I used to chalk this up as due to my "post-feminist liberalism." But I'm not beyond being covetous, sexually insensitive, and objectifying. But weren't previous generations of men sexually guarded or obsessed with protecting and upholding women's chastity?

In the post-women's-movement era: what kind of partner do women want us to be?

And: what do I feel during sex?

Men want longer orgasms.

Men worry: performance, performance, performance.

Some are performance artists. Some play performance artists: Michael Fassbender performed sex like a machine in Steve McQueen's movie *Shame*.

Men, even New Men, usually don't want to wear condoms. The issue is often performance anxiety. In WWII, GIs were provided with rubbers and used them, because they didn't want to get the clap, syph. Maybe then, during that war, "men were men." Since AIDS, there is less resistance to using condoms but performance remains a problem.

(Wasn't the "greatest generation" also a silent generation and is that what made them "manly"?)

In a noisy bar: atmosphere, raucous.

Any story about a woman he loved and lost gets to me. I wouldn't tell them, it's my effort to maintain some distance, some bit of objectivity, not to stain the playing field.

Guys might debate whether women are really cool with dads playing moms. Or if the new woman thinks, gazing at her man folding the laundry—even for a sec—I'd rather be dominated. Question: how will people live with gender unsettledness, survive their voluntary undoing?

Subject 23: I was raised in a house full of women, so there's a lot of feminist support built into my everyday perspective, which it's easy for me to take for granted.

Subject 24: The obvious differences between me and my father are expectations, like not having a "wife at home" whom you support as the sole breadwinner. And if there is that situation, the woman is more uncomfortable than before, as she knows it's maybe not the norm anymore, so that must (may or can?) affect her self-image/esteem.

Subject 11: My mom was married at twenty and had to quit college so she could have me. Dad demanded that she marry him in the Catholic church even though she was Methodist. Her parents disowned her. That was the Bronx in the 1960s, like in *Goodfellas*. She found herself stuck in the suburbs with no driver's license or college degree and two bored kids to manage.

He thought it was fine to cheat on her, since he earned all the money. When he was home, all she did was fight with him.


I'm alone in a bar, listening to Lee Dorsey's "Ride Your Pony": "Get on your pony and ride . . . Stay in the saddle"; I'm looking around. Like my sample, I had ideas about the women I could love, "types," and about the type of life I wanted, but didn't and couldn't know: Where did those types come from, parents, movie stars, etc.

Oh, man, the psyche is a prison, every one of us his own guard on the top floor of the panopticon. Our living dreams, even them, are so routinized, and can't we live bigger, and not be delusional?

Being educated levels the economic (and marital) playing field, which is another reason why public education is being destroyed (I think). Stats show that what college you attend determines your future mate.

College-educated men are a lower percentage of the male population than they once were. In general, college dwellers in dorms, in 2010, the *Times* reported from Census Bureau figures, outnumbered people in adult correctional institutions: 2.3 million to 2.1 million. That's a positive shift from 2000.

Sick shit, totally.


## STORIES ARE EXISTENTIAL FACTS

Three of my subjects played in high school bands. One turned pro, plays tenor, but needs a day job since his employed girlfriend split, because he was too caught up in his music, was never there, when he was there. He didn't listen. He says, "What can I do about that? It's true."

Feminist mothers homeschooled, to some extent, couldn't do it all, may have indulged their sons. Or, hated them?

My subjects suggest or explain that their girlfriends have left them often because of their lack of commitment; or, their straying—or cheating—which doesn't mean they didn't love the girlfriend, they just couldn't commit. Some have used cheating to end it all. Most find "confrontation" near-impossible. One, whose best friend is a gay woman, has tried "lesbian processing," talking it through. Lesbians do that, according to her. But he's lousy at talking about his feelings.

Some note, as they have grown older, playing the field isn't what it was, since guilt and consequence have entered their minds. They feel more responsible. Again: "owning your shit."

Also, with age, they know they won't as easily attract younger females for bed or wed, unless they have money, power, institutional power, or some quality that shows their prowess, intellectual or otherwise. Most want babies—at the least, they want to know their sperm can penetrate an egg and make one. Older, more look for comfort, companionship, from a woman. Comfort means less risk, and some subjects face that moment, a crossroads, and some want to blame females for imposing that—a need for safety.

They're getting worn down standing, pitching, swinging for the stands. They get old, and it gets old.

•

(My relationships haven't worked out. I might always be a single straight white male. I've read the stats, those guys are the least happy on the planet, and I know that's true, because anything straight men believe about themselves needs to be supported by having a woman. The guys I see on the street, unwanted men, become bums, and year by year look crazier. No female wants this male, because he doesn't offer anything. Their clothes are filthy, they stink, they let their teeth go, they have no money, they're done. Sometimes, I believe women keep men from becoming bums.

Curious my thoughts, worries. New men, or newish ones, might think women will keep them sane or from losing touch with the world, being human. Like their mothers, when they were caring for them?)

In groups, new men mostly don't discuss their feelings. Or with the woman they're dating, until they feel safe. It's an issue, though I might argue that the new woman doesn't want to hear about the new man's feelings, because the "old man" talked all the time.

Subject 3: One big difference between my father and me might be that while I am concerned with my relationship with women, with my wife, with my friends, he is not. I look at him and assume that he is sad, that he is unsatisfied with his relationship with my mom. But hard as it is, I have to realize, sometimes, that he is actually just fine. He is satisfied, even happy. He just isn't interested in having some of the things

that I want. I look at him and think: He's so sad, so unful-
filled. But when I really look at him, he's fine, more or less.
He has a different set of values, and most of the things I mentioned in my first note—friendships with women, etc.—aren't
that important. It makes his life easier in some ways, more
difficult in others. I do sometimes wonder what my kids will
think of me, both in terms of my personality, but also in terms
of my era, such that it is. They will probably see things that
I just don't, and they may attribute feelings to those things
in ways that I do not (fail to?) feel. That's the way, right? But
I think that if I aim for some sort of satisfaction (not always
easy for me), that will be enough, and if they are vaguely decent (which I hope they are), they will recognize that too.

There was a discussion of owning guns. In my sample, only
one does. But would he use it?

Subject 20: Where I live now, hunting is a big sport for men.
Sometimes I feel a little unmasculine when I'm asked if I hunt,
and I say, "No, I'm not really into guns." I mean, come on,
what man doesn't like guns, right? There's usually not much of
a response, maybe a change in subject. In our fathers' generation, men didn't get away with not participating in masculine
activities, for fear that they would be shunned or beat up or
called a sissy or gay, and if they weren't good at those activities they were forced to do more of them to toughen them up
and make them more of a "man." Although it isn't as common, that mentality still exists. The funny thing is that even

though I know I have no interest in guns, I still catch myself thinking that maybe I should learn to shoot so I can go out with the guys and do "guy" stuff, but it's really not me and I let the thought pass. It's nice to not have the pressure of doing something that you don't really want to do just because it's what you "should" do to fit into your gender group.

The ex of a friend of mine kept a baseball bat by her bed. She said she'd swing at the head of any man who broke into her apartment. Would she, he wondered, and would she swing it at him? Under what conditions? They broke up before he could find out.

## MATING RITUALS: PRETTY COMPLICATED

Subject 3: When I was dating a woman in my early thirties, my dad once told me it was time to make things right, but I was so put off by this; the relationship wasn't working out, but he had no interest in that, only in the "duty" to marry.

Subject 7: My view of women, a very heterosexual manful perspective, still to some degree, sees women as objects of desire, to be admired, looked at, and at best had. I do that in my head, go through the process of imagining being intimate with them, what that would be like. My father was not—or at least when he taught me and my brothers—I have three—how to look at women for beauty—he was not relaying intimacy as much as the idea of purely fucking them, using them sort of, though he personally needed them for more than their bodies.

Subject 2: I went to [an Ivy League] college, where, at the tender age of nineteen, I once drunkenly said to a girl (woman?) whose company I enjoyed, "You're a really cool chick." To which she replied, "Do I look like a fucking *bird* to you?" It may have been the last time we spoke.

I asked two from my study what they saw as the biggest difference between men and women, in their experience (I insist on "in your experience").

Subject 22: Take a guy and put him in a room alone, and he will masturbate. I don't know about women. But don't imagine that's the same.

Subject 15: I'm definitely not an expert on feminism. The aim of creating equality between the genders makes a lot of sense, a still-unfinished project. But, in my experience, it seems as if this notion of equality has been taken to a literal extreme, in which to recognize any difference at all between the genders is considered a deep and horrible slight (especially coming from a man). This seems to me an unfortunate turn. It seems to me that the very real, inescapable differences between the genders (even though anyone now can medically alter their own sex) should be celebrated, if anything. Men are, in fact, fundamentally different than women, and vice versa. I just don't see any reasonable counter-argument to this. And I don't think there's anything wrong with that. Fran Lebowitz has said some great stuff on this, and she, of course, can successfully speak about it (as a lesbian and, well, because she's Fran Lebowitz), whereas if I did I imagine I would be drawn into some regressive sixties-style Norman Mailer shouting match (which I can't help but secretly think might be healthy). Now that men and women no longer actually need one another to reproduce the species, what does a man see when he looks at a woman? What does a woman see when she looks at a man? Can heterosexuality even any longer claim the status of normal? On the bright side! Thanks to our personal freedom, etc., it's very important to me that I learn how to become a mature, responsible adult male (still working on it!). I hope to find myself in a loving, mutually respectful mature relationship someday (not there yet!) and I am totally optimistic that I will.

(Subject 15 strongly argues that the use of sperm donors is unethical.)

## THE NATIVES ARE RESTLESS: NEW MEN AND RECIDIVISM

Behavior changes: men carry their babies on their chests, do the shopping, change diapers. But thousands of years of male behavior and expectations, and the unconscious—these don't change as fast. Women, they're caught, also, in mixed messages, they're seeing images of strong, indie women mixed with nearly naked women shaking their booties. Change isn't one-sided, never entirely.

Subject 19: I hear women say all the time, "I just want to be taken care of." I've wondered sometimes if women have experienced an existential disappointment, having fought so hard to obtain certain jobs and for professional equality, only to discover corporate America is a soulless, empty wasteland. I wonder if that's played a part in this nostalgia.

(In this study *Mad Men* [2007–2015] is regularly cited, Don Draper's fedora, smart suit, endless smoking and drinking, cavalier treatment of women, his infidelity to his little wife in the suburbs.)

What is independence? Mother talked about her independence from Father, about being "more than a wife and mother," but she was both of those, and also had a gig outside the house, which she usually brought home. She was the one who made dinner. She said Father came home too late to do it. She did attach a schedule on the refrigerator door, for us kids, our chores. She did try to get it across to us. Still, I saw her doing trad things, not much happening from my father. Now there are couples and marriages who do this mutuality biz better, and a chore can depend upon who's better at doing it. Some guys like cooking and are better at it.

Subject 3: At one point in my life I would occasionally say "I don't want to be a man," which confused some people—they thought I wanted to undergo gender reassignment. Really, I just wanted to be free to LOOK at men and women without so much interference. I still believe in all of this, but as time has gone on I have also realized that I didn't want to engage in a particular relationship with men, either: I didn't want to compete. My dad always wants to compete. And the fact that I dodged this has been something of a problem for me. (Freud would probably think so.) I think that men—particularly fathers—benefit from holding on to some of the old tropes of masculinity. Because it's still part of the world, and if you ignore it too much, then you wind up with your own dissatisfactions. Feminism helped me circumvent tons of bullshit. (For one thing, I've found very rewarding friendships with men as well as women—not always an easy thing.) But had I competed with my father, that would have probably cleared more area for me to distance myself from my parents. But it's a subtlety that some are better at than others.

Subject 20: I think feminism has affected how I relate to myself as a man because it's blurred the lines of femininity and masculinity. It's broken down the walls and the boxes of labels and expectations. Because of that people are redefining what it is to be a man or a woman, and identifying as a man or a woman isn't reduced to just being masculine or feminine.

Freud: "Fantasy is a protective fiction."

For the older dude, fantasy gets tougher to sustain and support, in all senses; and, mostly it has to be lived in secret, except, say, fantasy football.

The Dude: Jeff Bridges in *The Big Lebowski*. The adored loser. Everything he did was wrong, but he remained rebellious, an outlier, and his kick-ass diffidence, his never going to give in to The Man, rates high, still. The desire to "drop out of the game," leave the "rat race," never ends. A loser who wins by not competing is OK.

Fantasies turn into secrets: adults are expected to leave their fantasies behind or make enough money to buy them (secretly). It's why watching porn is normative: it's available, affordable fantasy (there is also sympathy-porn, which encourages do-gooders). Porn is frowned on, always accessible, on the internet, in hotels, accepted practice, not mentioned at the breakfast table unless an all-male group, gay, straight, bi. Some guys tell me they're addicted; but to an ethnographer, social customs are not addictions. In addiction, chemicals change the body's functioning, and neural pathways.

I suppose it could be hypothesized that porn—since when excited, blood rushes to the brain, and penis or clitoris—affects body chemistry, and when frequently indulged might build those neural highways similar to ones for drugs.

Subject 17: Pornography seems like such a standard thing, not usually discussed too much, but just there between the cracks. I imagine it's changed the way men think of women, but I'm not sure exactly how. On the one hand, there's the standardized sexual ideal, but in reality, my suspicion is that because of porn's wide range, there's actually quite a spectrum of ages, bodies, and activities that men look at and let themselves be curious about. A lot of that is private and not discussed, but I think it's there. And even more so with men (I'm talking about straight guys here) about ten years younger, in their twenties.

Fantasy is part of daily reality. Some things don't clock. Some of us humans keep it/our clocks/our cocks closer in our lives. For some, the fantasy IS reality, it's how they live, what they live for, the illusion.

Like my sample, I had ideas about the types of women I could love, about the type of life I wanted. Typical fantasies. Can't we DREAM bigger and not be delusional?

Subject 6: It is beautiful to see men being tender with children, with the women in their lives, and with their male friends. A gay male friend of mine recently sent me a video of a bunch of guys having an afternoon sex party in a private park. Dozens of guys sharing a few hired women. Some of the women were tough, laughing, between sucking dicks and getting fucked all over the place, counting their money, etc. The guys heard in the audio of the cameraman's camera was revealing. Guys made fun of other guys not being able to get off because too many people were around. Men teased each other about the pleasure they were receiving, just received, or were about to. There was a genuine respect for this need, and the willingness on behalf of the participants and the voyeurs to be in the moment without a terrible lot of negative judgment. Particularly interesting too was the lack of misogyny. The guys were partying, drinking beers, smoking pot, and all the while really quite respectful of the women's professional space. It was intriguing to watch not from a sexual standpoint but more from a sociological standpoint. My friend wrote to me about it saying that he was surprised that heterosexual men could be so free with each other, so uninhibited and celebratory of male sex and pleasure in front of each other very much in the same way that homosexual men can be and do. He remarked how much of the misunderstanding around sexuality came from people holding very limited views of sex, particularly of heterosexual sex from a male perspective. As paradoxical as it may be, the video did reveal a nuanced engagement that men have with each other. This is an extreme example but could be taken into consideration, with a range of coded male behaviors (e.g., the etiquette and conventions observed in male professional sports).


I have questions and thoughts about his perception. But I will leave his response free of my commentary.

## DAILY DESIRE

Existential facts on the ground, going farther out into the field, making street observations: Unusual, even rare, to see unlike males together (or females)—Armani suit with uniformed soldier, say, unless related or having a goal—drugs. Images exceed a frame on the wall or a place in a file. The platforms disseminate what's seen exponentially; images pile on, views of dailiness (thickening). Life's thick and shallow.

Street cruising: older gay men once employed overt signals, keys, color of handkerchiefs, now almost extinct, at least in urban sites, because of apps. Younger men, in trans-gen era, openly flirt.

Heterosexual cruising: "Ass men" have little trouble. She passes, they turn, stare. Breast men cast their eyes down, then lift to her face: large-breasted women know their breasts come first. Many get annoyed, but with cleavage the trend du jour, women expose everything; and, breast men have a field day. "Overwhelming in the summer," Subject 22 said.

The "first look," though, is not a distant memory to the New Man, who will, like older men, pursue her on first sight.

That first look, OK, a mirage of transference, and powerful, which is why movie stars still cause pulses to race. She or he represents a lost love, a lost hope.


A typical Friday night, in the field: I decided to watch couples, all kinds, all the varieties. Stood on a corner, at about seven p.m. and then midnight, witching hour, when drunkenness and being high let guards down. Cool observational platform. Beginning of night: heterosexual couples walk a foot from each other, unless they know each other. But "first daters," those before they've had sex, are trying to make an impression on each other. (Have to choose one. Hard call.) Younger women laugh, smile a lot. Kind of annoying, really. The guys, well, they're waiting. At midnight, they're walking much closer to each other. Guys flagging cabs. Impatient. The women, they're harder for me to read.

Used to make me feel sad, dating, not to know how she felt. Now I'm chill, more indifferent, anyway, guarded, have to be.

## OLD NEW MEN, NEW OLD ONES

The urge for sex, or lust, manifests itself; the approaches can be more subtle than whistling. Buying a woman a drink in a bar. Come-on lines. Again, new men are making it up as they go along. New women are too.

Guys like me—my sub-subculture peers, late twenties to early forties—have problems our fathers, grandfathers, etc., didn't have. Especially around sex. Sure, it's "easier" than it was for our elders in some ways, but harder in others. Attitudes have changed, because of the pill, the sexual revolution, less unwanted pregnancy, legal abortion: advantages. There's also recidivism. There's religion. There's backlash. CONFUSION.

Subject 17: One of my first girlfriends asked me if I fantasized about her when I masturbated, before we started sleeping together. I told her I hadn't because I thought it was objectifying. She was offended that I hadn't held her in higher sexual esteem.

New women are meant to know when they want it, know better, anyway, best-case scenario. Young women are also confused, and their hormones act on them too, social pressure, etc. New Men, males generally, have been very slow in getting it. Their fathers or grandfathers, the older gen men came on hard; they might have rammed it in, literally. Boys are still encouraged to be boys, to act like "men." To be assertive. Tough. Study the behavior of boys in playgrounds, their war play, their stances, notice how parents are undecided about when to stop it. They want their boys, and girls, to stand up for themselves. But to what degree— how to decide and set limits, which, along with their peers, game culture, etc., determines what kind of "men" are being grown.

Subject 12: Masculinity is as complex and nuanced and confusing for thoughtful men as I imagine femininity is for thinking women. It's not just about being strong and capable and steady and good, but it's also about murder, and overcoming fear, the self-hatred it engenders, and putting the needs of others above oneself. The final result of this is the male equivalent of childbirth: killing another human being. This is the essence of masculine heroism, the sublimation of the self so that one may commit an evil act. Gilgamesh and Enkidu, Cain and Abel, Grendel and Beowulf—one man lives, the other dies. I see very few men who have any

notion of their place in the world—I think it's particularly
difficult when a central component of masculinity is service
to society, and society has told men to abandon traditional
notions of masculinity.

## BRIEF NOTE TOWARD MALE FRIENDSHIP

I wrote to the group about best friends, the buddy movie,
bromance phenom.

Subject 12: My relationships with other men are quite varied,
as are my relationships with women. I suppose the only constant for me is a state of confusion and lack of clarity about
how I should be living. This is something my father's generation, and particularly his father's, did not have to deal with,
and I think their choices were more straightforward. They all
joined the army, they all cleaned their plates, they all married before twenty-five, none of them divorced, and I've never
heard of an affair (or at least if they produced children they
were taken care of somehow).

Most of my sample say bromances are dumb, like "chick
flicks" for guys, playing to the lowest common denominator.
Father/son stories appeal more.

No one mentioned a best friend betrayal. Nothing like
my situation.

Betrayal comes in all sizes and shapes, though, and telling

bad stories, recalling bad memories, is not for the easily down-hearted. Some would be deniers of their own history. Some want to remember only the good stuff. Can't blame them.

## "ACTING LIKE A MAN"

Men are made, unmade, done, undone.

Are men ever unmade beds? Do-overs?

Manly/womanly; mannish, womanish.

Churlish. Fetish. Newish.

I quiz myself:

What if I lost my apartment and had to live on the streets?

What if, before the pill, in the 1950s, I'd gotten a girl pregnant: would I have married her? (Those days returning to U.S.A.?)

An invading army—sinister enemy drones fly low (though who can tell now?), monster nuclear submarines rise at the coast like behemoths, landings on the beaches.

What would you do? Fight? I think I would. Hide? Run? They sweep block by block, what's your move? You may wonder: It might already be over. (There should be a one-minute warning.) Panic in the streets.

I'd have bought an Uzi or another attack weapon. I'd be armed.

Maybe my sample would awaken like sleeper cells. Maybe we/they are not immune to instinct.

How do you know the enemy? Is that an instinct? Fear is, right? But enemies disguise themselves, and might be your best friends.

I stop imagining. Shake my head, shake it, shake it out, shake shake shake.

Whatever comes, whoever, whenever, however, no one wants to be disappeared, imprisoned, offed.

One night, in the hood, I watched a scene between two twentysomethings, white, male and female arguing. She looked drunk or high, she's talking at him, he keeps silent, he is walking faster and faster to get away from her. She starts shouting: YOU HAVE TO CARE ABOUT ME. YOU HAVE TO CARE ABOUT ME. Over and over. Pretty intense. It was about two in the morning, no one else around, I stayed with the drama, a private performance in public. No one else mattered, they did their thing, and I stood behind the trunk of a tree, then in my doorway, and watched, right, a voyeur. But, hell, it was amazing: You have to care about me, you have to care about me. Isn't that it, isn't that it, isn't that what we all want. And what I felt, and never said aloud.

It came to an end, down the end of the block, under a harsh streetlight, he held her in his arms. He did care. Then, anyway. What would happen, eventually, I'll never know, but I still see it, and wonder about them. About her.

In the future: My genderqueer friend is optimistic. She thinks "there is a big shift coming, we're in it, it hasn't arrived, anything static or fixed denies it, no identity politics but lots of identities, language is way behind, language doesn't 'get' it (or at least any language that isn't poetic, any language that seeks to define), middle America is closer than we think because it actually isn't hard to see we're all just sacks of skin—but also, it's impossibly far off because it's about power, always about power holding itself."

I wrote her: "I'm not sure about history, but I'm probably on the wrong side of my body."

> People unfortunately are seldom impartial where they are concerned with the ultimate things, the great problems of science and of life. My belief is that there everyone is under the sway of preferences deeply rooted within, into the hands of which he unwittingly plays as he pursues his speculation.
>
> —Freud, from *Beyond the Pleasure Principle*

These pages, this field report and survey, contain other men's thoughts, but always my preferences, because unwillingly I participate in everything I may want to change. And, everything I am, and may not want to be.

## ACKNOWLEDGMENTS

My gratitude to the MacDowell Colony and the Chinati Foundation for the space, time, and solitude to write this novel. Thank you to all of the men who responded so generously and intelligently to Zeke's questions. Thank you, Colm Tóibín, for suggesting I look into Henry James's friend Clover Hooper Adams, that I'd like her. You were right. Thank you to everyone at Soft Skull/Catapult for your help and devotion. Thank you, Joy Harris, agent and friend, for being with me through this weird ride. Elizabeth Schambelan, thank you for your careful and helpful reading of this novel in its early days. Thank you, Thomas Beard, Patrick McGrath, and Josh Thorson, for your astute comments. I want to acknowledge here, to remember, Paula Fox, Harry Mathews, and Denis Johnson, who all died in 2017. Great, astonishing writers. I am very grateful to have known them as friends. Thank you, DH, for your love and incredible sense of humor, the ridiculous in life and in me.